Time of Death

Riverdale PD Series

J.I. O'Neal

Published by River Walk Press, 2020.

This is a work of fiction. Similarities to real people, places, or events are entirely coincidental.

TIME OF DEATH

First edition. March 31, 2020.

Copyright © 2020 J.I. O'Neal.

ISBN: 978-1393285427

Written by J.I. O'Neal.

ACKNOWLEDGMENTS

I would like to gratefully thank Detective Beal of the Grant County Sheriff's Office and IWU Campus Police Department for his input into campus security.

I would also like to thank all the doctors who so thoroughly documented the side effects of chloroform as a sedative, from the 1800s on.

Thanks also to the Mayo Clinic and the National Institute of Mental Health websites for information on male depression.

CHAPTER ONE

The victim's red scarf draped over his shoulder and down his light blue dress shirt. Her blood spattered through his short, black hair and flecked the right side of his face in a pattern that mimicked the scars he bore on the left. This image, reflected in the large window at the back of the room, distracted him a moment.

He took a breath before turning his attention back to the audience before him.

"As you can see from this case," Noah Harkham said, gesturing toward the photos on the screen in a way that, he noticed, blocked the projector's beam so that part of the images displayed on the right side of his body instead, "valuable evidence was lost due to lack of training and inadequate crime scene preservation techniques." He stood before a class of uniformed officers in one of the precinct's conference rooms, presenting a particularly gruesome and unsolved double murder from 1989.

He shifted his stance and the images returned to the screen. "The perimeter was set too close and too late – not until after more than half a dozen officers had already trampled all over the premises. Some items were collected before photographing them *in situ* and with incomplete labels to identify where they'd been collected from. Not all the officers' shoeprints were taken for elimination purposes. Mistake after mistake compounded on top of each other. Had this case been handled correctly, who knows what might have happened. But, as it went down, it has remained unsolved for nearly twenty-five years."

1

An officer toward the back raised the pen in his left hand to interrupt. "So, do you think it's the cops' fault it went cold?"

Noah regarded the young man a moment, trying to decide whether he was asking out of genuine curiosity or to stir up trouble. He was sick of having to make these kinds of judgments, but he'd long ago learned not everyone in the station was happy with having to take his classes. The hardest thing he'd had to deal with after his career-ending injuries – apart from the physical difficulties – was the reaction from some of his former colleagues to his new position: pity, derision and juvenile amusement, just to name a few.

He decided to cut to the chase. "Yes. To an extent, I do."

Murmurs rippled through the room. He held up a hand. "But don't get me wrong – I am not saying they were bad cops or inept. Just inexperienced. If you remember, this homicide occurred in a rural town that hadn't seen a murder of any kind – let alone one this brutal – in years. If they'd had some sort of forensic training, or if they'd had access to the technology we have today, they would have had a better understanding of the dynamics of a crime scene and the half-life of physical evidence."

"So, you're saying that if you'd been the one on the case, you'd have solved it," the same officer said, a slight smirk tugging at his thin lips.

To stir up trouble. He shrugged, forcing an indifferent demeanor. "No, that's not what I'm saying, but who knows? All I can say is that by the time crime scene technicians were called in, the responding officers had already walked all over multiple items of evidence, including a shoeprint in the yard that likely belonged to the killer. I can't say this case would have been solved had that evidence been properly collected. I will say that it would have stood a *much* better chance."

The officer said something under his breath to the female officer next to him. To her credit, the second officer – Ryzowski, he recalled – tried very hard to ignore her classmate. Hot anger surged inside him, and Noah struggled to clamp it down. He glanced at the roster on the podium to the right of the screen and located the annoying officer's name.

"Tell me, Officer...Spicer, have you ever been on a homicide scene?" He raised one eyebrow as the young cop looked up at him.

Apparently, Spicer remembered some of the rumors about Noah's teaching methods; he shifted uneasily in his seat. "No. Sir."

"Don't worry, son, I wouldn't let you anywhere near one." A few of the officers laughed. "But since you feel qualified to pass judgment on cops who have been on the job a lot longer than you, I'm going to give you the opportunity to prove to all of us how much better you are." He tried, and failed, to keep the irritation out of his voice.

"I never said I was –"

"Come up here, Spicer."

The officer's brown eyes burned with anger and he clenched his rather weak jaw, but he nevertheless walked up to the front of the room. Noah stepped aside and gestured toward the podium. "Go on. Tell the class how you would have handled this case."

Noah could hear the other cops snickering at their classmate, but he ignored them, keeping his attention fixed on the defiant young officer before him. Spicer blushed and turned toward his fellow officers. He cleared his throat, opened his mouth to speak, then shut it and turned toward Noah instead.

"Do I really have to do this?"

"So, you get to the couple's house and find them like this." He gestured to the crime scene photographs on the screen. "What do you do first?"

Spicer let out a breath. "I would set up crime scene tape around the house. Then I would call for backup."

Noah sat on the edge of the closest conference table and crossed his arms. "So, while you're getting the tape out of your cruiser alone, the killer exits the house, comes up behind you and slits your throat like he did theirs and backup only arrives a few hours later when the neighbors report your body."

Some of the officers hissed at Spicer mockingly, eliciting more chuckles from the others. Noah held up a hand to shush them, keeping his eyes on Spicer. "Come on, this is basic Academy training. What do you do *first*?"

"Okay, first I would call it in and check the rest of the house to make sure the killer wasn't still on the premises." He flicked his gaze toward Noah for confirmation. He merely looked back. Spicer let out a frustrated sigh. "Then I would set up the tape perimeter while I wait for CSU and a Major Crimes detective."

"How far?" Noah prodded. Spicer gave him a blank stare. "The perimeter, Spicer. How far do you set it?"

"As far as possible –"

"How far?" Noah gritted his teeth.

"I don't know – all the way to the street and all around the property line, I guess."

Noah gave an ambiguous dip of his head. Spicer's answer was close enough to right. "What do you do after that?"

Spicer scrunched his brow. "Uh, I should...assess the scene? Try to determine what happened and where the evidence might be."

"And all that tramping through the house you did when you were looking for the suspect has contaminated the scene and potentially destroyed evidence. How do you plan to remedy that?"

Noah could see Spicer getting frustrated, a feeling he shared. "First, I'm stupid for not checking to see if the perpetrator is still on the scene, then I'm screwing up the scene if I do! What do you want?"

"I want you to think!" Noah yelled, crossing the distance between them to slam his hands on the opposite side of the podium. Spicer flinched, and the room fell silent. "I want you to use your head before you screw up our *one* shot at getting the evidence that just might make sure a murderer doesn't go free!" He jabbed a finger toward the screen. "Look at them, Spicer."

Noah waited until the cop tore his startled gaze away from him and looked at the photographs. "For over twenty-four years the guy who did this has been laughing at the cops who screwed this case up so royally there wasn't a chance in *hell* he'd ever be caught. Would you want that to be on you?"

"N-no, sir." Spicer raised his hands and took a step back. "Okay, I get it. Can I sit down now?"

Noah took a deep breath and collected himself. "Yes. Sit."

As Spicer hurried to his seat, Noah took his place at the podium and turned to the class. The officers looked back at him with stunned expressions and he made a conscious effort to soften his voice before speaking. "I'm trying to teach you how to do your jobs without making it impossible for the crime scene units to do theirs, so we have a better chance at putting away the bad guys than we have in the past. Yes, secure the scene, but do it carefully. Watch where you step, avoid the central paths through doorways, rooms and stairs and touch nothing without gloves."

The tension was slow to dissipate, so he forced a smile. "I think we should stop there for the day. We can pick it back up here next time." The smile withered, but he held their gazes. "Copies of the case notes are available in my office for anyone interested. And read the sections on trace evidence in the handbook." He paused another moment before dismissing them with his usual, flippant, "Now, get out."

They all seemed to breathe a collective sigh of relief and rushed out of the conference room. All except Officer John Reynolds, who stood in the aisle waiting to be acknowledged. The two had initially met during the very first case that Noah and his former partner, Detective Alan Franks, worked together eight years ago, when John was only eighteen and his little sister's best friend was killed in a hit-and-run; they only met again a few months ago during the first major case John had been involved in as a cop. He had potential, and Noah considered the young officer as his unofficial protégé – and a friend.

Seeing him now, however, made Noah sigh to himself. "Hey, John. What's up?"

"I was gonna ask you the same thing." His amiable face was clouded with concern as he approached. "What just happened up here?"

Noah shook his head. "I just get so fed up with some of these jackasses coming in thinking they know everything there is to know about everything just because they went through the academy. I just thought he needed taught a lesson."

John nodded. "Look, I'm not sayin' that guy didn't have it comin', but I gotta say that got a little...tense there for a minute."

"Yeah. Sorry about that." Noah gripped the edges of the podium.

The younger man's brow furrowed, but he shrugged. "Don't worry about it. Listen, I had a thought about this case I wanted to run by you: You said there was a shoeprint the cops trampled – is there a way, like some sort of computerized analysis that could scan the images and extract the layers of the officer's shoeprints? Whatever was left would be the killer's shoeprints, right? Sort of like how you said overlapping fingerprints can be digitally separated sometimes."

Noah nodded as John spoke. "Yes. There are digital enhancements around that can do that – but not in this case. Unfortunately, we don't have enough elimination prints and the scene just wasn't preserved well enough. But your head is in the right place. You're thinking like the kind of cop we need at crime scenes."

Though John smiled at the compliment, his dark blue eyes still looked troubled. "So, there's no way this case could be solved?"

"There's always a chance someone could come forward with more information," Noah replied with a shrug. "Or the killer could commit another crime and we'd be able to link him to this one... but, barring that, no. Probably not."

"Have you ever worked a case you didn't solve?"

"A few, actually." He gestured around the room. "Contrary to popular opinion, I don't think I'm some sort of super cop."

"I know. Like I've said before, ignore the ignorant and remember that some of us are glad you're here."

"Thanks, John. That means a lot." He was still learning to make do with this instructor's position and knowing at least one person was getting something out of it made it a little more bearable.

"Yeah, well..." John's shoulders hitched up in a self-effacing shrug. "I'm due for patrol. I'll see you later, 'kay?"

"Okay." Noah smiled. "Better get out there before your sarge comes looking."

"Yes, sir," John replied with a smile of his own as he turned to leave.

Noah shut down the projector and disconnected his laptop. He glanced up at the sound of John exchanging greetings with Detective Franks as they passed each other in the doorway. He closed out of the presentation, and ejected the flash drive it was stored on.

"Hey, Frankie," he said as his best friend approached.

"Hey. That was quite the lesson plan."

Noah glanced up but went back to powering down his laptop without comment.

"Wanna tell me what's really going on? I mean, I heard what you told the kid, but you should know by now I can see through your B.S."

Noah shrugged as Frankie regarded him with his 'good cop' interrogation face. "I got angry. It happens; no big deal." He shoved the laptop into its carrying case then grabbed the box of files and looked to see if he'd forgotten anything. "Ah, crap." He jutted his chin toward his orange notebook and pen on the table. "Can you grab those for me?"

Frankie laughed, and it sounded a little forced, but grabbed the items anyway and dropped them into the box. "You're mastering the absent-minded professor role, huh?"

"I'm not absent-minded," Noah protested as they headed out the door, still trying to shrug off his irritation. "I just couldn't see them at first."

Frankie winced, as he did every time Noah's one-sided blindness was brought up. "Oh. Sorry."

"You have got to learn I'm not going to break down every time someone mentions my condition."

"Okay." He lowered his voice as they passed a group of uniformed officers going the opposite direction. "But what about the other condition?"

Noah shot him a look. "What are you talking about?"

"You know," Frankie leaned in to say, "the *other* condition... I mean, Alzheimer's in someone so young...shame really..."

Noah threw an elbow into Frankie's gut, eliciting a pained grunt. "You are such a jerk." He laughed anyway. "Let me drop this by my office and I'll be ready." Noah turned down the next intersecting hallway, leaving him behind to wait.

Frankie called after him. "Are you sure you remember the way?"

Noah's only response was to lift the hand carrying the laptop and raise a one-fingered salute.

CHAPTER TWO

The room was far too crowded for his liking. If it weren't for Frankie and Neil guilting him into coming, he'd have been somewhere much more appealing – like home, or the gun range. Or even the dentist's office. It wasn't that he didn't like Conrad Ward or wish him a happy birthday, but he just didn't get why the party had to be *here*.

What grown man had his birthday party at a hotel pool?

Of course, looking around, Noah could see one reason. He doubted that Conrad knew even half of the bikini-clad women strutting around, and he seriously doubted most of them even knew what a criminalist was. Not that Conrad would mind too much.

"Hey, Thunder Cloud, what's with the grim face?"

He looked up to see Robin "Shots" Dorian handing him a can of Coke. He took it and tried to give her a smile in return. "Thanks. Thunder Cloud?"

She shrugged. "If the nickname fits... So, why aren't you having a good time?"

He sighed and took a drink. "I guess I'm too old for this, Shots." At least *she* was dressed, in a tank top and shorts.

She pulled a mock-serious face and nodded, her auburn-brown ponytail bobbing behind her. "Yes, I can see the wrinkles forming as we speak." She laughed. "Come on, lighten up a little. I got you your second-favorite drink – sorry, no ginger ale – and there's music,

10

sort of, and people you know and even like here. It's called fun. You should try it."

He frowned. "I know fun. I've even had it a time or two, believe it or not."

"Well, then, time to give it another try."

The sound of a splash followed by Conrad and Frankie laughing floated across the room over the way-too-loud top forty rock playlist. Conrad had apparently knocked Frankie into the pool. *Accidentally, I'm sure...* Noah looked back at Robin. "I'm sorry; I guess this just isn't my definition of fun. Thanks for the drink, though."

"You're not leaving, are you?"

"Yeah, but I've already wished Conrad a happy birthday, and I even got him a gift." He gestured around. "Honestly, I don't think he'll notice."

She smirked. "You might be right. Do you even know who any of these people are? Besides us, obviously."

Us. He smiled at how she always lumped the cops of the Fifth Precinct and the criminalists and techs at the Calera County Crime Lab together as one big team – and how she still included him in that team. "No, not a single one."

She sighed. "Yeah...can Neil and I come with you?"

"Sure," he said with a laugh. "Where is he, by the way?"

"Um..." She looked around. "Oh, there." She pointed to the corner where his cousin lounged in the hot tub. The ever-serious younger man had his eyes closed and seemed completely untouched by the chaos surrounding him. "Actually, that looks kinda nice. You sure you don't want to at least hang out with us in the hot tub for a bit?"

"I'll leave you to it. I didn't exactly dress for the venue." He gestured to his dress shirt and trousers; he'd left straight from work and didn't have any other clothes to change into. "Can you just tell Conrad I hope he's having a good birthday for me?"

"Of course."

"Thanks." He gave her a quick hug. Now that she and Neil were dating – inseparable, more like – that made her family in his eyes. But, even though hugging was the norm in his family, he'd never been all that comfortable with it. "I'll see you guys tomorrow, then."

"Okay. Good night, Noah."

"G'night."

Just walking through the doors into the hotel lobby made him feel better. It was cooler, emptier and much quieter out here. *Maybe I am getting old...* He finished his drink and threw away the can before walking to the bus stop and checking the time. Another bus should be arriving in one minute.

A man walking up the sidewalk slowed as he neared the bus stop. Noah moved over a little inside the shelter and gave the man a tight smile as he joined him to wait. He looked familiar, but Noah couldn't place where he'd seen him before. He was slight, younger than Noah with mousy-brown hair, darker brown eyes and was sporting stubble he no doubt thought made him look more mature.

"Couldn't take it anymore either, huh?"

Noah looked up. "Excuse me?"

The man gestured toward the hotel. "The party? Weren't you just there, too?"

"Oh, I thought I'd seen you before. Yeah, it isn't really my idea of a good time."

"Yeah, me neither."

They lapsed into awkward silence. When the bus came, Noah let the other man get on first. As he passed by where the man had taken a seat, he heard him say, "Have a good weekend, Noah Harkham."

He stopped and looked back, but the man was already speaking to the person seated next to him.

CHAPTER THREE

The blue orb spun away higher, making a graceful arc before it sped back toward him. Just before it landed, Noah caught the ball and tossed it up into the air again. He was lying on his back in the middle of his living room floor, performing a depth-perception strengthening exercise that Dr. James Weymouth – the doctor that was teaching him to better function in the world with only one working eye and ear – had taught him.

Movement in his peripheral vision made him look away. The ball fell with a hard *thwack* on his forehead and rolled away. He grunted and rubbed the sore spot above his brow, silently cursing himself and the stupid fly that had distracted him. He got up, a little sullen, and retrieved the ball, putting it back in the shallow dish on the footlocker-turned-coffee table in front of his couch. His grandfather's footlocker was one of the few items he'd brought with him when he moved here from his old apartment.

The apartment where he'd nearly watched Neil die...

It was late Thursday night – or, as the clock on the wall told him, very early Friday morning – two weeks after Conrad's party. Three-thirty in the morning, and he was as wide awake as he had been at three-thirty that afternoon. Not that he wasn't tired; he was exhausted, but he hadn't been able to sleep well for the past couple of months. At first, he chalked it up to nerves about starting the new teaching position. But even after that had faded, he was still having trouble.

Then he thought maybe things would only go back to normal once Simon Turner and Tony Barrett were convicted and sentenced. But now, with Turner long dead and Barrett sentenced to life, he had only one explanation for his sleeplessness: August 31st was only two days away. This would be the first anniversary of the day Bobby Avalon ended his career with a single gunshot.

There was no way he was going to sleep again tonight. He picked up the book he had been re-reading – Frank Herbert's *Dune* – but couldn't summon the concentration to keep up with interplanetary intrigues. He tossed it on the sofa and sat next to it, considering turning on the television instead. Once he realized that infomercials and shopping channels would be the only things still on the air, he discarded that idea, too.

Instead, he went into his bedroom and settled into the armchair before his desk, firing up his laptop to review notes for his upcoming class. Using real unsolved cases helped point out all the ways an investigation could go wrong, so he was using cold cases from around the country and his own precinct if no one objected. It was his hope that the cops he taught would learn from real-world examples – and maybe one day someone would see something everyone else missed and breathe new life into a dead-end case.

He was deep into the case notes of a twenty-seven-year-cold rape/homicide when his phone rang. He frowned at the clock, but the caller ID showed it was Frankie. He answered on speaker, something he did most often now that he could only hear out of one ear.

"Yeah, Frankie, what's up?"

"Sorry to wake you–"

"Don't worry, you didn't. Whatcha got?"

"I just got called to a homicide on the RiverWalk." He sounded stressed, his voice tinged with anxiety. "The victim was found with the image of a clock carved into his forehead."

Noah sat up straighter. "A clock?"

"Set at one o'clock."

He swallowed hard, his heart beginning to pound. "He's back."

"Looks like," Frankie said with a sigh. "I'm gonna need you to come to the station, take me through the old case."

"Whatever you need." Noah gripped the chair arms tighter. "I'll be right there."

———————

3:56 am

"He was known as the 'One O'clock Killer.' Extremely obvious, I know," Noah said, handing Frankie one of the two cups of coffee he'd poured, "but the press needed something to call him and, apparently, that was the best they came up with." He took a sip of his coffee. He didn't need the caffeine, but the bitter taste matched his mood.

Frankie, on the other hand, looked like he'd been asleep when he caught the call and was still a bit bleary-eyed. Being the on-call detective at night or the weekend was one thing Noah did not miss about the job. They were at Frankie's desk at the station and Noah pulled an extra chair from along the wall and sat facing his old partner. He'd thrown on a long-sleeved black shirt and jeans before catching a cab to the station, but he hadn't thought to take a jacket. But the warmth of the mug in his hands helped stave off the slight unseasonable chill of the early morning.

Frankie had the original case file in front of him and flipped through some of the pages. "There were just the two victims?"

"Yes. Paula Stevenson, age twenty-four and Will Messer, twenty-three. No connection was found between the two of them, just the clock carved into their skin. The press was quick to call this a serial killing, given the dramatic signature, but we were very careful to avoid that label since we only had two victims." He rubbed his eyes. "Looks like the press got something right for once after all."

"You worked this case with Rob Meares, didn't you?"

Noah had to turn his mind away from the painful memories associated with that name. "Yes. We tried everything we could think of: Rob interviewed the families and friends, I canvassed the neighborhoods where they lived and where they were found, we dumped phone records of anyone who looked remotely good for it, and we went over the crimes scenes with a fine-toothed comb..."

He shook his head, weary and defeated. "Nothing. We pulled one partial print off the button of Will Messer's jacket, but it was too incomplete to be of any use. Other than that, there was nothing to go on. This guy was quick and brutal and then...gone."

"No one saw or heard *anything* either time?"

He shook his head again, then fixed his friend with a piercing look. "You have to catch him this time, Frankie."

"That's the plan."

He took another sip of coffee. "Tell me about the new victim."

Frankie cleared his throat and consulted his notebook. "Young Caucasian male. He was stabbed multiple times in the chest, throat and face. He had a Riverside University student ID on him. Name's Nathan, no Nigel, uh, Warner. We're trying to –"

Noah's head jerked up. *"Nigel Warner?"*

Realization dawned on Frankie's tired face. "I can't believe I didn't make the connection. I'd forgotten that was his name." He gestured to his notes. "All he had on him was a school ID with a faded picture, no wallet, and his face... I didn't recognize him." Frankie groaned and wiped a hand across his face. "I'll get the address; Gerald should hear it from me in person."

He opened a database and typed in the attorney's name. Noah glanced at the entry. "Benton Springs. That's by the lake."

"You know it?"

"Yeah, my aunt and uncle live in that neighborhood. I can help you find it."

Frankie sighed and threw a miserable look at him. "Man, I wish I didn't have to do this."

"I know." He rose from the chair he'd sunk into earlier. "Come on, if it were me, I'd want to know right away."

———

It took them less than half an hour to get to the lakeside suburb and to navigate the winding streets of the gated community to Gerald Warner's house. It was a handsome, two-story colonial, complete with columns supporting the roof over the porch. It was now roughly a quarter to five, and the street was dark and silent.

Frankie shut off the Chrysler and led the way up to the front door. He hesitated a moment, then rang the doorbell. He let several seconds pass before knocking. A dog began to bark at them from across the street, which led to another one barking a few houses down. A light came on somewhere inside the house, and then the porch light switched on, nearly blinding them. Gerald Warner's sleepy face appeared in one of the door's small, decorative glass panes. He frowned and opened the door, dressed in a robe, pajamas and slippers, his hair still awry from his pillow.

"Detective Franks? Noah? What are you doing here?" Gerald frowned in confusion.

Frankie had trouble meeting the prosecutor's eyes. "Gerald, can we come in?"

He opened the door further. "Of course, please." He stood aside as Frankie and Noah entered the stylish but comfortable living room. "What is this about?"

Frankie took a breath and forced himself to look Gerald in the eye. "We need to talk to you and Miriam. I'm afraid I have some terrible news."

"Oh..." Gerald Warner looked from the detective to Noah and back. His hands trembled. "Oh, please, no."

CHAPTER FOUR

"How? How did it happen?" Gerald gripped Miriam's hand tighter as they sat side by side on the overstuffed couch. His other hand was still shaking, so he squeezed it into a fist on his lap.

Frankie shifted in his chair opposite the grieving couple. "Dr. Lee has only done a preliminary on-scene exam so far, but it looks like he was stabbed." He gave them a moment to digest this before continuing. "He was attacked along the RiverWalk early this morning – somewhere after midnight – but Lee will be able to tell us more after the, um – later."

"Stabbed..." Gerald closed his eyes. "Mugging gone bad?" His voice broke and his eyes were red when he opened them.

Frankie flicked a look at Noah before answering. "He didn't have his wallet on him, so we're not ruling that out, but we don't know anything for certain at this point. Gerald, Miriam, I can't tell you how sorry I am."

Miriam raised a trembling hand to brush a strand of greying brown hair off her face. "Thank you. Do you know who did it?"

He hesitated. "Not yet, but I promise we will do everything we can to make sure we find that out."

"Where did you say it happened?" Gerald furrowed his brow at them.

"On the RiverWalk. Just south of Spring Street."

"Why there?" He wiped his hand over his mouth. "What was he doing there this time of night?"

Frankie and Noah exchanged a look. "We were hoping you could tell us," Noah said.

Gerald scrutinized their faces. Then he rubbed his hand across Miriam's back, turning toward her. "Miriam, would you give us a moment, please?"

She looked at him, then at Frankie and Noah. "I'll put some coffee on. You boys look like you've had a long day."

Noah stood. "Let me give you a hand."

Once the two were out of the room, Gerald scooted forward on the couch and leaned toward Frankie. "What aren't you telling us?"

"I don't have much information yet –"

"Alan, please. I need to know."

He was employing one of his courtroom tricks: address the reluctant witness by first name to forge a bond and coax out the answers. Even at a time like this, Gerald Warner couldn't stop being a lawyer. Then again, it was probably the only way he could cope.

"I can't tell you much more than I already have yet. But if you could answer a few more questions, it could help us know where to go next."

Clearly not satisfied, Gerald sighed. "All right."

"Is there *any* reason you can think of why Nigel would have been on the RiverWalk so late?"

"No, as I said. Although we don't know what he does with his time nowadays. When he lived here, his curfew was ten-thirty, and he very rarely ever broke it. If he wanted to, he would ask first, and we usually let him. But once he went to college...well, you can't expect a young man on his own for the first time to check in with his parents like he used to."

"Has he ever told you that he'd been out this late before? Any parties or road trips or anything that he told you about after the fact?"

His brow furrowed. "Actually, yes. There was a concert out of town that he went to with a few friends once. This would have been...maybe early first semester last year."

"Do you remember who he went with?" Frankie got out his notepad and pen.

"Let's see, it was his roommate Justin Pierce and his best friend, Brent Miller. Ah, Brent – he'll have to be told. He'll be devastated..." Gerald's stare grew unfocused and his lower lip quivered.

"I'll have to talk to him and the roommate, anyway. I'll break it to them, easy like."

Gerald seemed to come back to himself. "Thank you... I think the girl Nigel was interested in at the time, Veronica – no, Vivian, went with them. They didn't get back until three in the morning. We asked them if they got into trouble, with campus curfew being eleven o'clock for freshmen and sophomores. He just laughed and said even newbies knew how to get around that."

Frankie made a note to follow up on all this with the roommate and friends. "Do you know what he meant by that?"

Gerald shook his head. "No. He started talking about something else, and we didn't press it."

"That's okay. Do you have a last name for Vivian?"

"No." He ran his hands across his face. "I'm sorry, Alan. I wish to God I had more to tell you." He looked down at his shaky hands. Tears finally broke through his shock, and a few fell onto his lap.

Frankie reached over and touched his arm. "It's okay, Gerald. You've given us a lot to start with. We'll find who did this."

Noah and Miriam returned, and she laid a steaming cup of coffee on the mahogany table before him. "Thank you, Miriam."

She nodded and smoothed the front of her robe as she sat next to her husband once more. Noah threw Frankie a familiar look as he sat back down: he had something important to tell him. He nodded back and took a sip of coffee.

"Can we see him?" Miriam asked.

"It will probably be later in the afternoon before Dr. Lee has him ready," Noah told her gently before taking a sip of his own coffee.

Frankie's heart ached for them. "I'll call you as soon as he does. I could pick you up, if you prefer it." He drank more of her fine coffee. He needed the caffeine.

"Thank you, but I think we'll be able to manage it," Gerald answered.

"All right." Frankie exchanged a look with Noah. "I have to get back and continue the investigation, but I promise I'll call you as soon as we know anything more." He stood and everyone else followed suit. "Try to get some rest, okay?" He placed a hand on each of the

Warners' shoulders, trying to will some comfort and reassurance into the contact.

"Thank you, Detective Franks. Noah." Gerald's voice broke and he swallowed back more tears.

Noah gave Miriam a sympathetic smile. "If you need anything – anything – don't hesitate to call." He gave her his card. She accepted with a grateful nod and then he and Frankie left the Warners to their grief.

Once back in Frankie's Chrysler, Noah told him what Miriam had said in the kitchen. "She doesn't have any idea why he'd have been there so late tonight, but Miriam says Nigel would often go to the RiverWalk to clear his head. So, it's possible he'd walked there late at night before now." Noah rubbed his eyes. "He could have been chosen because of that – watched, stalked a while – or it could just have been a case of wrong place, wrong time."

Frankie *hmm*ed as he drove out of the neighborhood. "He's younger than the previous victims were, from a higher socioeconomic class. The first was female, the second and now the third were male. What is it that ties the victims together? Why is he targeting the people he is?"

Noah gave a short, bitter laugh. "If I knew that, Frankie, I would have caught him eight years ago."

CHAPTER FIVE

"Spicer! Keep your eyes on that perimeter," Criminalist Simon Lewis glared at the young officer. "I want these gawkers held back." He kept glaring until the officer returned his attention to the crowd that had gathered around the site where Nigel Warner's body had been discovered. He turned to his partner, Jake Saddler, and jerked a thumb back toward Spicer. "Can you believe this guy?"

Saddler looked up from behind his camera, his tired green eyes appraising the rookie. "I think this is his first homicide." He shivered in the cool air.

"Yeah, well, as long as he remembers he's just here for crowd control and not to actually touch anything, we'll be fine." Lewis went back to cataloging the evidence they'd already collected. Not that there was very much so far, other than blood.

There was a lot of blood.

Saddler snapped a picture of a section of the RiverWalk, the boardwalk lining First Street from River Street to University Drive. "He's just green. Hey, I think we may have just gotten lucky. This looks like skin and blood. Maybe there was a bit of a scuffle and the killer got snagged on this splinter."

"Hmm." Lewis turned, eyeing the bit of railing in question. Saddler pointed to the splinter that held a lump of what looked like organic tissue. "It could belong to the victim. We'll have to have Dr. Lee check the body. Or it could be from someone else completely unrelated to our case." He bent his head to resume his catalog entry for some cast off blood spatter. "And he's not just green."

"What?"

"Spicer. It's not that he's a rookie." He nodded toward the other side of the crime scene, where another young officer was maintaining the perimeter there. "Look at Reynolds. He's only been on the force a couple months longer than Spicer, but he's a much better cop."

Saddler nodded in agreement. "Yeah, Neil told me Harkham thinks he'll make Detective in no time. He's acing those forensics classes."

Lewis harrumphed. "Great. That's all we need: more cops thinking they can do our job."

Saddler shrugged. "Personally, I think it's great. The less we have to worry about uniforms screwing up the scene, the better. Remember the mess they made of that murder-suicide scene last October? Compare that to tonight – Reynolds secured the scene, set up a decent perimeter and started isolating witnesses almost single-handedly, before Frankie and Townsend got here." He nodded toward where Townsend was speaking to the group of late-night partyers who had found the body. "All without compromising a single thing that I can see."

"Good for Harkham, Jr. Now can we get back to work?"

"You're the one that brought up Reynolds being the better cop." He knelt a few feet further down the boardwalk.

Lewis went back to cataloging. This section of blood evidence was unusual. It had a few sharp, clean edges, as if something lying there had been removed after the murder. He placed an evidence marker next to it and started to ask Saddler to photograph it when he heard the younger man take a sharp breath. He turned to find him looking at a business card with an odd expression.

"Simon...look at this."

Lewis read the name on the card. "Better get Townsend over here."

CHAPTER SIX

On their way back to the precinct, Frankie put in a call to the University's campus police department. After explaining the situation to the officer on call, Lieutenant Peal, they arranged to meet at Tetherton Hall – Nigel's dorm – at seven o'clock to interview Nigel's friends. He wanted to search Nigel's room as well. Even though he may have been a random target, Frankie wanted to be sure to rule out any connection to his personal life and the campus.

Noah was quiet. It must be beyond frustrating, having this cold case re-emerge now that he can no longer pursue it himself. "Still with me, partner?"

Noah looked over at him. "I'm here." He sounded exhausted.

"Hey, I know this whole thing must – " Frankie's phone rang. "Sorry." He dug his phone out of his pocket. "It's Townsend," he said before answering, "Franks."

"Is Harkham still with you?"

"Uh, yeah. Why?"

"Listen to me, bring him back to the precinct and keep an eye on him until I get there."

"Okay... You wanna tell me what's going on?" He glanced over at Noah, who was watching him with a questioning expression.

"Just please don't let him out of your sight. And don't tell him anything."

"Well, that's going to be easy since I have no idea what you're talking about." They were at the stop light at the intersection of Reed and Jepson. A moth fluttered in the beams of his headlights. "Look, I'm a block away. How soon will you get here?"

"Ten minutes."

"Okay. Townsend..."

"Yeah?"

"Should I be worried?"

"I'll see you in ten." He hung up.

Frankie put away his phone with a frown. The light turned green and he continued toward the precinct, a knot forming in his gut. He flicked another glance at Noah.

He looked back at him, raising one eyebrow. "Does he have a lead?"

"I don't know what he has, but we're supposed to wait for him at the precinct."

"Okay."

Something was going on, and his gut was telling him it wasn't good. He pulled into the precinct's lot and they got out. As they walked toward the door, Frankie decided to ignore Townsend's instructions. He stopped Noah just inside the lobby.

"Listen, Hark, I don't know what's going on, but Townsend wanted me to keep an eye on you until he gets here."

"On me? Why?"

"He wouldn't say. Something's not right, though. I can feel it."

Noah took a moment before replying. "Well, we'll know when he gets here. Come on."

5:17 am

A little less than ten minutes later, Townsend arrived and joined them at Frankie's desk. His expression was closed, a tightness around his blue eyes, which was a contrast to his usual demeanor toward them. This was his cop-mode face, and Frankie was confused to see it levelled at Noah.

He pulled his desk chair over and sat facing them. "I hear you two went to Gerald Warner's house to deliver the news."

"Yeah," Frankie said. "We just came from there."

He switched his attention back to Noah. "Did you speak to Gerald or Miriam at any time?"

Noah's brows drew down sharply. "What's this about, Townsend?"

"Just answer the question, please."

"Yes. I spoke to them both."

"Alone?"

"Just Miriam. I helped her make coffee."

"What about?"

Noah leaned forward in his chair, regarding Townsend, no doubt trying to figure out where this line of questioning was going. Just like Frankie was doing. "She told me that Nigel sometimes walked along the RiverWalk to clear his head. Like when something was troubling him."

"Anything else?"

He shrugged. "She cried, of course. And she made me promise that we – you would find who killed her son. I told her you would do everything you could."

Townsend made a slow blink. "Do you have any business cards?"

Noah sat back, letting out a deep breath. Then he stood. "Look, I'm not sure where you're going with all this, but if you don't start explaining –"

Townsend rose to his feet, blocking Noah's path. "I would think very carefully before finishing that sentence, Mr. Harkham."

Noah frowned. "I was going to say I'm going home. Casey, I really don't understand what's happening here."

"Neither do I." Frankie maneuvered himself in between the other two men and forced Townsend to back up. "What's gotten into you, man?"

Townsend reached into his jacket pocket and withdrew a small evidence bag. Inside was a bloody business card. Frankie saw whose name was on it and the knot in his gut constricted. "What is that?"

Townsend looked past him to Noah. "Well, Mr. Harkham, care to enlighten your old partner?"

"Wait – me? Why?"

Frankie turned toward him. "It's your card, Hark."

"What?"

Townsend shoved the evidence bag closer to Noah's face. "It was found two feet from where Nigel Warner's body was discovered. It has his blood on it. Can you explain why that is?"

Noah shook his head, backing up a step. "Wait – you're not seriously implying –?"

"There has to be some explanation, Casey. Maybe Gerald gave it to him." A thousand different thoughts raced through his mind, but he couldn't find one good one to figure out what was happening. "I mean, the killer took Nigel's wallet, maybe he found Noah's card and tossed it."

A strange expression came over Noah's face. Townsend gave him a predatory smile. "You know that's not how it happened, don't you, Mr. Harkham?"

"What's he talking about?"

Noah looked like he was about to be sick. "The blood spatter. It's medium velocity cast off, not transfer."

Frankie's mind raced. "What are you saying?"

"The blood got on the card as Nigel was being murdered. So, unless the killer took his wallet, tossed the card, all while Nigel just waited patiently, and *then* killed him, the card had to be dropped by the murderer as he butchered that young man."

"Oh, come on, Casey, you can't seriously be saying – you think *Noah* had something to do with this?"

Townsend flicked his gaze back to his partner, his expression softening a little. "I'm sorry, Franks. I gotta take him in for questioning."

"What?" Frankie and Noah said simultaneously.

Townsend pushed past him toward Noah, but Frankie grabbed his arm. "You can't do this."

"I have to." Townsend gave him a grim frown.

"It's okay, Frankie," Noah said. "This is all just a misunderstanding." He waved a hand toward the aisle between desks. "Let's get this over with."

Townsend took Noah by the arm and started walking him toward Interview Room One but stopped and looked back at Frankie. "Oh, and you should think about recusing yourself from this case."

"This is absurd," Frankie scoffed. "Townsend, wait!"

Noah shrugged the detective's hand off his arm. "Just call Ziehring, for me, will you, Frankie? And Cecelia."

CHAPTER SEVEN

———

<u>Friday, August 29, 2014 6:03 a.m.</u>

Townsend was staring him down from across the table. "So, Mr. Harkham, care to explain how your card ended up at the crime scene?"

This whole thing would be laughable, if it weren't for the fact that there was no solid explanation other than coincidence – something cops were trained not to believe in. "Someone had it and dropped it. It happens. I give my card to witnesses, victims and their families all the time."

"You mean, you did."

"What?"

"You said you 'give' your cards. Don't you mean you 'used to give' your cards? You know, when you were still a detective."

Noah gritted his teeth at the condescending tone in the detective's voice. "Yes, I used to give my card to witnesses, victims and their families. But I gave one to Miriam Warner earlier this morning, too."

"Why?"

"So she – or Gerald – could call me if she needed to."

Townsend's mouth quirked. "Why would they need to call you?"

"I've known the Warners for years. I thought they might want someone to talk to."

"Where were you between eleven pm last night and two o'clock this morning?"

Noah's lawyer, a deceptively fragile-looking black woman named Cecelia Baker, placed her hand on Noah's wrist. "Detective Townsend, are we really here – at six in the morning – because of a business card?"

"Yes, ma'am. And unless your client can explain how it got at my crime scene or provide an alibi, then I'm going to have to charge him."

She laughed. "Okay, Detective. You try that and see how fast this case falls apart on you." She sat back, crossing her arms, and stared him down.

Townsend looked away, back at Noah. "Where were you between eleven and two, Mr. Harkham?"

Noah swallowed. "I was home. Alone."

There was a glint in Townsend's eyes that made Noah want to punch him. "So, no one can verify that?"

"My building has security cameras in the lobby and at both exits, and a desk clerk in the lobby. Both will confirm I didn't leave until Frankie called me."

"But this is your business card, correct?" He slid the evidence bag across the table.

Noah looked at the card. The knot of anger and anxiety that had formed in his gut melted away. He smiled.

"Something funny, Mr. Harkham?" Townsend sounded as annoyed as Noah had been feeling.

"Yes, actually." He pressed a finger to the evidence bag. "That *was* my card, not is."

"What are you saying?"

Noah gestured toward his back pocket. "I'll show you the ones I have now."

He waited until Townsend nodded, then got his wallet out and withdrew one of his current business cards. He laid it on the table next to the evidence bag, then pushed the two across to the scowling detective. "The one from the scene is from when I was on the job. I haven't used those since – since I retired. I use these now," he tapped the other card.

They were very similar, and in fact were ordered using the same template. But he had dropped his rank and old desk phone number, replacing this with his new title of "Consultant and Forensics Training Instructor" and his new office number. His cell number was also on the new ones. Townsend looked them both over.

"Do you still have any of these old cards in your possession? At home or here at the precinct?"

"No." The muscles in his jaw tensed and relaxed as his teeth clenched in response to the unpleasant memory. "I threw away most of them. Then I sort of burned the rest when I realized I'd never be a cop again."

The look Townsend gave him was actually a little sympathetic. "All right."

Cecelia leaned forward. "All right? Do you mean, all right, my client can go home now?"

He frowned at her. "For now. I'll have to confirm your alibi still, Noah, but, yes, you can go for now."

The three of them stood up. Noah shook Cecelia's hand. "Thank you for coming."

She nodded with a tight-lipped smile. "I'll be in touch. Call if you need anything." She eyed Townsend with disapproval.

"I will. Thank you again."

Townsend stepped toward the door. "I'll, uh, walk you two out."

"We know the way out, Townsend," Noah said, pushing past the detective and accompanying his lawyer out of the room.

———————

Frankie caught up with him by the front door. "You okay?"

He scoffed. "Fine. What day is complete until you're accused of murder?"

Frankie winced. "You know he had to question you."

"Are you seriously defending him?"

He shifted his stance but didn't look away. "No. Well...I mean, it's protocol. That's all. He doesn't really think you did it."

Noah barked a short laugh. "Oh, that's very reassuring."

"I'm sorry, Hark. Do you want me to drive you home?"

"Thanks anyway. Probably shouldn't be seen hanging out with your prime suspect."

"Noah –"

He shoved the door open. "See you around, Frankie."

CHAPTER EIGHT

———

Noah walked to the nearest bus stop, about a block away from the precinct, still fuming. Townsend was an idiot. They weren't friends, but Noah never would've thought the man would believe him capable of murder – especially of Gerald Warner's kid. And all because of a bloody business card. *I thought he was a better cop than that...*

He glanced at his watch: 6:17. Three minutes until the next bus. And just under two hours until he had to be right back here for work. That is, if they even let him work today. It didn't make sense to go home, so he decided to walk to the coffee shop at the other end of the block instead and bought a newspaper on the way. He hadn't stopped by yet today, and, since it was only about fifty degrees out, the warmth of the shop would be a nice change.

The waitress, a petite black-haired woman in her mid-twenties, gave him a tired smile as he came in. "Good morning, Mr. Harkham."

"Not really, Lynn. How about you?"

She chuckled and shook her head, setting her long ponytail swinging. "Not this early. Wanna talk about it?"

He shrugged. "Just a misunderstanding." When she lifted an eyebrow to show he wasn't getting off that easily, he elaborated. "Someone thought I was involved in something I wasn't."

Her eyes widened. "Involved in something... something illegal?" She laughed. It reminded him of a bicycle horn.

His jaw clenched in a flash of irritation, but he forced a smile. "Thank you." He then ordered his usual Friday indulgence: black coffee and a cinnamon swirl doughnut.

She gave him his change, then brightened as she glanced at his receipt. "Oh, hey, you won!"

He frowned. "Won?"

She smiled and reached under the counter to retrieve a small box, which she placed in front of him. When she opened the box, he saw a mug with the shop's logo inside. She withdrew it with a small flourish. "Ta-da! We're doing a promotion. Every day, a previously selected random order number gets a free mug."

Noah's mouth quirked. "My lucky day."

She laughed again, then took the mug to the sink behind her to wash before filling it with coffee. The handle was still wet, so she set it down and wiped it off with a towel. "There you go. I'll just grab that doughnut and you'll be all set." She retrieved the doughnut from the glass case under the counter and gave it to him on a small paper plate. "Last one – it is your lucky day," she said, handing him a couple of napkins.

He forced a smile. "Thanks."

He took his doughnut, coffee and newspaper and chose a table toward the back of the shop. A few other regulars nodded to him as he passed by, but no one seemed inclined to talk today, which was fine with him. He settled into the chair to read the early edition. As expected, the press had already gotten wind of the Nigel Warner story, although all it said was that a young man's body had been found on the RiverWalk, the victim of foul play, that the RPD was not releasing any further details at this time but that they would keep on top of this story as it developed. He wished he had thought to warn Gerald and Miriam about reading the papers. But Gerald knew how these things worked, he would no doubt shield his wife from it as best he could. But who would shield Gerald?

He sucked some icing off his fingers and took a sip of coffee. How did his business card end up at the crime scene? Did someone drop it earlier in the evening and it was just a coincidence it was there when Nigel was killed? Or did the killer leave it there? If the killer was so meticulous about taking whatever he used to carve the clock into Nigel's skin with him, was the card, then, left behind on purpose? To implicate him?

But then that raised the question: Why? Who would do that?

Was there anyone with a big enough beef with him to want to frame him for murder? To be honest, he had put away many bad people over twelve-and-a-half years on the job, and several had made threats at the time. He would have to look into – no. No, *Frankie and Townsend* would have to look into recently released inmates Noah had put behind bars. If it was a frame up he was looking at, more than likely it would be one of them behind it.

He popped the last bite of doughnut into his mouth, and then licked the icing off his fingers. After wiping his hands on his napkin and washing down the sugar overload with coffee, he dug out his phone and dialed Frankie's number. His old partner answered on the first ring.

"Hark, you okay?"

"I'm fine. I've been thinking about Nigel's case –"

"Don't."

"What?"

"I'm sorry, man, but you have got to stay clear of this. You can't be part of this one. Not now."

"That's the thing, Frankie. I think I'm being deliberately set up for this."

"Yeah, I know."

His brow furrowed as he frowned. "You do?"

"Well, obviously I don't think you really had anything to do with it, and finding that card was a little too... neat, wouldn't you say?"

"Absolutely," he said with a relieved sigh. "So, I was thinking it might be someone I put away. Someone who would know I was on the One O'clock Killer case. I think you should look into anyone I arrested who's been recently released."

"Doing that right now. Great minds and all that."

"And?"

"So far, nothing stands out. But I'll keep at it. Something's bound to shake loose."

Noah smiled. "Okay, then. Thanks. I guess just keep me posted?"

"As much as I can. Uh, where are you right now? Home?"

"No, at Jumping Beans. Why?"

The was a muffled sound, like Frankie was cupping the phone with his hand. "Listen, Hark," his voice was much quieter, "Townsend's like a dog on a scent whenever he works a case. He may be convinced about the business card, but he's on your trail now. He's gonna be keepin' tabs on you, showin' up randomly wherever you are. He's gonna try to rattle you and he'll keep at it until he's completely convinced someone else did this."

He shrugged, even though Frankie couldn't see him do it. "Let him. I have nothing to hide and I did nothing wrong."

"Just fair warnin', s'all."

"Frankie, your accent is starting to show. Get some sleep."

He laughed. "Yes, sirree, I'm fixin' to get raht on that in jest a minnit." He over-exaggerated his native Alabama accent, the one he had worked so hard to negate in his everyday speech before moving 'up north' here to Riverdale. It always leaked out some when he was tired or really stressed. Today, Noah bet he was a good deal of both.

"You do that," Noah replied with a laugh. He started to sign off, but then thought of something. "Oh, hey – my classes...uniforms are going to hear about this, aren't they?"

Frankie was quiet for just a second too long. "Well, there were a few officers in th' room when Townsend took ya in. Geesh. I didn't think about that. Uh, y'know, no one would blame you if you cancelled your classes today." He muffled a yawn.

"And make them think I'm guilty?"

"No one is gonna think you did this."

"Townsend thinks it's possible." He picked up his cup and frowned into its empty interior.

"He doesn't really, I don't think. He just has to be thorough. If you were guilty and he didn't come at you so hard to prove it, he'd get accused of trying to cover for his former colleague. I think he's just covering his bases – just maybe a little too well."

"Whatever. Let whoever think whatever they want. I don't really care. I just wondered if Ziehring or Greenaway had said anything about it to you."

"No, not to me. And if neither of 'em have called to say otherwise, I say just go on like normal."

"Okay. Thanks, Frankie. I'll see you around."

"You betcha. See ya."

Noah hung up, then went back to the counter to order a coffee to go. Lynn filled a Styrofoam to-go cup and plopped it inside his mug with a grin. She wished him a fantastic day, the irony of which would have been humorous, if it weren't so horrible. He thanked her and left the shop.

As he stepped into the early morning and out onto the sidewalk, someone collided with him on his left side, sending scalding hot coffee sloshing onto his hand. He dropped the mug, shattering it across the concrete, and sucked in a breath from the pain. Stepping back, he turned more toward the person – a pretty, young blonde woman – so he could see her with his good eye.

"Sorry! You okay?"

The coffee had splashed her, too; she was busy swiping at a spot on her white blouse. She threw him a glare like he'd insulted her and her mother. Pushing past him and on into the shop, she muttered, "Jerk."

"I said I was –" He sighed as the door swung closed. "Forget it."

Shards of navy blue porcelain and bits of Styrofoam and plastic lay in a puddle of coffee at his feet. With a growl of frustration, he knelt and started to pick up the pieces. One sliver jabbed deep into his finger, drawing blood. He pulled it out with a hiss and stuck his finger in his mouth, sucking a drop of blood out of the puncture.

"Let me get that for you."

He looked up to see Lynn exiting the shop with a broom and dustpan. With a grateful sigh, he stood. "Thanks, Lynn."

She was already sweeping up the mess. "No problem. But you lost your mug...Tell you what, lemme get you a new one."

"I appreciate that, but don't worry about it."

She stiffened a little. "You sure?"

"Yeah. Thanks anyway. See you later." He started back down the sidewalk toward the precinct when he remembered his laptop was still at home. With a groan, he went on to the bus stop instead.

Oh, yes, it was going to be a *fantastic* day.

CHAPTER NINE

"I'm going with you to the University."

Frankie looked up at Townsend standing next to his desk. "What happened to 'I should think about recusing myself from this case'?"

Townsend rubbed his forehead. "I had to question him, you know that, right?"

"I know. But, really? Noah Harkham is the last person who would do this. He'd never hurt anyone." Townsend's eyebrow twitched upward before his face regained its neutral expression. Frankie frowned. "What was that look for?"

He took a breath and let it out before answering. "I know you're probably right. But, you have to admit that Harkham's got a bit of a... volatile side."

"Oh, come on." Frankie started to laugh, but it died out when he saw that Townsend was serious. "Look, I know Noah can be a little...gruff, but so was my grandpa and the only thing he ever killed was a few chickens for Sunday dinner."

Townsend gave him a small smile, but then shrugged. "I don't know him as well as you do, so I'll take your word for it. But, there have been complaints. Official complaints."

Frankie scoffed. "About what? By who?"

"Officer Spicer, for one."

He blinked. Okay, that one made a little sense. "He's just upset that he got called out on being a jackass. I was there, Casey; Noah got mad and raised his voice. It was *not* a big deal."

"Yes, apparently Captain Ziehring agreed. He filed it away with barely a word."

"Well, then..."

Townsend tapped his fingers on the edge of Frankie's desk. "So, are we going to the University or...?"

Frankie looked at his watch: going on 6:30. "We can go ahead on over there, but campus police won't let us in until seven. Might be good to get a look around for ourselves first."

Townsend nodded. "That was my thinking."

With a groan, Frankie got up and stretched his stiff back. As soon as he got the chance, he was going to take a very long nap. "Let's go."

By 6:48, Frankie and Townsend were parked in the lot outside Tetherton Hall. The temperature was finally getting back up to normal. He guesstimated it was right around sixty-five degrees already. His windows were down to enjoy the nice weather while it was still decent and not too hot, and a light breeze wafted through the car now and then. The campus lawns had been mowed recently, the scent of clipped grass tickled his nose, threatening to trigger his allergies, but otherwise, the stillness of the campus, the warm breeze and his lack of sleep were conspiring to make him drowsy.

His eyelids were about to close for the third time in a row when Townsend tapped his arm. "Hey, check this out."

Frankie took a deep breath, stretching, and looked where his partner was pointing. A young man was weaving his way across the green between buildings toward Tetherton, concentrating more on the text he was typing than his surroundings. After nearly colliding with a tree, he brushed a leaf out of his mop of curly auburn hair, steadied himself and then resumed his unsteady trek toward the dorm. He lurched to lean against the wall next to the emergency exit door and waited with eyes closed.

"Something tells me he's been hitting something a little stronger than his morning coffee," Townsend said.

A minute passed, then the emergency exit door opened, and another student stepped halfway out, grabbed his inebriated friend and hauled him inside. When the door shut, Frankie turned to Townsend. "I guess that's what Nigel meant by knowing how to get around curfew."

"Disabling the emergency exit alarm..." Townsend shook his head.

"Is not what we're here about." An idea struck him. "Although we may be able to use that as leverage if these guys know something but hold out on us."

Townsend nodded, considering this. "That might work." He looked around. "So, while we're waiting, tell me why you're so convinced Harkham's innocent."

Frankie squinted at him. "I already did."

"Yes, but I mean, tell me why you didn't even have to think about it. Why the possibility never even occurred to you." He was watching Frankie closely.

"Because I know him. I trust him – with my life. He may not be the easiest guy to like some days, but he is... I don't know how to describe it. Honorable, I guess. Hark believes in the law, in order and justice. I mean, really believes in it. He would never kill anyone, especially not Nigel Warner. Gerald is a colleague, a friend, he would never want to cause him this kind of pain. Besides, he barely knew the kid."

Townsend was quiet a long moment. "What if I told you he already has?"

"Has what?"

"Killed someone."

He twisted in his seat to face Townsend more. "What are you talking about?"

"I did some digging."

"You gotta be kid–"

"Hear me out." He held up his hands, cutting Frankie off. "I looked into him right after our interview, like I do every other suspect. Okay?" Frankie fumed, but nodded for him to continue. "And I learned two things: First, his alibi checks out. The night clerk in the lobby confirmed he didn't leave until after you called. Second, Harkham killed a guy holding up a bank back in 2000, his first year on the beat. Hostage situation. It was ruled clean, and he even received a commendation for saving the lives of multiple hostages, but he does have blood on his hands."

Frankie thought back. Had Hark ever told him about this? "You're talking about in the line of duty, Casey. We all know that's different."

"Is it?"

Was it? Could he do what Harkham had, if it came down to it? If it meant preventing the death of an innocent, yeah, he knew he wouldn't hesitate, just like Hark hadn't. "If there had been any other way, I know he would have done it different."

Townsend shook his head, an incredulous look on his face. "You believe in the guy that much, huh?"

"Listen, guys like Harkham – and me and you – we do this job for the right reasons, okay? If someone was accusing you of this thing, do you think for one second Noah or I would believe it? Would you believe it if they were accusing me?" Townsend merely dipped his head. "Okay, then, what does that weird radar thing you got tell you?"

"Weird radar thing?"

"You know, how you 'read' people." He made air quotes with his fingers.

Townsend went quiet for another long moment. Then he nodded. "Okay."

Frankie scoffed. "Okay?"

"Yes. Okay. I believe you."

"Yeah? Well, good. You should. You know I'm right about this." He noticed a campus police car pulling into the lot. "Here we go." He got out of his car as soon as the officer's car parked.

A middle-aged cop with dark brown hair and wire-rimmed glasses got out and hitched up his trousers before coming around to greet the detectives. "Detective Franks? Lieutenant Peal."

Frankie held up his badge and ID. "Good morning, Lieutenant," he said, shaking the man's hand. "This is Detective Townsend." Peal shook Townsend's hand. "Sorry to call you out so early, and under these circumstances."

"I'm sorry, too, fellas. I was surprised to get your call about Nigel. It's all just...tragic."

Townsend exchanged a look with Frankie. "So, you knew him?"

Peal waved a hand. "Not really, but, you know, we were alerted when Nigel enrolled, told to be aware of the possibility that someday someone might wanna take a shot at his daddy by hurting the boy. It's standard procedure whenever we get someone here with a connection to any high-profile types. Nigel was on our EPP list."

Frankie furrowed his brow. "I'm sorry, your what list?"

"EPP. Extra Precautions Patrol. All that really means is that we drive by the dorm a few extra times each patrol sweep, keep an eye out on the kid when we see him or her walking on campus. That sort of thing."

"I never realized Riverside had that many high-profile students."

Peal winked. "That's the idea, boys. Nobody does. Come on, I'll get you inside."

CHAPTER TEN

Peal led the way to the dormitory and used one of about three dozen keys on a retractable keyring attached to his belt to unlock the door without using the keycard reader. Townsend and Frankie followed him into the dorm's lounge area, furnished with groups of tables and chairs plus a large central couch and scattered bean bags. A large, flat-screened TV adorned the wall opposite the couch and vending machines and water fountains lined the one opposite the door, next to a hall that led to a set of stairs and the dorm rooms beyond. A restroom and the RA's desk filled the wall behind the seating area. The lights were off, and all was quiet.

As he led them through the lobby toward the hall leading off to the first-floor suites and stairs, Peal kept up a running commentary. "Riverside has been gaining prestige steadily for the last two decades, and we've had some fairly important people attend here. Paul O'Dwyer, the pro baseball player, graduated from here in '95 after leading the Ospreys to the top of the division four seasons in a row."

"Really?" Townsend feigned interest.

Peal started up the stairs. "Oh, yeah. And the police Chief's granddaughter graduated just two years ago."

"I heard she was as smart as she is easy on the eyes."

They had arrived at the second-floor landing and Peal paused before leading them further. His expression remained friendly on the surface, but a tightening around his eyes told Townsend he'd hit his mark. "I really couldn't tell ya much about that – she's not much more than a kid, Detective."

"Of course. I just meant that good genes of all kinds run in that family. Her grandfather is quite proud of her."

Peal forced a smile, but it didn't quite erase the look of protective distaste in his eyes. "He sure should be, that's right. Come on, Warner's dorm is just up the hall." He tromped on around the corner.

"What was that about?" Franks' voice was barely audible as they followed the officer down the hall.

"Just taking a 'read' on him."

"And?"

"Good man. Or at least, not a pervert."

"Here we are, gentlemen." Peal was stopped outside a closed door.

Before the two detectives caught up to him, the door to their left opened and a frazzled-looking student rushed across the hall to pound his fist on the closed door opposite. Franks murmured a polite 'excuse me' as the oblivious kid nearly backed up far enough to bump into him. It was only then that the kid realized they were there. He froze, wide-eyed as he took in their attire and bearing.

"Good morning," Franks said with a nod as they passed by.

The closed door opened, and another student sleepily asked, "Whaddaya want, Blake?"

Townsend heard the kid – Blake – say to the other, "Dude, it's the Feds."

Franks smirked. "Hear that, Townsend? We've been promoted."

Townsend frowned, his mood souring. "That depends on how you feel about the FBI."

Franks chuckled. "Touché."

Peal waited until they approached and raised his hand to knock on the door, but Franks stayed him a moment. "We'd like to break the news to his roommates ourselves, if you don't mind. And we'll need to search the room, as we discussed on the phone."

"Like I said, whatever you need. But with him being..." He glanced over their shoulders to where the two students were still peeking out the doorway at them. They quickly shut the door. "With it happening off-campus, I'm not sure what you expect to find here."

Townsend nodded. "You're probably right, Lieutenant, but we need to cross all our t's. You understand."

Peal rapped his knuckles on the door then stepped aside. Franks stepped forward, then pointed to one of a pair of dry-erase boards hanging on the door. The one he indicated had Nigel's name underlined at the top. A couple of messages were written on it, one a short, angrily scrawled note:

Let me know when you're sick of being a fool. – Brent

"Brent. That's the best friend."

Townsend scoffed. "Doesn't sound too friendly."

They heard a muffled voice say, "Minute." Then, after several more seconds, the door opened to reveal a guy around eighteen with bed-tousled blond hair rubbing his eyes with the palm of one hand. He wore plaid pajama pants and a tee-shirt featuring a chili pepper wearing a sombrero and mustache over a suggestive leer, a word balloon asking the inevitable, 'Hot enough for you?'

The young man's eyes went wide when he saw Peal and the detectives. "Whoa...um, hi?"

"Are you Justin Pierce?"

The boy's eyes shifted to Franks. "Uh, yeah?"

"My name is Detective Franks. This is my partner, Detective Townsend." They both showed Justin their badges. "Do you mind if we and Lieutenant Peal here come inside, please?"

Justin looked over his shoulder at the messy room: clothes thrown everywhere and stacks of books overflowing the desk by his bed and teetering in piles on the floor. "Yeah, of course...place is a wreck, though. Sorry." He stepped back and opened the door further for them to enter.

It was easy to tell by the contrasting states of the different sides of the room that Justin and Nigel had nearly opposite views on cleanliness. Nigel's bed was made, there was no trash or dirty clothes anywhere and all his books were at least placed on the bookshelf next to a drafting table, even if they weren't precisely organized. Justin eyed Nigel's empty bed and began chewing on his lower lip, his arms hugged around his middle.

"What's this about? If you don't mind me asking."

Townsend finished taking stock of the room before turning his attention back to the young man. "Justin, can you tell us when you saw Nigel Warner last?"

Justin shifted his weight from one foot to the other repeatedly. "Last night. At dinner. Uh, I finished before he did so I came back to the room to study and I, uh, must have fallen asleep."

"So, you didn't notice that he didn't come home last night."

Justin paled and sucked in his bottom lip as he shook his head. "Is he in some kind of trouble?" He looked at Lieutenant Peal.

Peal threw a pointed look at Franks, who cleared his throat and said, as gently as one can in this situation, "Justin, I'm sorry, but Nigel Warner was murdered last night."

Justin froze, all the color draining from his face. His breathing turned rapid. "What?" His voice came out strained and tears were already flooding his eyes. He looked at their grim faces, each in turn. "Nigel's dead?"

"I'm very sorry." Franks gave him a sympathetic look as the boy sank to sit on the edge of his bed.

"Justin, we need to ask you some questions, if you don't mind." The boy was shaking now, and Townsend knew he needed to direct his mind, get him to focus or the kid was probably going to end up heaving on the floor.

"Yeah...Yeah, of course. What, uh, what do you wanna know?"

"First, I'd like you to tell me when the last time you saw Nigel really was."

Justin jerked his head up, then his expression crumpled. Tears streamed down his face. "I, uh, it was around midnight." He threw a worried glance at Peal. "We were at, um, this club downtown... A friend's band was playing, so we – we snuck out to go see them."

Townsend nodded. "Okay. Now, who is 'we,' Justin?"

Franks cut in. "Was it just you and Nigel? Or were Brent and Vivian there, too?"

"How do you –? Um, Brent was there, but not Vivian. It was me, Nigel, Brent and Trevor." A flicker of what could be guilt flitted across his face.

"What happened around midnight?" Townsend pressed. "Why didn't Nigel come back here with the rest of you?"

There was a knock on the door next to Justin's bed and then the door opened. A tall, thin African-American kid with glasses, and a stockier Caucasian kid with brown hair peeked into the room. "Hey, Justin, we were going to run to Breakfast House, d'you wanna –" The African-American boy stopped mid-sentence when he saw the three cops.

Justin started crying in earnest when he saw his suitemates. The third boy's gaze went directly to Nigel's empty bed. "No," he said, coming into the room and pointing a shaking hand at the other side of the room. "Justin?"

Justin shook his head, wrapping his arms around himself tighter. "Brent, Trevor..." he sniffled, "Nigel's dead."

The first young man – Trevor, he surmised – turned to Townsend and Franks. "No, that can't be right. You've made some kind of mistake."

"I'm sorry, son, but we're positive it's him."

Brent put a hand to his stomach and leaned forward, his other hand braced on his knee. Franks was at his side instantly, but Brent pushed him away, although he kept hold of his arm. "How? What happened?"

"He was murdered," Franks told him. "Not too long after he parted ways with you three at the club."

Trevor, who had gone stock still at the news, now seemed to snap out of it. "You told them we broke curfew?"

Justin gaped at him, incredulous. "Nigel's dead, Trevor! I think that's more important than the freakin' curfew!"

"I know, I know...it's just... I'm sorry, officers, but I don't think any of us should say anything else until we have lawyers with us."

Franks expression was of unmasked irritation. But it was Peal who answered, stepping in smoothly. "We're not going to bust yer balls for breaking curfew, boys. This is a murder investigation, though, so you best answer the detectives honestly and everything will be all right."

Franks made a sweeping gesture toward all three boys. "Someone wanna tell us what happened last night?"

Justin sniffed. Without looking at his friend, he said, "Brent?"

Trevor sputtered, "Justin, stop talking!"

"This isn't one of your stupid mock trials, *Counselor*, so I think you should just shut up and –"

"It's my fault." Brent sucked in a breath. "Oh, God, it's my fault, isn't it?"

Franks put a hand on the boy's back. "Just tell us what happened."

"We got into a fight." He sniffed. "I, uh, I tried to tell him that his girlfriend was cheating on him, but he wouldn't listen. He didn't believe me, like I would lie to him. He's my – he's my best friend, and we – and now –"

"All right," Franks said soothingly. "You had words. Did it get physical?"

Justin cut in. "No, sir. The bouncer kicked us all out because of the arguing. The last any of us saw of Nigel was as we were leaving."

Trevor nodded. "He went one way, we went the other."

"Did he say where he was going?"

Trevor looked at Townsend as if he'd already said too much. Instead of replying, he simply shook his head. Townsend then turned to Brent. "Nigel's girlfriend, this is Vivian?" Brent nodded. "And she's cheating on him?"

Justin gave a short, bitter laugh. "Oh, yeah. That girl will flirt with anyone with a pe–" he stopped short. "Pulse," he amended quickly.

Brent nodded. "No surprise she was caught with her tongue down some other guy's throat. But Nigel, he's blind when it comes to her. He doesn't – he didn't listen..." He closed his eyes and groaned. "The last thing I said to him was, 'If you think I'd lie to you, maybe we aren't friends after all. If you want to throw your life away on this girl, I'm done with you.' But I didn't... he died thinking that I..." He tried taking another breath, but it caught in a sob.

Franks looked at Townsend. "I think we have everything we need for now, don't we?"

Townsend pressed his lips together. If these guys knew Nigel was dead before they arrived, they were extremely good actors. "Yes, we're done." He looked at each of the boys. "But we'll need y'all to come down to the station and give your statements."

The grief-stricken young men nodded. Townsend turned to Peal. "Is there somewhere you can have these fellas wait while my partner and I take a look around Nigel's things?"

"Sure thing. Justin, why don't we all step over into Brent's room over here and let these boys do their job?"

Justin and the others stood and dutifully filed out of the room. Before Peal left with them, Franks held him back a moment. "When we got here, there was a student clearly under the influence sneaking back into this dorm, with the help of another student. These boys just confessed to breaking curfew last night. Our victim once told his father that, quote, even the freshmen know how to get around that, end quote. I think it would be a good idea if you let us talk to the rest of the students in this dorm, let them know what happened. And that it could have happened to any one of them."

Peal bristled but was doing a great job of not showing just how much. "If you're suggesting that –"

Franks held up his hands. "I'm not suggesting anything. Maybe one of the other students saw or heard something these guys didn't. Maybe they can tell us something that will help. Maybe not. Either way, letting these guys know what happened might scare them off sneaking out, might prevent what happened to Nigel from happening to anyone else."

Peal took a breath. Then he nodded. "All right. I'll talk to the RA and have all the boys in this dorm meet you in the lobby. You can make an announcement and make the appeal for anyone with information to contact you, but I won't have you interrogating any of these kids."

Franks nodded. Peal threw a glance at Townsend on his way out the door. There was guilt and anger etched into the lines of his face. *He feels responsible...*

Franks sighed. He had walked over to the drafting table on Nigel's side of the room and was now staring at the unfinished building designs there. The sketches looked like plans for a church, a beautiful neo-gothic structure. "Kid had talent," Franks said.

"Yes, he did. Why don't you take the desk and I'll take the closet?"

"Yeah, sure..." But he didn't move away from the sketches. "He was a kid when I met him, you know? Last time I saw him, he hit me up to buy popcorn for some fund raiser his class was doing. Gerald said it was good for him to learn not to take money for granted, that it had to be earned."

"Franks."

He looked up. "Right, the desk. I said I got it."

"Yes, I heard you. But I gotta tell you that, from here, it doesn't much look like you've got your head in the game."

Townsend could almost feel the anger rising inside the other detective as he answered, "Excuse me?"

"Look, I've known Gerald for a long time, too. My heart breaks for him and Miriam, it does, but we're not helping them or Nigel by standing here feeling sorry for them." He paused. "Maybe I should just finish up in here while you go tell the others what happened. Give your little 'it coulda been you' speech."

Franks glared at him. "Do you want me off this case?"

"That's not what I –"

"Do you want me off this case or not, Casey? It's a simple question."

"No. But if you're on it, you're on it. Anything else is just wasting time we don't have."

"Right. Like this conversation." He turned and grabbed the door handle. "Don't take too long in here. I'm gonna go give my little speech."

Franks left without slamming the door, which, Townsend had to admit, was a testament to his professionalism. He sighed. If Franks hadn't needed to get angry to get him out of whatever fog he was in, Townsend would never have spoken to him like that. But Franks at the top of his game is exactly what he needed – what the Warners needed – if they were going to solve this thing.

"Sorry, pal," he said to the empty space where his partner had been standing.

CHAPTER ELEVEN

He had gotten to his office without incident. That he was aware of this fact made his teeth clench so hard they ached. *How dare you do this to me?*

He rubbed his fingers across his left eye, which felt swollen and scratchy. It had been sore off and on over the past week since his last surgery, but never this bad. Maybe it would be better to admit defeat and just have Dr. Barnes remove the useless thing rather than keep subjecting himself to this tide of hope and despair when surgery after surgery failed to restore his sight.

He'd made his peace with the loss of hearing in his left ear, why couldn't he just do the same for his eye? Because no one had said it was impossible. And if there was even one chance in a million he could see normally again, he had to try for it, no matter the toll it would take when it failed.

His laptop was open, the rape/homicide case notes displayed on the screen, but he found it too hard to focus on that. But he had to at least try to have something to present in class, provided anyone would listen. He opened the top center drawer of his desk, looking for a pen to make notes with, shuffling through random pencils and unused flash drives. There should've been a letter opener in there, too. If his eye would stop burning, he could find it – and a pen – a lot easier.

He was wiping away the tears that scratching at his eye had welled up when there was a light knock on his door. His cousin, Neil, stood in the doorway. "Hey," he said.

"Hey, Neil. What's up?"

"Is it true?" He came in and closed the door, but remained standing, his arms crossed over his stomach.

Noah's brow drew sharply down as indignation rose up inside him. "How can you even ask me that?"

Neil blinked. "What?"

He suppressed a growl. "What do you mean 'what'? How can you think it's even remotely possible that I had anything to do with this?"

"What are you *talking* about?"

He paused. "What are *you* talking about?"

Neil shifted his stance. "Nigel Warner. Saddler said he was murdered."

Noah waited for him to get to the part where Noah was accused of being the murderer, but he didn't say anything else. "That's all he told you?"

Neil frowned slightly. "Yeah. What else would he –? Wait, did someone think you had something to do with it?"

"Yeah." Noah nodded, raising one eyebrow. "Saddler. And Lewis. And Townsend."

Neil came further into the room and dropped into the chair in front of Noah's desk. "Are you serious? Why?"

Noah scoffed. "My business card – one from when I was on the job – was found on the scene. With Nigel's blood on it."

Neil shook his head. "But that's circumstantial at best."

"Exactly."

"Did he question you? Townsend." Noah nodded, and Neil's eyebrows raised slightly. "Officially?"

"He didn't place me under arrest, but it was a formal interview, yes."

"Because of a business card."

"That's exactly what Cecelia said."

"Your lawyer was with you? That's good... But I still don't see why you were even remotely suspected." He leaned forward, resting his elbows on his knees. "What am I missing here?"

"It was done the same way the One O'clock Killer had killed his first two victims."

Neil processed this for a minute. As usual, his expression betrayed very little of what he was thinking. "So, the idea is what? You're creating a case for yourself to solve?"

"That's about the gist of it."

"Ridiculous," he scoffed, but then grew quiet again. "That was years ago. Why is he back now?"

He couldn't help but laugh. "Yeah, answer me that and you'll have solved the case."

"I guess that explains why you looked so upset when I got here."

Noah frowned, thinking back. What had he been doing right before Neil knocked? "What do you mean?"

"Sorry, I couldn't help but see you through the glass door." He gestured toward Noah's face.

"Oh. That. No, that was just my eye. It's sore again."

Neil quirked one eyebrow. "Still? It's been over a week now. Have you told Dr. Barnes yet? You can't afford to let anything out of the ordinary go unchecked."

"Or what? I could go blind? Oh, wait, too late."

"You could lose it completely."

"No. God wouldn't even be that cruel."

Neil sighed and stood. "It isn't God that's cruel, Noah. Humans have the market cornered on that trait."

His jaw was aching again. He forced his muscles to relax, his teeth to stop clenching. "Yeah, that makes a convenient excuse, doesn't it? Blame it all on free will, don't make Him answer for anything." It felt good to pour out the venomous words, but in their wake was guilt. He closed his eyes a moment and made a negating gesture with his hand. "I'm sorry. I know you were just trying to help."

Neil's mouth turned in a small, sad smile. "It's okay. I can imagine the kind of morning you've had – believe me." He glanced at the clock on Noah's wall. "Look, I've got to get to the lab, but I'll check in on you later, yeah?"

"Yeah. Okay. And Neil? Thanks. You know, for not believing it."

"Of course. See you later?"

Noah felt himself smiling. "Yeah. See you later."

Once Neil had left, Noah tried to go back to working on his presentation for class, but the words and images on the screen failed to hold his attention. Even though he hadn't been directly involved, it still boiled down to it being his fault that Nigel Warner was dead. Whoever killed him had done it to get back at Noah for something, and they chose Nigel for that purpose. But why? He shut the laptop, set his elbows on the desk and buried his face in his hands. *What have I done?*

He wriggled his fingers through his hair, then yawned. If only he could sleep, maybe he could think this through. But no, it was already eight o'clock. His first group of officers would be in the conference room, waiting for him. Did he even want to deal with that today?

He sighed. Just get it over with.

CHAPTER TWELVE

———

Apparently, the word had gotten out. The boys of Tetherton Hall were mostly silent, sitting in various places all over the common room lounge, thousand-yard stares on their faces. Some, Frankie presumed they were the ones who had known Nigel well, had tears in their eyes. Everyone looked stunned.

"I can see that I don't need to tell you all why we're here." He swept his gaze over the crowd. "And to those of you who knew Nigel Warner, I want to say I am sorry for your loss. The RPD is doing everything we can to find his killer." He looked them over again, but no one looked like they might be trying to hide anything. "I can't discuss the details of the investigation at this time, but I do want to make you all aware that the attack that claimed Nigel's life occurred off-campus, near the river, after curfew."

This caused a wave of murmurs to sweep through the crowd. He waited until it subsided. "I realize that breaking curfew, sneaking out of the dorm, is not an unusual occurrence in this and probably all the other underclassmen dorms. I realize that it has probably been happening as long as this University has existed and will probably continue for as long as this University remains, but I urge you all to remember this: what happened to Nigel could happen again. I don't want to cause any kind of panic here, I just want you all to be aware of the possibility of danger in this city."

Everyone just stared at him, glassy-eyed. "Does anyone have any questions?"

One young man standing against the back wall with his arms wrapped around his stomach, looked up. "Yeah, I got a question." All eyes turned to him. "Where were you? If you all know how dangerous this city is, where were all the cops? Are you telling me there wasn't even a single cop patrolling the river?"

He had expected this. It was always easier to blame cops for allowing something like this to happen. "There were officers in the area, but the attack happened very quickly during a time when no one was in the exact location. First responders were on scene as soon as the – as soon as he was discovered, and we have been working hard ever since to track down any information that may lead to a suspect. Which brings me to my next point: if any of you knows anything that might help us with that," he sought out the high-flyer he and Townsend had seen sneaking in and fixed his gaze on him, "it could greatly affect the outcome of this case."

The boy's face flushed, and he looked away. No one else met Frankie's gaze. Either nobody knew anything, or nobody wanted anyone else to know that they did. He noticed a bulletin board covered in fliers and posters near the vending machines. "I'm going to pin my card to the notice board. If anyone has any information – even the smallest detail could help – call me. You don't need to identify yourself; if you'd prefer to stay anonymous, that's fine. But, please, call if you know anything relevant. You're all free to go now."

As they filed out of the lounge, he went to the notice board and tacked one of his cards to the cork, next to a flier about job openings across campus. Peeking out from under that flier was a notice offering term paper editing services. The contact listed was none other than Nigel Warner. Several of the little slips with his number on them had been torn off.

Frankie took a glove from his pocket and used it to pull the notice off the board. It was a long shot, but it was possible that someone had been very displeased with Nigel's services and confronted him, then things just got out of hand. The clock could have been added afterwards to confuse the investigation. There was a fantastic criminal justice program here; they may have even covered the One O'clock Killer case in class...

But that still wouldn't explain what Noah's card was doing there. Unless...Noah had done a few guest lectures before he was injured. More than likely, he had left behind some of his business cards. Whoever had killed Nigel could have planted the card at the scene, again, just to muddy the waters. But that begs the question of why. Was it because they were really trying to frame Noah? Or did they think that he'd would be just enough of a distraction to let them go free without Noah being in any real danger?

He frowned at Nigel's flier. It was probably a long shot...but it was the only lead he had.

CHAPTER THIRTEEN

———

<u>Friday, August 29, 2014 8:04 a.m.</u>

A hush fell over the room the moment he walked in. Ignoring it, he walked to the front of the room, opened his briefcase and removed his laptop. As he began trying to hook up the laptop to the projector, someone started whispering again. It ceased the second he looked up, but several of the officers were eyeing him with a variety of expressions: suspicion, anger and pity being the most readily identifiable ones. He took a deep breath and let it out through his nose, concentrating only on getting the laptop to plug into the fricking projector.

Once that was finally done, he faced his class. He stared them down a long moment, just long enough for them to start fidgeting. "I'm sure all of you have heard about Nigel Warner's murder, and that Detective Townsend interviewed me this morning. Let me be clear: my business card was found at the scene and Townsend had to ask me if I knew how it might have gotten there, but that is the end of the story. I could stand up here and proclaim my innocence, but I won't, because doing so would give credence to the idea that I am even remotely considered a suspect in his death." He fell silent, letting that sink in with everyone. "Now, can we all concentrate on the case I am presenting to you today instead of Nigel Warner's?"

A female officer in the second row raised her hand. He didn't recall her name, but he'd seen her and officer Spicer hanging around together. He let two heartbeats pass before acknowledging her. "Yes?"

"So, let me get this straight, Mr. Harkham," she said in what he figured she considered her best 'cop' voice, "something belonging to you was found at the scene of a murder and Detective Townsend just cut you loose?"

"I'm standing here, aren't I?" He flipped on the projector. "Get the lights, Officer...?"

"Gomez," she answered, but made no move toward the light switch.

"Get the lights, Officer Gomez."

She settled further into her chair and glared at him, one eyebrow raised in challenge. Another officer toward the back sighed and got up. Noah held up a hand to stop him. "Wait. Gomez will get those."

She scoffed, then forced a sickly-sweet smile on her face. "Oh, I'm sorry, I didn't hear you *ask* me to, *sir.*"

"And you won't. I'm your instructor and I instructed you to turn off the lights." His breathing was starting to quicken, and an angry coil twisted in his chest. He composed his features and just stared back at her. Eventually, she made a 'whatever' face, got up, and turned off the lights.

The screen showed the brutal crime scene photos from the cold case. "Right, then. Twenty-seven years ago, Martha Sanders was raped and murdered. Blood found at the scene belonged to the twenty-three-year-old victim, but blood and tissue found under her nails and between her teeth belonged to a yet unidentified male. She was found, partially clad, in a Dumpster in downtown Riverdale. Water Street, near the port."

He paused and advanced to the next photo. "This photo collage is all the potential suspects, all of whom were ruled out due to blood typing and/or alibis. All these men were either related to the victim or knew her well: coworkers, friends, and former classmates she kept in touch with. Can anyone tell me why the investigators considered their leads exhausted at this point?"

Some of the officers were whispering to each other; only about half were paying attention. He got the roll sheet for this section out of his briefcase and picked a name at random. "Officer Byers, thoughts?"

A slightly older female cop in the front row with a bearing of natural authority shifted her hazel eyes from the screen to him. She cleared her throat. "Because four out of five rapes are committed by someone known to the victim, and about forty-seven percent are committed by men the victims consider friends."

"Absolutely correct." Thank God one of them has a brain. "Now, with no concrete leads to point them in the direction of the stranger who raped and murdered the victim, there was very little else they could have done at that time. However, the DNA from this case still exists. Whether it was preserved correctly and what condition it's in currently is a question no one was too eager to answer when I asked – "

Someone snickered loudly on the left side of the room. He looked but couldn't tell who it had been. "Which leads me to believe that budget cuts, staffing shortages, and the lack of a proper storage warehouse for cold case evidence may mean this DNA hasn't been preserved. Either way, CODIS didn't exist back then, and neither did widespread use of DNA testing, so the killer's DNA isn't in the system. Now, here is the lesson from all this: cases go cold despite good police work. No one did anything wrong here, they just lacked the tools that might have given them a shot at closing this case. The only way the blood from this case will ever get tested for DNA –

if it still even exists – is if new evidence comes to light to warrant opening this case, or if another case with a similar MO occurs."

"Like Nigel Warner's murder."

The officer who spoke sat near Gomez, so he figured he was cut from the same ignorant cloth as she and Spicer. Noah glanced at the roll sheet, then stepped away from the podium and gestured toward him. "Fine. Go on, Patrolman Tritt. Say what you've got to."

The officer smiled innocently. "I just meant that now there's another body, your case will be reopened."

"It has been reopened. Detectives Townsend and Franks are working it. Not my case anymore. Do you have a point?"

He retained his innocent expression. "So, when you say another case with a similar MO, could that mean a copycat, too?"

Gomez smirked at Noah. He ignored her. "Yes."

"How can you tell the difference? I mean, unless the copycat happens to, say, leave something of his behind at the scene that indicates this crime was committed by a different person–" Gomez started laughing into the back of her hand, and the patrolman struggled to keep a straight face. "Ahem, unless that happens, how can you know this guy isn't the original killer?"

This time, it took several heartbeats and controlled breaths before he could answer. "Time is a consideration, how long it has been since the original case and how old that would make the original perpetrator now. Geography is another, whether or not the new case occurs somewhere near the old –"

Gomez snorted, and her cohort lost his composure. Noah talked over them. "You also have to consider whether or not what was left at the scene is too convenient or too obvious. Sometimes, what looks like a copycat turns out to be a frame up."

Byers threw a dirty look at her comrades. She turned to Noah. "How easy is it to frame someone, sir?"

He focused on her, blocking out the distraction the others were trying to cause. "Very easy. The question is: how easy is it to frame someone well? And the answer to that is it isn't. People tend to like what is obvious and easy. The path of least resistance, so to speak. Our – your job is to look beyond the easy answer to find the right one. If a personal item is found readily at your crime scene, but other evidence is meticulously removed or destroyed, then that *should* be a big red flag to you that something else might be going on."

"That the person the item belongs to might be being set up, you mean?" She said this very pointedly.

"Exactly."

"Couldn't it also mean that the criminal screwed up and isn't as perfect as he thinks he is?" Gomez asked. "Maybe he is a copycat. Maybe, his life is just pathetic enough he thinks if he can create a buzz around a case and then, oh, I don't know, help solve it himself, he'll be some kind of hero?" She stared him down, one pencil-thin eyebrow raised over her gaudy eye shadow. Tritt's face was turning red from suppressing laughter so hard.

"What do you want, Gomez? Do you want me to say it for you? Fine, if you must hear it, I'll say it. Once. I did not kill Nigel Warner."

"Whoa, I didn't say anything about you or Nigel. I was posing another angle to the hypothetical case you and Byers were talking about. Why would you automatically assume that was directed at you?"

"Why would you assume that I'd be stupid enough to leave my business card at the scene? One I haven't used in over a year and don't own any of anymore?"

She shrugged. "So how would you do it, huh? How would the Great Noah Harkham pull off the perfect murder?"

He clenched his teeth. "I'm not doing this with you."

"But we're here to learn from you, Oh Wise One."

The patrolman chimed in. "Yeah, teach us all about this amazing forensics crap you get off on and that I've gone five years on the job without having to care about."

His hands curled into fists and he could feel blood rushing to his face. "I didn't have anything to do with this." His voice was getting louder than he could control. "Because if I did, there would be no way in *hell* anyone *here* would ever know it."

As soon as the words left him, he wished he could call them back, make everyone unhear them. But he couldn't, just like he couldn't stand looking at their gawping faces a moment longer. "Get out," he said, though not in his usual flippant dismissal. "Everyone get out of my sight. I'm done trying with you people."

Everyone started talking, Gomez and Tritt's laughter drowning them all out as they led the way out the door. Noah slammed his laptop closed and jerked out the cords, taking the door to his right out of the room. Ten feet down the hallway, he was still fuming – but now his anger was directed at himself. *Stupid, stupid move, Noah. Way to sell your innocence...Frick.*

He didn't know what had come over him. Usually, he could ignore the bad attitudes some of the cops gave him in class, but today...

Granted, it had started getting ugly without his help, but that was no excuse for letting it get so out of hand. Again. *What is wrong with me?*

CHAPTER FOURTEEN

Noah hesitated, his hand poised to knock. He took a breath, then rapped his knuckles on his former Captain's door. Ziehring's voice told him to enter, so he did.

"Noah?" He sounded surprised. "What brings you by?"

His hands were trembling, his heart beating too fast. He went to the chair across from Ziehring's desk but gripped the back of it instead of sitting. "You're going to hear about it, so I want it to come from me first."

Ziehring frowned, his red eyebrows making a deep V over his green eyes. "Have a seat."

Noah shook his head and began pacing. "I never should have lost control of the situation. I screwed up, Captain."

"Slow down, Noah." He stood and stepped in front of Noah, stopping him mid-stride. "What happened?"

"I lost my cool with a couple of the uniforms. It was just like with Spicer..."

"Okay, okay – just take a breath and start at the beginning. Who were the officers?"

"Gomez and Tritt."

Ziehring scoffed. "Those two would try the patience of Job. Go on."

78

Noah took another deep breath and felt his heartbeat slowing a little. "They'd heard about me being questioned by Townsend and wouldn't let it go and focus on the case I was presenting. They as good as accused me of being guilty. They baited me and I – I fell for it." With an effort, he unclenched his fists. "Stupid, it was so stupid..."

Ziehring put his hand on Noah's shoulder. "Listen to me: no one really thinks you did this. But you know the drill. Every T has to be crossed, every I dotted. Townsend had to follow through so we could rule you out. And you know how cops deal with this kind of thing. Gomez and Tritt were just covering their own asses by vilifying you."

Noah nodded. "I know, I know, but *I* shouldn't have lost my composure. I never should've said –" He closed his eyes, reliving the moment.

"Said what? Noah?"

He sighed and looked his former boss in the eye. "I said they could be sure I didn't do it, because I know how to make sure no one would ever know it was me if I had."

Ziehring raised his eyebrows, but then shrugged, removing his hand from Noah's shoulder. "So what? We've all said stuff like that."

"Yeah, but I think I'm being framed for this. What if, next time, whoever's doing this does a better job? Or, even if nothing points to me next time, it still won't matter. They could just say I made good on my claim. I've opened myself up to more suspicion now, no matter what happens."

Ziehring chewed on the inside of his cheek while he thought this over. "Okay. I see your point..."

"And? What do I do?"

Ziehring had been looking off into the middle distance, but now his eyes turned back to Noah. "Hmm? Umm, well, you're not going to like what I would suggest."

"You want me to go home. Cancel my other classes."

"It would just be for now. I mean, I'll make a statement, let everyone know you are officially not a suspect, and I'll formally rebuke Gomez and Tritt, but I'm afraid you might still be a target of more incidents like this as long as you're here."

Noah suppressed a growl. "Fine," he said through gritted teeth.

"Just give it the weekend, Noah. Come back on Monday. Maybe by then, the worst of it will be over. Okay?"

"Yeah, sure. Whatever you say."

"Perfect. I'll let Greenaway know."

Noah's mouth turned downward. Yorton Greenaway was technically his boss instead of Ziehring now that Noah was a civilian employee. The guy was the epitome of bureaucratic paper pusher. And what kind of name was that, anyway? Sounds like a brand of algae killer... Noah couldn't stand the guy, and he suspected the feeling was mutual.

"Thanks, Captain."

Ziehring smiled in sympathy. "Yeah. Go home, get some sleep – you look like crap."

Noah couldn't help but laugh bitterly. "Thanks, that is exactly what I need to hear right now."

Ziehring shrugged. "I cannot tell a lie."

"Right." He shook his head. "I'll see you on Monday, then."

Ziehring clapped him on the arm and steered him toward the door, opening it for him. "Take care of yourself, Noah."

"Always do, Cap."

———————————

As soon as he got back to his office, there was a knock on the door. He half expected it to be Frankie or Townsend and was pleasantly surprised when he looked up to see Joyce Collins instead. Her hands were full, carrying a stack of paperwork, an oversized purse, and a drink carrier with two large Styrofoam cups. He opened the door with a smile. "Joyce, good to see you."

"Hello, my boy," she said, giving him a motherly kiss on the cheek. He ushered her to the chair opposite his across the desk and helped her set her stuff aside.

He sank into his chair and absently rubbed at his left eye. "So, I guess you heard."

"Yes, the poor boy. Gerald and Miriam must be devastated."

"They took it hard. Not that there's any easy way to take something like this." He shook his head. "And I guess you know about the other part, as well. Did Frankie send you to check on me?"

She frowned. "I don't know what you mean."

"Really? I figured it was all over the building by now." He sighed. "Somehow, one of my old business cards found its way to the crime scene. Townsend pulled me in for questioning this morning. Now half the uniform rank thinks I'm a killer. Or, at least a suspect."

Her deep chocolate eyes regarded him sympathetically. "Oh, honey, that's just wrong. No wonder God put you on my heart so strongly today." She removed one of the cups from the carrier. "Here, this is for you. I didn't know how you take yours, so it's just plain."

He took the proffered cup with a smile. "Thank you, Joyce. That's perfect." He noticed that her black hair was starting to show traces of silver, and the ebony skin around her eyes was crinkled more than he remembered. *This line of work ages us all before our time.*

"No offense, honey, but by the look of you, you could use the caffeine. When's the last time you slept?"

He shrugged. "What month is it?"

She didn't crack a smile. "Noah Harkham –"

"I'm just kidding. Do I really look that bad? You're the second person to comment on it today."

"Well, you're far too handsome to ever look *bad*." She had one leg crossed over the other and was tracing circles in the air with her toes. "You know, my Danny used to go through phases of insomnia. It got so bad one time that he was lucky to get four hours of sleep in an entire week."

"Wow."

She arched an eyebrow. "You know what helped?" He shook his head, so she went on. "He started talking about what was on his mind. And once he realized he could tell me anything and I wouldn't judge him, he started sleeping better."

He regarded her a long moment. "I'm all right, Joyce. Really. I think it's just because of Sunday."

She looked puzzled for a moment, and he felt irrationally offended. But then, realization dawned in her eyes. "Oh, honey, I am so sorry I didn't realize sooner. Are you going to be okay?"

He took a sip of the strong black coffee before nodding. "I'm not sure I should put this on you, but I want you to know that I'm really glad it was you that day, in what could have been my final moments. You were always my rock out there." He rubbed at his eye again.

She closed her eyes and shook her head slowly side to side. When she opened them, there were tears on her lashes. "Hearing that shot and then you screaming like that...my heart nearly stopped. That was one of the worst days of my life. I prayed so hard for you that day I was almost afraid I drowned out anyone else's prayers. Good thing the Lord has excellent hearing." She winked.

He had to swallow past the lump that formed in his throat. "You prayed for me?"

"Of course I did. I pray for all my boys and girls when I have to send them into a bad situation." She suddenly looked at him more closely. "Noah, your eye..." She reached into her purse and pulled out a compact mirror. "Take a look. It's really bloodshot."

He took the mirror but found it too difficult to hold it close enough to his left eye but still able to see it with his right. From what he could tell, she was right: the white of his eye was extremely red. "Yeah...it's just irritated. Been itching a lot."

"What does your eye doctor say?" She took the mirror back and slipped it into her purse again.

"Ummm..."

She rolled her eyes. "Men. You really ought to have him look at it, at least."

"Now you sound like Neil."

"Hmpf. And yet you haven't gone to see him." She glanced at the clock and sighed. "Time to get back down in the trenches." She stood and fixed him with a maternal stare. "Promise me you will get that checked out."

"Promise." He stood and started around his desk. A sharp pain lanced through his eye and his breath caught in a sharp hiss. He stumbled and put a hand over the left side of his face, leaning hard on his right hand on the desk.

"Noah!" Joyce tentatively touched his arm. "I'm calling an ambulance."

The sharpness of the pain was subsiding, now just a throbbing ache. But it left him panting and more than a little shaken. "No, I think I'm all right now." He lowered his hand and blinked a few times.

Concern and doubt were etched in the lines of her face. "Please, please call your doctor, Noah. Something is obviously wrong."

He tried to smile. "I will. I promise." She crossed her arms and threw a very pointed look at his telephone. "You're going to stand there until I call Dr. Barnes, aren't you?"

She nodded. "Somebody's got to make sure you take care of yourself, Noah Harkham."

He sighed, not about to admit he was glad she was staying, and dialed Dr. Barnes' office on speakerphone. Within minutes of describing what happened, with Joyce filling in the pertinent details of his male stubbornness, he was given an appointment for nine o'clock.

CHAPTER FIFTEEN

———

Townsend had left Brent, Trevor and Justin sitting in separate interview rooms, each reviewing their official statements about the previous night. Franks had shown him the flier Nigel had posted, offering editing services, and shared his theory about a disgruntled customer. He was now in another room with an inconsolable Vivian Markos, Nigel's girlfriend of ill-repute.

A longshot, he'd called it. That didn't begin to describe it, but protocol is protocol. He decided to approach Justin about it first. As Nigel's roommate, he should have the best idea of what, if anything, might have happened with Nigel's customers.

Justin looked up as Townsend entered the room. He had changed his clothes before coming to the precinct, now wearing a black long-sleeved tee shirt and jeans. His eyes lowered immediately after seeing who had come in, staring at the paper before him. "I keep reading over it, and it just seems... so stupid. I mean, the last hours of someone's life should be... meaningful, you know?" He looked up at Townsend again.

He nodded. "Life doesn't always give us that choice, unfortunately." He took a seat in the chair across the table from Justin. "My partner found this," he said, laying the evidence bag with the flier in it on the table. "Did you know Nigel was offering to edit other students' papers?"

A flicker of amusement flitted across his face, followed very quickly by both fear and shame. But the expression he presented Townsend

86

when he answered was carefully neutral. "He told me before he put the poster up. Said he was giving me a heads up because he'd be a lot busier and wouldn't be able to hang out as much."

"Do you know who his customers were? Which students hired him?"

He shook his head, his brow furrowed. "No. Nigel never said. He'd just get the paper ready and say he was going out to drop it off. I never asked." Again, a flash of fear flickered in his eyes.

"How long had he been doing this?"

"Since second semester freshman year."

"Did he have many clients?"

Justin shrugged stiffly. "A few, I guess. I don't really know."

Townsend stared at him a long moment. "And how much did he charge for his services?"

"Hundred bucks. The usual rate." As soon as the words were out of his mouth, he paled.

"That's a lot of money for proofreading a paper. Especially with spell-check and all those grammar checker programs out there. Riverside University even offers three different programs on the student portal, all for free."

The boy began fidgeting with his pen. A bead of sweat trickled down his temple. "Nigel was really good at that sort of thing..."

"What sort of thing is that?" Townsend lightly tapped a finger next to the evidence bag. "Selling papers to other students?"

Justin's lower lip began to tremble as he tapped the tip of the pen on the paper before him in a rapid staccato. He pressed his lips together in a hard line, a flush of red creeping across his cheeks. He eventually nodded, blinking free a tear that he wiped away.

"Please don't tell his parents." He crossed his arms around his middle.

The lazy buzzing of a fly in the room's one small, barred window was the only sound for a moment. "Is it possible that at least once Nigel didn't produce as good a product as he advertised? That someone might have gotten upset with him – maybe because it cost them a grade?"

Justin's eyebrows drew downward. "He never said... Do you think that might have had something to do with his death?" He sniffed. "I guess I just assumed it was, like, a mugging or something..."

"We have to pursue every possibility until we know for sure."

"I can't imagine anyone at the school would do something like this. Not anyone that Nigel would have known, anyway."

Something about the look in his eye suggested otherwise. "Are you sure about that?"

He chewed on his lip. "Yeah...except..."

Townsend leaned forward. "Except?"

"There was one guy, about a month back, from one of Nigel's classes. He found out who Nigel's dad is and went off on him for not telling everyone. Accused him of being a 'stuck-up snob goody-good that was just waiting for something he could go home and tell his daddy about.' That's what Nigel told me he said."

"Do you know the name of this guy?"

"Ummm... Barlow. Ryan Barlow. He's a real loser, and I don't mean cuz he's here on the poor kid's grant. This guy has this great opportunity handed to him and he couldn't care less. Nigel says he rarely shows up for class and when he is there, he treats everyone like garbage."

"Would he have hired Nigel to write his papers for him?"

"I wouldn't think so. I doubt he'd want to, but even if he tried, I seriously doubt Nigel would have done it." He looked back down at his statement. "Do you think it would be okay if I called my parents now? They're back home in Ohio, and I really wanna talk to them before they hear about this from someone else."

"Of course." He pointed to the bottom of the statement Justin had just signed. "Do me a favor first and write down the class this Barlow guy had with Nigel?"

"Uh, yeah, sure." He wrote a quick note at the bottom and then laid the pen on the statement and pushed them both over to Townsend.

"Thank you. Go ahead and call your folks, and then, if the other guys are done, I'll drive y'all back to the University."

Justin's mouth quirked. "No offense, Detective Townsend, but I think we'll just get a cab or take the bus. Everyone is already gonna be staring at us like we're the latest attraction without being escorted back by a cop."

Townsend smiled. "Right. In that case, just be sure to sign out at the front desk when you boys leave."

"Will do."

Townsend took the statement and pen and left Justin to make his phone call. "He's free to go," he told the uniformed officer by the door. "All three of 'em are."

The officer nodded, and Townsend moved down the hall to enter the observation room adjoining the room in which Franks was interviewing Vivian Markos. The girl was crying still, and he could tell by the set of Franks' shoulders that it was probably more for show and that he'd had enough. On a whim, he dug out his phone and texted Franks:

Ask her if she knows Ryan Barlow.

A moment passed before Franks looked down and pulled out his phone. He read the screen, glanced at the one-way window and then over at Vivian. Townsend turned on the speaker.

"-a guy named Ryan Barlow?"

Vivian stiffened at the name. She wiped away a few tears, shook back her long mane of coal-black hair and pouted her large lips. "Uh, I think he's in one of my classes, maybe...Or maybe Nigel mentioned him..." Her accent was thick Brooklyn. "I don't know for sure."

Townsend texted Franks again: *She's lying*

Franks frowned down at the phone screen. He typed a quick reply: *Wanna sit in?*

He replied in the negative and went back to watching Vivian. Franks tilted his head at her. "Just a guy from class, maybe. Did he and Nigel ever have any problems?"

She looked everywhere but at Franks. "I mean, yeah, maybe. I don't know, you'd hafta ask –" she froze, and few tears leaked down her face. "I started to say you'd hafta ask Nigel... Oh, gawd, this doesn't seem real..."

She should've been an actress... It did look like some of her grief might be real, though. He texted Franks again: *Nigel was selling papers, not editing*

Franks eyed her again after reading the message. "Did you know about Nigel's side business, Vivian?"

She went still. "Whaddaya talking about?"

"Nigel was selling term papers, wasn't he? Was this Barlow guy one of his customers? Maybe he didn't like the grade Nigel earned for him. Or was it that Nigel refused to sell to him at all? Something like that?"

Townsend smiled. Franks was quick on the uptake, as usual. Vivian crossed her arms and legs and jiggled her foot. "Look, I don't know what somebody told you, but Ryan's not a bad guy. He wouldn't-a done this."

"So, you do know him."

She sighed. "A little, yeah."

"So, tell me again: how long had you been dating Nigel?"

"About a year, on and off." She shrugged.

"On and off...why off?"

She wiped at her already dry eyes. "Nige was a good guy, a really nice guy, ya know? But sometimes... nice gets a little boring. No offense."

Townsend chuckled as Franks pointedly ignored the slight and favored her with an indulgent smile. "You like the bad boys, huh? And Ryan is one of 'em you like in particular?"

She shook her head. "It was only a coupla times. But he had all these rotten things to say about Nige, and so I told him to go to hell. I haven't seen him in, like, a month."

"So, you wouldn't know where we could find him, then?"

"He lives in one of the Quads." She shrugged. "He works in the dining hall a few days a week. Try there. But I don't think he woulda actually hurt Nigel."

Franks glanced toward the one-way window, then gave Vivian a tight-lipped smile. "Okay, then. You've been a lot of help. Thank you." He got up, taking the notepad with her handwritten statement in it with him. "Sorry for your loss."

The cool formality of his tone was not lost on the girl. "Detective Franks, I know I shoulda been a better girlfriend to 'im, but... I really did love Nige. I hope you find whoever did this."

"Thank you for coming in, Miss Markos. You're free to go."

As Franks headed for the door, Townsend turned off the speaker and opened the observation room door. "You're getting cynical in your old age, Franks," Townsend said as Franks entered the room to join him.

"Is that right?"

"Poor girl crying her eyes out and you didn't once say, 'there, there' to her."

Franks scoffed. "Please. Nigel Warner deserved a lot better than that girl. I'm starting to see why Brent was getting so frustrated with him."

Townsend was still watching her. Now that she was alone, she had let her guard down. There was real sadness in the downturn of her mouth and set of her brows, but it wasn't the grief Justin and Brent were experiencing. "She was telling the truth. She did care about Nigel, just not the way he apparently cared for her."

Franks frowned, but otherwise didn't share his opinion on the matter. "So, who's this Barlow guy? And when are we bringing him in?"

"Someone who made it known he didn't like that Nigel was a prosecutor's son, and now, if you're ready."

He stifled a yawn behind his fist. "Sure. But I wanna swing by Noah's office first."

"Of course."

Franks looked at him sidelong but said nothing. Instead, he walked out of the room, telling a uniformed officer to get Vivian signed out and back to her dorm. Townsend was just glad he didn't offer to let her ride with them.

CHAPTER SIXTEEN

<u>Friday, August 29, 2014 8:53 a.m.</u>

Noah sat in the waiting room, rubbing his eye. A sharp pain burned deep inside, and his whole eye area felt sore and swollen. Nadia, Dr. Barnes' receptionist, kept giving him sympathetic looks every few minutes, along with extra tissues as his eye kept running. He'd asked her for aspirin or something for the pain, but she said that Dr. Barnes would have to see him first before any pain medication could be administered.

So, now he was just waiting. And miserable.

Finally, Nadia opened the door that separated the waiting room from the exam areas. "Mr. Harkham, you can come on back."

He got up and followed her to exam room two, where nearly all his appointments had taken place. She got him seated and laid his file – which was thick after the last year of dealing with this – on the counter. Another minute or two passed before Dr. Barnes came in, his flop of brown hair hanging over his friendly blue eyes. He held a clipboard with the paperwork that Noah had filled out when he first arrived and was reading over it.

"Noah, what seems to be going on today?"

He took the tissue away from his eye and pointed one finger at the bloodshot orb. "This. It's been sore for almost a week and now it's red and hurts like crazy. I think..."

Barnes shifted his gaze from Noah's eye to the rest of his face. "Yes?"

"I'm thinking something went wrong…like rejection or something. But this doesn't feel the same as last time."

"It's been too long since the last cornea transplant for rejection to be an issue again now."

Noah let out a breath. That either meant whatever was happening was treatable, or something worse was going on and he could still lose his eye. "Then what could this be?"

Dr. Barnes smiled. "We'll just have to take a look and find out." He flipped off the light and retrieved the ophthalmoscope from a drawer in the counter. He seated himself on a low stool and turned on the scope's light. "Now, just look straight ahead."

Noah sat still while Barnes shone the light in his left eye. It took a few seconds before he appreciated the fact that there was a red fuzziness in his vision. He gripped the arms of the chair and waited one more second before voicing the words he never thought he'd say: "I think…I think I can see something."

Barnes froze, then backed up to look at Noah. "Tell me."

Noah blinked. The red haze was gone now. "Just for a moment, it was like when someone shines a light at you when your eyes are closed – like a fuzzy redness."

The doctor leaned forward and passed the ophthalmoscope light across his left eye again. "Anything?"

"Barely, but it's there." His heart was beating rapidly. "Does this mean I'm going to see again?"

"Slow down, Noah. That was the point of all those surgeries, but I need to do a full exam before we know anything for sure."

"Of course... Okay." He took a few slow breaths to calm his heart rate and waited while Barnes pulled the slit lamp over in front of him.

"Go ahead and place your forehead against the top bar and put your chin in the cup for me."

Noah got into position and Dr. Barnes turned on the lamp, throwing a tightly-focused, bright light into his left eye. Again, he was able to detect the light. "I can see it," he whispered, almost afraid saying it out loud would make it not true and he'd be condemned to half-sightedness forever.

Barnes *hmmm*ed and continued looking through the apparatus. "Lots of inflammation, some edema and the beginnings of some hypopyon..." He sat back and moved the slit lamp to the side. "It looks like we're dealing with an infection, most likely endophthalmitis." He sighed.

"Infection? Okay, then what? We start antibiotics?"

"Yes. An intraocular injection now, and then a course of oral antibiotics." He frowned. "I wish you had come to see me when you first began experiencing symptoms."

"Intra-" Noah's heart skipped a beat. "You're going to put a *needle* in my *eye*? Here? Now?"

"Don't worry, there are drops that will numb your eye. You won't feel it."

Noah stared at him. "You can still fix it, right? The antibiotics will clear it up?"

"Most likely, yes. But endophthalmitis is – or can be – serious and can lead to vision loss." He held up a hand. "*Permanent* vision loss, I mean. But the fact that you were able to detect the light of the scopes is very promising."

His hands were shaking. "Promising..."

"If it helps," Dr. Barnes smiled, "I am cautiously optimistic. But, first things first: let's get you that injection. Come with me." He stood and turned the room's lights back on.

Noah got up and followed him out of the exam room, down to another room at the end of the hall. When the doctor opened the door, the first thing Noah saw was a chair that looked like the one at his dentist's office. A stainless-steel counter lined one wall and a rolling cart full of shallow drawers stood nearby. Barnes unlocked a cabinet on the wall and removed a small packet, which he handed to Noah. "This is a mild sedative to help you relax."

Noah opened the packet and swallowed the pill inside before Barnes could fill a small cup with water. "I know the drill, Doc." He gave him a nervous smile.

Barnes motioned to the chair. "Have a seat, then. I'll be right back."

He left Noah alone in the room for about half an hour, long enough for the sedative to kick in. When he returned, his assistant came with him. The younger man's name eluded Noah now – the sedative was fuzzing his brain – but it was the way they were dressed that was foremost in his mind: surgical gloves, drapes over their lab coats, and masks. His heart sped up again. This was hardly his first procedure, but this one felt like it had the most at stake.

Dr. Barnes retrieved a bottle from one of the shallow drawers and removed its lid. There was a dropper attached and he drew up the clear liquid into it. "All right, Noah. This is the anesthetic. I'll put a few drops in first, then some iodine to sterilize the surface of your eye before the needle goes in."

Noah nodded and swallowed hard. "All right."

Barnes lowered the back of the chair until Noah was looking at the ceiling. "Now, look straight ahead and hold still."

Noah gripped the arms of the chair as the drops hit his eye. He blinked rapidly, but soon the slight sting went away and his eye went numb. The assistant propped his left eye open with a little metal device he'd learned was called an eye speculum. He'd also learned to hate the thing after his third surgery. It didn't hurt exactly, because of the anesthetic, but he could still feel the weight of it and wanted so badly to blink it away but couldn't.

The iodine drops hit his eye next. After that, he decided to close his right eye – he didn't want to see the needle coming at him or he knew he'd have nightmares.

CHAPTER SEVENTEEN

"This doesn't mean anything," Frankie told Townsend as they walked across the lot to his car.

"I didn't say anything."

Frankie looked over at his partner. "Yeah, sure." Despite his assurances, Frankie was far from certain that Noah's outburst – the second one this month – meant nothing. Something was going on with his best friend, something that was making him act like someone else. Someone not Noah. At least, not the Noah he had known all these years. The fact that he'd been advised to go home meant Ziehring was worried as well. But there was one thing that Frankie was certain of: whatever was going on with Noah, it had nothing whatsoever to do with this case.

Townsend's phone chimed, just as Frankie unlocked the car. "Got a number for Ryan Barlow's employer," Townsend said as they got in. "I'm gonna give 'em a call to see if he's there or at the dorm." He dialed the number while Frankie started the car and pulled out of the lot to head toward the university. "Could I speak to the manager on duty, please?" A moment of silence passed. "Hello, this is Detective Casey Townsend with the Fifth Precinct. Could you tell me if Ryan Barlow is working today?"

Frankie threw a look over at his partner. Townsend gave him a thumbs up. "Uh, no, I don't need him to come to the phone, but I do need to speak with him. My partner and I will be there in about ten minutes... No, no, we just need his help with something, just ask him a couple of questions... Yes, thank you. You, too." He hung up and put his phone away again.

"Straight to the commons, then?"

"Yeah. His boss says Ryan's scheduled until ten, just after they stop serving breakfast."

The whole way over, all Frankie could think about was the way Ziehring described his conversation with Noah. He'd said Noah had been agitated, shaky, and his eyes were bloodshot. *He looked mad...or possessed.* He hadn't come right out and said it, but Frankie knew his captain was thinking about ordering Noah to see the department psychologist, an order that would go over about as well as trying to bathe an angry cat.

When they arrived, most of the seats in the commons were full. One of the servers showed them through the kitchen, where the manager met them in the hall. She was a slim, tall woman with flame-red hair, wearing a crisp white blouse and black pants. She offered her hand to Townsend. "Good morning, Detectives. I'm Margaret Cooper."

Townsend shook her hand. "I'm Detective Townsend, we spoke on the phone. This is my partner, Detective Franks."

"Anything I can do to help, just let me know," she said, shaking Frankie's hand.

"At the moment, all we need is a quick word with Ryan Barlow," Frankie said. "Can you tell us where he is?"

She nodded and gestured toward the kitchen area. "Right this way. Ryan's working in the kitchen, washing dishes."

She led the way. The kitchen was separated from the dining hall by a thick wall and the conveyor belt contraption where students returned their trays to be transported back to the dish washer. Despite this separation, the noise from the seating area mixed with the chatter of the cooks and other workers and the sounds of the various machinery created a constant chaos of sound.

The young man at the sink was dressed in a white tee shirt and black pants, a plastic apron covering from his collarbone down to his shins. He wasn't quite as tall as Frankie and was...what was the word? Swarthy? Swarthy. Dark brown hair, dark green eyes that shot them a dark look as they approached, dark olive skin. He didn't look nervous, he didn't look angry...just dark.

Townsend and Frankie held up their badges. "Ryan Barlow?"

Ryan shifted his eyes from Townsend back to the rack of dishes he was rinsing. "If something happened to my mom or sister, don't tell me here."

Frankie and Townsend exchanged a look. "Actually, Ryan," Frankie told him, "we were hoping to get your help on something. Do you have a minute for a couple of questions?"

The boy looked at Margaret. She nodded, so he put the sprayer back on its hook on the wall above the sink, dried his hands on the towel tucked into his back pocket and tore off his apron. He threw it in the trash can under the dish return and turned to face them. "Sure."

Frankie leaned toward Margaret. "Is there somewhere quieter where we could talk?"

"You can use my office."

She led the way and they all crowded inside her little office. Ryan stood eyeing his surroundings with detached interest. The room was clean and too warm, both in temperature and in color scheme.

Margaret's red hair clashed with the earthy orange walls and red-brown high traffic carpet. At least her desk was black, giving their eyes something to rest on.

As Margaret made no move to indicate she was going to leave them in privacy to talk, Frankie nodded to Townsend to begin the interview. "Ryan, do you know Nigel Warner?"

Ryan's eyes hardened. "Yeah. The lawyer's mole – sorry, son. Why? What's he saying about me now?"

Frankie shot a look at his partner. Townsend turned down the corners of his mouth and raised one eyebrow, which Frankie interpreted as saying it was up to him how to tell Ryan about Nigel's death. He turned to the boy. "Nothing. He was murdered last night."

Margaret's sharp intake of breath distracted him from Ryan's reaction a little, but it did look like the news shocked him. But the shock was quickly replaced by a glower of resentment. "So that's why you're here? Somebody kills the lawyer's brat, so you find the nearest Barlow to blame it on?"

To everyone's surprise, Townsend laughed. He caught a breath and waved a hand apologetically "I'm sorry," he said, still smiling.

Ryan's hands curled into fists. "Did I say something funny, Detective?"

Townsend's expression softened. "No, son. You didn't. You just remind me of someone I used to know. Always thinking the world was out to get him and that its sole purpose was to put him down and keep him down – him and his whole family. But here's the thing, Ryan – the world didn't even give a crap about that guy and it doesn't give a crap about you, either. Here's how this is going to work: we're going to ask a few easy questions, and you're going to put that chip on your shoulder away and give us some honest answers. We're only here because we were told you and Nigel had some kind of confrontation when you found out who he was. Did the two of you have words at any time after that?"

The darkness was still in Ryan's expression, but now it lacked conviction. "No."

"Were you sleeping with his girlfriend, Vivian Markos?"

Ryan glared defiantly at Townsend. Townsend merely looked back, a slight smirk lifting one side of his mouth. Frankie sighed. "Answer the question, Ryan."

"Sometimes." He glanced at Margaret, his cheeks reddening.

"Did you ever try to hire Nigel to write term papers for you?"

Ryan stared at them a beat. "Are you serious? The lawyer's kid was selling papers?" He laughed, and it was as bitter and joyless as Frankie expected. "Guess he wasn't so perfect, after all."

"I didn't say he was selling papers," Townsend said. "I asked if you ever asked him to write a paper for you. And you didn't answer."

Ryan scoffed. "No, I didn't. I may be from the wrong end of town, but, contrary to public opinion, I've got a brain in my head. I don't need Nigel Warner to do anything for me, let alone write my papers."

Margaret touched Ryan's arm. "Ryan, I think you might not want to answer any more questions until you have a lawyer with you." She gave the detectives an apologetic smile.

Ryan ignored her. "Before you ask, I stayed with my mother and little sister last night." He turned to Margaret's desk and used her pen to scribble something on a sticky note, which he then slapped into Frankie's hand. "There were plenty of witnesses to corroborate for you that I was there all night. That is, unless he was killed around eight o'clock, because then I was driving, alone, from my Probabilistic Systems Analysis class to that address."

Frankie looked at the paper, then up at Townsend. "Thank you for your time, Mr. Barlow." He then led his partner back out of the dining hall and commons. Once they were back in the car, Frankie showed Townsend the address Ryan had given him.

His eyebrows shot up. "Wasn't expecting that."

Fifteen minutes later, Frankie parked in front of the Lantern Lane Women's Shelter.

CHAPTER EIGHTEEN

Friday, August 29, 2014 9:47 a.m.

The anesthetic was wearing off. He couldn't feel where the needle had gone in, but the pain and irritation that had already been there was coming back. That irritation and redness had caused several people, mostly women, to look at him like he was some sort of freak or druggie when he happened to make eye contact. So, now he was trying to avoid looking at anyone at all and sat on the bus, keeping his face turned toward the window.

He had wanted his sight back for so long, and now the idea that it might actually be happening was... a little frightening. The thought had seized him while Dr. Barnes gave him the injection and hadn't let go. It didn't make any sense, but he was scared. He chewed on his bottom lip as he turned this over in his mind, trying to see it from all angles.

This is what he wanted, right? So why was he so anxious about getting it?

Because what happens after? What happens when he got his sight back, but still couldn't be a cop? Without his hearing in his left ear, he could never go back to the job. He'd still be stuck teaching classes to a bunch of cocksure idiots who don't care about any of it. How exactly was he supposed to feel about it, given that? Was he supposed to be grateful?

He sighed. That's the thing – he *was* grateful. He had all but given up hope of ever seeing out of his left eye again, and now it seemed

that what he thought impossible was going to happen. And soon –
within days, not just someday. It was happening *now*.

And that was a miracle, despite what the cynic in him said. If he
could just endure this pain and irritation for one week, he would be
almost normal again. Almost whole. And he was afraid of ever being
less than whole again. *That* was why he was scared, he realized. It
wasn't that it wouldn't change his circumstances, wouldn't give him
his identity back. He would have to deal with that, and he knew
he probably could come to terms with it someday. But the real fear
was, what if it happened again? Or what if something even worse
happened?

He'd heard of cops who'd been shot in the head and survived, only
to be brain damaged. He'd heard of cops getting shot in the back and
left paralyzed. And then there was Kenny, the guy who owned the
Blue Line Bar. He retired from the force as a lieutenant, in perfect
health, only to get in a motorcycle accident two months later, losing
his right leg below the knee and two fingers on his right hand.

*But that didn't stop him from doing everything he loves. Didn't stop
him from living.* These thoughts came to him, but it didn't feel like
they were his. And he knew whose voice he was hearing. It had just
been years since he'd last listened to it.

He sighed and gave in, slightly lowering the shield he had put up so
many years ago, and prayed. *Okay, God, so what do you want? If you
want my gratitude, fine, you have it. If you want my forgiveness... I'm
not ready for that. I just don't –* Did he really want to get into this
now?

He closed his eyes and leaned his forehead against the glass. *I just
don't understand why they had to die. All of them. Losing my job
because of the injuries...I could have handled that if they were still here.*

But you've taken everything from me. And now you throw me a bone and give me my sight back, potentially. What am I supposed to do with that, when it changes nothing?

The bus pulled over. He opened his eyes and saw that it was his stop. Wrestling with God would have to wait a little longer. He got up, taking his briefcase, and started down the aisle toward the exit. A man waiting to get out into the aisle smiled at him as he passed by. Noah nodded in reply, though he didn't recognize him. Once off the bus, he crossed the street and headed up the block toward his apartment building. But his mind kept buzzing, cycling through the mixed emotions and thoughts over and over.

He was putting his key into his door when he realized he did recognize the man on the bus. The guy who ducked out early from Conrad's party, too. He went inside, shut the door and just stood there for a long moment, willing the stress out of his body. When that didn't work, he kicked off his shoes, threw his briefcase on the couch and went into the bathroom to take a shower.

His feet felt like concrete blocks and his shoulders felt connected to his neck by twisting and tightening steel cables. It took ten minutes under the hot water, eyes closed and forehead leaned against the tiles, before he felt the least bit of relief. Then he stayed in for a while longer, washing up. Once dried and dressed in track pants and a tee shirt, the lack of sleep caught up with him like running into a wall. He crawled into bed, flopped onto his back and was sound asleep in seconds.

Thirty-seven minutes later, he woke up.

CHAPTER NINETEEN

The woman who greeted them when they came into the reception area reminded Townsend of a wolf. Not that she looked like one – she was all of about five feet tall and a bit doughy around the middle, with lank dishwater-blonde hair pulled back in a bun – but she had a look he'd seen too many times before. It was the feral sort of wariness some women had whenever a man entered their space, tempered by a survivor's unbending will.

She rose from a desk overflowing with paperwork and placed herself between them and the door leading further into the shelter. Her gaze swept over them both in efficient calculation, then a smile touched only her lips. "Detectives. What brings two of Riverdale's finest to my neck of the woods?"

The corners of his mouth quirked upwards as he and Franks showed her their badges. "Nothing serious, Mrs...."

"*Ms.* Rhodes. Lilah." She crossed her arms over her checked button-front shirt, which made the lacy undershirt beneath it slide down just enough to reveal the top edge of what must have been a big and nasty scar across her chest. She caught him noticing and lifted her chin as if daring him to pity her.

"Ms. Rhodes. I'm Detective Townsend and this is my partner, Detective Franks. We just need to verify the whereabouts of Ryan Barlow last night."

She made a noise in her throat. "Whatever you think he's done now, he didn't. Like all the other times. He was here, with his mother and sister." She shrugged. "Technically, it's against the rules, now that he's an adult, but the three of them...they're all each other has. I let it slide now and then. He's a good kid."

Franks gave him a sidelong glance, then asked the wolf lady, "Can we speak with his mother?"

She pressed her lips together in a tight frown and *hmm*ed low in her throat. "I don't think she'll go for that. She doesn't trust cops. Especially not male ones."

Townsend expected this reply. "May I ask what her story is?"

"You can ask." She eyed him a long moment, then took a deep breath. "The short version is that the Barlow name was tarnished by her husband's daddy and uncle, which made it hard for him to get a fair shake. So, he moved them to a new state and went into the military, to get away from all that. But, like too many others before him, the person he was when he came back was very different from the good man who went over. He took to the bottle and fought his demons by beating on Ryan and his mamma. But the cops only saw a war hero and never got to see the bruises, so they weren't exactly responsive to the situation." She paused a moment. "She was lucky to get away and come here. He'd tracked her down twice before and things got...bad. It is vital that he never finds her again, so I will demand that you keep all this to yourselves."

"Of course," Townsend said.

"You have our word," Franks added.

She gazed at the floor a moment, then looked up at them. "I'll ask her if she's willing to talk to you, but don't get your hopes up." She started to leave the room but stopped in the doorway and turned back. "What is it you think Ryan's done?"

Townsend and Franks exchanged a look. "At this point," Franks said, "we just need to verify his whereabouts last night."

"But I've already done that. Do you really need to put her through the stress of answering your question again?"

"Is there any way Ryan could have left here at any time during the night?"

She put her hands on her hips and frowned at Townsend. "No. Lockdown begins at ten and isn't lifted until six-thirty. Do you really need Susan to tell you the same thing?"

"It's all right, Lilah," a voice said from the room behind Ms. Rhodes. "I'll talk to them."

Ms. Rhodes moved aside as a slim, pretty woman with dark hair and olive skin came into the room. She wore nice jeans and a short-sleeved shirt with a floral pattern stitched around the neckline. A blue and white bandanna kept her hair off her face. The combination made her look like a little girl, instead of a grown woman with two children. "What do you want with Ryan?"

Franks put on his most amiable expression and gave her a respectful nod. "Mrs. Barlow, we appreciate you taking the time."

Her smile was a bit crumpled. "Time is the one thing I've got plenty of these days. Why do you want my son?"

"Oh, we don't, ma'am," Franks assured her. "We've spoken to him already, but we just need to verify a few details, if you don't mind."

"But why do you want to know about him? Why are you asking about him now?" A hardness was forming around her eyes.

Townsend stepped in. "We don't have any reason to believe he's done anything wrong at this point, Mrs. Barlow, but we need to be able to officially rule him out."

She glanced at the television mounted on the wall in the shelter's common room behind her, then turned back to them with wide eyes. "You're here because of the lawyer's boy. You think Ryan – *my Ryan* – could have had something to do with that?" She shook her head. "No, you're wrong. He would *never-*"

Franks held up his hands. "We're not saying that, ma'am. We're just trying to make sure we know where everyone who had any recent contact with Nigel was last night, that's all. It's anyone we can't account for who will be looked into."

She stared at him, anger and fear making her gaze brittle. "He was here. All night. He stayed with me and Maddie."

He nodded congenially. "Okay. Has he had any trouble with his classes lately? We've been told he's been missing some classes."

"Missing some–" Understanding registered on her face. "You must be talking about his Engineering Physics class."

That was the class Ryan and Nigel had both been in, the class where their altercation had taken place. It was also the class Justin had said Ryan missed several days a week. "Yes, ma'am, that's the one," Townsend said.

"No, no, he's not missing it. He has an arrangement with Dr. Tillotson. Ryan has to work to help support us, and he has to work during the time that class meets twice a week. Tillotson meets with him later in the day to go over the material, grade his homework or give tests or quizzes. My boy is smart, smarter than anyone I've ever met, and Tillotson says he's going to be a master electrical engineer. He's the only one who's ever seen Ryan for who he is and recognized how gifted he is."

"He's his mentor," Townsend said. "We truly do appreciate you talking to us, Mrs. Barlow. Ms. Rhodes, thank you." He took one of his business cards out of his pocket and gave it to Mrs. Barlow. "If you ever need anything, give me a call."

CHAPTER TWENTY

<u>Sunday, August 31, 2014 4:42 a.m.</u>

Nearly five hours in, and nothing had changed. Noah sighed and stared at the ceiling. He wasn't sure what he was expecting but feeling the same was not it. It was all still there – the tiredness, the irritability, the insomnia and heavy feeling in his chest hadn't increased or disappeared now that the anniversary of That Day had come. He thought about getting up, since he was clearly not going to sleep again tonight, but a part of him whispered, *it's not like you have anywhere to go.* So, he rolled over onto his side and stared at the wall instead.

<u>8:38 a.m.</u>

He must have eventually dozed or just zoned out, because the next thing he was aware of was bright sunlight dancing on the wall opposite his bed. He glanced at the clock and saw four hours had passed. With a frown, he forced himself up and into the bathroom. After he brushed his teeth and ran a comb through his hair, he considered going for a run. The very idea exhausted him.

His cell phone rang. He left the bathroom and retrieved his phone from the nightstand. The caller ID showed that it was Dr. Weymouth. He answered it on speaker. "Harkham."

"Noah? It's Dr. Weymouth. James. How are you?"

"Did I miss a session?" He sat on the edge of the bed and laid the phone on the nightstand again.

"Well, yes, yesterday's actually. But that's not why I'm calling."

"Okay."

"I ran into Joseph Barnes yesterday."

Noah felt a scowl pulling at his features. "You did?"

Weymouth cleared his throat. "Well, yes. We've been keeping each other apprised of your progress, as you know."

"I forgot about that." It felt a little like the two were conspiring behind his back.

"Um...He told me about your good news. I just wanted to call and congratulate you personally."

He ran his hands across his face then held them in front of him, checking if he could see them with his left eye yet. He couldn't. The light in the room was too dim. "Thank you, James."

"Noah— is, is everything okay? You don't sound pleased. Is this not what you wanted?"

How could he explain how he felt to a man who would no doubt give anything to have his right eye back? "It is, but...It really doesn't change anything. Even if my sight does come back, I still can't be a cop again."

There was a pause on the other end of the line. "Come see me. Today, if you can. I think it will be good to start tailoring your training to reflect your potential new situation. You'll need to adjust to being able to see again. I can still help you with that." When Noah didn't reply, he said, "It may not change your prospects for being a police officer again but, believe me, it will change everything else. This is... it's a miracle, really."

A lump formed in his throat and he had to close his eyes and swallow hard before speaking. "I know. I'm sorry."

"You don't have anything to be sorry about, Noah. It's a lot to process. I understand that you might be feeling a little conflicted about it right now. Especially with today..."

"Yes, today..." His hands formed fists on his lap and he chafed his knuckles over the fabric of his sleep pants. His heart was beating faster, but it weighed a ton, like a stone sinking in his chest.

"I'm serious about meeting with you, if you feel up to it. If not, will you be at your session on Tuesday?"

"Yes. Yes, I'll be there." *Although I don't see the point.* "Thank you for calling, James. I appreciate it."

"Of course. I'll see you Tuesday."

"See you Tuesday." He hung up before Weymouth could make him feel any worse for not feeling better about this whole thing. He wanted to be happy about it, but instead, he just felt indifferent, disconnected. Like it was someone else's miracle and not his.

He got up and went to the kitchen for breakfast. As usual, there wasn't much food in there and he made a mental note to stop forgetting to go to the store. He ended up throwing out some grey bacon and settling for coffee and toast with peanut butter on it. It wasn't much, but he wasn't very hungry anyway. He had just swallowed his morning dose of antibiotics and was washing his cup and knife when there was a knock on his door.

The knife slipped from his hand to clatter against the bottom of the sink. For a moment, he panicked that it would be Bobby Avalon come to put a bullet in his head to finish the job he started a year ago. *Don't be stupid. Avalon's in jail.* He turned off the faucet, dried his hands and went to see who it really was. One look through the peephole was enough to make him wish he could crawl back into bed. Instead, he took a breath, faked a smile and opened the door to his aunt, uncle, Neil and Robin.

"Good morning, Noah," Aunt Helen said in her usual warm way.

"Good morning. Uh, come in." He stepped aside and let them all in. Neil gave him an apologetic nod, and Robin gave him an awkward smile. This wasn't their idea, at least.

Uncle Michael surveyed the state of his apartment before turning to him. "We're on the way to the zoo for the day. Would you want to come?"

Noah glanced at Neil before answering. Neil nodded and half-shrugged. "Uh, sure. Just let me get dressed." Without waiting for a reply, he went back to his room and shut the door. Great. Forced family bonding time. He changed clothes and came back out to find them all huddled near the door, talking low.

The anger flooded through him before he could contain it. His glare stopped them all mid-sentence. "I don't need any handholding today, if that's what this is all about."

"Noah, no one said–"

"I'm fine, Uncle Michael. In fact, I'm getting my sight back."

They all stared at him a moment. Then Aunt Helen came forward to place her gentle hands on his face. "Is it true? Can you see me?"

His irritation melted away a degree. He smiled at her and closed his right eye. The faintest light, blurred and greasy, filtered through. His pulse quickened. A shadow moved. She had taken one hand off his face and was no doubt now waving it in front of him. He followed the movement, a tiny thrill of excitement fluttering inside him. "Not completely. Not yet, but I'm almost there."

He opened his other eye. There were tears in her eyes as she pulled him into a hug. Robin and Uncle Michael look stunned and even Neil's placid features registered surprise. "Then today is a celebration," Uncle Michael said, coming up and patting Noah's back.

Noah smiled, but he could tell by their expressions that it was less convincing than they wanted it to be. The stone in his chest dropped a little further. "I'm ready when you all are," he mumbled.

9:33 a.m.

By the time they got to the zoo, which was twenty minutes west of the city, the oppressive heat of the day had already settled in. There were plenty of shaded areas around the exhibits, however, and seating areas with umbrellas to keep off the sun and rain were scattered here and there. But even in the shade, the temperature was pushing eighty-some degrees.

After a few minutes of trying to decide where to start, they all drifted toward the tiger exhibit. This was one of the zoo's five big cat exhibits, each enclosure covering three acres. Noah used to love coming here when he and Neil were younger, loved seeing these incredible, powerful beasts up close. Today, however, the only thought that kept running through his mind was how trapped they must feel, how far from home they were.

The male tiger lay listless in the dappled shade a few feet into the enclosure. His predatory eyes were half-lidded, his sides heaving slowly with each breath. He looked...miserable. Noah walked closer to the thick glass separating the huge animal from the gawkers and laid his hand against the cool surface. He tapped a finger on the glass softly, and the tiger glanced his way before closing his eyes again.

"Isn't he beautiful?" Aunt Helen's voice sounded awed.

His uncle's approach was reflected in the glass, and when he stood next to Noah, Michael said, "I don't know... he looks a little sad to me. Or like he's not feeling well."

"Maybe he's just too hot," Robin said, flapping the neckline of her shirt to cool herself.

"He should be used to it," Neil said, pointing to the tiger's information sign. "Says here he's from 'the eastern part of India, where the climate is very hot and dry'. Could be the humidity, though he should be used to that by now, too."

"Just because you can get used to somewhere you don't belong doesn't mean you're happy about being there." When everyone fell silent, Noah looked back to see them staring at him. He forced a smile that just as quickly withered. "I, uh, I bet the otters are out now."

He turned away and headed to the river otter enclosure just up the walkway. Halfway there, he remembered to see if they were following. They were, but by the plastered-on smiles they all gave him, he could tell he'd caught them talking about him. Again. He clenched his jaw, the irritation mounting inside like the needle rising in a temperature gauge.

He forced himself to breathe out slowly through his mouth and let them catch up. He noticed Neil watching him as they approached the exhibit, his arm around Robin's waist. She slipped her arm around him, too, and leaned her head on his shoulder. Neil looked away when she giggled and pointed to the otters. Aunt Helen was laughing at the little critters, too, and Noah was struck by the sudden urge to walk out of the zoo, away from them and everything else. He pictured himself running down the highway, not back toward Riverdale, but away, toward somewhere, anywhere else.

His body turned, as if it were going to give into that impulse, and that's when he saw Bobby Avalon heading toward him from the tiger enclosure. His heart jackhammered and sweat beaded on his forehead that had nothing to do with the heat of the day. He reached for the gun at his waist by instinct before once again remembering he didn't have one anymore. A thousand different scenarios played out in rapid fire succession in his mind, each one culminating with Avalon's gun going off in his face.

It took a full ten seconds or more before he realized that the man he saw was not Bobby Avalon, and that he didn't have a gun, and he wasn't even remotely interested in Noah. What was wrong with him? Why was this happening?

"Noah? You okay?"

He jerked around toward the voice, hands balled into fists with one readied to swing. It was only Neil.

"Take it easy. It's just me..." Neil backed up a step, hands up in defense. "I didn't mean to surprise you."

Neil, with his unmarred face and perfect girlfriend and wonderful life. Neil, who wasn't losing his mind because some low-life thug nearly shot his head off a year ago. Neil, who had been the one there with his parents when they were shot dead, who had lived instead of them... The desire to make him hurt for that, even a little bit, was overwhelming.

"Noah?" Confusion, hurt and fear clouded Neil's grey-green eyes. "You gonna put that away or what?" He nodded toward Noah's fist.

Noah forced his hands to relax. They were shaking when he shoved them into his jeans pockets. "Neil... I didn't– I..." He had to swallow to get his breathing to slow down.

"It's okay. Just, are you all right?" His posture was still defensive, still braced for the punch that hadn't been thrown. "You looked like you saw something."

His teeth clenched. This wasn't him. What was happening? "I just... I need to get out of here." He stalked off toward the indoor aquatic exhibits, shoving through the doors and startling a young girl and her parents as he almost ran into them. "Sorry," he mumbled, walking past them, deeper into the darkened and cool interior.

He stopped when he got to the jellyfish hall, which was unlit except by a dim strip of lights along the walkway and the dark blue-tinted lights inside the tank. Here, he could disappear for a minute and get his head together. Breathe.

His thoughts slowed from the tangled jumble they'd been a few moments ago, and he could now rationally assess the situation. He had to calm down or this, this...panic-fueled anger would overwhelm him. How to get a handle on it? Could he keep it together enough to get through the day? Everything would go back to normal tomorrow, it had to, and if he could get any sleep tonight, it would be like waking from a nightmare when he woke up tomorrow morning.

He focused only on the jellyfish, watching their globular, amorphous bodies swaying through the dark water, and listening to the white noise of all the tanks' filters running. The dark blue bulb lighting the tank seemed to work like a black-light, making their pale bodies almost glow in the darkness. They were hypnotic, and soon his pulse slowed to normal and the shaking in his hands subsided. In their absence, he felt exhausted and heavy.

A minute or two later, his uncle found him. Noah sighed. He didn't know what to say, so he just stayed silent. Uncle Michael stood a couple of feet away, hands in his pockets.

He looked at Noah a long moment before saying, "We don't have to stay here. I – we all understand if you'd rather not."

The stone in his chest sank even further. "I'm sorry. It was nice of you guys to want to do this. I'm sorry I'm ruining it." His throat felt tight and his eyes welled up. He blinked a few times to clear them.

Uncle Michael stepped closer to allow the foot traffic to curve past them, and to place a hand on Noah's shoulder. "You're not ruining anything. Okay? If you don't want to be here, that's okay. You have every right to be angry or sad or anything else you're feeling."

Noah rolled his eyes. "Please don't do this right now."

His uncle's clear blue eyes registered confusion. "Do what? I'm just trying to talk to you."

"No, you're being a shrink. This isn't your office and I am not one of your patients. Just…let me worry about how I'm feeling today, all right?"

Another stretched moment passed before his uncle removed his hand and stepped back. "Okay."

"Okay." Noah looked away from his pitying eyes. "You catch up with the others. I'm gonna call a cab."

"Noah–"

He headed for the exit. "I'm fine. I just can't do this–" he gestured vaguely around at the tanks, "right now." Then he pushed through the door and kept walking, determined to get through the rest of the day, literally praying to get through the rest of the day, without further incident. Because, despite his assurances to the contrary, he wasn't fine.

And he was *very* worried about how he was feeling today.

CHAPTER TWENTY-ONE

Noah still wasn't answering. Michael Coates had sent Frankie a text half an hour ago saying Noah had taken a cab, leaving the zoo and the rest of the family. Apparently, something had happened to throw a sour note over the excursion and Michael wanted Frankie to keep an eye on him.

He'd tried calling twice and texted three times, but there was no response. So now, Frankie was at Noah's door. He took a breath and let it out before knocking, a dreadful sense of déjà vu slithering in his gut. After a moment, he heard footsteps inside the apartment, then silence, and then Noah opened the door.

Frankie let out a shaky breath and felt a goofy grin stretch his mouth. "Hey, partner."

Noah's brow furrowed. "Hey." He didn't step back to let Frankie in. "I guess it's your turn now, huh?"

The grin slipped. "I tried to call you. And text. When you didn't respond, I..."

Understanding dawned in Noah's eyes, along with anger. "I see. Because of today and everything, you thought I finally gave up and did it, is that it?"

He started to deny it, but all he could think about was that night almost a year ago. "I didn't know what to think. Not after last time."

Noah was fuming now but trying to suppress it. He shook his head in disbelief and started to say something, some sharp retort, but instead he just...sagged. His shoulders dropped a few inches and all the anger in his expression melted, leaving him looking worn out. "I'm fine, Frankie. Really. My phone died while I was out, and I forgot to turn it back on when I put it on the charger. I'm sorry if I worried you."

Something wasn't right, and it went beyond it being the anniversary of the day Noah got hurt and the stress of being implicated in Nigel's murder. He was obviously exhausted: his gray eyes were sunken and bruised and his posture looked like he was being held upright by sheer will alone. This could even be worse than last time.

"It's okay." He forced a smile. "I thought maybe you might want some company for a while. We could order Gianni's and watch one of your movies where people end up dead in space."

This elicited the barest hint of a smile, but, again, he made no move to let Frankie in. "Actually, I've got a million things to do here. I've been so busy lately that I let things slide, and now the place is a wreck. Maybe tomorrow after work? Or whenever Townsend lets you stop investigating me."

"Ah, okay, that's what this is about. Look, I told you–"

"What *this*? I'm just not in the mood to sit there while you pretend you aren't only here to make sure I don't blow my brains out all over my apartment. You don't have to bother, because that is not going to happen. Ever. Okay? Just go back to Townsend and keep *him* company. Maybe you can keep him from playing right into the hands of whoever is framing me." Noah stepped back and started to close the door.

Frankie slapped his palm against the door panel. "Wait! Just let me in, Hark."

Noah froze. "Go home, Frankie." Then he pushed the door closed.

After listening to the lock engage, Frankie stood there with a knot in his gut telling him he'd just failed his best friend in some major way. He'd expected Noah to be less than agreeable to what essentially amounted to being babysat, but he never saw this level of hostility coming.

Noah had to know Frankie was on his side, right? That he believed he was doing everything he could to make Townsend see Noah's innocence, despite what the evidence might say? He probably just wasn't thinking clearly because his emotions were too amped up because of what today was. Tomorrow would be different; things would be back to normal...

Right?

Without knowing what else to do, Frankie left. Back out in his car, he considered staking the place out. Just because Noah didn't want him in the apartment didn't mean Frankie couldn't still watch out for him. But, if Noah found out he'd sat there surveilling him like a suspect, what was left of their friendship would be destroyed.

Then again, what if Noah did get back to the point where he was last year? Despite his angry assurances that it would never happen, all Frankie could think about was the time it almost had and worried that it could happen again. What if he didn't get there in time to stop it this time? Should he then stay and risk ruining their friendship or trust Noah when he said he would never end up there again?

The blinds covering Noah's window twitched to the side. He glared down at Frankie until he gave in and started the car. As he drove away, concern and guilt gnawed at his stomach, but he knew the best way to help Noah was to get back to working the case. If he could figure out who was framing him, if he cleared his name, then he might get his friend back in one piece. If he couldn't solve this thing...

That was not an option.

CHAPTER TWENTY-TWO

———

<u>Monday, September 1, 2014 5:28 a.m.</u>

Another one. Why another one, so soon? Frankie sighed as he and Townsend joined Dr. Lee in the parking lot behind the Adams Avenue convenience store. A second body bearing the signature of the One O'clock Killer had just been found.

"What's the story, Marvin?" Townsend asked the old ME, who stood next to the Dumpster taking notes by the light of a security lamp.

Lee glanced up. "She was reported almost half an hour ago." He pulled a face. "This'n's rough, boys. Like the last, but even worse."

"Same MO?"

"Nah, Frankie," he said, shaking his head. "This time he used a baseball bat or somethin' similar. Beat her so badly I can't even hope to use dental records to identify the poor lamb. Hope her prints are in the system or you can find some ID."

Frankie grimaced and peered around the ME. The woman's body had been wedged behind the Dumpster, and, for one moment, seeing her legs sticking out from between the hulking gray metal trash bin and the faded white cinder block wall of the store made him think of another body from seven years ago. Another woman who had died because he failed to put a killer away.

When he forced his eyes up past her waist, his stomach seized and his breath caught in his throat. He heard Townsend letting out a tightly-controlled breath next to him. Lee was right, this one was rough. Her skull was so misshaped it was hard to tell it had once been part of a living human being. He *destroyed* her...

"Sirs, you're going to want to see this," a uniformed officer told them, interrupting his thoughts with a grim set to her squarish face. He glanced at her nameplate: *Officer M. Byers.*

"What is it?" Frankie asked.

She gestured a few feet up the concrete sidewalk leading around the building to the space next to a withered little shrub where criminalist Jake Saddler was kneeling. A floodlight on a tripod lit the area and he reached a gloved hand into what appeared to be a woman's purse. Byers turned back to Frankie and Townsend. "We may have found the victim's purse. Thought you'd want to see before CSU takes it to the lab."

Townsend nodded. As he and Frankie approached the criminalist, Townsend said, "Tell me we've got a name for our victim."

Saddler looked up from the clipboard he was using to fill out his crime scene report, the expression on his face tired but focused. "We do. I think." He squinted at the driver's license he had just put into an evidence bag. "Her name is Jennifer Sealey. From Riverdale." His eyebrows shot upward. "Her address is about four blocks from the Fifth precinct."

Frankie went still, ignoring the look both men were giving him. "What about a phone, any kind of mobile device?"

"Uh, no, sorry," Saddler told Frankie. "But I did find this." He held up another evidence bag containing a receipt. "It's from that coffee shop, Jumping Beans. From Friday morning."

A flush crept up his neck. *It doesn't mean anything,* he told himself a couple times. "What time?"

If Saddler noticed the constriction in his throat that Frankie forced his voice past, he didn't show it. Instead he just glanced at the receipt. "Uh, six forty-two a.m."

"Can you hold up the license again for me?" Townsend asked. When Saddler did, he snapped a picture of it with his phone. He frowned at it before showing it to Frankie. She had been young and pretty, though somewhat stern looking, with long blonde hair. "Hard to believe that could be the same person lying over there."

"Yeah." A sort of cold weight settled into his gut. It was hard to believe what one person could do to another. Hard to believe that someone could take this living, breathing person with a whole life and probably someone or several someones she loved and laughed with and turn her into a pile of gore shoved behind a Dumpster.

Townsend's expression as he left Frankie to show the ID to Dr. Lee was guarded. Saddler may not have noticed his discomfort, but Townsend sure would have. Would he just chalk it up to the grotesque condition of the body or would he be able to divine his true dilemma? As far as he was aware, Townsend could only read people's faces and body language, not their minds. But still... He forced a neutral expression as Townsend came back.

"Dr. Lee is pretty confident the girl in the license photo and the victim are one and the same, but he'll confirm with prints or DNA. Come on, let's get over to Jumping Beans and see if anyone remembers seeing her Friday morning."

Frankie nodded and followed Townsend back to the car, because there was nothing else he could do.

He started to tell his partner three separate times on the way to the coffee shop. Every time, he talked himself out of it because all it would do was add fuel to the fire that was already burning out of control. It didn't mean anything anyway. Lots of people from businesses in the area were in that shop at any given time of day. Just because Noah had been there when she had been didn't prove anything.

"You okay?" Townsend asked as he turned off the car.

They had arrived already. Frankie didn't remember anything about the drive over. "Yeah...just trying to work it all out."

Townsend stared at him, but then smiled and opened his door. "Come on."

Frankie followed him into the shop. As usual, they were met with warm air and the earthy scent of coffee. Soft acoustic music filtered out of the speakers in the ceiling and their shoes thumped dully on the light-colored laminate wood flooring. Frankie usually felt relaxed coming in here. The navy wainscoting and golden-brown walls combined with the quiet music and warm scents and sounds had always made him feel at home. Today, he couldn't breathe. The air was too stuffy and the walls seemed to be closing in.

Lynn, the woman who worked mornings wasn't in her usual place behind the register. Instead, an older gentleman with a paunchy gut and thin, white hair wiped down the counter with a dish towel. He smiled broadly when they came in. There were no other customers at the moment, so Frankie bet he was all too glad to see the two cops. Frankie, however, wanted to leave as quickly as possible.

"Detectives, good morning! What can I get Riverdale's finest this morning?"

Townsend smiled. "Actually, we're here on official business...Mr. Rohrman," he said, eyeing the man's nametag that identified him as *Walter Rohrman, Owner/Operator*. He dug out his phone and pulled up the photo of the victim. He showed it to the proprietor. "Do you remember seeing her in here Friday?

He leaned over the counter for a better look, eyes squinting in concentration. "No sir. When was it she was supposed to've been here?"

"A little before seven a.m."

Walter shook his head. "Nah, it'll be Lynn you're wanting to speak with then. She's mornings, I'm afternoons." He shrugged. "Well, usually, anyway."

Townsend put his phone away and got out his notepad instead. "And what is Lynn's last name?"

"Hopkins."

He jotted this down. "And why isn't she here this morning?"

Walter waved the meaty hand holding the towel. "Ah, somesuch about a doctor's appointment that got rescheduled at the last minute."

"Do you have contact information for Lynn?"

"I have a cell phone number for her, if you need to speak with her. But she's at a doctor's appointment, like I said." His eyes squinted. "What do you need with Lynn?"

"She's a potential witness material to a case we're working on. So, we'll actually need her full name and address, as well, if you don't mind." Before letting Walter answer, he pointed his pen toward the discreetly positioned security cameras over the counter and seating areas. "And we'll need the surveillance footage from Friday as well."

Walter jiggled a nod. "Of course, of course. All in the office here." He lifted the hinged section of the counter. "Right this way, gents."

Frankie closed his eyes a moment before following his partner into the office. The room was small, with a desk that held a computer and stacks of paperwork and catalogs against one wall. A couple filing cabinets and a set of lockers for the employees' belongings flanked the desk and the opposite wall was lined with floor to ceiling shelves that held extra supplies for the shop. Walter seated himself in the red, plush rolling chair at the desk and wiggled the wireless mouse to wake up the computer. After clicking around on different icons and folders, he pulled up a program that showed surveillance footage from the last several days.

"Friday, you said?" Townsend nodded, and Walter clicked on the entry dated Friday, August 29th. "Here you are."

He clicked Play and the footage began rolling, the screen split between three camera angles covering the door and register, the seating area, and the back door. The timestamp started at midnight. "Can you advance it to about six-forty-five, please?" Townsend asked.

Walter fast-forwarded the footage to six-forty-five and let it resume playing. Frankie went still, and a coldness traced his spine when the tape showed Noah at the counter, getting a coffee to go. Lynn smiled and plopped the Styrofoam cup into the navy-blue porcelain mug Noah held. Townsend gave Frankie a pointed look, then placed his hand on the computer's mouse, tapping it to pause the tape. "Walter, do you mind if I drive?"

The old man looked like he could tell something was wrong but didn't know what. "Uh, sure. Be my guest. I, uh, I'll just get you her contact information." He stood and let Townsend take the chair while he opened one of the filing cabinets and flipped through some files.

Frankie felt heat rising to his face. If he had only told Townsend first... *Now he's gonna think– he's gonna take me off the case...* His gut roiled.

Barely noticeable above the café rod curtains in the centers of the windows flanking the door was the victim, Jennifer Sealey. She was standing outside on her cell phone but put it away and headed for the door just as Noah was heading out. The two collided just outside the door, and Noah's coffee splashed over them both and the mug dropped from his hand. He said something to her, and she responded in what looked like a less than friendly manner.

Townsend tried turning up the volume on the computer, then when they still couldn't hear what was being said, paused the footage again. "No audio?" Walter shook his head. Townsend sighed. "So, there's no way to tell what they're saying."

"Sorry. This system was expensive enough as it is. The version with audio was ridiculously overpriced." He took out a file and brought it to the end of the desk and copied over her name, address and phone number onto a piece of scrap paper. "Here you go," he said, giving the information to Frankie. "Here's her address and other information."

"Thank you." He absently glanced at the paper, watching his partner out of the corner of his eye instead.

Townsend held his tongue and rewound the tape to when Noah first entered. He and Frankie both watched intently as Lynn looked at his receipt, then produced a box from under the counter, which she opened with a flourish to reveal a navy-blue mug. Townsend pointed at the screen. "What's this about?"

Walter frowned. "I don't know. Looks like she's giving that guy one of my mug design prototypes." When the detectives just looked at him, he went on to explain. "I ordered several different designs for a new logo on some mugs, just to see 'em in person to pick the best one. That mug she's giving him is one of the designs I was considering."

"But you didn't authorize her to give the mug away?"

"No way! I still haven't decided on which design to go with." He ducked out of the office and went to the counter, swore under his breath, and then came back to glare at the screen. "What was she up to?"

"Now that is a very good question," Townsend said. He skipped the footage ahead to where Noah and the girl collided and had their exchange again and let it play on from there. Noah brushed the coffee off himself and then knelt to where the broken mug lay in pieces. The curtains obscured their view of him now.

Inside the shop, Lynn was speaking to Jennifer Sealey, who still looked upset by the incident. The barista handed the girl her change and a bagel from behind the counter, then grabbed a broom and one of those long-handled dustpans that swivels shut when lifted but lays flat on the floor and went outside. The camera showed her from behind, so they couldn't see if she and Noah were speaking. She swept up the mess, then stopped and gestured toward the shop. Her posture stiffened, and she walked back inside with the broom and dustpan, which she took back to the office where they were all gathered now. Noah walked past the shop back toward the precinct.

Frankie glanced around the office and located the dustpan. It was empty now. Townsend skipped the next ten minutes of footage, until Jennifer Sealey exited the shop, heading in the same direction Noah had gone. He paused the tape again. "Can we get a copy of this, Walter?"

"Of course."

Townsend stood and moved out of his way as Walter opened a drawer in the desk. He fished out a new flash drive and inserted it into the computer. "Just one second, fellas." He saved the file over to the flash drive, removed it and handed it to Townsend. "Can I ask what this is all about? Is that young lady in trouble?"

"Actually, Walter, she's dead."

He paled and lifted his eyebrows. "Oh. Wasn't expecting that." His brow then furrowed. "You're not thinking Lynn had anything to do with it? Or maybe the guy she gave the mug to? I guess I'm just not seeing how her being here Friday has anything to do with her being dead now..."

"We're trying to get a timeline of events leading up to her death. This is just the last known place she was seen alive." Townsend shifted his eyes to look at Frankie with that last sentence. *Tell me this doesn't mean anything, either, pal,* his expression said.

It was too hot in this little office. The unease in his gut was turning into a tight ball of writhing nervousness. Maybe he could still salvage this. Maybe Townsend would see the truth here: Noah is innocent, and Frankie hadn't told him he was here because... *because I was*

*trying to protect my friend, our only suspect...There's no way I won't be
taken off the case. Or worse.*

His thoughts were interrupted by Townsend taking their leave of
Walter and ushering Frankie out the door. Once outside, Frankie
risked looking his partner in the eye. "Townsend, I–"

"Just get in the car," he said with a curt gesture.

Frankie got in and jerked the seatbelt so hard that it jammed up. He
let out a frustrated sigh and slowly pulled the buckle down across
his chest and fastened it. Townsend got in and put the key in the
ignition but sat with his hands wrapped around the steering wheel
a long moment. His eyes were half-closed, and his breathing was
unnaturally slow. Eventually, he turned to Frankie.

"You knew Harkham was here." It was stated as a fact, neither
accusatory nor questioning. "You knew *when* he was here, and you
knew how it was going to look the second Saddler read the time
stamp on that receipt." He held up a hand to forestall Frankie's reply.
"You wanted to tell me but didn't. Why?"

"Because it doesn't prove anything," he replied, trying to keep his
voice as calm and neutral as his partner's, without a ton of success.

Townsend's jaw muscles twitched. "Of course it proves something,
Alan. It proves you don't trust me to do my job. I don't know what to
do with that."

Frankie felt some of his anger and fear ebb away, replaced with guilt.
"That's not what this is about. I trust you, I do, but–"

"No, see, if you did trust me, there would be no 'but' in that sentence.
Look, I know I'm not Harkham. We're not friends. Okay, fine, I get
that. But we are partners, and I have trusted you implicitly on every

case we've ever worked together. I thought I could count on the same from you."

"I trust *you*. What I don't trust is that whoever's doing this won't pull it off." He shifted in his seat to face him more squarely. "Casey, we both know that it doesn't matter what you or I know to be true if the evidence doesn't bear it out. All that matters is what the lab and the attorneys can prove in court. I know Hark is innocent. I think you do, too. He'd never even raise his voice at a woman just for accidentally bumping into him, let alone kill her for it. But what will the evidence say?" He lifted a hand in a defeated gesture, then let it fall on his lap. "I don't like this thing with the mug. And it's a little too convenient that Lynn's not here for us to question today. This whole thing is sitting wrong with me."

"I know."

"Not just because it's Noah, though."

"No, Frankie, I *know*. The barista, Lynn, she's got something to do with this. You're right."

Frankie blinked. "Oh. Well, then we have to get her in a room where you can use that weird radar of yours on her."

"I plan to." Townsend smirked, but then pulled a serious face. "But you have to step down from this case. You know that, right?"

He sat back in his seat. "Yeah. I know." He glanced back at his partner. "Casey, I'm sorry."

He shrugged, starting the car. "I get it. The things we do for best friends and all. Here on out, though? You pull anything like this and I go to Ziehring for your badge. Clear?" He pinned Frankie with a sharp glare.

"Clear."

"And you know I still have to bring him back in for questioning? Despite what your gut or my...radar is telling us. He is still our primary suspect, according to the evidence. It's just–"

"Protocol. Right, I know."

Townsend nodded and eased the car out into the flow of traffic. Franks fidgeted with the paper containing Lynn's information. He started to set it aside, but something about the address caught his eye. He pulled up the map app on his phone and saw his suspicions were correct.

Holding up the paper he said, "I think you're going to need to put a BOLO out on Lynn if you want to talk to her. The address she gave Walter is fake, unless she rents out the storage room of Cardwell's pharmacy."

CHAPTER TWENTY-THREE

Noah had already been awake for seven hours by the time the knock on his door came. He closed the pages of search results he'd found online about the Nigel Warner case, but left his laptop on while he went to see who was at the door. The quiet knock sounded again as he leaned toward the peephole, startling him for one jarring second. He gritted his teeth and frowned when he saw Frankie in the hallway.

The man is like a puppy: even if you kick him, he'll still come back. The thought was both a source of comfort and of self-recrimination. He hadn't meant to be so, well, mean to his best friend yesterday. But what Noah meant and how he ended up acting were often two different things these days. He opened the door but couldn't look Frankie in the eye.

"Hey," Frankie said, sounding every bit as wary of Noah as Noah was of himself.

"Hey."

Frankie looked around the empty hallway. "Sorry to bother you so early, but I really need to talk to you."

Noah stepped back. "Sure."

At least Frankie had the decency not to be obvious about evaluating the state of his apartment, which at least wasn't as bad as it had been. He hadn't lied when he told him yesterday that the place was a wreck, but now it was only a little untidy. Noah shut the door and cleared a scattered newspaper off the couch so they could sit.

139

Only Frankie didn't sit.

Noah stopped halfway down to a seated position and straightened back up. "What is it? What's happened?"

Frankie sighed. "It's happened again."

Dread settled into his bones like the ache of a flu. "You found another one already?"

Frankie nodded, shoving his hands in his pockets. "We – Townsend and I – just left the scene a while ago. Does the name Jennifer Sealey mean anything to you?"

He frowned. "Should it?"

"Please, just– do you know the name?" Frankie looked tired, or, more accurately, weary.

"No. I don't." He tossed the newspaper onto his coffee table and crossed his arms. "What's going on?"

"I only came here to give you a heads up. Townsend will be coming to take you in again for questioning."

"What? Why?"

Frankie looked at the floor. "I'm off the case officially now. I just wanted you to know so you wouldn't be blindsided." He went stiff and looked up at Noah, his expression sheepish. "Ah, geesh, you know what I mean."

Noah dismissed it with a wave of his hand. "Frankie, tell me what's going on."

"I can't, not really. Like I said, I'm off the case. But someone is going to a lot of effort to put you in the noose. I didn't see anything that stood out when I went through the list of released inmates you arrested. There has to be someone who made a credible threat somewhere along the line, I just haven't found it yet. You sure you can't think of anyone who would go this far for payback?"

He laughed, though there was nothing funny about this thing. "Who do you think I am, a superhero with an arch-nemesis? I'm just– I was just a cop. Yeah, people get angry when they get arrested and they say stuff. But no one takes that too seriously."

"Well, maybe you should have. At least once."

His eyebrows shot upwards. "So this is *my* fault?"

Frankie sighed. "No, that's not what I meant."

"So, what?" Noah scoffed. "I had to have done something to deserve all this? It can't possibly be that someone is doing this just because they can, right? No criminal has ever simply gotten off on the power they had over somebody else. There must be a reason. I had to have done *something* to someone that warrants them framing me for murder, is that it?"

Frankie waited him out. "Noah, listen to me: that is not what I said. Usually, someone doesn't go to these kinds of lengths unless they have a grudge against their target. I'm not saying the grudge is justified, only that they would believe it is. Okay?"

His pounding pulse started to slow as he realized the truth of what Frankie was saying. Still, the feeling that he was being blamed for all of it lingered. "Fine."

"I wasn't trying to babysit you yesterday, I just needed to know you were okay. And today, well, I only came by to warn you. I've done that, so I'm gonna go home." He turned toward the door.

"Frankie, wait." Noah waited until his friend looked at him. "I don't know who is doing this. I mean, sure, there are plenty of people who wouldn't hesitate to break my face if they cornered me in a dark alley, but to want to ruin me so completely like this?" He shrugged.

"Okay. I'll keep digging."

"I thought you were off the case."

He dipped his head. "Yeah, but that doesn't mean I'm gonna just walk away and let this play out. I'm gonna find out who's behind this. You'd do the same for me."

Noah felt sick. "Actually, I wouldn't."

Frankie couldn't have looked more hurt if Noah had literally stabbed him in the back. "What?"

Noah spread his hands, beseeching. "The more I would try to help you, the more I would end up compromising the case, the more likely the bad guy would win." Even though it was true, saying it out loud felt like he was slapping away Frankie's offered hand. "The best way to help me now is to let Townsend do his job. I have to trust he'll get to the bottom of it all and keep me from going to prison. But he can't do that if you're working the case off book."

Frankie shook his head and started to say something, but Noah cut in. "I know you want to help me, and I can't tell you how grateful I am, especially in light of how...off I've been, but I can't let you jeopardize your career or this case for me."

"Coming from the guy who had me risk my badge to get him in a room with Bobby Avalon a few months ago."

It was like the floor dropped out from under him. "That was– this isn't the same thing. You have to see that, right?"

Frankie glared at him for a drawn-out moment. But then he nodded, his face glum. "Yeah, I get it. And you're right about another thing: something has been off with you. I don't know what's going on, but it's something big. If I can't help with your case, at least let me try to help with that."

Tears stung the backs of his eyes. "You can't."

"Then what am I even doing here, man?" The look he gave Noah was defeated, done.

"No, it's just– I mean, no one can help because I don't even know what the hell is wrong with me." He blinked, and a tear fell free of his lashes. He flicked it away irritably. "Even I can't predict what I'm going to say, how I'm going to react or, or feel, or– It's like I have no control anymore..." He held up his tear-slicked finger as proof and let out a shaky laugh. A few more tears slid down his face before he could stop them, and he sniffed loudly. "I'm scared, *terrified* that I'm losing it, man. Like, *really* losing it. And I'm sorry for how I– I'm just sorry for everything–"

Frankie reached out and pulled Noah into a hug. "Don't worry about all that, okay? I'll help you figure this out. You're gonna be all right."

He swallowed hard before trusting his voice to speak, hating how he was falling apart in front of his best friend. "Yeah? Cuz it doesn't look like it from here." He sucked in a breath to keep from sobbing.

Frankie stepped back and levelled a stern look at him, a hand gripping one of Noah's shoulders. "Hey, shut up. Just because you don't know what's wrong yet doesn't mean it can't be fixed. Just stop trying to go it alone, okay?"

Noah sniffed and nodded. "Yeah. Okay."

A knock on the door startled them both and they exchanged wary glances. Noah rubbed the cuff of his navy-blue dress shirt across his eyes and cleared his throat. "Who is it?"

"Detective Townsend. Open up."

Frankie opened the door for him. Townsend looked only mildly surprised to see him there. "Franks."

"Townsend."

"What are you doing here?"

Frankie shrugged. "I'm off the case now. I can hang out with my best friend again."

Townsend half shook his head as he pushed past Frankie toward Noah. "What did he say to you?"

Noah frowned. "Only that you'd be coming for me."

Townsend sighed and looked back at Frankie, who shrugged. "I didn't say anything else, Casey. That's your job now."

"All right." He took out a pair of handcuffs, snapping one onto Noah's right wrist. "Noah Harkham, you are under arrest for the murder of Jennifer Sealey. Anything you say can and will be used against you–"

Noah turned to Frankie, panicked. Frankie laid a hand on Townsend's shoulder. "Wait, what? What's happening here, Casey?"

Townsend kept his eye on Noah. "Dr. Lee found shards of that mug on Jennifer Sealey's body. There was blood on some of them and I had him run it against your blood type. It matched."

CHAPTER TWENTY-FOUR

———

<u>Monday, September 1, 2014 7:49 a.m.</u>

Now what are you doing to me? Noah wasn't sure if he was asking God or whoever was framing him, or if it even mattered at this point. The cuffs were heavy on his wrists and seemed to stay cold no matter how long he'd worn them. He tried resting his hands on the table before him but that made the metal dig into his skin more, so he ended up waiting with his hands on his lap. Even then he could feel the cold metal through his dress pants.

Townsend had dumped him in this interrogation room unceremoniously, leaving to have a head-to-head with Frankie. All Noah had gotten to say so far was that he wanted his lawyer. He had to laugh a little at the role reversal. How many times had he cuffed someone and left them to cool their heels in this very room? He'd lost count.

Being on the receiving end gave him new perspective. If this was happening to him, could he have ever gotten the wrong man himself? Almost every person he'd had in this room had said they were innocent. What if that had been true, at least once? Could that be why this was happening? Someone wrongfully convicted was giving him a taste of his own medicine?

Dr. Lee found shards of that mug on Jennifer Sealey's body. There was blood on some of them and I had him run it against your blood type. It matched.

What mug? The one from the coffee shop – the one that broke? There was nothing about that that made any sense. Unless...the only explanation was that someone had taken the broken mug out of the trash at Jumping Beans. But they would also need access to his old desk at the precinct, the one that was now occupied by some newbie detective he hadn't met yet. What's his name? The tall, thin black guy? He shook his head. That didn't matter now. He needed to focus on getting himself out of this frame.

His thoughts were tumbling all over themselves, getting tangled. The more he tried to sort one out from the others and follow it to the end, the more other irrelevant thoughts clung to it. His stomach growled. He hadn't eaten much since Sunday after abandoning his family at the zoo. Why did he always forget to go to the store until he was out of everything? Neil was always getting onto him for that.

He closed his eyes. He hadn't spoken to Neil since he almost threw a punch at him. Would he visit Noah in prison after that? Provided he even survived twenty-four hours in with the people he'd put away, that is.

Be still.

The thought came unbidden, and from somewhere *outside* himself. With it came a sort of enveloping quiet that, somehow, calmed the tumult in his mind. At least long enough to allow him to think.

If that's you, he prayed silently, *why don't you tell me something a little more useful? Like who's doing this to me?*

The voice was silent. Maybe he was going crazy after all. But a small sense of peace remained. Think this through, Noah... The only people who had access to the main office where all the officer's and detective's desk were – what they called the bullpen – were the cops themselves, some administrative personnel like dispatch, payroll, mailroom staff and...That was it, right? Of those, only the higher ups like Ziehring could get into his locked desk to steal his business cards, and it sure wasn't the Captain doing this. Who else? What was he missing?

Before he could get any further with that line of thinking, the door to the interrogation room opened. Townsend's expression gave nothing away as he entered and took the seat opposite Noah. He placed a file folder on the table and unbuttoned his grey suit jacket, revealing a sweat-dampened pale blue shirt and his shoulder holster.

Noah's gaze fixed on the gun, his heart rate suddenly skyrocketing. A hand was squeezing his heart and lungs, it was too hot and there was no air. *The gun was aimed, he had to move fast. There's no air. The fall to the ground knocked the wind out of him.* Can't breathe. *The thunderous crack was the last thing he heard clear-*

"Noah!"

His whole body jerked, and he swiveled his head up and over to look at Townsend so fast it hurt. "What?" His breathing was still too fast, his heart pounding and sweat prickling his skin, but the drowning, panicky feeling was already fading.

The detective was looking at him like he was deranged. Townsend's calculating stare bored into him like icicles. "I asked you if you know Jennifer Sealey."

"What?" He tried to swallow, but his mouth was dry. "No, I don't know that name. She's the victim?"

"She's the woman we found brutally murdered, yes." He opened the folder and pulled the first of a stack of crime scene photos out and slid it across the table.

Noah looked at it, but the damage to the victim was so extensive he couldn't tell what she may have once looked like. He pushed the photo to the side and glared at Townsend. "Where's my lawyer?"

Instead of answering right away, he picked up the photo and put it back on the stack. "You know, I've always heard it said that it's usually the guilty who lawyer up immediately."

Noah scoffed. "Yeah, I used to think that, too. But now I'm starting to see how little guilt or innocence mean in the right circumstances."

Townsend smirked. "She's about five minutes out. I thought I'd give you a chance to tell me...anything you might want to before she gets here."

He sat back and stared Townsend down. "I have invoked my right to have my lawyer present during interrogation. I am exercising my right to remain silent until then."

"Okay, then." Townsend got up and walked away, leaving the folder on the table.

Even though he knew it was part of the detective's plan, Noah still couldn't resist opening the file. Paperclipped to the inside front cover was a photocopy of the victim's driver's license. It only took a fraction of a second for Noah to recognize her as the woman who'd run into him at Jumping Beans.

Sorry! Are you okay?

Jerk.

I said I was – Forget it.

When Noah looked up, Townsend was standing by the door, scrutinizing his reaction. He smiled coldly and walked out of the room, and Noah was left alone with his confusion and dismay.

What did this mean? The real killer had to have been there, watching him. He picked this girl because she bumped into him. He thought back to Friday morning, trying to recall who else had been there. But other than a couple of regulars – older men with a lifetime habit of getting up with the sun and nothing better to do – the place had been empty. There had to be someone else... *Think, Noah.*

Unless he had been watching from outside. If that was the case, then there was no way Noah could find him. It was literally hopeless. With his blood on the victim and their previous run-in, there was no way Townsend would look at anybody else for this.

He heaved a shaky sigh and flipped through the case file again, desperate for something he could point to and say, *See? This proves it wasn't me.*

What he saw instead looked like just another nail in his coffin.

CHAPTER TWENTY-FIVE

<u>Monday, September 1, 2014 8:00 a.m.</u>

"He recognizes her," Townsend reported.

Ziehring pulled at his narrow chin, staring at the thinly-carpeted floor. "Are we absolutely sure about this? I mean, *Noah Harkham...*" He cast his gaze around his office as if seeking comfort in its familiarity.

"I know, sir, but that is what all the evidence is saying." And that was the problem, wasn't it? Townsend didn't know Harkham all that well, but what he did know shouted that this was all wrong. But he was acting odd...

"What? What is it?"

He looked up to find his captain peering at him, a hopeful look in his eyes. Townsend took a slow breath, gathering his thoughts. "In all the years I've been doing this, sir, I have never once doubted my skills. Until now."

Ziehring's brow furrowed. "What do you mean?"

"You selected me for your department because my training would be 'highly valued' and that I could make a difference here, you said. And I feel like I have, when working a legitimate case and not using it to spy on my colleagues."

"I never asked you to *spy* on anyone," the captain protested, shifting his position in his creaky chair.

Townsend smirked. "Oh, no, you never used that word. You were very careful about that." Ziehring started to say more, but he overrode him. "That's not really my point here, Captain." But then he frowned. "Or, I guess it sort of is. What I mean to say is, even though I have never liked being your ferret, I have always been able to trust what Frankie calls my weird radar."

Ziehring sat forward, one hand outstretched. "Wait, Franks knows about your training?"

"Is that really what you want to focus on right now? Sir." He couldn't help but glare.

"Fine. Go on."

He took a moment, scratching at the nape of his neck, then got up from the stiff-backed chair opposite the Captain's. "My radar tells me Noah Harkham did not do this. I'd swear it in court and shout it to anyone and everyone. And yet, there is something going on with that guy. Something psychological, I'm thinking. Because of that, I don't know if what I'm picking up from him is the Truth, with a capital T, or just what he *believes* is true, you know?"

Ziehring thought this over. "You want a psych eval."

"No, I don't want one, I *need* one. If he's had some sort of psychotic break, it could be possible that he's doing this and just not able to face it. Right? I mean, that could be possible. People repress memories successfully enough that they honestly can't remember them." He stood there, hoping his captain would throw him some other explanation as a lifeline.

"You know more about that than I do, Casey. But I agree that the evaluation needs to be done. If for nothing else than to give us something more than we've got to work with. If he's cracked up, then we can explore the idea he's doing this and unable to remember it afterwards. If he's fine, we can explore the idea he's being framed more aggressively."

He shook his head. "Shouldn't we be doing that anyway, just in case? If he's being framed, any delays could mean the real killer slips through our fingers."

"Relax, Casey. It's not an either/or situation until we know for sure. I'll order the eval. You inform his lawyer. She may throw a fit and I guarantee he will, but if you explain how it can help him, maybe he'll see reason. In the meantime, follow up anything to do with the possibility this is a frame job." He got up and walked Townsend to the door. "I'm just trying to cover all the bases." He opened the door and smiled at Townsend in what he probably thought a friendly, I'm-on-your-side kind of way.

To Townsend, it just looked smarmy. Yeah, he was trying to cover something all right, but it sure wasn't his bases... He stalked out of the Captain's office and saw Cecelia Baker talking with the desk sergeant. "Cecelia," he called out.

She looked up, her infamous you're-in-for-it-now glare set firmly in place as she stomped across the bullpen toward him. "What is it this time, Detective? Was there a newspaper article about my client found within five miles of the crime scene? Or maybe he was simply in town when it happened, along with a hundred thousand other people?"

He held his hands out. "Cecelia, calm down. I don't like this any more than you do, but this time it's bad."

She took a breath and forced her posture to relax a fraction. "Tell me."

"We found shards of a broken mug on the victim's body. A mug just like the one Harkham got from the coffee shop at which he and the victim had a literal run-in on Friday."

"Circumstantial. Other people probably bought that mug, too."

"It isn't one anyone can buy. It was given to him by the barista as some sort of promotional thing. It got knocked from his hands and shattered on the sidewalk when the victim ran into him as he was going out and she was going into the shop. They had words, he cleaned up the shards and stormed off."

She quieted. "I'm listening."

"There was blood on one of the slivers recovered from the body. I had the lab run it against Harkham's blood type. It matched."

She processed all of this for a long moment, her deep brown eyes flicking from one part of the room to another without seeming to take anything in. Townsend noticed that her black hair was expertly coiffed, and she was dressed in a tailored suit. He figured she must have a court appearance this morning.

"You matched it to his blood type, but not his DNA?"

"So far. The lab is running the full comparison as we speak."

"Where is he?"

"Interrogation Three."

"You *booked* him?"

"Yes. He was Mirandized in front of witnesses and reminded of his rights when I brought him in, on tape. He invoked, and we've just been waiting for you before going any further."

She looked at her watch. "I'm due in court in an hour. Let's get the preliminaries out of the way, then I want him arraigned no later than this afternoon. I'm not leaving him in booking, not here." She started past him toward the interrogation room.

He put a hand on her shoulder. "There's something else I need to run by you first."

"What now?"

"We're ordering a psych eval."

Her eyebrows shot upwards, crinkling her forehead. "You're *what?*"

"I need to know he's competent, that there's not a mental illness at play here."

She shifted her weight to one leg and tilted her head. "Why on earth would you even think that's a possibility?"

"I have something to show you. I think you'll understand."

CHAPTER TWENTY-SIX

The next time the door opened, the first person Noah saw was Cecelia Baker. He smiled, but the expression on her face made it soon wither. Her scowl seemed meant for him instead of Townsend, which worried him.

"Cecelia, thank you for coming," he said, standing to greet her.

She squeezed his arm and gave him a tight-lipped smile. Then she noticed the handcuffs and turned to Townsend. "What idiot handcuffed him?"

Noah relaxed a bit. She was still on his side, after all. That was promising.

"I did," Townsend answered, unfazed by being called an idiot. "It's protocol."

Cecelia's laugh was humorless. "Right." She patted Noah's shoulder. "Sit down. Let's get these things off you."

Noah sat and the two of them stared expectantly at Townsend until, with a sigh, he got his keys out of his pocket and unlocked the cuffs. Noah rubbed his wrists once the cold metal was removed, glad to be free of their weight. He noticed then that Townsend had brought a laptop with him and set it on the corner of the table. After pocketing his keys and the cuffs, he opened the laptop and turned it on. He also flipped on the tape recorder built into the tabletop.

"This is Detective Casey Townsend, badge number 2262. It is eight-twelve a.m. on Monday, September first, two-thousand-fourteen. I am interviewing Noah Alexander Harkham, in the presence of his lawyer, Cecelia Baker. I have a couple of videos to show you before we begin, Mr. Harkham."

"Videos?"

Townsend clicked the touchpad a couple of times, then turned the laptop to face Noah. "This first is from the security feed here in the precinct." He clicked to play the video.

It was the feed from inside his classroom, the day he went off on Spicer. Noah clenched his jaws so tight sharp pains were shooting up from his molars. He should have known this would be thrown back in his face. But with the anger came shame. Seeing it from the outside, he saw how volatile he had looked; how out of character he'd acted.

"Do you recognize the incident recorded on this video, Mr. Harkham?"

He shot a sharp glare at Townsend, but the fire behind fizzled out. "I–" His voice croaked. He cleared his throat and started again. "I do. This was Friday, the, um, August fifteenth."

"Talk me through what happened. That *is* you, yelling at one of your students – Officer Spicer – correct?"

Noah swallowed hard and closed his eyes. When he opened them again, the looped video feed was just getting back to the part where he had slammed his hands on the podium. He heard himself, through the speakers, say, *"I want you to use your head before you screw up our one shot at getting the evidence that just might make sure a murderer doesn't go free! Look at them, Spicer. For over twenty-four*

years the guy who did this has been laughing at the cops who screwed
this case up so royally there wasn't a chance in hell he'd ever be caught.
Would you want that to be on you?"

He tried to ignore the look on Spicer's face and on the faces of the
rest of the class behind him. In fact, he tried to look away from the
video altogether, but it was like he was glued to it, entrapped by it. "I
got angry, I admit..."

"Why? Why were you so angry at this officer?" Townsend asked,
pausing the playback.

Noah shook off the hold the video had over him and looked to
Cecelia before answering. At her nod, he said, "He wasn't taking it
seriously."

"It? Do you mean the class, or do you mean he wasn't taking *you*
seriously?"

"Well, both, I guess. I mean, it is my class..." He frowned. "What
difference does that make?" He glanced at the video. It was paused at
the moment everyone was leaving the room. Noah stood alone at the
podium.

"A year ago, you were injured on the job, forced into early retirement.
Before that, you had been a cop for what? Twelve years?"

"Almost twelve and a half," he answered cautiously. Which way was
he going with this?

"Seven, sorry, seven and a half, of those years you were a detective.
You had an impressive record –"

"Detective Sergeant," he corrected automatically.

"What?"

"I was a Detective Sergeant." He waved a hand. "Never mind, I guess it doesn't really matter now, does it?"

"Why would you say that? That it doesn't matter?"

Noah narrowed his eyes. "This isn't a therapy session, Townsend. If you want to ask me a real question, get to it."

Townsend's left eyebrow raised, but he otherwise didn't acknowledge his attempt to shift the power play. "Well, that actually brings me to my next 'real' question: is it because you no longer feel important, or taken seriously, that you reopened the One O'clock Killer case?"

"I didn't reopen it."

"But you did check the case file out of archives three weeks ago, did you not?" He opened the file folder he'd left with Noah earlier, flipped to a page toward the back and spun it around to show him. It was the sign out sheet from the records archives with the case number and Noah's signature.

He stifled a groan. How could he have forgotten about doing that? This was going from bad to worse fast. He looked to Cecelia again. She nodded, though her expression was troubled. He turned to Townsend. "I thought about using it for class."

"Thought about it."

"Yes."

"But didn't."

"No."

"Why is that?"

Noah's throat and chest felt tight. "Because–" The great heaviness he'd felt looking through those notes settled over him again. "Because it was too hard." He put his elbows on the table, cupped one hand around the other fist and pressed them both against his mouth, struggling to keep the tears he felt coming at bay. His emotions were never this raw. Why were they now?

Townsend paused, and Noah thought there was a glimmer of sympathy in his eyes. But then his interrogator expression took over again. "What was? Seeing the case you failed to solve?"

He glared. "Seeing Rob's handwriting. I thought after all these years I could handle it, but I was wrong, okay? All I could see was how I failed him," he added in a small voice.

"So then, let me ask you this: is that the reason you killed Nigel Warner?"

Cecelia laid a hand on his arm to keep him from reacting. "We've already been down this road, Detective. And we've already established that your so-called evidence for that theory is laughable, at best. Besides, we're not here about Nigel Warner, are we? Keep your questions limited to the scope of this arrest and investigation."

Noah's breathing had quickened, too fast. A flush was creeping over his skin, and a prickling like sweat itched up his scalp. Maybe it was seeing himself on the video, maybe it was hearing Townsend's accusations, but he did feel it, he felt...guilty. He had to get himself under control before Townsend smelled blood in the water.

As if he could hear his name in Noah's mind, Townsend looked at him, his scrutinizing eyes taking everything in. He then clicked another couple of buttons on the laptop and swiveled it back toward Noah. "This is from this past Friday, August twenty-ninth. Again, this is your classroom. Again, you lose your temper, this time with a couple of uniformed officers. Your students. Want to tell me what happened?"

Noah gritted his teeth. "You have the video right there. You have eyes and ears, you know what happened."

Townsend smirked, making him look even more like a shark. "Yes, of course, but I mean, can you tell me what was going through your mind? Why did you lose your cool this time?"

"Are you seriously asking me that?"

"Noah," Cecelia warned.

"They accused me of murder!"

"And that made you angry?"

"Of course it fu-" He bit his lip to keep the profanity, the one he *never* used, from slipping out.

He had to keep calm. He had to remain in control. But he felt his world slipping through his fingers. Everything – what little he had left – was dangerously close to being ripped from him. If Townsend made the connection with the crime scene...it would all be over. It wouldn't matter that he was innocent, he would end up on death row, with only a lethal injection waiting for him.

Why bother to fight? It was only a matter of time. It didn't matter how hard he might rail at the injustice, how hard he might throw himself against the cage being built around him, he would just end up exhausted and alone and, eventually, dead. Why not just give in now and save himself the futile effort? Would it be such a bad way to die? It was designed to be humane. He'd just go to sleep, and never wake up.

If he wasn't shanked or beaten to death in prison first.

There was a falling sensation in the pit of his stomach, a cold, electric pulse coursing through his body. He wasn't sure what to call the emotion, but it was overwhelming, crushing. Some combination of fear and helplessness, only amped up by a factor of, like, a hundred.

"Mr. Harkham? Noah?"

He lifted his head to look at Townsend, and if was like lifting a boulder the size of the entire room. *Just breathe...Be still.* He took a moment to center himself before answering. "Of course it made me angry, Casey. But that does not mean that I killed Nigel Warner or Jennifer Sealey. I don't know her, why would I want to kill her?"

Townsend pulled up another video file and played it. "This is Jennifer Sealey. Do you remember her now?"

Noah didn't even look at the screen. "I didn't say I didn't remember her. I said I don't know her. Outside of that one incident, I have never seen or spoken to her before, to the best of my knowledge. I didn't know her name until you told me."

"Then how do you explain your blood on the pieces of that mug you were holding when she ran into you getting inside her shirt?"

Noah groaned. "I don't know what to tell you. That mug broke, I cut my finger on one of the slivers trying to clean it up. Lynn, the barista from the coffee shop, came outside and swept up the mess for me. Maybe someone got into the trash at Jumping Beans and took the pieces to plant them on her. Have you even talked to Lynn? Did you look at the surveillance of the back alley where the Dumpsters are? Or did you just get the footage of the victim's run-in with me and leave it at that?"

Townsend ignored the questions. "Why, Mr. Harkham, would someone want to do this to you? Why frame you?"

He sank his head into his hands, his elbows still on the table, and rubbed his fingers through his hair before flinging his hands toward Townsend pleadingly. "We've already been over this. I don't *know* why. All I know is," he said, slamming his fists onto the table, "I. Did not. Do. This. I *am* being framed, someone *is* doing this to me. Please. Tell me you see that."

Cecelia placed a hand on his shoulder. "Detective Townsend, perhaps we could take a break now before going any further? Maybe let my client have something to eat and drink? I am assuming, of course, that you haven't already accommodated him."

The look the two exchanged sent a shiver through Noah's stomach. Townsend turned away from her to regard Noah with an expression that was frightening for all its neutrality. Noah sucked in his bottom lip, unsure what the other man was about to say next but fearing to hear it.

"Your uncle is a psychiatrist, isn't he?"

Cecelia sighed. Noah sat back, stunned by this curveball. Whatever he was expecting their shared look to mean, it was not this. "He is."

"Have you ever been or are you currently one of his patients?"

He planted the balls of his feet on the floor, removing his hands from the table. "No." His brow furrowed. "Where are you going with this?"

"Would you say that the behavior you exhibited in these videos is typical of the way you normally act?"

"No," he whispered, more in denial of what he could now see was happening than in answer to the question.

"Was that a 'no,' Mr. Harkham?"

"Yes," he said, shaking inside, "that was a 'no.'"

Townsend leaned forward, adopting a gentler demeanor. *Here it comes...* "Mr. Harkham, Noah, I've spoken with Captain Ziehring and Ms. Baker. We're ordering a psychiatric evaluation for you."

Even knowing this was where it was headed, he still felt gut-punched. "This is insane–" *Bad choice of words.* "This is ridiculous." He stared at each of them, disbelieving. "A psychiatric– so you think, what? I've gone completely insane and am killing people without knowing it? Is *that* your working theory? Or that I've just flipped and turned complete psychopath all the sudden?"

Cecelia placed one hand on his shoulder, her other around his arm, as both a soothing gesture and, he suspected, a restraining one. "I didn't like it either, at first. But hear him out before you get all in a lather."

"*In a lather?* I'm not some teenager who's mad he can't borrow the car this weekend – you're talking about having me committed!"

"No, that's not what we're talking about," Townsend said. "I just need to know, without a shadow of a doubt, that there is no scenario in which you are doing this and not remembering. The way you've been acting lately has a lot of people concerned about your state of mind and –"

"My state of mind is that I'm being set up for two crimes – two *murders* that I did not commit and all I can see is the noose that's being tightened around my neck – and *you all* are the ones doing the tightening." It was hard to breathe again, and the room was too small. No air, no way out. *Where are You now, huh? How can I 'be still' if you've abandoned me?*

"This is happening, so I need you to calm–"

"Detective, maybe we should–"

"How can you even think that I had–"

A sudden, sharp tapping on the one-way mirror startled them all into silence mid-sentence. They turned to look, but, of course, could see nothing through the mirrored glass.

"Stay here, I'll be right back," Townsend said, his voice sharp, as he stood. He stopped long enough to tag the recording, "Interview interrupted, eight forty-seven a.m. Will resume momentarily." He paused the tape then stalked out the door.

Noah blew out a breath and rubbed his hands across his face. He noticed they were trembling and tucked them under his arms to still them. He didn't even look at Cecelia, though he could feel her eyes on him. "I'm not crazy," he eventually said.

She sighed. "I know, hun. But you haven't exactly been yourself lately, either, have you?"

He closed his eyes, wanting to disappear, to escape. But, as things stood, there was nowhere to go, no way out of this. Whoever was doing this just might win. And what then? How long could he survive on the inside?

The hopelessness of the situation weighed on him. He was so tired. Tired of being tired, of not understanding what was happening to him or why. Tired of fighting. Already. But what was the point of fighting, anyway? Right now, he could only see two outcomes: either he'd go to prison or get put in a psych ward. Either way, his life was over. So why fight?

He pressed the heels of his hands to his eyes. *What is* wrong *with me?*

"No, I'm not sure *who* I am anymore." He opened his eyes and looked at her. "Not my uncle. I don't care who, just...not my uncle."

She nodded, sympathy and compassion in her warm eyes. "No, it can't be him. I suggested someone to Townsend already. I believe you've spoken with her before, after your injury: Dr. Maria Frazier."

"After Rob," he corrected. "Ziehring forced me. And it...didn't go very well."

She'd asked him if Rob's death was dredging up past abandonment issues from his parents' deaths. Surprised and angry she even knew about his past, he had unleashed on her, yelling at her that she knew nothing about him or anything else. His parents hadn't abandoned him, God had stolen them. God was stealing everyone he ever cared about. He'd stormed out of the session forty minutes early, telling her to stay out of his head.

Cecelia held his hand. Hers was warm and strong, his was cold and listless. "This can only help you, Noah."

Dear God, something had to.

A couple minutes later, Townsend came back into the room and closed the door, his back to them. He stayed there a second or two, then turned around, his expression closed, and crossed the room to turn the tape recorder back on. "Interview terminated, eight fifty-one a.m. Mr. Harkham, you are free to go."

A full three seconds elapsed before Noah could fathom what had been said. "I'm– what? What happened?"

"You remain a person of interest, so we ask that you not leave the city until further notice. But, as of this moment, you are free to go."

"Detective Townsend, not that I'm not elated," Cecelia said, "but why exactly are you letting my client go when you were ready to put him behind bars just a few minutes ago?"

"We have a new development. A witness has come forward."

CHAPTER TWENTY-SEVEN

———

<u>Monday, September 1, 2014 8:37 a.m.</u>

Frankie threw another glance toward the hallway leading to the interrogation rooms. Townsend had escorted Noah's lawyer, Cecelia Baker, into the conference room when she'd first arrived, but he didn't know why. A few minutes later, they both went into the interrogation room. That was over half an hour ago.

He drummed his fingers on his keyboard before trying to continue with the report he had been filling out. But the words he typed and read didn't make sense to him anymore. After stretching and yawning, he decided he was in desperate need of caffeine. He got up and started toward the break room area across the room.

"Detective Franks?"

He turned back toward the unfamiliar voice and had to fight to keep surprise from showing in his expression. It was the kid from campus, the High-flyer, that he and Townsend had witnessed sneaking back into the dorm. "Yes? How can I help you, Mister....?"

The boy raked a hand across the back of his head. The unbuttoned cuff of the open red and tan plaid shirt he wore over a stained concert tee mussed up his curly hair. "Oh, um, I'm just Kevin, uh, Kevin Scruggs."

Frankie watched the kid for signs of being under the influence again, but, from what he could tell, he was sober. Ish. "What can I do for you, Kevin?"

His eyes darted around the room, he shifted his weight from one foot to the other and back. Frankie's hand stayed near his sidearm, just in case. When someone gets this jittery, it was difficult to predict their next move. "Hey, Kevin? Why don't we go sit at my desk, all right? You can take your time and tell me what's going on. Okay?"

Kevin nodded, and Frankie led him back to his desk, pulling an extra chair from along the wall for the kid to sit in. He waited until Kevin was seated before sitting himself. The kid's legs bobbed up and down at a furious pace.

"Um, I think I need to tell you something." He chewed on the side of his thumb, his pasty face drawn and pale. "You said if we knew anything.... you know, about Nigel Warner.... that we, um, should contact you, right?"

Frankie leaned forward. "That's right."

"I, uh, I was in the same sorta area that night. Meeting a friend," he added too quickly. "And I saw something." He started looking around again, chewing on his other thumb now.

"Hey, Kevin? Look at me." He waited until the kid looked at him. "It's all right. Just tell me what you saw."

"There was a guy. He was running down the RiverWalk, back toward Chandler's Row. I don't think he saw us, he was pretty intent on booking it out of there. When he got to the where the RiverWalk ends and all those bushes and sh- sorry, stuff, is, he threw something." His words tumbled to a complete stop and he looked at the floor. The jiggling of his legs increased in speed.

"Did you see what he threw?" Frankie grabbed a pen and notebook and made notes.

The boy shook his head, his lips pressed tightly together and his face flushing bright red. "No." His voice cracked, and a string of spit connected his lips. He sucked in a breath, not quite a sob, and continued, "I walked down the RiverWalk a little while later and, uh, I could s-see that, um, there was some-someone on the ground..."

The tears came now, and Frankie grabbed a tissue from the box on his desk and gave it to him. "It's okay, Kevin. You're doing good. What exactly did you see?"

He sucked in another half-sob. "I think it was Nigel." He plopped his hands on top of his head, flattening his hair down his forehead, before wiping them down his face. "I think I saw Nigel dead."

"Hey, it's okay. You're doing great here, okay?" He smiled reassuringly. "Do you remember what time this was?"

He looked up at the ceiling. "I don't know...I was, I was pretty messed up already by then, man." He looked at Frankie sharply, his face gone white. "Oh, shi- I mean, crap, I didn't– I mean–"

"Don't worry about it, kid, I don't work for narcotics. Just your best guess, what time would you say it was?"

He took a deep breath and let it out, fluttering his lips. "Um, okay, I met Darryl– I mean my buddy around twelve and this was a while after that... I'm not sure how long I waited. We sorta argued about whether I should stick my nose in it. I'd say it was maybe one-twenty, one-thirty?"

Frankie wrote this down. "So, you saw the man running a little after midnight, but before one o'clock, then saw the body maybe twenty or thirty minutes after that? Ish, anyway."

Kevin nodded and wiped his nose on the tissue. "That sounds right."

"What did you do after you saw the body? Did you look for what the guy tossed into the bushes?"

He shook his head and a fresh wave of tears poured down his face. "No. I was scared. I never seen anything like that, man. And my buddy, he was all like, 'we gotta get outta here before the cops show up.' So, I– I just left with him." He sniffed loudly.

"Okay. Where did you two go?"

Kevin stopped jiggling his legs abruptly. "Aw, man, I tell you that and I get myself in some serious sh- trouble."

Frankie put down his pen and leaned closer to the kid. "Look, buddy, you gotta see this from my perspective, okay? You come in here and you say you were there, in the same area where the victim was killed. You tell me you see a man running from the direction of the crime scene and throw something in the bushes, but you don't know who he is or what he threw away. Then you tell me you saw Nigel Warner's dead body. Okay?"

"Yeah. That's right."

"Okay, but you also tell me you were with somebody else and that you–both of you–were high. You don't remember the time so well, you don't know what you saw. Now, what is to keep me from thinking you either, A: made this all up–"

"I'm not making this–"

"-or B: either you or your buddy or both were involved?"

He sat stock still. "That's—no you can't think–" He shot up out of the chair. 'I never shoulda come here.' He sniffed and rubbed the back of his hand across his nose.

Before the kid could bolt, Frankie got up and blocked his path to the door. "Hey, Kevin, I never said you were involved. Okay? All I was asking was for something to help me know your story is true as you told it. All right? Can you give me something like that? What about the guy you saw? Race, height, weight, hair color? Anything can help."

He still looked spooked, but he closed his eyes and furrowed his brow in concentration. "It was dark, so it was kinda hard to tell, but I think he was wearing, like, camouflage pants...they were patterned something like that. And, um...his hair...I don't think he had any...or not much."

"Like bald? Or just close-cropped?"

Kevin opened his eyes. "Like a buzz cut, maybe."

Frankie gestured for him to take his seat again, and once he did, sat back down himself and recorded this new detail in his notebook. "Could you tell, then, if he was white, black, Hispanic, Asian, or...?"

"Um, he was a white guy, I think. Look, I'm not a hundred percent about all this, it happened so fast and I was... I wasn't in the best shape to really notice this stuff."

"Okay," Frankie said, tapping his pen against the notebook. He glanced back at the hallway to the interrogation rooms. He then opened a drawer in his desk and removed the digital tape recorder he kept there. "Come with me."

The boy looked utterly confused now, but he pushed himself up out of the chair and followed him. Frankie led the way to the observation room adjoining Interrogation Room Three, where Noah was. The light was already off, so they could see Townsend, Cecelia and Noah in the middle of a full-blown argument. Everyone was still seated, but from their postures, Frankie would've sworn it looked like the detective and the lawyer were both ganging up on Noah.

"What the–?" He couldn't focus on that. He'd brought Kevin here for a reason. "I'm going to record our next bit of conversation, okay?"

He looked nervous but nodded. "Okay."

Frankie pressed the Record button. "This is Detective Alan Franks, badge number 2914, with Kevin Scruggs. It is," he glanced at his watch, "eight forty-five a.m. on Monday, September first, twenty-fourteen. Kevin, will you please state your name and age for the record?"

He leaned close to the tape recorder as Frankie held it out to him. "Uh, Kevin Dale Scruggs. I'm twenty."

"Thank you. Now, Kevin, tell me again what you saw in the early hours of August twenty-ninth?"

"Uh, I was at the RiverWalk, and I saw some guy running toward Chandler's Row. He threw something in the bushes. A little later... I, uh, I saw someone lying on the ground further up the RiverWalk."

"And you believe this was Nigel Warner's body that you saw, is that correct?"

"Yes, sir."

"Okay. We are in the observation room associated with Interrogation Room Three, in which Detective Casey Townsend is interrogating suspect N.H. in the presence of his lawyer. Now, Kevin, can you take a good look at the suspect in there, the man in the dark blue shirt, and tell me if he is the man you saw fleeing the scene of Nigel Warner's murder?"

He didn't even hesitate. "No way. That dude is a lot taller and thinner, like in better shape. Plus, he's got a lot more hair than the guy I saw."

"Thank you, Kevin. We're just going to go back to my desk and finalize your statement. Then you are free to go with the Fifth Precinct's thanks."

"Uh, yeah, sure. You're welcome. Who is that guy in there, anyway?"

"Sorry, I can't discuss an ongoing investigation. Interview terminated eight forty-six a.m." Frankie stopped recording and tucked the recorder into his pocket. He led the way back to his desk, where he gave Kevin a notebook and pen. "Write down everything you told me a few minutes ago, exactly as you told me, start to finish. And I'm going to need Darryl's last name."

Kevin, who had already started writing, suddenly stopped. "What? No way! You never said I'd have to rat anybody out!"

"Kevin, it's okay. Like I said, I don't work for narcotics. I just need to have him tell us what he saw, too. Maybe he noticed something you didn't see, something that can help us find who killed Nigel. He'd be a hero. You both will."

Still, Kevin wrestled with the decision. "All right. But I can't guarantee he'll talk to you." He continued writing for a second, then stopped and looked up. "Do you... d'you think that–" his voice faltered. "I saw the news and I just keep thinking, if I'd come here sooner... maybe that lady would still be alive."

"We don't know that. You can't think like that, okay? You're here now, and you're doing the right thing. Just focus on that, all right?"

"Okay," he said, not appearing convinced. But he carried on writing his statement anyway.

Frankie looked around until he spotted a familiar uniformed officer walking across the room. "Hey, Byers!" She looked over at him. "Got a second?"

She changed course and headed to his desk. "Yes, sir?"

Frankie stood. "I'm sorry to ask, but can you stay here with Kevin for just a minute? I've got to go stop an interrogation."

"Uh, sure. Not a problem, sir." She eyed the boy with a puzzled frown.

"Be right back." He rushed back to the observation room. Things had gotten even worse since he last looked in and, when he tapped the recorder on the glass, everyone stopped mid-sentence to look toward him. Townsend said something sharply to Noah, paused the interrogation tape, and stormed out of the room.

A few seconds later, he entered the observation room. "You had better have a hell of a good reason for interrupting."

"The best." He rewound the recording and played it. When it got to Kevin's declaration that Noah was not the guy he saw fleeing the scene, Townsend's eyes narrowed as he processed the information. Then his countenance brightened with excitement.

"We have a suspect. Got a name?"

"Not yet, but we've got a description. I'm sure Kevin will sit with a sketch artist." He gestured the recorder toward the glass, through which he could now see Cecelia and Noah in subdued conversation. "What was going on in there? It looked like two against one."

"Don't worry about it. If this pans out, the whole thing is moot, anyway. Where is this witness now?"

"Writing up his statement in the bullpen. Byers is watching him."

"Byers, huh? Surrounding yourself with Harkham supporters now?"

"What?"

"Never mind." He headed back to the interrogation room.

Frankie turned on the speaker to listen in. "–terminated eight fifty-one a.m. Mister Harkham, you are free to go."

Noah didn't move, apparently stunned. "I'm– what? What happened?"

Townsend remained standing, his hands on his hips, staring at a point in space just over Noah's shoulder. "You remain a person of interest, so we ask that you not leave the city until further notice. But, as of this moment, you are free to go."

"Detective Townsend, not that I'm not elated," Cecelia said, "but why exactly are you letting my client go when you were ready to put him behind bars just a few minutes ago?"

"We have a new development. A witness has come forward."

Frankie, even knowing beforehand that, because of this, Noah would be set free, still felt the surge of relief and excitement at hearing the words come out of Townsend's mouth. He watched as Noah and Cecelia exited the interrogation room with Townsend, then followed them out. Noah looked mid-collapse.

Captain Ziehring, along with Yorton Greenaway and a uniformed officer, met Noah before he was even twenty feet outside of the interrogation room. "Noah," Ziehring said, and to Frankie, the sound was akin to a death knell, "I've spoken with Mr. Greenaway, and we have determined that it is best for everyone if, pending this investigation, you were relieved of duty."

Noah looked from Ziehring to Greenaway, a frumpy pencil-pusher with a bad seventies haircut. "What?"

"I'm sorry, Noah. I'm going to have to ask you to turn over your ID card and keys."

CHAPTER TWENTY-EIGHT

"You're *firing* me?" Noah couldn't believe his ears. On top of everything else, now this?

"Now, Mr. Harkham," Greenaway answered, spreading his clammy hands in a placating gesture, "no one said 'fired.' Just think of it as a leave of absence. You are still very much on the payroll." He smiled, a wormy twist of his pale lips. "Speaking of which, I'm still waiting for your timesheet, so if you could submit that ASAP as possible, that would be great. Before you leave, please."

Noah didn't even try to keep the disgust and incredulity out of his expression. This was beyond ludicrous... "I already did it," he said.

"Well, actually, no, you didn't, I'm afraid."

Noah shook his head and stormed past the group toward his office. He halfway registered that Frankie was standing just outside the observation room door, which meant he must have had a hand in interrupting his interrogation. But his mind could only process one thing at a time right now, or he would simply drown.

Timesheet... He unlocked his office door and slammed his chair away from the desk, jabbing his finger on the buttons to power up the computer and monitor. He stabbed at the keys, typing in his password to unlock the screen once it finally booted up. When he pulled up the time entry management program to the current pay period, he saw Greenaway was right. The entire sheet was blank. "What the-?" *How did I forget to do this?*

Greenaway cleared his throat, standing just outside the door. "Did you find it?"

"Yes," Noah answered, typing in the general in and out times he typically worked into the appropriate fields, then clicked to sign off and submit it for approval. "There. You have it now."

"Thank you. Although, it is you who benefits from it, not me." He wheezed a laugh.

Noah ignored him, intent on getting his stuff – *ASAP as possible,* to borrow Greenaway's ridiculous, redundant pet phrase – and getting out of the building before this whole fiasco became a precinct-wide spectacle. He pulled his ID badge out of his pocket and slammed it and the keyring that held his work keys onto the desktop. He then tore open the top middle drawer of the desk, where he kept some of his class notes and other personal effects.

What he saw inside the drawer now instead caught him completely off-guard. He jerked his hand away as if the handle had burned him. He froze, staring at the little white rectangles with their neat print and horrible brown splotches, lying next to the navy-blue porcelain shards.

"Mr. Harkham?"

"Greenaway, get Ziehring. Now." He glanced up to see his boss starting to edge away from the doorway. "Wait! Don't leave the room; please, just call out for him. I need you to keep me in sight. Okay? See? My hands are up, I'm stepping away from the desk."

"Mr. Harkham," Greenaway's voice was pinched, "what is going on?"

Noah eased away from the desk and backed away to the wall nearest the door, nearest Greenaway. "Please, just get Ziehring and Townsend in here now."

Greenaway leaned out into the hallway and asked a passing uniformed officer to get the captain and detective. A moment later, Ziehring arrived, though Townsend was just a beat behind. They stepped past the civilian supervisor at his gesture. They looked to Noah for explanation; he simply pointed to his desk.

"I haven't touched anything other than the handle to open the drawer. I have no doubt you'll find my fingerprints on everything inside all the same, though."

Ziehring frowned and approached the desk cautiously, as if expecting to find a bomb inside. When he saw what *was* in there, he jerked his head up to gape at Noah and his hand strayed toward the gun at his hip. Noah braced himself, heart pounding, waiting for his former captain to draw on him. But Ziehring eventually just motioned for Townsend to look.

Townsend stared at the bloody business cards and remnants of the shattered mug a long moment. "You said you threw them away or burned them all," he said, peering at Noah. "You said the barista cleaned up the mess."

"That's right."

"How do you explain all this being in your desk right now?" His voice was calm and even, the total opposite of how Noah was feeling.

Noah licked his lips with a dry tongue. "If you were going to frame me, you'd want to make absolutely sure I go down hard for the crimes, right? And most people would think: what better way than to have an excessive amount of evidence implicating me? Please, just think for a minute. Even if there was any possible motive for me to kill Nigel, why would I have old business cards with me, all over the ground when I did it? And why then pick up all but one and put them in that drawer? And why would I keep the broken mug when I'd have to go back to the coffee shop to get the pieces out of the trash? Why then would I have them with me when I killed Jennifer Sealey? None of this makes any sense!"

Townsend closed his eyes for a moment. When he opened them again, his expression was resolute. Noah's heart sank – until Townsend spoke.

"Captain, we're going to need to pull the surveillance footage of this area, see who has accessed this room in the last couple of days. I also think we need to get Noah out of here. Whoever did this could be in the building right now, and they probably won't be too happy we aren't locking him up and throwing away the key."

Ziehring turned his thin lips downward, drawing his long face even longer. "You think he may become a target."

"Right, I think it's possible. If the frame up didn't work, this guy may just decide to take him out directly."

Noah's head was reeling. First, he's sure he was going to be put in an institution or maybe put to death, then he gets a reprieve from that, only to get faced with the prospect of losing his job. Now, his head was on the chopping block again, but for a whole different reason. He put the heel of his palms to his temples. "What do you need me to do?"

Townsend and Ziehring exchanged a look. "For now, we'd better get him home," Ziehring said. "If this guy decides to make a move, I'd rather it be with as few bystanders around as possible."

"But surely," Greenaway said, "a precinct full of cops would be the safest place for him, wouldn't it?"

"Exactly the problem," Townsend told him.

Noah nodded. "You're going to use me as bait. Or is it that you still think I'm going to go all Mr. Hyde on you?"

"Don't worry, we won't send you home alone," Ziehring said.

"Just consider it protective custody." Townsend smirked. No doubt the irony of the situation was not lost on him.

"Right." A thought occurred to him. "Is there a spiral-bound notebook with an orange cover in there?"

Townsend looked back inside the drawer. "Not that I can see. What else was in here?"

"Um, a digital voice recorder, a couple of pens and pencils, flash drives, and a silver letter opener. It has my initials on it."

Townsend was shaking his head as Noah spoke. "None of that is in there."

Noah thought back. He hadn't taken his notebook to the ill-fated class Friday morning, just his laptop. Come to think of it, he hadn't seen the letter opener in that drawer on Friday, but everything else had been there. So, it had to have been taken before then, maybe the notebook, too. The rest could have been set up at any time after his run-in with Jennifer at Jumping Beans.

Ziehring went to the door and nudged Greenaway out ahead of him. "I'll call in CSU," he told Townsend. "and get the surveillance pulled. I'll send a uniform over to secure the scene until the techs arrive. You get him out of here."

"Yes, sir."

Once they were gone and it was just Noah and Townsend left, Noah said, "This is a crime scene, how about we step into the hall?"

Townsend nodded and followed him out. "What's in that notebook?"

"Notes on the cold cases for class – pointers on how not to contaminate the crime scene. Lots of things someone looking to get away with murder and frame someone else for it could use." He made a frustrated sound low in his throat. "Basically, everything he needs to know to get away with this."

"This isn't your fault, you know that, right?"

Noah scoffed. "That's why everyone keeps asking me who I pissed off to deserve this."

Frankie headed up the hallway toward them, a uniformed officer Noah knew well in tow. "Noah Harkham, still causing a ruckus around here, I see," Kenneth Stiles said with a grin that made his graying mustache lift like bird's wings.

Noah shook his hand. "Stiles. Ziehring send you?"

"Yessir, until the lab rats get here."

Frankie frowned at him. "What's going on? Ziehring tore through like a bat out of hell, ordering Stiles to secure your office so CSU can search it."

"He planted evidence in my desk," Noah told him.

"What? He was here, in the precinct?"

Townsend nodded. "And now we're getting Noah out of here."

"Let me do that," Frankie offered. "My witness is in with Byers waiting for the sketch artist, I've got Reynolds, Ryzowski, Cox and Adelmo out canvassing the end of the RiverWalk. The only things left to do now are find Lynn and follow up with Dr. Lee about Nigel's autopsy."

"All right, but call me when you get him secure."

"Copy that," Frankie agreed, then tapped Noah on the chest. "Let's get you out of here."

Noah nodded and started to follow him but turned back to Townsend. "Casey, thank you for finally believing me."

Townsend's smile was guarded. "Don't prove me wrong. Remember what happened to Mr. Hyde."

CHAPTER TWENTY-NINE

———

<u>Monday, September 1, 2014 9:30 a.m.</u>

Frankie made him wait in the hall while he cleared the apartment. Once satisfied no one was lying in ambush, Frankie let him in and locked the door. Noah stood in the middle of the living room, unsure what to do with the yo-yoing emotions in the wake of this morning's events.

"How long do you think it'll be before this guy realizes I've been released?"

"Probably not long, if he hasn't heard already."

Noah took a seat on his couch and gestured for Frankie to do the same. "Well, until he comes here looking for me," he said, tossing the remote to his friend, "maybe you can find something to watch to kill the time."

Frankie turned on the TV and flipped through a couple of channels but threw a concerned look his way. "You look terrible, Hark. Why don't you go try to get some sleep?" As if in protest, Noah's stomach growled. "Food first, apparently," Frankie said with a smirk. "Do you have any eggs?"

Noah gave him a sidelong look. "Yes," he answered cautiously.

With a grin, Frankie got up from the couch. "Good. Then I'm making us some of my world-famous omelets."

"*World*-famous?"

"Well," he shrugged, "they liked 'em back home and in Atlanta." He started toward the kitchen.

"Hey, you ever miss it?"

He stopped and turned back. "Miss what?"

"Georgia. Central Investigations. Fraud, robberies, embezzlement...not having to deal with death all the time?"

Frankie furrowed his brow. "Sometimes, I guess. But putting away a killer is a lot more satisfying than putting away a guy who fleeced his own company out of money it could afford to lose anyway." He came back and sat on the arm of the old grey armchair adjacent to the couch. "What happened in your interrogation? It looked like you were outnumbered in there."

Noah looked down, chafing his hands on his thighs. "They want me to see a shrink."

"Ah."

"Yeah. Townsend thought it was possible that I was killing people and not remembering doing it. Like a split personality thing or something."

"Is that why he made that Mr. Hyde reference?" Noah nodded, so he asked, "What are you going to do?"

"You mean now that I'm not being forced into it?" He shrugged. "I don't know. I mean, I had resigned myself to it just before they cut me loose, but now..."

"Look, Hark," Frankie leaned forward, resting his elbows on his knees and lacing his fingers together, "I'm not going to tell you what to do, but given what you told me this morning, maybe just... give it some thought?"

"You know, Frankie, my whole life since the day my parents were killed, people have been trying to get inside my head, analyze me. Even those who aren't qualified to." He rubbed his tired eyes and then gave his friend a smile. "Especially the ones who aren't qualified. But not you. You never have. Maybe it's the lack of sleep making me all sappy, but I want you to know I appreciate that. I think it's why I eventually considered you a friend, not just my partner."

"Yeah? Cuz I'm still trying to decide whether or not to call you *my* friend."

Noah laughed, and though it was still sort of forced, it was the closest thing to a real one than he'd had for quite a while. "Thanks. I *was* trying to be serious."

"Yeah, me too. I mean, I hate to break it to ya, pal, but you're kind of high-maintenance. I mean, between you getting hurt and forced to retire and now being framed for murder, I'm not sure I'm up for all your drama." He tried to keep a straight face but ended up laughing.

"Oh, thanks, that's exactly what I need to hear right now. Jerk." He aimed a kick at Frankie's shin, but he dodged it. Even though he thought Frankie was only joking, a part of him worried he might mean it, on some level. "For what it's worth, I'm sorry I dragged you into all this and put you in the middle against Townsend."

"I was kidding, Hark. And you didn't drag me into anything, it's part of my job description."

"Not anymore; we're not partners now."

"I meant as your friend." He got up and went into the kitchen. "Oh, and by the way, my granddaddy always said, 'never kick the cook unless you have good health insurance,'" he called out over the sound of pots and pans clanking against each other. "Hey, where do you keep your arsenic?"

Noah grinned. "Top drawer to the right of the stove."

He heard the drawer open. "Nah, that's sea salt, but I guess that'll do."

<u>10:37 a.m.</u>

About an hour later, after they had eaten what were admittedly good omelets, Noah went to his room and changed into a tee shirt and track pants, intending to try to get some sleep. But all he could do was lay there and turn everything about the case over and over in his mind instead. The thing that kept eating at him was the victim choice. Why Nigel? Why Jennifer?

Granted, she was probably chosen because of their run-in at the coffee shop, but that would mean that the killer had to have seen it happen. Which brought him back to the idea that he was being watched, followed...stalked like a deer just before the hunter brings it down. And if that was the case, then it was just a matter of time before this hunter caught up with him.

But why Nigel? How did he tie in with the original victims? Or did he? There was an itchy feeling in the back of his mind that said, if he could answer those questions, he'd have all the answers he needed to unravel the whole case. Nigel was first this time around, and Noah was certain there was a deliberate reason for that.

He lay there, staring at the ceiling, until he figured he wasn't going to sleep now any more than he had the past several weeks, so he grabbed his cell phone off the nightstand and got out of bed. He opened his bedroom door, slipping the phone into his track pants pocket. He couldn't hear the TV anymore, but it did sound like Frankie was on the phone with someone. He stopped at the end of the hall to listen before interrupting.

"–her there now? Great. Let me know how it goes. Yep, bye."

Noah entered the living room. "Was that Townsend?"

Frankie stood near the kitchen doorway, putting his phone back in his pocket. He looked up at the sound of Noah's voice. "I thought you were asleep."

Noah shrugged. "Would if I could." He rubbed his eyes with a thumb and forefinger, coming over to sit on the couch. "Was that Townsend?"

"Sorry, yeah. Uniforms found Lynn. He's talking with her now."

Noah frowned, remembering that they had mentioned her name back at the precinct this morning. "Lynn...the barista? Do you think she's part of this?" he thought back to the way she had laughed when he'd told her someone thought he'd been involved in something illegal. Had it been because she thought the idea was laughable? Or was she glad to see that her plan to frame him was working?

"Something's up with her," Frankie said, seating himself in the armchair. "That mug she gave you? The manager confirmed there was no free mug promotional thing. She made it up."

His thoughts were churning. "Why, though? What would make her hate me so much?" He rubbed a hand down his face and stifled a yawn. "Wait– would that mean that Jennifer Sealey was in on it, too, or was the run-in just a happy coincidence? I mean, if the end-game was to get pieces of the mug with my prints or blood on it to plant on the next victim." He shook his head, his brain feeling thick from the lack of sleep.

"I don't know, but Townsend's with her. He'll crack her, if there's anything to find inside." He sent off a quick text, no doubt telling Townsend to ask her about how Jennifer Sealey became a target.

"I bet if you pull her phone records, you'll find a connection to the killer. Even if she's only supplying him information on me and my whereabouts or whatever, she must have a way to contact him. Unless she only spoke to him in person..." He growled in frustration, leaning his elbows on his knees. His throat felt constricted, and his eyes were starting to tear up and he wasn't sure why.

He took a breath to calm himself. He had to keep trying to work it out, he couldn't fall apart now. A thought occurred to him then, though, and that same feeling from earlier – the helpless, falling sensation – washed over him. He laced his fingers together and rested them against his mouth. *Better to get it out in the open now...* "Frankie...the convenience store where you found Jennifer Sealey's body...it's less than three blocks from my old apartment. I went in there all the time."

"I know."

Noah looked up quickly. "You– Did Townsend put it together, too?"

Frankie shrugged. "Not that I'm aware of, but it wouldn't have taken much digging for him to."

"You didn't tell him?" Frankie shook his head. "Why not?"

"It was irrelevant. You didn't do this."

Noah raised an eyebrow. "But it is significant. I haven't lived there for three months. I haven't had those business cards for a *year*. This guy has been planning this for a very long time. If he knew where I lived before, if he was able to get into my *office*, wouldn't he already know where I live now? We're sitting ducks here as much as, probably more than, at the precinct. I know the idea was to flush him out, but are we sure this is the best place for it?"

"Here I can see him coming." He seemed completely unfazed.

"I just keep getting caught on one thing: why Nigel? I mean, he was the beginning of it all this time around. The Sealey girl may have just been a crime of opportunity, maybe not...but Nigel? There has to be some sort of connection between him and the original two victims."

Frankie frowned. "I don't see how. He would've been just a kid eight years ago."

"I need to see the original case file." He bounced his leg in a jittery rhythm. "I need to see my notes."

"I have copies of yours and Rob's notes in the car."

"Yeah? Would you mind grabbing them?" His almost excitement was quickly doused. "Except, if this guy's been in the precinct, he's going to recognize you if he's watching the place now."

"If you need them, though...I can be five minutes, tops. Besides, I'm armed."

Noah thought it over. "Having the notes would really help, but if he's watching the place..." He shook his head. "Maybe Townsend can email me some scans later."

"They're right downstairs." He pulled his backup piece from his ankle holster. "It wouldn't make sense to have Townsend copy them again." He handed the revolver to Noah. "I'll leave this with you, just in case, but I'll be quick."

Noah nodded, and Frankie walked out of the apartment. Noah followed him and locked the door but stayed peering through the peep hole. He closed his left eye to look out into the empty hallway and realized after a moment that it wasn't itching or hurting as much anymore. That made him also realize that, with the events of the morning, he hadn't taken his next dose of his meds.

He walked into the bathroom and flipped on the light, the built-in exhaust fan rattling to life in loud fits and starts. He laid the revolver on the sink and ran his hands across his face. The medicine cabinet door squeaked as he opened it, and he left it open while he opened the dose packet, shook out the pill, tossed the packet and turned on the faucet. He swallowed the pill down with a handful of water from the sink, closing the cabinet door with his other hand. He then splashed some water on his face and ran his wet fingers through his hair.

When he straightened back up to grab a towel, he'd only just registered that someone had come up behind him from the doorway when a pungent, sweet chemical smell filled the small room and a wet rag was clamped over his nose and mouth and an arm wrapped around his chest. He grabbed for the gun, but his arms were pinned, and it ended up getting knocked off onto the floor instead. He then slammed his head backwards, trying to bash it against the attacker's face, and stomped on the man's foot. The attacker dodged the blow to the head but didn't move his foot in time. He yowled but tightened his arms, preventing Noah from slipping out of his grip.

He was trying not to breathe, but he'd already inhaled a lot of the chloroform in the shock of the initial attack. The panic right after made him take a few more breaths. There was so much of the chemical on the rag that it was leaking into his mouth. He swallowed involuntarily, and immediately gagged and coughed, breathing in more before he could hold his breath again.

He clawed at the attacker's face, but his fingers hit against something hard like plastic. Mask? He tried to pry it away, but the man shoved him into the wall, whacking his head on the door frame. The blow made him gasp, taking in more chloroform, and left him dazed.

The man pulled him out of the bathroom away from the mirror, so Noah couldn't see his face in the reflection. He was tiring too fast, the lack of sleep left him weaker than normal to begin with, and now his heart was already slowing. Everything he'd done to try to throw the attacker off felt like he'd been moving underwater. And still the man maintained his grip on the rag over Noah's face.

He tried one last time to throw the man over his shoulder, but his lungs forced him to take in a deep breath first, and he ended up collapsing on the floor instead. An overwhelming lethargy immobilized his limbs, a grey fuzziness ringed his vision. The man followed him down and knelt looking at him, but Noah couldn't move. The rag was stuffed over his face again.

Moments later, his vision went black.

Unconsciousness took him.

CHAPTER THIRTY

The door was unlocked and halfway open. Frankie slowed to a stop a couple feet away, put the case file folder on the floor and drew his gun. Staying to the side of the doorway, he used the end of the gun's muzzle to nudge the door the rest of the way open.

He listened a moment.

The apartment was quiet inside.

He went in, eyes darting to take in the room: each of the corners, the obscured areas behind the couch and chair, beyond the doorway to the kitchen and the hall leading to the bathroom and Noah's bedroom opposite. There was no sign of anyone.

He cleared Noah's bedroom and approached the bathroom. He detected traces of a sickly sweet, sort of damp, chemical smell in the air. His heart began to pound. This can't be happening. He was only gone five minutes! He took cover next to the bathroom door, then ducked inside, sweeping his aim across the interior. The shower curtain was half-open. He pulled it the rest of the way back.

Empty.

The light was off, so he got his mini flashlight out of his pocket to shine into the darker areas of the room. That's when he saw the revolver. The end of the grip was barely visible between the sink and trash can. Panic rose inside, but he clamped it down to focus. He started out of the room and almost missed seeing the tiny smear of blood on the door frame. But once he noticed it, a cold fear pulsed through his body. "No. Please, no."

He charged out of the room, muttering, "No, no, no," under his breath and searched the hallway outside the apartment in both directions. He ran down the stairs and pushed through the door to the street – there was no one except the cars rushing by.

"He wouldn't have brought him this way, too many people," he mumbled to himself, thinking it through. "I would've seen them if he had, anyway."

He ran around the building. Was there a side door or back door? He didn't see one. Wait, there was a maintenance door. But the handle was locked, and the sign said, "Restricted Access." The only other door on the back of the building had a fire alarm attached, and it, too was locked. He rushed around to the front and entered the lobby. The clerk wasn't at the desk this early in the day. He charged back upstairs, digging out his cell phone and dialing.

The call connected almost immediately. "Townsend."

"He's gone," he said, out of breath. He stopped just outside the apartment door. "I don't know what happened, but Noah's gone. He was here. He was *here* and... I don't know where he is." His heart was beating so loud he could barely hear himself speak.

"Slow down. What happened?"

Frankie put his hand to his head, the cold metal side of the gun resting heavy against his skin. "I swear, I was only gone five minutes."

"You left him *alone*?"

He closed his eyes. "I left my backup piece with him, just in case. I was literally just downstairs."

"Okay, okay. So, what are we looking at here? Harkham bailed?"

"What? No! He was taken. The guy was here. The door was open, my gun on the bathroom floor. Somehow, this guy got to him." He took a breath. "I smelled something, like ether or chloroform. It was faint, but I smelled it."

"All right. I'm calling in CSU. Don't touch anything, I'm on my way."

Townsend disconnected before Frankie could say any more. Not that there was anything left to say. This was his fault. He *never* should have left the apartment. Whatever happens to Noah now...

He leaned against the wall, then slid down to sit on the floor. How did this happen? How had the guy gotten in here? He'd distinctly heard the door lock behind him before he had headed to the stairwell. *I never shoulda left. Noah knew it, he knew the guy would be watching the place...*

The folder with the copied case notes was lying next to him on the muted gray, blue and burgundy carpet. 'Why Nigel?' Noah had asked. If he could answer that, maybe it would lead him to the killer. He pulled the folder onto his lap and opened it. His hands were trembling, shaking the pages as he leafed through them.

He forced himself to read through the notes slowly, both those Noah had taken and the ones Rob Meares had made. Noah's were meticulous and complete, but there weren't very many. It seemed Noah had been given the grunt work while Rob worked up the major leads – not that there were very many of those.

Rob's notes were more problematic; he tended to use short phrases and incomplete sentences. Comparing them to the typed reports showed that many of his notations didn't seem to make it into the final report. One note that intrigued him most also never made it into the report, but was only jotted down in the margin of a notebook page:

Meet with ℓ. Wed. 11:15

From the handwriting, he couldn't tell if the initial was a capital I or L. The page of notes wasn't dated but some of the rest of the info on it lined up with a report dated the day before Rob had died, Tuesday, February seventh, 2006.

He checked the rest of the pages, but there was no other mention of anyone with either of those initials, and Rob must have either died before the meeting or just never wrote down any notes from it. His first instinct was to call Noah to ask him about it and it took a second to check himself from doing just that. He blew out a breath and checked his watch: 10:56. Where was Townsend? Where was CSU?

He got up and began walking the hall, looking for anything he might have missed the first time around. His stomach was in knots, but the shaking in his hands was starting to dissipate now that the initial surge of adrenaline was wearing off. A couple more minutes passed while he searched in vain for some sign of where Noah was taken before Townsend texted him that he was on the way up with Lewis and Saddler.

Lewis was a little out of breath, his round face bearing a sheen of sweat and exertion. He didn't waste time complaining, however. "Franks," he said in terse greeting. Saddler arrived next, with Townsend in tow, and the two criminalists pulled out Tyvek shoe covers from their kits and slipped them on. Lewis pointed toward the open door of Noah's apartment. "You sure the place is clear?"

"Yes. It's empty." Impatience made him a little gruffer than he intended, but he didn't have the time or energy to care.

The pair put on their nitrile gloves and nodded their readiness to each other. "Let's go, then," Lewis said.

As soon as they were out of sight, Townsend pulled him aside. His hands were tightly balled into fists, one resting on his hip. "What the hell happened?"

"Noah said if he could connect Nigel to the first two victims, he would know the who and why behind this. I had copies of the case notes in the car, so I– I went downstairs to get them." He held up a hand, beseeching him. "I was only gone five minutes, maybe less."

"You left a known target unguarded," Townsend said, rubbing a hand down his mouth and chin. "Do you even understand what protective custody means? It means you protect the guy in your custody. It doesn't mean you give a half-blind, half-deaf guy a *gun* and say, 'don't worry, I'm sure you'll be fine,' and leave him out in the open." He kept the volume of his voice under tight control, but the disgust and anger were unmistakable. "What were you thinking?"

Everything Townsend was saying was what he had already been saying to himself. Even still, hearing the words, the accusations from someone else's lips drove the knife deeper into his guilty wound. "Do you honestly think I don't know how seriously I screwed up here? He's my *best friend* – how do you think I feel right now? If anything happens–" He sucked in a breath. Tears pooled in his eyes and he sniffed. "I'm going to find him. I'll get him back."

Townsend stared him down a few seconds. "No, you won't," he said, relaxing his stance. "We will."

Relief made a tear slide down his face. He simply nodded, then cleared his throat to buy time before speaking again. "Okay. Thank you, Casey. I mean it."

"Now," he said, shifting into total focus mode, "you're absolutely sure he didn't leave of his own free will? There's no chance he could've just run?"

"No way, not a chance," he sniffed and wiped his hand over his face. "Even if he were guilty – which he's not – and if he was going on the run, he would want my gun with him. And if he had somehow figured out who's doing this while I was gone and was going after this guy on his own, for whatever reason, he would definitely want the gun. There is no reason for it to be where it was unless there was a struggle. And...there's blood on the doorframe."

Townsend's eyes narrowed as he frowned. "Tell me everything Harkham said."

Frankie rubbed his forehead; a headache was forming above his right eye. "He said he thought Jennifer Sealey was a crime of opportunity, thinks Lynn put the killer onto her because of their run-in at the coffee shop. But Noah said Nigel had to have a connection to the first case because he was where all this started up this time around."

"Okay," he said, drawing the word out as he processed this information. "But Nigel would've only been a kid back then. The original victims were in their twenties."

"Yeah, I know. But he was so sure about it."

"All right, then. I didn't get very far with Lynn yet, but I'll take another run at her. There's definitely something she's trying to hide."

"What's she said so far?"

He snorted a wry laugh. "That she gave Harkham the mug because she has 'a thing' for him and was trying to find an excuse to talk to him more. But then she saw 'the way he acted toward that poor woman' and has since reconsidered her affection."

"How he acted towards her? What did she mean by that?"

"She's saying he screamed at her and that the 'poor thing' was crying by the time he was done. Oh, and that he yelled at her, Lynn, when she tried to help clean up the broken mug. She say's he took the pieces with him."

Frankie gaped at him. "She doesn't know about the security cameras?"

Townsend smirked. "Apparently not. In her defense, they are fairly well hidden and probably harder to spot from her side of the counter." He shrugged. "Anyway, I was giving her a minute to cool her heels and rethink her story before showing the tape to her, but then I got your call."

"Then I say we go have a little film festival with our favorite barista."

"I'll go after her," he said, putting a hand on Frankie's chest to stay him. "You should follow up Harkham's theory. If there is a connection, find it."

"Copy that." A thought occurred to him. "Casey, I don't remember seeing his cell phone in there. He may have it on him. If so..."

Townsend went to the apartment door and leaned his head in. "Lewis, any sign of Harkham's cell in there?"

A moment passed, then Lewis replied from the further side. "That's a negative, Detective."

Townsend dug out his cell phone and speed dialed. "Tyler, it's Townsend. I need you to ping Noah Harkham's cell. Call me or

Franks when you've got something. Yep. Thanks." He hung up and turned to Frankie. "Pray the killer hasn't found it yet."

"Oh, that's not all I'm praying for."

CHAPTER THIRTY-ONE

———

Almost half an hour after leaving Harkham's apartment, and delivering the building's security footage to Tyler, Townsend was again seated with Lynn in Interview B. Her arms were crossed and she was hunched over, almost hugging herself. She had been chewing on the end of her thumb nail when he had first entered the room, but now she just stared at him.

He stared back, waiting her out. The longer he maintained eye contact with her, the less defiant and confident her demeanor was becoming. Her eyes kept darting to the clock high up on the wall behind him. He resisted the urge to glance at his own watch, not taking his eyes off hers.

Finally, she shifted her weight in the uncomfortable chair and asked, "Are we going to keep having a staring contest, Detective, or are you gonna ask me something? If not, I think I'd like to go on back home now."

He let the room fill with silence again before speaking. "Who are you working with?"

She frowned. "Um, well I mean, I usually work alone, most of the morning shift. There's a couple part-timers that come in a few hours each day. They kinda float wherever and whenever we need them, though, so I don't really work with any one over the others. My boss, Walter, he does the afternoons. We don't usually work more than about ten minutes or so together at the shift change. Is that what you mean?"

Her expression was almost flawlessly innocent. Except for the eyes. Her eyes told him she was enjoying this, that she could play this game all day, if she had to.

"Why did you lie earlier about the incident between Noah Harkham and Jennifer Sealey?"

"I didn't. I told you what happened." She shuddered. "I wish it weren't true, because that was pretty...unpleasant. You should have seen it."

He smirked. "Well, now, it's funny you say that, Lynn." He reached over and opened his laptop, which had been positioned rather prominently between them. He queued the video from the coffee shop, the very same clip he'd shown Harkham this morning. When he turned it so the screen was facing her, she went rigid. "Because, as a matter of fact, I did see it."

He clicked Play and the whole scene unfolded before her in grainy color. Her gazed flitted across the screen, to the clock, to his face, back to the screen and froze, becoming unfocused as she no doubt cooked up her next lie. "There's no audio," she finally said. "You can't hear the horrible things he said to her."

He paused the tape and rewound it, zooming in on Harkham and Jennifer Sealey, then playing it again. "Here, they collide. Harkham turns to her and says, 'Sorry, are you okay?' She replies, 'Jerk,' and storms past. Harkham here, 'I said I was -forget it.' She goes on into the shop. That's where we lose out, because the sign for the special deal on caramel macchiato obscures yours and hers mouths just enough our lipreader couldn't make out what you and she talked about."

He stared her down again. She was shaken by being called out on the lie, but that conniving brain of hers was still churning, trying to find a way to wriggle out of all this, no doubt. "We know Harkham didn't yell at her and we know she wasn't in tears. We know you are lying. Now, then: who are you working with? Who did you tell about this incident, about her? Who killed this woman?"

"Who did I– I don't know what you mean. *You* are the one who told *me* she was dead."

"So, when the tech guys pull your phone records, they won't find any calls to someone about the same time as this incident? Someone a nice girl like you," he sneered the words, "shouldn't be associating with?"

"You can't do that. Not without a warrant." Her eyes glinted with triumph.

"You're right. Not everyone knows that, but you–you're smart. But here's what you may not know: the man you and your friend tried to set up and have now abducted is one of us, and we take care of our own. We have exigent circumstances here and you are our best lead at the moment, so how long do you think it took to get a judge to sign off on the warrant? And not just for your phone records, but for your apartment and your car. What do you think our Crime Scene Unit will find?"

She paled but kept her cool. "You're lying."

He raised his eyebrows in a little shrug. "Maybe. Maybe not. But let me tell you, if I'm not, and you don't tell me now about something our techs turn up, it's gonna look bad for you in court. Are you willing to bet your future that I am lying?"

She licked her lips and glanced at the clock again. "I have nothing to say because there's nothing *to* say. I haven't done anything wrong. You said I was here to help, that I was a witness, possibly one of the last people to see that woman alive. Now you say you're searching my home?" She shook her head. "Nah, I don't buy it. No judge would let you search my place or vehicle without me being under arrest."

He didn't react or respond right away. Instead, he kept regarding her with an even, nonchalant stare. Once she started jiggling her knees up and down again, he asked, "Who killed Jennifer Sealey?"

"How should I know? Maybe it was him," she gestured toward the laptop.

"We know it wasn't him. We know he's being framed. We think–no, I know that you are involved somehow. Yeah, you're in it up to your pretty blue eyeballs. But what I don't know, yet, is why."

A flash of seething hatred and deep anger darkened her face for a full second before she regained control. This was personal, deeply personal. He just had to keep pushing her.

"Why am I here, Detective? Am I under arrest?"

"Give me the name of your partner and I'll see about getting you a decent deal."

"I never heard you read me my rights, so I can't be under arrest. And that means I'm free to go." She stood up, glaring defiantly at him.

He rose, never breaking eye contact. "Lynn Hopkins, you are under arrest on suspicion of conspiracy to commit the murders of Nigel Warner and Jennifer Sealey. You have the right to remain silent. Anything you say can and will be used against you in a court of law. You have the right to an attorney. If you cannot afford an attorney, one will be appointed for you by the court." He smiled. "Sit down."

She lowered herself back onto the chair. "I want a lawyer," she said, crossing her arms, her face smug.

"I'll put in the call." He looked at his watch. "Nearly lunchtime on a Monday, shouldn't take the court more than six hours or so to find you one. Sit tight; I'll let you know when one gets here." With that, he shut the laptop and tucked it under his arm. "Interview suspended, eleven fifty-one a.m." He stopped the recorder built into the table and headed toward the door.

"*I've* got all the time in the world, Detective. Not sure the same is true for your guy."

The flat coldness of her expression chilled him. "What did you say?"

She smiled. "That I'm not saying another word until my lawyer gets here."

He exited the room and instructed the uniformed officer stationed outside it to take her to a holding cell. The girl was good, knew how the game was played, she was used to going toe-to-toe with authority and holding her own. How that came to be was a story he fully intended to know before this was over. He went back to his desk and put in the call for her court-appointed attorney. As soon as he hung up from that, his cell phone rang.

"Townsend," he answered before the second buzz.

"Sir, it's Officer Reynolds. Um, just wanted to let you know we located Nigel Warner's wallet. I've got Conrad Ward from the lab here to take it in for processing." There was a muffled voice in the background and he heard Reynolds say, "What? Okay, one sec. Um, Detective Townsend? Ward wants to talk to you."

"Okay, put him on. Oh, and hey, Reynolds?"

"Sir?"

"Good work."

"Thank you, sir. Here's Ward."

There was a moment of muffled sounds, then, "Townsend, hey, listen: this wallet is missing cash, but the credit card is still here, so no need to track its activity. There are no visible traces of blood, but he could have taken it, pocketed it and then killed the kid, I suppose. But I keep asking myself, if the whole point of this was to frame Noah, why toss the wallet? Why not plant it with the other evidence?"

He frowned. "That's a good question." His phone beeped. "I've got another call coming in. Let me know what you get off the wallet."

"You got it. See ya."

"Yeah." He hung up and connected to the second call. "Townsend."

"Detective Townsend, Dr. Lee," the ME's voice drawled.

"What've you got for me, Doc?"

"Well, now, if you'll remember, our young Mr. Warner suffered multiple stab wounds and young Miss Sealey was beaten with a blunt object, like a baseball bat or somethin' like."

"Right..."

"Well, then, I think you ought to come take a look at what I found when I opened them both up."

"I'll be right there."

He stopped by Franks' desk, but saw his chair was empty. He was about to call him to let him know about the wallet and have him meet up at the morgue, but his cell phone rang again. "Townsend," he answered, heading on toward the hall leading to the parking lot.

"I got a location on Noah Harkham's cell," Tyler Hendricks informed him.

His heart sped up with both dread and hope. "Where?"

"System's showing it at the corner of Main and Market."

"That doesn't make sense. That's one of the busiest parts of town...unless," he said, slowing to a stop outside the precinct's back door.

"What?"

"I bet it's a dump job. The guy found the phone and tossed it. I'm headed there now. Have Lewis meet me there if he's through at Harkham's place, will ya?"

"Sure thing."

"Anything off the surveillance cams outside Harkham's office or from his building?"

"Still working on it. I've been working backward from this morning on the footage from the precinct, but it's slow-going since we don't know who this guy is or when exactly he got in there. As for the apartment footage, nobody suspicious looking went in or out the front entrance, and the footage from the two cameras to the rear of the building was all blank, like the cameras were broken. I'll need to find our man here at the precinct before I can compare him to anyone on the apartment footage."

Townsend rubbed his forehead wearily. "It had to be this weekend, after Harkham left on Friday. It can't take that long to go through two and a half days' worth of tape." He pinched the bridge of his nose and paced a circle. "Don't you have someone going through it with you?"

"I normally would, but Pete's on vacation and no one else comes in until the evening shift at five."

"Then get somebody, *anybody* else! The longer we stand around twiddling our thumbs, the less likely we are to bring Harkham home alive, *you do realize that?*"

"Of course. I'll– I'll find somebody. I'll let you know as soon as we get something."

"Thank you," he said in exasperation. He hung up before Tyler could reply and rushed to his car.

The meticulously restored Limelight Green 1971 AMC Matador stuck out like a sore thumb among all the Chargers, Impalas and Explorers. Strictly speaking, he wasn't supposed to take it out on calls because it wasn't department approved, but he didn't think anyone would care this time since he was only securing the phone for CSU and then heading to the morgue.

Franks' Chrysler 200 wasn't in the lot and he considered calling him again. But, if he was going to yell at an overworked, under-appreciated lab tech for wasting time, he'd better not do it himself. He would just have to fill him in later.

12:20 p.m.

When he got near the intersection, Townsend pulled into the parking lot of a church and walked the rest of the way. He wanted to be wrong. He wanted to find this guy sitting with Harkham in the Market Street Grill, ready to give himself up, or not know Harkham had his phone and wouldn't be expecting a takedown but knew the chances of that were...nonexistent. And before he got to the intersection, he saw he was, unfortunately, right. The phone was lying right next to a storm drain grate, just below the sidewalk. Another two inches and the phone would've gone down into the water and been ruined, and they never would have found it. Even expecting this, he still muttered a curse. He just hoped they could get *something* off it that would help.

A black Explorer pulled into the lot of the Grill, and Simon Lewis exited with his crime scene kit in hand. "Detective Townsend. Twice in one day, I suppose I should feel honored."

"Yeah, well, feel whatever you like, Lewis, as long as you can get this phone processed. I'm holding out hope the killer forgot to wear gloves when he tossed it."

Lewis aimed a camera at the phone and grunted. "I still hold out hope of being six-foot-three and married to a supermodel. I think we're both bound for disappointment." He took a couple more photos of the phone and surrounding area, then collected it into an evidence bag. "I'll let you know what we find, or don't find."

"Thank you."

He nodded. "You'll find him."

The knot in Townsend's stomach twisted. "Yeah, but will it be too late?"

"We can only hope it won't be," Lewis said with a grimace that belied his optimism.

"I suppose you're right." He turned and walked back to his car, hoping that the killer's endgame required Harkham to stay alive a while longer.

CHAPTER THIRTY-TWO

———

Dr. Marvin Lee picked up a metal bowl covered with a towel off the autopsy table on which Nigel Warner's body lay and brought it over to the counter where Townsend was standing. "Here we are," he said, lifting off the towel.

Inside the bowl was a rusty one-inch nail and a sliver of pale green glass about two-inches long. He used forceps to lift out the nail. "January twelfth, 2006, Paula Stevenson, aged twenty-four years, was found dead around three a.m. outside the nightclub where she worked part-time. She'd been bludgeoned to death with a chunk of broken concrete from the parking lot. The concrete was left at the scene, in a puddle that degraded the majority of the evidence. The clock that was carved into her chest contained traces of iron oxide and dirt."

Lee put the nail back in the bowl. "The nail used to carve the clock image, as I determined it most likely to have been, was removed from the scene. Never made sense to me."

Next, he picked up the large sliver of glass. "On January twenty-third, 2006, Will Messer, aged twenty-seven years, was found dead at a bus stop on Water Street at one-fifteen a.m. by a bus driver. His head had been smashed into the sidewalk so many times all that was left back there was mush. The clock image carved into his arm held the tiniest fragment of pale green glass. Again, the glass was removed from the crime scene." He placed the glass sliver back in the bowl.

"Are you telling me these are the same nail and piece of glass the killer used?"

"I believe so, yes. Of course, you'll need to have Ward or Saddler confirm with trace analysis."

"And these were where, exactly?"

Lee led him over to Nigel's body and pulled back the sheet. Now that he'd been cleaned up and autopsied, the full extent of the damage to the boy's face and torso was revealed. It was easier to take in, though, without all the blood. Lee pointed to the one large gash in the boy's abdomen. "All the other wounds are stabs," he made a stabbing gesture with his right hand, "straight in, straight out. That one, however, went in and sliced downward, making the gash. Peri-mortem. The nail and piece of glass were inserted into the gash."

"The killer put them inside Nigel?"

"That's right." He put the metal bowl back on the table next to Nigel.

"On the phone you said you wanted to show me what you found inside each of them."

"I did." He walked over to a second autopsy table, on which lay Jennifer Sealey's body.

Townsend didn't look at her face; once at the crime scene was enough to last him a lifetime. A rectangular metal tray lay next to her hip. Lee picked it up and used the forceps to retrieve what looked like a letter opener. "I believe this was used to kill Nigel Warner, and to carve the clock into Jennifer Sealey's arm. I pulled it out of what used to be her mouth and throat."

Lee turned her left arm so Townsend could see the signature for himself. The clock was carved into her skin with care, the hand set at one o'clock, just like the others. The killer was telling them something, no doubt about that, but what exactly that something was, he couldn't begin to say.

"Are the initials NAH on the handle?"

His eyebrows lifted. "Yessir."

"Harkham mentioned that there should have been a letter opener in his desk. It isn't there now. This guy swapped it and some other things for evidence implicating Harkham in these two murders. Now I know why."

"Lord above," Lee drawled. "Can I show you somethin' else I noticed about these two?" Townsend nodded, so Lee continued, pointing to the clock on Jennifer's arm, "See here? This clock is neater, more...precise than the one on the Warner boy's body." He hurried back over and pointed to the one on Nigel. "See how his is a little lopsided? Like it was rushed?"

"So, he had more time with Jennifer than he did with Nigel," he surmised, not liking the implication. "Can you tell if she was held captive before death? Any signs of ligature marks on her wrists or ankles? Anything unusual about her condition?"

"No, nothing like that. The only thing of note is that her clock was done post-mortem, whereas Nigel's was peri-mortem." He glanced back at her body. "But now that you mention it, she didn't have any defensive wounds on her. Now, the Warner boy, he had cuts on his hands and arms from trying to fight off his killer. But either she was caught completely off guard by the first blow or was already unconscious when he attacked."

"Unconscious? Like maybe he used chloroform on her first?"

Lee tilted his head as he thought about this. "Unlikely, but possible. It's not like in the movies; it's very hard to knock someone out with chloroform, unless you know how to handle it. Just a minute." He walked to the head of the table where she lay and leaned close to her face. With both hands, he pressed down on her chest and inhaled deeply. He blew the breath back out forcefully and passed the back of his wrist across his nose.

"Oh, yes," he said, turning back to Townsend, "she was rendered unconscious by chloroform first, no doubt." He frowned and wiped his nose again. "She wouldn't have felt a thing with the dose he had to've given her. Small blessing. I'm surprised she was alive at all before the first blow landed, though, poor lamb."

Townsend went cold. "Why?"

"From the smell of her, he used far too much. That high of a dose would've nearly killed her on its own." He then seemed to notice the detective's unease. "What made you ask about chloroform specifically?"

"Franks smelled it at the scene where Harkham was abducted. I thought it was because he needed him alive, but now..." A coil of nervous energy buzzed in his gut.

Lee laid a hand on the autopsy table to steady himself. "Oh...oh, no. Even if his intention was to keep him alive, if he used that much on Noah...Even if he somehow survives the initial dosing, that stuff has horrible, often lethal side effects." He shook his head slowly. "Oh, Lord, help that poor man."

CHAPTER THIRTY-THREE

―――

He became vaguely aware of a voice and something hitting his face. He tried to move his head, but that required an enormous amount of energy that he just couldn't summon.

―――

Somewhere, someone was shouting.

―――

There was now something pounding on his chest. It probably should have hurt, but it didn't. Nothing did. He felt...nothing; suspended, senseless. Breathless. Limbless. Sightless.

―――

Monday, September 1, 2014 11:56 a.m.

A hand hit his face, the sting of the slap clearing away the fog in his brain. He groaned and pried his eyes open. His sight was blurry, like looking through greasy lenses, and blinking did little to improve things. His heart tried to start pounding, which caused his head to ache so hard he thought it would explode.

All the various aches and pains in his whole body seemed to come alive all at once then. His head, his chest, his shoulders and knees—everything burned with pain. Inside his mouth tasted like copper; his throat felt raw. Nausea roiled through his stomach, and, before he could stop it, he pitched forward and vomited.

He tried to wipe his mouth but couldn't move his hands. He blinked again and slowly, slowly a low-lit room swam into focus. He found himself sitting on a metal chair in the middle of a large, open space. His hands and feet were bound to the chair's frame. The smell from the puddle of what remained of Frankie's world-famous omelet at his feet threatened to trigger another ejection of the same, and he rolled his head to the left to escape the worst of it.

That's when he saw him.

A man, slight of build and mousy. Brown hair, brown eyes, stubble. He knew him from somewhere, didn't he? Noah licked his lips and tried to speak, but it came out a croaky whisper instead. "Hey..." The skin around his mouth and nose felt irritated, raw.

The man stood a couple feet away, his hands held out like he'd just quick-stepped backwards, staring at the puddle of vomit between them. "That was nasty," he chided, wiping his hands down his shirt. "Hope you don't expect me to clean that up."

"The bus...the party...I remember you." His breath tasted sweet and metallic under the sourness of stomach acid. *Chloroform...I was knocked out.*

The man tilted his head. "Really? For a detective you are not very observant."

Noah looked around, his head still swimmy and his vision a little bleary. The room was large and open, smelled of disuse and mold from the wooden crates stacked on the concrete floor here and there. It must have been part of a factory or warehouse, but one that hadn't been used in a long time. The one window he could see from where he sat was high up on the opposite wall, long width-wise and narrow height-wise, and covered in dust and grime. Sunlight filtered through, revealing floating dust motes, but the rest of the weak illumination came from a few battery-operated lanterns sitting on top of the crates.

Another wave of nausea clenched his gut. He double over and coughed, gagging up the meager remains of his stomach contents. He swished saliva around in his mouth and spat out the last of the vile taste. His eyes were watering and his nose running, his head pounding. He groaned. "The chloroform..." he said in a hoarse half-whisper. "How long did you keep me under?"

"Well, I had to be sure you'd stay out long enough to get you here. I had to dose you a couple times, so, close to an hour total, I suppose."

"*An hour?*" His heart was now chugging to race, making his pulse pound so hard he could see the throbbing in the blood vessels in his eye. "You used too much, too long. It's a miracle I woke up at all."

The man scratched at his chin. "It did kinda worry me some, when you wouldn't wake up all the way there for a while. Had to jumpstart you a bit. But you seem right as rain now, so we can get this show on the road." He clapped his hands and rubbed them together with an eager grin.

"Buddy, I am far from right as rain," he replied, sniffing. "If you don't get me to a hospital soon, my liver and kidneys will fail. When they do, I'm going to get septic and die." His voice was still hoarse, and he had to swallow to continue speaking, but his vision was finally clearing. "I don't know what you have planned, but if you wanted me dead, I'm pretty sure I already would be."

The man paled but covered his uncertainty behind a cocky smirk. "You can't talk me out of this. My sister may have gotten picked up by your old partner's new partner – that's gotta suck, by the way, being so easily replaced – but that's why there are two of us. I can still see this through, with or without her."

Sister? Did he mean Lynn? Was that how she tied in to all of this? Noah was almost positive the man hadn't meant to let that slip. He filed it away. Maybe he could try to use that against him later. Somehow.

"You said before I wasn't observant. I admit, if I know you from somewhere else besides the bus and the party, I don't remember. Why don't you set me straight?" His throat felt hot and scraped. He would've given his left eye for a drink of anything right then. The thought left him feeling hollow inside. Of course this guy would take him and probably kill him horribly now, right before he got his sight back.

The man laughed and dragged over another chair from behind one of the crates. Noah noticed with a sinking feeling that he was wearing gloves. There would be no fingerprints or touch DNA, and, unless he left some other traces of himself behind, nothing to tie him to this location. He sat in the chair and leaned toward Noah.

"December fourth, 2000."

Noah's blood chilled. He swallowed hard, trying to keep the memories he'd worked so hard to forget buried. "What about it?" *What does that have to do with this?*

The man's eyes turned dangerous. "Really? You're going to pretend you don't remember? Or did you seriously forget the day you destroyed my family?"

"*Your* family?" His mind raced. No, there wasn't a second brother. It was just the one guy and the girl, the brother and sister. Donnie was the man who he– was the brother. The girl's name had been Raelynn. Raelynn...Lynn?

"Oh, you didn't know about me, did you?" His eyebrows lifted, then furrowed as he glared at Noah. "Yeah, the papers left me out, too.

And you know what? That really upset me. That really upset my sister. But it's turned out to be a blessing, because no one thought twice about hiring me to pick up your trash."

Now it clicked. "You work for the precinct's janitorial crew. Uh, Jerry, right?" How often had they passed each other in the halls, how often had Noah seen him without paying him any attention?

The man shook his head with a wry chuckle. "Ian," he corrected, tapping the name tag on his work shirt. Noah's eyes struggled to focus on it. "Jerry's the boss the company's named after. Wow, I really fail to see why everyone is so damned impressed by you."

He ignored the insult probably meant to rile him. "Ian, right. I'm sorry, of course I remember now. But I don't understand, the investigation never turned up any other relatives, especially not another brother."

"Oh, so you do remember That Day now, huh?"

Noah could hear the capital letters as he said this, and a chill ran through him. 'That Day' is how he thought of both the day Bobby Avalon ended his career and the day his parents were murdered. And now, to know this family had their own 'That Day,' and that he was to blame...

"Technically, I'm her stepbrother." He tilted his head. "Well, sort of. My dad was banging her mom for about five years before she drank herself to death. My old man went out in a bar fight a year later and, bam, the three of us were left on our own. I scraped by taking care of 'em, until Uncle Sam gave me a better way to keep a roof over their heads. But, I'm not surprised the RPD never figured any of that out. It's full of lazy, useless cops." He grinned. "Speaking of..."

He got to his feet and walked to the far side of the room. There was a door there that Noah hadn't noticed before now. When Ian opened it, there was no bright sunlight. It must have led to another interior room instead of outside. That didn't mean it couldn't lead to an exit, though....Another thing to file away for later. Provided there was a later.

All thoughts of future escape vanished from his mind when he saw the dazed, beaten cop Ian dragged back in with him. "Spicer?"

The younger officer lifted his head lethargically. His eyes were unfocused, and Noah figured he must have been drugged or chloroformed as well. His hands were bound with what looked like his own cuffs and a bandana had been used to gag him. He wasn't fighting back, not even a little, and it took a moment before Noah saw why: a dull glint of lantern light reflected off the gun Ian held in his left hand, pressed against Spicer's ribs.

Ian shoved the officer to sit in the second chair and was using zip ties to bind him to it. When Spicer's eyes finally focused on Noah, they went wide then narrowed and hardened with anger. He tried to say something, but the gag muffled it to an unintelligible growl.

"Spicer, listen to me–"

"Shut up," Ian ordered.

"I'm sorry, Spicer, I didn't–"

Ian leveled the gun at Noah's face. "I said shut up. No talking."

Noah flinched and fell silent but didn't take his eyes off the surly officer. *All because I yelled at him... How many more people are going to die or get hurt because their paths crossed mine?*

Once Spicer was secured, Ian came around behind Noah's chair. Noah tried to keep him in sight, but Ian smacked the back of his head with the gun. "Hold still," he said.

Noah froze as Ian held the gun alongside the left side of his face, bringing his own face down to sight along the barrel. "Looks about right to me," he said. But then he clucked his tongue. "Silly me," he switched to Noah's right. "You're right-handed."

"What is this, Ian?" He strained against the multiple zip ties holding his wrists to the chair.

He chuckled. "Oh, you'll see. It's going to be perfect," he said into Noah's ear, his breath hot and stale.

Noah tilted his head away. "Let him go. He has nothing to do with this. He was just a kid back then."

He grabbed Noah by his hair and jerked his head backward. "So was my sister. So was my *brother*. But that didn't stop you from killing *him* in cold blood and ruining her life."

Stay calm. He had to stay calm. "I did everything I could to get Donnie and Raelynn out of there safely. I didn't have a choice, Ian. If I hadn't–"

"Shut up!" He yanked on Noah's hair harder, his face twisted with rage. "You don't get to play the innocent. Not here. Not today. You've gotten away with this for too long already. It's time you finally pay." He pushed Noah's head back down and walked away, running his hands through his hair. Then he blew a breath out slowly and shook his hands, like a runner gearing up for a sprint.

"Gotten away with what? What do you think happened in there that day?"

Ian chuckled. "You really are a piece of work. Are you trying to tell me my little sister lied to me about how it all went down? Or are you–like everyone else – assuming she doesn't know the truth because of her illness? Isn't that how you did it? Because they locked her up in the loony bin and you got to tell everyone whatever you wanted, 'cuz who would believe her if she contradicted you?" He regarded the gun in his hand a moment. "You know, I thought doing it the way we planned would make it more satisfying, but now I'm starting to think just killing you now will feel a whole lot better."

He took a step toward them and Noah's heart began to race, sweat beading on his skin. "Ian, wait. Please, listen: I have regretted that day every moment since. I've played it over and over in my mind, thinking, how could I have done it differently? But I had no choice-"

"Yes. You. Did," he said, aiming the gun at him. "You could have let Donnie go, walk out of there like he wanted, for a start."

Noah sat back, confused. "Walk out? What are you talking about?"

Ian tilted his head to regard him, an incredulous half-smile on his lips. "I read how they ran the stories in the papers. 'Hero Cop Saves Hostages.' Bullshit. More like 'Lying Cop Shoots Surrendering Suspect.'" He eyed Spicer and a sly smile spread across his face. "Okay, yeah, this is going to be a lot better. Either way we end up slicing it, it all looks good to me."

"Ian, please, whatever you want me for, you've got me, all right? But you don't need him. Just let him go."

"You gettin' nervous I'm gonna let the cat out of the bag, Harkham? Scared I'm going to tell him the truth and destroy what pathetic legacy you had in the RPD? Oh, you betcha, that's exactly what I'm going to do."

He walked over to kneel next to Spicer's chair, his elbow resting on the chair's arm next to the cop's, the gun casually aimed at Noah. "You see, Officer, your illustrious hero over there not only lied to my little brother and sister, he tricked my brother into a situation that gave him an excuse to kill him. All so Harkham here could get the hero's treatment. All the glory. They gave him a damn *medal* for it. And then a promotion, and then he makes Detective before the age of thirty – the youngest in the history of the precinct – and all because he lied."

Spicer's eyes looked doubtful, but he still looked at Noah with suspicion.

"That's not what happened, Spicer."

Ian threw him a glare. "You deny killing Donnie?"

"No, that's not what I meant–"

"So, you admit it then?"

He tried taking a deep breath but felt like he was breathing through mud. "Yes. Yes, I killed Donnie." He saw Spicer's eyes go wide. "But I never lied to him, I never tricked him, and I certainly did not kill him in cold blood."

"Tell you what," Ian said, standing up, "I think we should play a little drinking game. You're going to tell Spicer here all about that day. December fourth, 2000. And every time you say something I don't like, instead of taking a drink, Spicer here is gonna take a bullet. This revolver holds six, but I have plenty more if we run out."

"Ian, don't do this," Noah said, fighting panic, "It won't work, no one will believe that I did this, just like they didn't believe I killed Nigel and Jennifer."

"Oh, you don't get it, do you?" He pried Noah's hand up off the chair arm, turning it thumb up. He forced the gun into his grip and wrapped his own around it, holding Noah's fingers in place. "You are going to do this one."

"Stop, please– Let him go. There's no reason for me to kill him. This whole thing is just going to fall apart on you."

"No reason? Everyone saw you yell at him for daring to think he could be a good cop without the great Noah Harkham teaching him. You threw a fit in front of your entire class of sworn officers, and you think no one will believe you wanted him dead?"

"You think that would make me want to *kill* him? I only wanted him to take the job seriously, to make sure the techs don't have to process a contaminated scene. I just want him and the others to think about the fragility of the evidence–"

"Blah, blah, blah. God! No wonder you hate his class," he said to Spicer. "Now, enough of all that. Let's get on with the show."

Noah began to tremble. "No."

"No?" Ian grabbed Noah's face and turned it toward him. "Oh, I'm sorry. I didn't mean to make you think you have a choice. And you know what?" He let go of Noah's face and used both hands to force Noah's aim toward Spicer's right leg. The officer began pulling at his restraints, his cries muffled by the gag. "That officially counts as the first time you've said something I don't like."

"No! Ian, don't "

The gunshot echoed in the high-ceilinged room. The bullet entered Spicer's leg, just below the knee, and he screamed beneath the gag.

Noah panted, fear and adrenaline surging through his veins. He had to get them out of this, but how?

"Stop! I'll do it! I'll play along. Just don't hurt him again."

Ian threw an arm around Noah's shoulders. "That, my friend, is entirely up to you."

CHAPTER THIRTY-FOUR

Frankie had gone over the formal reports twice more to be sure, but there was nothing he could see that indicated who Rob Meares intended to meet with or if he ever got the chance. He was now at his desk, the report from Meares' death pulled up on his computer. The cause of death was listed as sudden cardiac arrest, with coronary artery disease as a contributing factor.

The report stated his body was discovered Wednesday, February eighth, 2006, slumped over on a bench by the pond in Mallory Park, by a woman who had come to feed the ducks. He had been taken to Calera County Hospital, where he was pronounced dead at eleven fifty-two a.m. He was only fifty-nine years old, but well past retirement eligibility with over thirty years on the job under his belt.

None of that was anything that helped with the current situation. Frankie clicked out of the report, frustrated with getting nowhere, and brought up Rob's personnel file instead. He had received several commendations going back to the early 80s and even a medal in 1998 for his heroic actions in an active shooter situation. He had saved the lives of several children by neutralizing the shooter, even though he had suffered multiple gunshot wounds himself.

No wonder the man was Hark's hero...No wonder it had hit him so hard to lose him unexpectedly. Especially given how unexpectedly he had lost his parents.

Then Frankie found what he was looking for: Rob's address. It was a long shot, but he wondered if the widow Mrs. Meares would know anything that might help. He just hoped she still lived there after seven years.

Townsend was coming out of the interview room where he had been in with Lynn all morning. Frankie got up, intending to ask his partner about the interview and let him know where he was going, but Townsend's phone rang. He decided not to interrupt, or waste any more time waiting until the call was completed, and so went on out of the building.

About twenty minutes later, he pulled up outside of a modest, dark green bungalow on the northern edge of James Park, the neighborhood east of the city. The very first case he'd ever worked with Noah had happened here. He smiled a bit to himself when he thought about how they hadn't gotten along then, at one point all but shouting in each other's faces in the middle of an interrogation. He was surprised, then and now, that it hadn't come to blows, and that they ever became friends afterward.

He hadn't been out this way much since then. This neighborhood usually stayed pretty quiet. When it wasn't, it was seldom anything the uniforms couldn't handle. A lot had changed in seven-and-a-half years; the city was expanding west and south more and more, and James Park was slowly being left behind. Businesses had folded up, and many houses had For Sale signs in the yard. The school was still there, though, and a couple of churches, and the Guzzle & Gulp still advertised the cheapest gas and coldest soft drinks around.

But the house where Mrs. Meares lived was nearly out in the country, away from all that. It was the last house on Carolina Avenue, with trees on two sides, the street to the front and open fields to the back. A woman was in the front yard, pruning a hedge of rose bushes that lined the walk up to the porch. She wore white canvas shoes, red pants, a white blouse, green gardening gloves, and a yellow sun-hat. The picture of retired bliss. He wondered briefly what his own retirement would look like and decided that colorful clothing and gardening likely wouldn't be part of it. Especially not with his allergies.

She glanced up at him as he approached. "Good morning, Detective. What can I do for you?"

He smiled, amused she had pegged him for police so easy. "Mornin', ma'am. I'm Detective Alan Franks with the Fifth Precinct," he got out his ID and badge and held them up, but she didn't bother looking. "Would you happen to be Bonita Meares?"

She stopped chopping out dead branches and set the blades of the pruning shears on the ground, resting her elbow on their long handles. One gloved hand wiped across her forehead as she regarded him with sharp, warm brown eyes. "I wondered when one of y'all would show up here once I read the papers." She took her gloves off, then her hat, and tossed the gloves inside it. Grabbing the pruning shears by the handle, she turned toward the house. "Come on inside, young man. I'll fix us some sun tea."

He followed her up the sidewalk, catching the sweet scent of roses. Like the damp-sweet smell he'd noticed in Noah's apartment. *God, please let him still be alive...*

She mounted the wide concrete steps to open the screen door, which emitted the universally requisite groan, and led him into a homey sitting room. "Make yourself t'home, Detective Franks. I'll get you a glass."

He knew better than to refuse her hospitality, especially when he would be asking her a favor, so he smiled and took a seat on the pale yellow and pink flowery sofa. She went into the next room and he could see her open the refrigerator and pull out a large glass jug full of tea. She sat this on the counter and opened a cabinet on the far wall to get down two glasses, which she filled with tea and brought back into the sitting room. "There you are, young man."

"Thank you, ma'am," he said, accepting his glass. The tea was sun-brewed and super sweet, just the way he preferred it.

"You're welcome, hun. Now," she said, folding her hands together on her lap, "just what is it you think I can help you with?"

"Well, ma'am, if you've read the papers, then you know two more people have been killed by the same killer your husband investigated eight years ago. But what you and nobody else outside the RPD knows is that this guy is going to a lot of trouble to frame your husband's partner for these two."

"Noah? You're meaning Noah Harkham?"

"Yes, ma'am." He had to take another sip of tea before he could put into words the worst part. "And now, because we didn't arrest him like the bad guy wanted, he's taken Noah. I don't know how it happened, exactly, but Noah's been abducted, and I'm going to do everything I can to get him back." He dropped his gaze to his glass. "You see, ma'am, he was my partner, too."

She put a hand to her chest. "Oh, lor'. That poor man..." She shook her head. "He's such a nice boy, why would anyone want to frame him for murder?"

"Once I figure that out, I'll be able to bring him home, I reckon."

She looked across the room at a photograph on the TV console. It was of a younger Noah in his uniform with an older, thickset man that must be Rob Meares. "He was as broken up about losing Rob as I was, poor thing. Rob was his first FTO right out of the academy, but he was also his mentor before that. Rob taught seminars at the University and took to Noah like a duck to water. Did you know that?"

Frankie shook his head, so she continued, "Rob made Detective in mid-2000, so he was only Noah's FTO for about eight weeks, but he still did all he could to prep and push that boy to earn his own gold shield. And he did it, a little under six years later. Rob was so proud; snatched him up as his own partner that same day..."

She shook her head again, her neat bobbed white hair flouncing a bit around her jaw. "I'll help any way I can, of course. I'm just not exactly sure what I can do."

"Did Rob ever talk about the One O'clock Killer case with you?"

She pursed her lips. "Some, and usually just in general terms, you know, but I could tell this one bothered him more than some of the others. It frustrated him to no end he couldn't find the connection between those two kids who were killed. And that there weren't any decent leads."

"Did he ever mention anyone with the initial 'I' or 'L'?"

"No, not that I recall..." She thought a moment longer. "No, I'm afraid not."

He took another sip of tea, buying time while he thought of a way to ask the real favor he was here for. "After he died... You were no doubt given his personal effects, am I right? What he'd had with him when it happened?"

Her lips turned downward. "What little there was, yes."

"Was there a notebook?" He got his own out of his inside jacket pocket and showed it to her. "Like this one?"

"Hmmm...Yes, I believe there was. But I'm afraid it was basically empty. A few notes in his usual shorthand, but not even many of those." She set her glass down on a cork coaster on the low, polished wood coffee table and stood. "I still have it; if you can use it to help find Noah, you are more than welcome to it. Rob and I loved that boy like our own. Wish we'd keep in touch more, but you know how life gets."

His hopes dashed by the grim prospects of the notebook, he nodded. "Yes, ma'am. Thank you."

She left the room for several minutes, but when she came back, she carried a small, dusty notebook with a black cover and yellowing pages. "Here you are, hun."

He took it carefully. "Thank you, ma'am." The first page was blank, but the second one had a note that caught his attention:

ℓ: CMB 2000 -connection?

He showed it to her. "Do you know what this means?"

She peered at it a moment. "CMB, 2000...Sorry, hun, that doesn't mean anything to me." She shook her head, but then looked again. "Wait... I...Of course, how silly of me." She laid a hand to her temple. "Can't believe I got that wrong all this time."

"Got what wrong, ma'am?"

"I thought he always referred to her as his eye, as in e-y-e, like a nickname. But it was 'I,' as in first initial of the word." She tutted to herself, then, seeing he was still confused, explained, "His informant. She's a homeless woman, doesn't speak a lot of English, or at least pretends not to. She's Portuguese. Minds her own business, so people don't pay attention to her. But she's whip smart, I remember that. A lot more than people think. I don't know for sure, but I think she informed for several cops, not just Robbie. But she always made sure she got a little bit by way of a reward for her information. I wouldn't be at all surprised if she were the richest homeless woman in the whole state."

A flutter of excitement filled him. "She's around fifty, now, five-foot-nothin' with black hair, brown eyes, and usually wearing a trench coat and red head scarf?"

She smiled. "Guess I was right. She's one of yours?"

"Yeah. Yeah, she is. Haven't seen her in several months, but I know where she usually haunts." He looked at the note again, taking one last sip of her wonderful tea, before tucking the notebook in his pocket and standing up. He took her hand in his. "You have been remarkably helpful. I can't thank you enough, Mrs. Meares."

She stood and patted her other hand on the back of his. "You just find Noah and bring him home. Promise me that, Detective Franks."

He nodded gravely. "Whatever it takes."

12:24 p.m.

After Bonita Meares had seen him out, Frankie had sped back toward the city. Neide, the Portuguese lady who had been Rob's informant and was now occasionally one of his own, usually holed up either near the river or by the bus station on Market Street. Going on one in the afternoon, he figured she was probably out scouting for food. He headed toward the bus station first and circled the area in vain for over fifteen minutes. He was just about to give up and head to the river when he spotted her.

She was sitting on an overturned trash can in a shadowy alley about six blocks from the station, fanning herself with a crumpled magazine. He pulled over up the block and walked back to her. "Olá, Neide."

She spooked at first, but then recognized him. "Oh, Mr. Frank, you give me a fright," she said, fanning herself harder.

"Sorry, Ms. Neide, but I hadn't heard from you in a while and when I saw you here, I figured I'd come check on you."

She squinted at him and lowered her voice. "If I know something, I come tell you. You know this. What do you need?"

He smiled. Looks like he needed to work on his poker face. Either that, or women's intuition was running particularly strong today. "All right, Neide, ya got me. I wanted to ask you about something that happened eight years ago. Do you have time to go to lunch with me?"

"I have all the time in the world for you, Mr. Frank. But eight years, nossa! Is a long time ago."

She got off the bent trash can and daintily set it upright again. Then she tightened the sleeves of the tan trench coat that was tied around her waist and took his arm when he offered it. He could smell her three feet away but knew the poor thing couldn't help it. There weren't many places in the city she could get a free shower, and most of those were too far for her to walk.

He opened the car door for her, then got in himself, driving back toward the Surfside Café on Market Street, where he knew they wouldn't try kicking her out, citing they didn't want the rest of the customers to feel uncomfortable. He never spent any of his money in those other places, even if they *would* tolerate her as long as *he* was with her.

Once they were seated at his regular table, his favorite waitress, Jean, came over and gave him a big grin and a squeeze on the shoulder. "How y'all doing today, sweethearts?"

"Just fine, Jean. You?"

She leaned closer and lowered her voice some. "So, what's the story with these two killings, Frankie? We got ourselves a real serial killer this time?"

"We're looking into it, Jean. How about some iced tea for me and my date here?" he said with a wink at Neide. She grinned and put a hand to her cheek.

"Sure thing. Y'all eating today, too, or just the tea?"

"Get her whatever she'd like. I'll have a burger and fries, please."

"Everything on that, sweet pea?"

"Yes, ma'am. Thank you." He hated when anyone called him sweet pea. That was what Carmen had called him – the woman from that first case with Noah. The woman he hadn't been able to stop thinking about ever since they found Jennifer Sealey's body. The woman he had failed to protect.

Jean had already taken Neide's order and scuttled off before he realized it. Neide was now looking at him expectantly. Had she asked something?

"Mr. Frank? You wanted to ask, eight years ago?"

He took out Rob's notebook and turned it to the note he'd made. "Do you remember a detective named Rob Meares?" He kept his voice low.

She went still. "Yes, God rest his soul, I remember. What about him do you need?"

He showed her the note. "Did you meet with him the morning he died? Wednesday, February eighth, 2006?"

"So long ago, I don't think I know..." She adjusted her head scarf, pushing her lank hair up under it.

He tapped the paper with a finger. "What does this mean? CMB, 2000?"

Her eyes narrowed in concentration. "I do not know what this means."

He pointed to the note. "You were his informant, right. I for informant – that was you? He never told anyone your name, but his wife, she met you, or at least saw you. I knew who she meant when she described you." He reached across the table and put his hand over hers. "Please, Neide, this is really important."

Jean brought them their drinks. She saw him remove his hand from Neide's and grinned. "Y'all don't go getting shy on my account. Even if you are breakin' my heart, Frankie," she said with a wink. "I'll be right back with your meals."

He gave her a smile and waited until she was gone before turning back to Neide. "Do you remember Rob's partner, Noah Harkham? He was my partner, too."

She smiled. "The girls on the street call him the handsome Yank. Yes, yes, I remember."

"Someone has taken him. Okay? And I think whoever did that had something to do with the case you were trying to help Rob with. If you tell me what you told him, it just might mean I can save Noah." He looked pleadingly into her weathered little face. "Pode ajudar-me. Por favor."

She looked around nervously. "I know nothing certain, I tell him," she finally said. "Only I hear a girl talking to herself. By the bus station. She was wandering around, crying and laughing. In her head, she is not right. Você entende?"

He nodded. "What was she saying?"

"I do not know most. But I heard her singing, 'they kill my brother, I kill them all. All the statues, I'll make them fall.' This she says many times. I will not forget this. She also was screaming and crying. She says, 'citizens first, my ass.' Perdoe-me. She also says, 'not good enough, not us. Didn't put us first.' Things like this. But strangest thing, she was saying numbers, again and again, many numbers. Ah...one, twelve, five, two thousand. She says all these things again and again, until man in bus station calls police." She shrugged. "I never see her again."

"Would you recognize her if you did see her again?"

She made a negative gesture. "I never clearly see her face. She was turning around and around, spinning like a...how do you say?... a pião, a...a spinning top. But I remember she looked young, teenager. Hair black and long. Thin...skinny. More, I do not know."

"That's okay, that helps. This all really helps." He had his own notebook out, jotting down everything she was telling him. "When was this?"

She thought back, mumbling to herself. "A week before I go see Mr. Rob."

"Which puts it just after Will Messer was killed..." He didn't want to press her too hard, but he had to ask, "Why didn't you come forward with this after Rob died? Noah would have followed the lead just as well as Rob."

"I read in papers he dies after speaking to me. I think, maybe killer got him, maybe killer get me. And I do not know what I told him has anything to do with One O'clock Killer. All I know is I hid, no more bodies."

"Until now."

Jean approached again, bearing their plates on a tray. "Here we go, sweethearts: steak and potato, salad and pie for the young lady," she said, laying the plates before Neide. "And a burger with everything and fries for the gent." She gave him his plate and tucked the empty tray under her arm. "Can I get y'all anything else?"

"Neide, can you find your way back from here?"

She snorted, unwrapping her silverware from the napkin. "I know all ways in this area, Mr. Frank."

"Okay. Sorry, Jean, can I get mine to go and the check? Please and thank you," he added with a smile.

"Cops, I tell ya," she muttered, taking his plate and glass back. A moment or two later, she came back with his tea in a Styrofoam to-go cup and his food in a bag.

She started to hand him the check, but he'd already dug out his wallet and handed her more than enough to cover the price. "Keep the change, Jean." Then he drew a hundred dollar bill out and pressed it into Neide's hand. "Take this, get a room in a hotel for the next couple of days. You have my number?"

"Yes, Mr. Frank, but I do not want–"

"Please, Neide. Get somewhere safe and let me know where once you've settled in. I may need you again before this thing is over." He squeezed her hand. "And thank you. You may have just saved my best friend's life."

He took the cup and bag from Jean, gave her a quick smile and ran out to his car. He dug out his cell phone as he started his Chrysler and merged into traffic exiting the parking lot.

Townsend answered on the second ring. "Where did you go?"

"Followed a hunch, or more like grasped at a few straws. Either way, I think I know where to start unraveling this thing."

"Where?"

"Actually, more like when. December, 2000."

"Okay...what happened then?"

"I don't exactly know yet, but once I figure it out, I think we'll know who has Noah."

"Great – I'll meet you at the precinct."

"Where are you now?" Frankie turned off Market Street onto Reed, heading back toward the precinct.

"Just leaving the morgue. Dr. Lee found something...interesting. I'll fill you in when I see you."

"Okay. I'm guessing Tyler wasn't able to locate Noah's phone?"

"He did, but it was no good. The abductor tossed it."

Frankie banged his palm on the steering wheel. "Where?"

"The intersection of Main and Market. Looks like he was aiming for a storm drain, but it landed next to it instead."

"So, basically, he could be anywhere in the city. Or even have left Riverdale altogether by now."

"Exactly why we need to find the beginning of this string you found and unravel it all the way to the end. See you back at the station." With that, he hung up.

Frankie tossed his phone down in the passenger seat, easing his speedometer up over the posted limit. December, 2000....it had to help. It had to be the key to all this. Good Lord willing and the creek don't rise, as his grandma used to say, they would have Noah home in time for dinner.

Something told him it wouldn't be that easy.

CHAPTER THIRTY-FIVE

———

Townsend got back to his desk a scant minute or two before Franks showed up. His partner was full of nervous energy, the kind that always builds up inside just before a case starts to come together. He pulled an extra chair away from his desk and plunked it down next to Townsend's and took a seat.

"The day Rob Meares died," he said without preamble, "he met with a confidential informant of his." He opened a dusty little notebook like the kind all the cops in the precinct carried and sat it before Townsend. He pointed to a scribbled note. "Based on what his CI told him, he made this note. 'CMB, two thousand.' He thought it might be connected to the One O'clock Killer case. See?" Franks pointed to the rest of the notation.

"Okay. What does that mean?"

Franks shook his head. "I'm not sure yet. Not completely."

He frowned. "Okay. Then how do you know we need to look back at December of that year, specifically? The note only says two thousand."

Franks looked around the room and leaned closer. "Rob's informant? She's one of mine, too. I met with her today and asked her what she told him the day he died."

"Which was?" He leaned forward in his chair, too.

"She said she had seen a teenaged girl having some sort of psychotic episode outside the bus station one night. Said the girl was talking about killing the people who had killed her brother, ranting about how she and her brother hadn't been good enough. That kind of thing."

"Good enough. Good enough for what?"

"I don't know, but I'm thinking it's what she said after that's really important. The CI said she was repeating the numbers 'one, twelve, five, two thousand' over and over. If Rob thought this had to do with the case, maybe the one is for one o'clock and twelve, five, two thousand is—"

"December fifth, two thousand."

His partner's eyes lit up. "Exactly."

Townsend sat back, processing this. "Okay...so we what? Go back over every case from that date and see what sticks out?"

Franks shrugged. "It's our best lead right now."

"But we don't even know if what this girl was saying has anything to do with the original case for sure, let alone our case now."

"Right, but...Right." Some of the fire went out of him. "But Rob put something together because of it. CMB." His eyes went unfocused as he thought about it. "Citizen's first..."

"What?"

"Citizens first. Something else the girl at the bus station said. Wasn't that a slogan?"

Townsend thought a moment but couldn't bring anything to mind right away. Franks stood abruptly and turned on his heels. "I'll look it up online." But then he stopped and turned back. "Before I do, what did you mean Dr. Lee had found something interesting?"

His mind immediately went back to the last thing he and the medical examiner had discussed. He decided to wait to tell Franks about the possible danger to Harkham until they had a solid lead to help find him. "He found a nail and a piece of glass that he thinks were used to carve the clocks into the original victims inside one of Nigel Warner's wounds."

His brow furrowed. "What?"

"*And* he found the letter opener missing from Harkham's desk shoved down Jennifer Sealey's throat. He believes it was used to carve the clock on her body and to kill Nigel."

Franks sat back down. "So, it is definitely the same killer from the original case. I mean, I know we were already operating on that assumption, but it's nice to have confirmation." He frowned, his blue eyes troubled. "But I don't get why he would do that. I mean, if the point was to frame Noah, the letter opener makes sense, but not the rest. There was nothing about the first two murders that remotely implicated him."

"I know. I've been thinking about that, too. I guess maybe this guy decided sometime over the last eight years that framing Harkham would be more fun than just killing again? Maybe he thought tying Nigel to the old killings would make us automatically assume that Harkham killed them, too? I don't know." He didn't like when things didn't make sense.

Franks started to respond, but both of their phones chimed at the same time. Townsend grabbed his off the desk first and read the message. A jolt of adrenaline rushed through him. "We might have another lead." He stood just as Franks was reading the message for himself.

"Oh, no," he said, following Townsend out of the precinct.

<u>1:52 p.m.</u>

Less than fifteen minutes later, they were back at Harkham's apartment building. A 911 call had come in from the apartment across the hall from his. A woman had been attacked and left for dead. Her husband had found her, and they were now at the hospital.

Townsend and Franks pulled one of the responding officers, Byers, aside when they arrived. "What happened?"

"Sirs," she nodded to each of them in greeting. "George Hermann came home for lunch and found his wife in and out of consciousness. The paramedics said it appears she had been bludgeoned on the back of the head by a yet unknown blunt object, and from what the husband said she had told him, it had happened around nine or ten this morning."

"Geesh," Franks said. "And she was still alive, what, almost four hours later?"

"Yes, sir, she was still alive when they took her to County. I alerted you two as soon as I realized where we were. I figured there might be a connection between this and what happened to Mr. Harkham." She gestured toward Harkham's apartment, then back to the new victim's place, where another officer was photographing the scene.

"Where's CSU?" Townsend asked her.

She shook her head. "Not here yet, sir, but on the way. I notified the lab myself."

"Good work, Byers. What's your partner's name?"

"Thompson, sir."

He brushed past her to the side of the doorway of the Hermanns' apartment. "Thompson, go ahead and step outside for me, will you?"

The young man looked offended, but he nodded anyway. Townsend backed up to let him exit without stepping in the middle of the doorway. The baby-faced cop muttered an 'excuse me' as he left. Townsend placed a hand on his shoulder. "I'm going to need you and your partner to start knocking on doors, see if anyone saw or heard anything. We'll wait here for CSU."

Thompson nodded and looked to Byers. She pointed him toward the apartments on the same side of the hall as the Hermanns' place, while she headed toward the ones adjacent to Harkham's. *That one is a good cop.* Townsend and Franks headed into the Hermanns' apartment, careful not to disturb anything.

Franks moved further into the interior, but Townsend focused on the living room. Not a lot was out of place. The living room was the first room they entered, just like in Harkham's. Here, the aesthetic was less Spartan than the former detective's, much cozier. There were photographs of the couple here and there on side tables, the TV console and on the walls. Many featured other people he presumed were their children and grandchildren. Still life and landscape paintings hung around the room, which was warm, inviting and well lived-in.

The most noticeably out of place thing amongst the comfortable clutter was a single metal plant stand and potted plant – a Boston fern, if he wasn't mistaken – lying on its side, dirt spilling onto a tired Oriental throw rug. Near this, on the beige carpet that covered the whole room, was a patch of blood. It was a large puddle, which was not uncommon with head wounds. He figured the attacker knocked on the door and pushed his way inside when she answered, then struck her over the head and she toppled the plant and plant stand over on her way down.

There was a purple dish towel on the couch, and it appeared soaked with blood. Perhaps, at some point, Mrs. Hermann came to enough to get off the floor and try to staunch the bleeding of her head. If this was all the work of the same guy who took Harkham, he would have been gone by a quarter to eleven. There was plenty of time for her to have gotten herself up onto the couch where her husband found her.

He looked back through the partially opened doorway into the hall. The door to Harkham's apartment wasn't visible from this far inside the Hermanns' place, so he walked over to the door, being careful of where he stepped, and used the end of the pen he kept in his jacket pocket to push the door closed. It was then that he could see the impressions in the plush carpet.

"Doesn't look like anything's been taken," Franks announced, reentering the room.

Townsend half-turned. "Nothing?"

"Not that I can tell. There's a jewelry box in the bedroom that has close to sixteen hundred dollars' worth of heirloom quality pieces plus some semi-precious stones and an antique pocket watch. Her purse is hanging on the coat rack by the kitchen doorway, still with cash and credit cards untouched." He gestured around the living room. "All the electronics are still in place and the paintings are all still on the walls. This wasn't a burglary."

It took him a moment to recall that this was what Franks used to do before coming to Riverdale. He pointed to the impressions in the carpet. "What do you make of that?"

After peering at the spot a few seconds, Franks said, "He was watching the apartment, through the peep hole. That's how he knew when I was gone." He turned away with an angry scowl.

Townsend got as close to the door as he could and dug his pocket flashlight out. When he clicked it on and shone it on the area around the peep hole, he could see slightly smudged greasy spots on either side. The attacker's nose had pressed against the door while his eye was close to the peep hole.

"Looks like he was watching a long time, without moving much, except to switch which eye he used to look out." He turned back to his partner. "He would have waited as long as necessary. He would have taken Harkham at some point."

Franks scoffed. "Well, I'm glad I saved him some time."

"Listen, Alan, I shouldn't have come down so hard on you earlier." He clicked off the flashlight and put it away, walking away from the door. "I know what you're feeling right now, but the truth is the only person here to blame is the guy who took Harkham."

Franks looked at him a moment, then dropped his gaze. "Thanks for trying, but we both know how bad I screwed up. If Noah – if anything happens to him, it will be my fault." He ran a hand across his mouth. "I don't know how I'll live with that."

Memories Townsend wished he could bury tried to surface, but he shook them off. "Let's just keep going. Hopefully, we'll find him before you ever have to find out."

He worried again about what Dr. Lee had said. Even if Harkham did somehow survive the initial exposure to the chloroform, he would likely suffer multiple organ damage. But at least that was treatable. Much better that than he never come home at all.

"Hello again, gents," Simon Lewis said as he pushed the door open with a gloved hand. "What do we have here?"

Townsend pointed to the impressions in the carpet. "The guy who took Harkham, we believe he was waiting here, watching for his chance."

The portly criminalist scanned the area with a critical eye. "Show me everything."

He came on into the apartment carefully, closed the door and set down his kit. Townsend gestured toward the door. "The victim was rendered unconscious by a blow to the head and fell there," he said, pointing to the bloodstain. "She then got herself up onto the couch at some point and used a towel to help stop the bleeding but passed out again. She was on the couch when her husband found her. Meanwhile, we think her attacker stood here behind the door, looking through the peep hole."

Lewis got out his flashlight and examined the door and the impressions in the carpet. "Looks like you're right." He eyed the path from the living room to the door. "I don't know how, but we got very lucky here. The husband, paramedics and first responders all missed completely destroying these imprints, though they are overlapped here at the end a bit." He flicked the flashlight beam toward Franks' face. "I'm guessing I ought to thank your pal for part of that."

Franks squinted and held up a hand to shield his eyes. "Finding something that helps bring him home will be thanks enough, I think."

Lewis grunted and went back to work. Townsend pulled Franks aside. "I think you should go to the hospital, see how Debra Hermann is doing. If she's still alive, get a description of this guy. I'm going to the A/V lab to light a fire under Tyler Hendricks' butt and get our surveillance footage of him to compare it to. I think once we know who we're after, we should take another run at Lynn. She has to know where he would've taken Harkham."

Franks nodded. "Agreed. I'll head on over now and let you know."

"Lewis, we're going to need out of here."

He scoffed. "Well, then, you're going to have to wait thirty more seconds or so." He was photographing the impressions.

"Okay, so I'll head on over there in thirty seconds," Franks quipped under his breath, just as his cell phone rang. "Now what?" He frowned at the screen when he saw the caller ID. "Crap, it's Neil."

CHAPTER THIRTY-SIX

Frankie cringed. "Crap, it's Neil. I didn't call him yet. Did you?"

Townsend frowned. "No. It didn't even cross my mind, I'm afraid."

With a sigh, Frankie answered the call. "Franks"

"Noah's missing?"

"Neil, I'm sorry I didn't call you yet–"

"He's been abducted, hasn't he? The One O'clock Killer has him."

"I–" He bit his bottom lip. "Yes. Yes, we believe so."

"I had to hear it from Tyler Hendricks, Frankie." In true Neil form, his voice betrayed little emotion, but Frankie could still detect a tremor of fear and anger. "I had to hear that my cousin has been taken by a man who has now butchered four people basically through the rumor mill, and now nobody will tell me anything more until I talk to you or Townsend. So, I'm asking you to tell me. Everything."

Lewis was done photographing, so Frankie gestured to Townsend that he was going to take the call outside. "Look, Neil, I'm sorry." He got out into the hall and headed down the stairs. "We've been busy trying to make sense of things, trying to find him."

"But what *happened*?"

Frankie was taking the stairs as quickly as possible, hoping that Mrs. Hermann wouldn't take a turn for the worse before he got to the hospital. "Looks like the killer forced his way into the neighbor's apartment, incapacitated the woman living there and then watched Hark's apartment. He waited for his chance and took it." He glossed over his own part in that, for now.

"I don't know how he got into Noah's place yet, but he used chloroform to take him down." He crossed through the lobby and exited the building, into the sounds of the city. It was the same as every day: car horns honking, engines running, people talking...Like nothing had changed.

There was silence on the other end of the line long enough he checked the phone's screen to make sure the call hadn't dropped. But then Neil said, "Okay. But how did he get him out of the building without being seen? He would have been lugging around about six feet and almost two hundred pounds of virtually dead weight."

"Uh..." He started circling the building, looking for anything he may have missed in his initial, frantic search.

"You don't know, do you?" Neil sighed. "Tell me what you do know."

Frankie was only half-listening as he examined the area. "We're working on it, Neil. It's only been a couple hours–"

"Don't handle me like some civilian family member, Frankie. I'm coming over. I'll find out how he got out of there."

"No, Neil, Lewis is working the scene. Just let us do our jobs, okay?" Silence. "Neil?" This time when he looked at the phone's screen, it was blank. "Fantastic."

He pocketed the phone and continued his search around the building. Noah's apartment and the fire escape that serviced it faced the busy street, so that plus the security cameras on the entrance and the traffic cams in the area all guaranteed this wasn't their route. Not to mention that they would have had to pass by Frankie. No windows in the Hermanns' apartment had been open, and he didn't remember seeing anything that looked out of place near any of the windows to suggest they'd gone out the neighbor's fire escape, though he'd have Lewis confirm.

He was just about to go back inside and ask the criminalist to do just that when he noticed the heavy steel maintenance door was now slightly open. Frankie drew his gun and cautiously opened the door further. Even though he knew this guy had Noah somewhere far away by now, he still entered on guard. The lights were off, the sunlight streaming in through the door throwing his shadow to stretch before him on the floor. He drew out his flashlight and followed the stuffy corridor to a flight of stairs leading down to the basement. He stayed to the edges of the hall and steps, keeping an eye out for potential evidence.

It got cooler as he descended. He stepped off the last step and swept the beam of his flashlight all around. The basement was large and noisy, and amber safety lights here and there offered sickeningly dim illumination. HVAC units, water heaters, and other equipment needed to keep the residents comfortable and safe filled the main room. Plumbing and duct work lined the ceiling and ran along the walls, and he noticed the elevator had a stop here, too.

He swore under his breath and pulled out his phone. Townsend picked up on the first ring. "He took him out through the basement, using the elevator."

"I thought you were on your way to the hospital."

"I was, but Neil asked me how this guy was able to get an unconscious, six-feet tall, nearly two-hundred-pound man out of the building without raising suspicion. I checked the whole perimeter of the building earlier and saw nothing. But this time, the maintenance door was open, with no building personnel anywhere around. Casey, there's a stop for the elevator down here, too. It has to be the way they came. It would've been easy to drag Noah into the elevator from his apartment without anyone seeing, then through the basement and out the maintenance door to the parking lot. It would've taken a while, but we were all preoccupied with the apartment..." he growled low in his throat, retracing his steps to the stairs. "If I had just stayed outside and waited, I would've seen them. I could've stopped him–"

"Alan, listen to me: you can beat yourself up all you want, but that won't change what's done. Okay? Use that energy to go forward instead, all right?"

"Yeah, okay," he said, trudging up the stairs.

"Now, I'm looking right at the elevator up here and it has a metal tension bar blocking the doors with a sign that says, 'out of order.' I'm mashing the button with a pen and nothing's happening."

"I don't know, Casey. He had to've gotten it to work long enough to get out of the building, somehow. It's the only thing that makes any sense." He went through the maintenance door and scanned the grassy gravel around it. It was faint, but it did look like there were drag marks. The parking lot itself was paved, but it was old, and gravel had been brought in to fill in pot holes here and there. "I think I'm seeing drag marks coming out of the doorway into the parking lot. Tyler hasn't seen *any* of this on the security tapes?"

"No, the rear cameras are busted, there was no footage."

"Yeah, I'll give you three guesses who made sure of that. Dammit!"

"It's going to be all right. I'll have Lewis take a look at the lot and basement when he's done here."

"Okay," he sighed, trying to calm down. "Good. Uh, Neil is on the way, too. He refused to sit it out."

Townsend was quiet a moment. "At this point, I think we can use all the help we can get. Technically, there's no conflict of interest, though the white shirts will probably have plenty to say about him being too close to the investigation when they find out..."

"No doubt. No doubt they'll say the same about me."

"Well, we'll worry about that later. For now, just get over to the hospital."

"Copy."

"And Franks?"

"Yeah?" He was out front now, getting into his car.

"Good work."

He smiled, shutting the door. "Thanks, partner." He hung up and started the car, then drove away toward the hospital.

CHAPTER THIRTY-SEVEN

When he looked back at Spicer, Noah could see the officer was more alert now. The pain and stress had cleared away any lingering fogginess from the chloroform. Noah figured the cop had been given a lower dose than he had, since Spicer hadn't thrown up and his skin wasn't burned. But shock and blood loss might get to him now before any side effects of the drug could.

Other than registering his obvious pain, the look in his eyes also held a note of something else, something that wasn't the anger and hatefulness of earlier. It was almost...resignation? There was fear, too, but he mostly looked as certain of their fate as Noah was. *We can't both give up, kid.* He would do his best to get Spicer out of this alive, but he would need the younger cop to fight for it, too.

Noah turned toward Ian again. "It was bad enough you killed the son of an Assistant District Attorney. But killing a cop and a retired detective is going to get you zero mercy. You may have seen combat, but I guarantee you, that did nothing to prepare you for being inside. And all of that is before they kill you by lethal injection. If you live long enough to get there, that is."

"Oh, keep going, I think you're really starting to get through to me, *Mister* Harkham. Is this how you talked to Donnie? Did you try to scare him down, too?" He pressed Noah's fingers tighter around the grip of the gun, reminding him who was in charge.

"No. I tried to save him, and the girl."

"Well, Spicer, I guess Noah here really doesn't want you to live much longer." He tried to force Noah's hand to aim toward the cop's shoulder, but Noah was more in control of his muscles now and resisted, keeping the gun aimed at the floor.

"Stop! It's the truth. I wanted everybody to go home that day, so I tried *everything* I could think of to get Donnie out of there alive. You want me to tell the story, Ian? Then stop making me shoot Spicer and let me tell the damn story!"

Ian smiled. He made a show of taking the gun out of Noah's hand and waving it and his other hand toward Spicer in invitation. "By all means, then. Please proceed." He sat on the edge of one of the crates a few feet away. "But you will put more holes in our pal here, if you make me mad."

"I won't tell you what you want to hear, Ian. I'm going to tell you exactly how it happened. Whether or not you like what I say is out of my control, but I am not going to lie to you."

"You better not." He gestured the gun toward Spicer. "For his sake."

———————

"It was Tuesday, December fourth, 2000," Noah began. "At three-fifty p.m. My then FTO, Sergeant Bill Bentley, and I stopped by the City Mutual Bank ATM, so I could withdraw some cash for food. Bentley was lazy, arrogant and always hungry, as long as I was buying, and I remember wishing that I was still working with Rob Meares when I realized the machine was broken. I told Bill that I'd have to go into the bank to get the cash instead."

As he had opened the door to the bank, he'd only had a moment to take in the scene before him before everything turned to chaos...

"I went inside and a young, Caucasian male, I thought maybe seventeen, eighteen years old, and a little girl, around twelve or so, were standing just behind the line of customers. I noticed he had one hand on her shoulder – she was holding it tight in her own – and he was raising his other hand toward the ceiling. I saw the gun just as he fired one round into the air and shouted for everyone to get on the floor."

He swallowed, his throat still dry and raw. "I drew my gun and radioed for backup as quietly as I could, but he still heard me somehow. He turned and saw my uniform and...he pointed the gun at me, ordering me to the ground."

"Put the gun down! Get on the floor!"

Noah held out his left hand toward the man but didn't take his gun off him. "Sir, just take it easy. I'm not going to shoot you or your little girl, okay? Let's just take a minute–"

"Shut up! Just drop the gun and kick it to me."

Noah cleared his throat. "He wanted my gun, but no matter what movies or television say, we don't ever relinquish our weapons. I told him, I said, 'If I give you my gun, I can't get these scared people home safely tonight. I can't get you or that poor little girl you got with you out of here safe. I won't use it if I don't have to, all right? Let's just work together and I promise to get you both out of here safe.' But that only made him angry."

Ian scoffed but otherwise didn't interrupt. Noah continued, "That's when he tells me if I didn't drop my weapon, he would start dropping bodies." He shook his head. "I didn't think he meant it. He just sounded scared, desperate...I could see from the way they were dressed and by their physical condition that they'd been living on the brink of poverty for a long time. The little girl, she looked like she was the guy's little sister, but I wouldn't know that for sure until later. After." He dropped his gaze to stare at the floor. He couldn't look Ian in the eye and relive this day.

He took another deep breath, noticing a painful hitch deep inside. *Not now. Just tell the story.* "I asked him to talk to me, tell me what was going on. He laughed – I'll never forget that laugh; it was almost hysterical – and he says, 'What's it look like?' And I told him it looked like he and that girl were in trouble. 'If you talk to me,' I told him, 'maybe I can help you.' But he just got this angry look on his face and said, 'You look like you just walked out of your Academy graduation. You can't do shit for me.' And I knew then that he could see right through me. I was in way over my head. I'd only graduated from the Academy six months before this, and I was green as a leaf. I was scared, too. There was a whole bank full of people looking to me to get them out of there safely, and I didn't know what I was doing, other than going by the script they tell you to stick to in training. And he knew it."

"You admit you didn't know what the hell you were doing in there?" Ian asked, his expression one of disdain.

"I was a rookie, Ian. I'd never responded to a bank robbery hostage situation in real life yet. We'd role-played the situation numerous times, though, in training and were given certain techniques, certain scripted lines to use, but I'd never seen the real thing before. But I did what I was trained to do."

"So, you're trained to lie to and murder suspects, is that it?"

"No! I didn't lie, I didn't–"

Ian aimed the gun at him before he could even blink. "If you say you didn't murder my brother, I will make you put a bullet in Spicer's head."

Noah shied away from the gun, hating that he couldn't move his arms to cover his face and felt the panic start to rise again. Gotta get control. Gotta get him stable. "Just-just put that down, Ian. Please. Please just let me tell the rest of the story."

Ian snorted in disgust. "Raelynn would love to hear you begging like this." He thought it over a moment, then nodded. "Fine. Go on."

He cleared his throat again. "Right then was when my FTO – Field Training Officer – that's when Bentley tried to sneak into the bank. But Donnie saw him and shot him. Bullet to the upper thigh. It nicked his femoral artery, but he managed to use his belt as a tourniquet to keep from bleeding to death on the sidewalk until the paramedics got to him. It took him months to recover. I found all this out afterward, of course."

Ian's expression was dark and angry again, so Noah skipped ahead in the story. "There were half a dozen adult females and teenaged girls, two adult males and two teenaged boys, and two little kids, including the little girl – little Raelynn – there with Donnie. I knew I had to handle this carefully, so I said to him, 'That was my superior officer you just shot out there. So, I'm thinking you're the kind of guy I don't want to jerk around, am I right?' And he says, 'You seen me, man, I will shoot you or anybody else in here unless I get what I want.'"

Noah sneaked a peek around the support column he'd taken cover behind. The guy was wild-eyed and twitchy. Nervous, scared. There was no way he had taken into consideration what to do if a cop walked into the middle of this thing. Noah had royally screwed up this guy's plans...

He was backing away, moving more toward the wall on the far left. From there, he could watch the hostages lying on the floor and Noah and the door but didn't leave himself in the line of fire from anyone outside. Smart.

"I asked him his name, so I wouldn't have to keep calling him 'sir,' or 'buddy,' but he refused. So, I said, just give me any name, it doesn't have to be your real one, just so we can keep things civilized. Then he told me to call him Ronnie, and I could tell by the girl's reaction that it was a fake name. That was fine with me. All I wanted was to keep him calm and buy time until the hostage negotiator got there to take over. Then I told him my name. The girl looked really scared and I asked him to tell me her name, too, but he just hugs her to him tighter and says not to worry about her." He swallowed. His voice was getting more and more hoarse. "I remember how tight she gripped his hand. Her eyes, they were dark blue, and had a… a bruised quality to them. Her face was dirty, and old, dried up tearstains streaked down her cheeks. She looked so scared."

He risked a glance at Ian, but the hand holding the gun was relaxed now, the weapon pointed at the floor. "I asked him to tell me what he wanted; how we could get the other people out of there. But he just ordered the tellers out from behind the counter and onto the lobby floor with everyone else. He shot another round into the ceiling to kick everyone into gear. The gun was a six-shooter revolver, so he only had three shots left. But I knew he could do a lot of damage with three shots."

He shivered as the scene played out in his mind again. "There was a kid, a little boy around five or six, and he started crying. I just kept thinking, don't make it worse, kid. Don't make it worse like–" He had to take a moment to repress the memory that had been triggered back then and was trying to resurface again now. His own first That Day.

"Donnie told me to get on the ground, too, out there with everyone else, but I told him that I couldn't do that. Not if I was going to be able to help him. That just set him off. He started yelling at me that he was the one in charge, and he was the one who said how it was going to work and that I was going to do what he told me, or somebody was going to die. And that kid, he was still crying, and Donnie pointed the gun at the mother and screamed at her to shut the kid up. I knew it was all about to hit the fan, so I stepped out from behind cover and told Donnie to look at me instead. He swung the gun around, like I hoped, and I just told him to ignore everyone else because they couldn't help him. 'I can help you, they can't,' I said."

He looked Ian in the eye. "I asked him if it was okay if I just sat down where I was, so he could focus on me and not the other people, not that little boy who was just scared like the rest of us. And Raelynn, she looks up at Donnie and says, 'He can play Still as Statues.' Donnie agreed, saying if I try anything, though, he'd put a bullet through my head."

A shiver coursed through him again. "I knew he wasn't bluffing then, I could see it in his eyes. The desperation. He didn't have much left to lose at this point, and he knew it. So, I tried to redirect his attention. 'They'll be sending more cops here any second,' I told him, 'and there's gonna be a negotiator with them. He's going to call the bank's phone, and when he does, I want you to answer it, because he's the guy who's going to be able to help you. But, in the meantime, tell me what I can do to help.' And Donnie says, 'I just need thirty thousand dollars. You let me have that, everyone goes home.' And I'm thinking, why only thirty thousand? This bank had tons more than that."

"You know why now, don't you?" Ian asked, his voice hollow.

"Yeah," Noah said. "Now I know why." He turned to Spicer. "Raelynn was diagnosed with schizoaffective disorder; Donnie just wanted the money to get her treatment."

The younger cop's eyebrows furrowed. He was getting pale, the amount of blood staining his pantleg and the floor under him had grown larger. "He needs to have that wound dressed, Ian. He'll bleed to death before I can tell the whole story."

"Talk faster," Ian said, aiming the gun at him again.

"Please, Ian. Whatever reason you brought him here requires him to be alive, or else he'd already be dead. Please. Spicer will die if you do nothing. There has to be something around here you can use to bandage his leg. Or was letting him die slowly part of Lynn's plan?"

He'd struck the right nerve, he knew in an instant. Ian heaved a frustrated sigh, then got up off the crate and disappeared between the stacks of crates along the wall. A moment later, he returned with a first aid kit, which he took over to the young cop. He began dressing the wound with efficient confidence, surprisingly even apologizing when Spicer groaned or whimpered. Noah figured he'd probably had a lot of practice patching up himself and his fellow soldiers overseas.

When he was done, he turned back to Noah. "There. Now, finish the story." He went back and sat on his crate.

Noah thought back to where he had left off. "Donnie said he needed thirty thousand dollars. I told him, 'Thirty thousand? Yeah, I think we can do that. I mean, the bank is insured, so it's not like they're really losing any money.' Of course, he was skeptical—"

"Because you were just trying to trick him."

"No, I wasn't. If I could get those hostages out of there alive by giving him the money, I was giving him the money. I didn't care about the repercussions of it. Thirty grand for at least seventeen lives? No contest. Did I think he would be able to leave that bank and keep the money? Not really. I figured backup would get there before that and he'd end up going to jail, but, even if he did get away, all I cared about were the hostages."

Ian gave a derisive snort, but Noah continued, "I looked at the teller closest to Donnie, a pretty, blonde...woman..." He stumbled to a stop as he called her face to mind. Ian was watching him closely, an amused expression on his face. It was making sense now. "I asked her to confirm what I had said." He closed his eyes a moment. It wasn't because he'd run into her at the coffee shop, after all. The tight feeling in his chest was getting worse.

He looked at the ground again. "She did, but before we could start getting him the money, backup arrived. There were sirens and lights everywhere around the bank, and Donnie, he just started freaking out. I tried to calm him down, telling him that they would have come no matter what, it was protocol. I told him it was going to be okay, told him not to let the sirens and lights rattle him. To just keep working together. And he did calm down a little, and he told–the teller," he couldn't bring himself to say her name yet, "to get the cash. She had to get it from the cash drawers, she said, because no one on staff that day had the combination for the vault."

Ian scoffed again but said nothing. Noah checked on Spicer and saw that the younger cop looked a little better now that the bleeding had been stopped. "He told her she had sixty seconds to get him the cash, or he'd shoot me. She was so rattled, so scared, but she did it. She emptied every single one of the drawers and came running back. But she tripped, dropping the money on the floor. Donnie, he thought she'd done it on purpose, and he hit her with the gun. But I stood up and had my gun aimed at him and told him to leave her alone or I would shoot him."

The little girl started crying. "Don't shoot my brother, please! It's all my fault, I'm sorry! It's all my fault." She sobbed so hard her words were almost unintelligible. "I'M SORRY!" She screamed, startling everyone, including Donnie. And Noah.

"Still as statues, quiet as a mouse," she said in a sing-song voice, pointing to each of the hostages. "Donnie? I want to go home..."

"Raelynn started crying, saying something about wanting to go home because the statues were staring at them. Donnie hugged her, said that they couldn't leave until he had her money. And he looks at me and says, 'Please, officer, just let me get the money and get out of here. My sister needs help and I can't afford it any other way.' And by that time, she was ripping out handfuls of her hair, scattering it on the floor like confetti. Donnie lowered the gun and began pulling the girl over toward the wall. I let him, because she was so agitated...and he, he looked *afraid* of her. He stroked her hair, shushing and reassuring her. But then he looked at me and said, 'See? I have to help her.' And I...I said, 'I know'. I didn't see a criminal in your brother; just a scared, desperate kid who was stuck trying to take care of a troubled little girl all on his own. I–"

"You're blaming me for all this?" Ian hopped off the crate and stared at him, incredulous. Furious. "Are you saying it's my fault that you killed my brother?"

"That's not what I said."

He closed the distance between them, pulled back the fist holding the gun and brought it down in a hard arc that ended at Noah's cheekbone. Noah grunted in pain, seeing stars for a full minute. "You," Ian's voice shook with anger, "had better just tell the rest of the story, before I forget the plan and end you now."

Breathing hard, his eyes cold and narrow, Ian walked back to sit on the crate. Noah winced and groaned a moment longer, trying to work out whether his cheekbone was broken, and deciding it probably was. Now he had a wound to match the one Donnie had given Jennifer Sealey all those years ago. There was probably something poetic in that.

"All right," he said. "There wasn't enough money. The drawers, they only had a little over $22,500. When he heard that, I thought Donnie would hit her again– or worse. I told him to just take what was there and let everyone go, that he could still walk away from this if he did that. I promised him everything would be okay, that I'd get them out alive."

He didn't want to go any further. He didn't want to relive what he'd done. But his and Spicer's lives somehow depended on this, so he had to keep going. "M-my radio, the others outside, they contacted me, asking me to give a report of the situation."

"2259, advise status."

"I have to respond, or they'll think I'm down. You don't want that, okay?"

"I told him I had to respond, or they would think I was dead, and I knew that if they thought that, they'd come in heavy and hard, and there was no way Donnie would survive. So, he let me tell them that everything was under control. But then someone else, the negotiator, I think, told me to stand down and let them handle it from there. That's when the phone rang. Donnie looked at me, that little girl with her arms wrapped around his waist, and I told him that it would be the negotiator, just like I had said before. I told him to answer the phone."

Donnie nodded and started toward the door dividing the lobby from the teller's area where the phone was. A red laser dot appeared on his chest. Noah couldn't let this girl witness her brother being gunned down right in front of her.

"They had snipers, already lining up the kill shot. I saw the bead on his chest and I warned him to stop, go back to the wall. This wasn't the protocol. Snipers were a last resort, after negotiation failed. I think, I think it was because he'd already shot Bentley. I think they thought he was too far gone to talk down...I don't know. But I didn't want Raelynn to see her brother gunned down in her arms."

Ian growled in frustration. "Stop trying to tell me how much you sympathized with my brother and sister, how you wanted to save him, how you wanted to save Raelynn. Just get to the part where you lied and tricked him and killed him." There were tears in his eyes. "I want to hear you say it, every detail of your deceit."

"That's not what happened, Ian. I told Donnie to get back, and then I radioed the team out front to have the snipers stand down. They'd just undone any progress I had made with him. There was no way he was going to trust me now, but I had to keep trying. He was freaking out again, asking how we went from negotiating his way out of there to snipers trying to take him out–and I, all I could do was apologize and try to get him to let the hostages go as a sign of good faith. Of course, he refused, so I asked for just the women and kids. That way, he'd still have the adult men and me. He would still have leverage."

The men and teen boys lying on the floor were looking at him like he was crazy. They began whispering to each other, and the one nearest Donnie made a gesture toward him. But Donnie was so focused on Noah that he didn't see or hear them plotting. Noah gave them a look and shook his head, ever so slightly. He had to resolve this before those kids could screw it up and get everyone killed.

"He agreed to the women and the teen girls and the little boy. But he refused to let the teen boys, the men, or me go anywhere. I wish to God that he'd told the older boys to go, too. But he didn't. All I could do was thank him and start getting everyone I could out of there. I holstered my weapon and came closer, my hands out in plain sight. I didn't want to spook him. Not then. I got almost all the women up and behind me without incident, but I had to convince the mother of the teen boys to trust me and leave her kids behind. And then, one of the girls refused to leave her father. She said that she wouldn't leave him there because Donnie and Raelynn were crazy, and she was afraid they would kill her dad. But her dad, he kissed her and ordered her to go, and I got her behind me with the others. Then I got all the tellers up and was just about to take them to the door, when–"

He couldn't do it. He couldn't think about it, let alone talk about it. He took a deep breath, felt the hitch inside again, and knew he didn't have a choice. There wasn't much time left. "One of the older boys, he suddenly got up into a crouch and lunged at Donnie. I shouted a warning not to do it, and Donnie pushed Raelynn away and kicked that boy in the chest. Sent him reeling. That's when Donnie accused me of tricking him, distracting him. But that's not–I had nothing to do with that. I would never let a civilian take a risk like that."

He paused again but had to push on. "I drew my weapon, and I tried to explain the truth to him. But he aimed his gun at that boy's head and I–"

Donnie looked from the teenager to Noah. "A trick, a distraction."

Noah drew his gun. "No, Donnie, listen to me: that was not–"

Donnie raised his gun and aimed it at the cowering teen's head.

"No!" Noah aimed his gun and fired three times.

Raelynn screamed. Donnie turned toward her before dropping to the ground. The women and kids behind Noah ran screaming for the door, where officers waited to get them to safety. The men and teenagers scrambled for the exit as well, leaving Noah, Raelynn and Donnie alone.

He couldn't take his eyes off Donnie. What just happened? What had he just done?

"I fired my weapon three times, like I was trained to do." Tears sprung to his eyes and slipped down his cheeks. "I had never shot anyone before, and I couldn't even understand what had just happened. But then I realized Donnie was breathing. I radioed for the paramedics and tried to help him the best I could in the meantime. There was so much blood, I tried to stop it, but...'Stay with me, buddy,' I said. His eyes were closed, but he was still alive. And I –She was just standing there, sobbing, hysterically sobbing. 'I'm sorry, honey. I'm so sorry.' There was nothing else I could say. Then the other officers and paramedics came in and I was pushed aside. One of the officers picked her up and carried her away. She was screaming and kicking until she saw me. She went...so still, and her eyes...she glared at me, not blinking, and said, in a way I will never forget, 'You promised.' And then she was carried out. And I never saw her again."

CHAPTER THIRTY-EIGHT

After Franks hung up, Townsend told Lewis about the elevator theory. The grumpy criminalist mumbled something unintelligible but nevertheless agreed to check it out. Townsend decided to check in with Byers and her partner before going back to interrogate Lynn Hopkins again. He found Byers finishing up with the last apartment on her side of the hall.

"Anything?"

She shook her head. Her light brown hair was pulled back in a bun, but a few stray strands framed her face. Everything about it was squarish, which could have ended up giving her a masculine aspect; instead, she was lovely in a capable, authoritative way that lent itself well to her chosen profession.

"Nobody heard or saw anything. This last guy," she said, jerking her thumb back towards the apartment she'd just left, "says he's only been home an hour. He did think he heard ours and the ambulance's sirens a little while ago, but he wasn't even a hundred percent on that." She rolled her hazel eyes.

"Great."

"I'm afraid Thompson will have a similar report, sir."

"Don't take this the wrong way, but is he a rookie?"

A slight smile of amusement tugged at her lips. "That obvious?"

"Kind of. But it was more how you were directing him. Which was good, by the way. How you didn't make him ask, didn't give him a chance to feel lost or stupid. You'd make a good FTO."

She smiled at the compliment. "Thank you, sir. I was supposed to be partnered with Spicer today, but he called in sick or something, so they stuck me with the greenhorn. He's a good kid, though, really. He'll be a good cop in a year or so. I lucked out."

"Glad to hear it. I don't want any babysitting or handholding to interfere with this investigation. Harkham is counting on us to find him and bring him home. I'd rather it not be in a pine box."

Her expression turned serious. "Copy that, sir." She started past him but stopped. "It's important to me to bring him home safe, too, sir. He was a damn good cop and he's a great instructor now. What he's doing for the department, it's valuable. At least to some of us." She held his gaze a moment. "We're going to find him, sir."

He smiled, tight lipped. "Let's hope so." His cell phone rang. "Excuse me," he said to her with an apologetic grimace. He dug out his phone and turned away from her. It was Ziehring. "Townsend."

"Please tell me you weren't serious with the Hopkins arrest."

"Why? What are you talking about?"

"They sent a lawyer down who took one look at her case file and demanded her release. Unfortunately for you, ADA Kirkwood agreed. She cut her loose about half an hour ago."

He closed his eyes and had to count to five before he could speak in a civil manner. "That's ridiculous, sir. I know Lynn's part of this."

"That may be, but you don't have enough evidence to charge her. We'll be lucky if she doesn't decide to sue for false arrest."

"I can't believe this, Captain," he said, running a hand wearily across his forehead. "We need her. We are so close to finding out who has Harkham and I need her to tell me where they are."

"Then you shouldn't have arrested her prematurely."

"Sir—"

"What's done is done, Townsend. Just move on and get back to work."

Before he could reply, Ziehring hung up. He had to fight the urge to throw his phone across the hall. Instead, he growled in frustration and squeezed it as hard as he dared without breaking it.

"Bad news?"

He turned, nearly forgetting that Byers had been there for all of that. "Yeah. Our only suspect in any of this just got set free."

She frowned. "So...what will you do now?"

He shook his head. "Hope we got a good look at this guy on the precinct surveillance."

"Sir? Ma'am— Uh, I mean, Byers?" They turned around at the sound of Thompson's voice. "Uh, there's a gentleman in apartment 209 down here who says he wants to know why the elevator isn't still working now. Says he saw a maintenance guy working on it early this morning, but the 'Out of Order' sign was back on now. I only mention it, cuz I thought, maybe, you know, Mr. Harkham might've been taken out of the building that way. If the elevator was working, I mean."

Townsend looked at Byers. She raised one eyebrow and shrugged. "Thompson, I'm putting you in for a commendation," Townsend told him. He clapped the officer on the shoulder as he passed by him. "209?"

"Uh, yes. Yes, sir. Mr. Fitzgerald is his name, sir."

As he went on toward the apartment Thompson had indicated, he heard Byers say, "There's hope for you yet, greenhorn."

———————

Mr. Fitzgerald was a gentleman about seventy-five years old who still retained traces of his native Irish accent. He had lived in the building since it was built nearly four decades ago. He said that the current elevator had replaced the original only two years ago and hadn't worked for over four months. The old one had only jammed up a couple times in the last year before it was swapped out for the newer, better model.

"Better model, my foot!" he'd added.

"But Officer Thompson says you saw someone working on it early this morning?"

"I did. Short, wee fella in a maintenance uniform. But I don't recall seein' him hereabouts before. So, I says to him, 'you gonna finally get that beast up and runnin' before I have meself a heart attack takin' them stairs?' And he says to me, 'Workin' on it, ain't I, sir?' So, I says to him, 'I'll believe it when I sees it.' And he just ignored me and kept on tinkerin'."

"Did you see his face?"

Mr. Fitzgerald shook his head. "Not really, no. He never looked away from his work, you see. But he had brown hair, and it looked like he had...not really a beard, so much, but like he needed a shave."

"Stubble," Townsend supplied.

"Yes, stubble. That's it. He wasn't very tall, like I said, but he looked fit anyways. Wiry strong, like my cousin Rory was. He was a boxer, you know."

"Ah. Anything distinctive about his voice?"

"He had a lovely singing voice, it's true."

"The guy fixing the elevator was singing?" He wrote this down in his notebook.

"Ah, no. I thought you meant my cousin."

Townsend struck through the note he'd just made. "Focusing on the guy fixing the elevator, Mr. Fitzgerald: was his voice distinctive in any way? Or was he wearing cologne or anything that can help us identify him?"

He thought for a minute. "Now that you mention it, he had a sort of chemical smell about him. Like he'd been working with solvents or somethin'. Cleaners, maybe."

"Solvents..." Townsend felt a thrill course through him. This had to be their guy. How would a maintenance guy get hold of chloroform, though? From what little he knew about it, it wasn't used in the medical field anymore because of how lethal it can be, so he doubted the hospitals would have any lying around. How easy would it be to make? Could it even be made at all? He'd have to ask Dr. Lee or someone about that. "Thank you, Mr. Fitzgerald. This really helps."

He dipped his head. "O' course. Hope you find your friend. I don't see him awful much, but he seems a decent fella. For a copper," he added with a wink.

Townsend smiled. "Thank you. You have a great day now."

Fitzgerald saluted Townsend, then went back into his apartment. *Okay, now I have a partial description to compare to the surveillance footage – if we ever get it.* "Byers, Thompson, I'll need you two to sit on the Hermann place and Harkham's until Lewis and Coates are done processing. I doubt it will happen, but just in case Lynn Hopkins or the elevator guy decides to stop by, I want you ready for them. Let me know if anything happens. I've got to get over to the A/V lab."

Byers nodded. "Got it, sir."

Townsend left them there in the hall and rushed past Simon Lewis and Neil Coates at the elevator. He didn't have time for Neil's reproaches now. The way he saw it, he could either coddle the upset criminalist, or he could work the case, but not both. He knew Coates would rather he work the case and bring his cousin home.

CHAPTER THIRTY-NINE

———

<u>Monday, September 1, 2014, 2:30 p.m.</u>

Frankie had to wait a few minutes before the doctors would let him in to see Debra Hermann. Her husband was in the recovery room with her, but he waved Frankie on in. "Mr. Hermann, I'm sorry to intrude. I'm–"

"Detective Franks," he said with a grin on his apple-shaped face. "I've seen you at Mr. Harkham's. He's told us good things about you."

He raised his eyebrows. "Really?"

"Yes. He gave us your card, told us to call you if we ever needed anything and he wasn't home." His eyes teared up. "I didn't expect it would be something like this when we officially met you."

He was holding his wife's hand and stroking her forehead where the bandages encircling her head crossed it. She appeared to be sleeping. Her heart monitor beeped in a relaxed, steady rhythm.

"I can come back in a little while," he offered. "She needs to rest."

Mr. Hermann shook his head. "No, she would want to help. We heard Mr. Harkham was abducted by the guy who did this to Deb. He is always good to us, we want to help bring him home safely." He gently kissed his wife's nose and said her name a couple of times before her heart rate made a slight increase. A moment later, her eyes fluttered open.

"Hey, beautiful," he said with a smile.

"Hey, handsome," she replied weakly. "What's going–" She groaned and put her hand to her head, her heart rate quickening. "There was a man," she said, gasping.

Frankie cleared his throat. She looked at him, startled. "George?"

"It's okay, honey. This is Detective Franks."

"Noah's friend," she said, calming. "I'm glad you're here." She looked around the room. "I need a pencil and paper."

Frankie pulled out his notebook and pen and handed them to her. "I'm afraid all I have is a pen, ma'am."

"Thank you, that's just fine." She took the items and began to make long strokes on the page he'd given her.

Mr. Hermann smiled at Frankie. "My wife is a gifted artist, Detective. I'm sure you saw the artwork on the walls in our apartment."

He had, but only peripherally, since none of them were missing to indicate a burglary had taken place. "I did. I had no idea they were your work, though, ma'am. Very impressive."

She frowned but didn't look away from the paper. "It's all amateur stuff, Detective; you don't need to play nice to an old woman."

"I didn't see anything that looked amateurish to me."

She flashed him a smile and then finished her sketch and handed it to him. "That's the man who attacked me."

Frankie was shocked by the quality of the sketch for no longer than it took her to draw it. The man was thin, with hair cut short but not buzzed and scruff just a bit more than a five o'clock shadow. There was a cast to his features that was a little... well, mousy was the only word that seemed to fit. This was not the same guy the High-flyer described.

"Detective Franks?" George Hermann asked. "Is something wrong?"

"Um, no, it's just that this man doesn't look like the same man another witness described." He smiled to show that this wasn't a big deal. "Witness descriptions often vary, though."

"That's exactly what he looked like," Debra insisted, "I promise."

"I have no doubt about that, ma'am." He dipped his head. "I learned a long time ago to trust an artist's memory. My mother was one and she remembered every detail about just about everything." He smiled. "Ma'am, can you tell me everything this guy said, what he was wearing...anything that might help us figure out who he is?"

She thought a long moment, her eyes growing troubled with the memory. "There was a knock on the door. I looked through the peep hole and saw that man." She pointed to the notebook in his hands. "I asked who he was, and he smiled and said that he was with building maintenance. He said he needed to check our bathroom plumbing." She looked up at her husband. "He mentioned the notice that we received last week saying there would be some updating this month."

George Hermann turned to Frankie. "He must have seen the copy of the flyer they hung up on the notice board by the mailboxes in the lobby."

She nodded and continued. "I could see he was wearing a gray work shirt...everything seemed okay, so I opened the door." She began to cry a little. "I knew the very second that I did that it was a mistake. He pushed his way in before the door was all the way open, and there was a wrench in his hand. One of those big monkey wrenches. I tried to run for the phone, but he must have used the wrench to hit me in the head before I could get there." She wiped her eyes. "I don't remember much after that. I'm sorry."

"No, ma'am, you're doing great. You said his shirt was gray, what color were his pants?"

"Darker gray. It was like a uniform."

"Okay, that's great. Was there like an emblem or company name or logo? Anything like that?"

She frowned in concentration. "I remember a J word...very scripty writing. I'm sorry, I didn't get a very good look."

"That's all right, ma'am. I think I have all I need here. Thank you." Something about her description and sketch felt vaguely familiar. He smiled at the couple. "I'll let you rest now."

He turned to leave but she called after him. "Detective Franks?" When he turned back, she looked very nervous and her heart rate had increased on the monitor. "That man...he didn't...try anything, did he?"

He was taken aback by the question for a split second. He hadn't thought through the implications of being rendered incapable of fighting back against a man that any woman would be concerned about. "No, ma'am. He only needed your apartment to watch Noah's." He shook his head. "I'm sorry, of course you wouldn't know yet. The man who attacked you; he abducted Noah Harkham."

She gasped and looked at George before turning back to him. "Why on earth would he do that?"

"That's exactly what I intend to find out, ma'am." He lifted the notebook. "And this will go a long way toward doing that."

"Then God bless you, Detective. I'll be praying you find him okay."

"Thank you, ma'am, sir." He nodded to each of them and left the room.

Once out in the hall, he ran a hand over his face. Great. Two different descriptions...two different suspects? And how did Lynn connect to either of them? He needed to get back to the precinct to try and help Townsend get that out of her.

CHAPTER FORTY

———

"Say that again?" Frankie was sure he'd heard his partner wrong.

"He let her go. Said I arrested her prematurely." Townsend shifted uneasily in his desk chair.

"Okay..." He drew the word out as his mind worked to solve this new problem. "So now we just have to hope the guy in Mrs. Hermann's drawing is in the system and try to go from there."

Townsend's phone chirped. He read the text and let out a relieved sigh. "Finally. Well, the good news on that front is that Tyler found us a couple usable still shots of our suspect at the precinct and Harkham's building." He clicked to view the attached photos and frowned. "You've got to be kidding." He held the screen out for Frankie to see.

"Wait, is that–?" He held Mrs. Hermann's sketch up next to the photos. Of course; that's why the guy had looked familiar.

He took the phone back and clicked to read the email. "Tyler says, 'Almost missed this because who would suspect the janitor, right? Well, he's the only one besides Harkham and a few other people visiting him who goes into the office all weekend. Unless Frankie, Neil or Joyce Collins did it – ha ha.'" He looked at Frankie and shrugged. "It would explain how he had access to Harkham's office and the elevator at his building. Jerry's Janitorial Services has contracts with nearly every precinct in the city, plus the hospitals, the University–" His eyes went wide.

"Which is how he met, or at least knew about, Nigel Warner. And probably how he got hold of the chloroform. Or the means to make it, if you can. Do you know?"

Townsend shook his head. "I don't know. But you're right on both counts, I'd wager."

Frankie was already pulling up the janitorial service's number in the precinct's directory. He dialed the number from his desk phone and waited through three rings before someone answered. "Jerry's Janitorial Services, this is Donna. How may I help you?"

"Hi, Donna, this is Detective Alan Franks at the Fifth Precinct. How are you doing today?"

"I'm just fine, Detective. How 'bout yourself?" Her voice was friendly, but wary.

"Well, I'm hoping you can help me with something. We need to get in touch with one of your employees who does some work for us out here and none of us can recall his name. Do y'all have records with photo IDs for your employees?"

"We do, sir, but employee information is confidential. I'm sure you understand."

"I do, but let me level with you, Donna," he switched to his cop mode voice, "we have evidence linking this man to murder and the abduction of one of our guys. Now, I need you to find out who this man is, where he lives and where he could be keeping our guy. Right now."

She gasped. "Just one moment, Detective."

She put him on hold, leaving him to listen to Kenny Chesney. He looked over to see that Townsend was on his cell phone, over at his own desk. The line connected again, cutting off the song mid-chorus.

"Detective Franks, this is Jerry Strathmore. How is it I can help you today?" Jerry's voice was all business.

"I need the name and address of one of your employees. He's wanted in connection to four murders and the abduction of one of our officers." Okay, so Noah wasn't technically an officer, but still...

"Of course. I'll help any way I can, Detective."

"Thank you, sir."

"Just come on by with your warrant, and I'll get you whatever you need."

"Thank you, sir. We're on our way." He hung up and got Townsend's attention. His partner held up one finger to stall him.

"No, sir, no one else. Just him...All weekend, that's right...No, sir, it isn't..." Townsend was looking ready to beat his head against a wall. But then, he smiled. "Thank you, sir. Yep, we'll swing by and pick it up right now." He listened a moment, going still. "Sir, if we wait until then, our guy will be dead. Literally every minute we lose could be his last."

Even knowing he was saying it mostly to speed things along, it froze Frankie's blood to hear him talk about Noah like that. But it was true, though, wasn't it? Every hour lost could mean the difference between a good ending to this thing or a tragic one. He shivered.

"We're on our way now, sir, thank you." He hung up with a frustrated scoff. "Judge Peterson wanted to delay us two hours because of an early dinner date across town, can you believe that?"

"But we're getting our warrant now, right?"

"Oh, yes, we're getting our warrant right now. Come on, you're driving."

3:27 p.m.

With a warrant for the information from Jerry's in hand plus the promise of an arrest warrant once they had the suspect's name to fill in, and an annoyed judge somewhat placated by their quick arrival and just as quick departure from his chambers, Frankie and Townsend now headed for the Jerry's Janitorial Services' base of operations near the docks on Franklin Avenue. When they arrived at the nondescript, single story brick building, it was Donna who buzzed them in. Her smile was tight and forced and she looked pale.

"This way, Detectives," she said, ushering them past the reception desk. "Jerry's on the phone right now, but he said to show you on in."

"We appreciate that, ma'am," Frankie said, following her through the drab lobby to an office down a short hall. She let them into the office and returned to her station.

Jerry Strathmore was seated in a leather swivel chair behind an overly-shined, dark wood desk. He wore the same two-toned gray uniform as the rest of his crew, but his looked spotless. It was doubtful he'd had to do any janitorial work himself for quite some time, now that his company had contracts with most of the biggest companies in the city. Still on the phone, he gave them a little wave and held up a finger to have them wait. "Okay, well, you just look into that for me and let me know, all right? Okay, thanks. My next appointment just arrived, so I'll call you later, okay? Okay, bye."

He hung up the phone and stood, coming over to shake their hands. "Jerry Strathmore. What exactly do y'all boys need?" His eyes were the palest green Frankie had ever seen, making them seem almost colorless. Paired with his salt and pepper hair and tanned coloring, the effect was a little unsettling.

Townsend held up a still shot of their suspect. "We know this man is part of the crew that works our precinct. We couldn't remember his name, so we'll need to know that and where we can find him."

Jerry took a good look. "That's Ian," he said in surprise. He looked up at them. "You think he kidnapped one of your officers? Why?"

"We can't say too much about an ongoing investigation," Townsend told him, "but we believe he may have some sort of grudge against our guy. What's Ian's last name?"

"Beaumont," he replied. "But he's one of my best guys. He's a war hero, for cryin' out loud."

Frankie's ears perked up. "War hero?"

Jerry scratched his neck. "Yeah. Been in the military for years. Did tours in Afghanistan, Iran and Iraq... I don't understand this at all."

"We need everything you have on him," Townsend said, handing over the warrant.

Jerry took it and gave it the briefest glance before laying it on his desk and going to a filing cabinet against the wall. He opened the top drawer and rifled through some manila folders before locating the one he wanted. He pulled out a folder and handed it to Townsend. "I had no idea, I swear," he said, shaking his head again. "I ran a background check, I interviewed him myself extensively, chased up every single reference – all had nothing but good things to say about him. We work in places with highly confidential materials – like the police departments, the hospitals, the University. I take security and the integrity of my crew very seriously. There was nothing – *nothing* – to indicate this guy was anything other than what he said he was."

"We believe you, Mr. Strathmore," Townsend said. "Trust me, people can be very good at hiding their true natures or motives."

"You did nothing wrong here," Frankie added.

Jerry nodded slowly. "Be that as it may, this is really going to cost me once the public hears about it." He swore under his breath. "Ian freakin' Beaumont, man! Of all people." He sighed. "Let me know if you need anything else, Detectives. I want to help any way I can."

"Thank you, sir, but all we need is to find where Ian may be holding our guy," Townsend said.

"Well, other than what's in his file, I don't know too much about him, apparently. I know his parents are dead; his mom when he was just a kid, and his dad died in '99 or 2000. He didn't talk much about his family. Uh, I think he once said he likes to hunt – or was it fish?" He waved a hand. "None of that helps, though, does it?"

Frankie looked at Townsend. "Actually, it might. Thank you, Mr. Strathmore. We'll be in touch."

"Any time," he said, showing them out.

Once back in Frankie's car, Townsend said, "We thinking maybe he's got a cabin or boat somewhere?"

Frankie started the car. "Pray that it's that easy."

CHAPTER FORTY-ONE

———

<u>Monday, September 1, 2014 12:42 p.m.</u>

Noah's chest hurt. His ribs were bruised from when Ian had to "jump-start" him, meaning his heart had stopped at some point, or his pulse had dropped so low that Ian thought it had. Either was possible with chloroform. But beyond the pain in his ribs was a deeper pain. One that he'd been trying to ignore the past hour. This pain made him more nervous than the ache in his lower back and the fatigue and nausea that told him his kidneys and liver were in the process of shutting down. This pain was different.

It was the pain that told him his lungs were filling with fluid.

This would mean death for him much sooner than his other organ failure, and much more certainly, unless he got medical attention soon. Within the next few hours. And it looked like the only way he was going to get that was to play along with Ian's game. He'd told the story, exactly as it happened, but he had no idea how Ian was going to react. It was possible he would still make him kill Spicer.

What if he stalled, gave his lungs time to fill up and kill him before Ian and Lynn's plan could be pulled off? There was nothing to guarantee Ian wouldn't kill Spicer anyway if he did, though. His only chance would be for both of them to get out together. Noah just had to figure out how.

There were tears in Ian's eyes. He dropped his head into his hands. "That's not what she told me, not how she remembers it." He looked up at Noah, tears sliding down his face. "That's not how she said it happened. You're lying!"

"I'm not lying, Ian. It's the truth. I told you the truth."

He gripped the gun tighter and brought it up to aim at Noah. "You, that girl who called them crazy, the teller who dropped the money and the kid who lunged at him – all of you were working together to get him distracted long enough for you to take him out." He flipped off the safety.

"Stop! Think about what you're saying, Ian! It's not even possible for that to be true. How could we orchestrate something like that? Huh? Donnie was right there watching us the whole time, with a gun – and if you knew anything about being a cop, you'd know we don't make elaborate schemes with civilians to take down armed suspects. Think about it!" He was panting with the effort of speaking like that. "I tried to help Donnie, I wanted to get them both out of there alive. That's the truth. I didn't–" His voice quivered with the pain of reliving that day. "I didn't trick him, and it wasn't a distraction. Just some teenager trying to be a hero, trying to do what he thought was right. The rest, that was just scared people not thinking straight because they were scared. It happens all the time."

He'd never learned the teenager's name – he'd distanced himself from the details and the aftermath of that incident as much as possible – but now he realized it had to have been a teenaged Will Messer. He mentally compared the guy from the bank and the man whose brains had been dashed out on the sidewalk and concluded they were one in the same. The teenaged girl, the one who called them crazy, she must have been Paula Stevenson. If he'd made the connection all those years ago...

"I was going to try to get him to give himself up once the hostages were out of harm's way." *The sharp, smoky smell from his fired weapon...the thick, musky, rusted smell of Donnie's blood slicking his hands.* "It was the only way I knew of to keep him alive."

Ian stared at the gun in his hands. "It took him eight hours to die. Did you know that? *Eight hours.* I didn't even know about any of it until three weeks later. I was in Afghanistan. Donnie's girlfriend finally thought to have the Army inform me." He wiped his eyes with the back of his hand. "They wouldn't let me come home to be with Raelynn because she and Donnie weren't legally family. I didn't even know where Raelynn had been sent for another six months. She was bounced around from one foster home to another before they finally got her committed to the nuthouse. A twelve-year-old girl, and they put her in Twinwood. I wasn't even allowed to see her for years And it was all because," he sniffed and looked up at Noah, his eyes hard. "You. Killed. My. Brother."

"I didn't want it to end that way. I never–" He swallowed, trying to control the quavering in his voice. "I'm sorry he died. I am. I told you: I never wanted that to happen." He had to wipe the tears off his face onto his shoulder.

Ian stood there, pointing the gun at Noah's head. "Do you understand what it was like for us? Having Donnie taken away like that? Do you have *any* idea what that did to us?"

He tried not to flinch away. "Yes. I do. My parents were both shot dead in a convenience store robbery when I was sixteen."

Both Ian and Spicer looked surprised. But Ian didn't remain sympathetic. "Then how could you, man? How could you ruin another family the way yours was?"

Noah closed his eyes and took a breath. Yes, it was happening, he could feel it. He was already short of breath. He had a few hours left, six or seven at most, probably. He wasn't sure how long it would take for him to drown, right there in the middle of that warehouse. The idea should have frightened him more than it did. Mostly, he was just tired and full of regret.

Frankie would take it hard, not finding him in time – if they ever found his body. He hoped his friend wouldn't blame himself. And Spicer...the man may not have been his favorite person, but he was innocent in all this and his family would never understand why this happened to him. And it was all Noah's fault, whether he could ever have foreseen this or not. All this was happening because of what he had done all those years ago.

He opened his eyes. "It was my job. I had to save that boy from being killed."

It was the wrong thing to say. He knew it the second the words left his mouth. Ian closed the distance between them in two quick strides. Noah expected him to hit him again and flinched, but instead, he forced Noah's hand open and shoved the gun into it again. Noah struggled, but Ian was running on pure rage.

"Say goodbye to your friend, Noah. You've just killed him."

"No, Ian, wait! Why did you want Spicer to hear the story?"

He paused. "What?"

"What was the point of having me tell him the story if you're just going to have me kill him now?"

"I just wanted you to admit what you did. How you killed my brother."

"But if I kill Spicer, who's going to know? That was the reason you wanted him alive, right? How will anyone know if I kill him now?"

He grinned. "You're going to tell them. It's going to be in your suicide note."

His heart stuttered. "My–?"

"Oh, I didn't tell you, did I? You see, we had two scenarios: One, you confess to being the One O'clock Killer and Spicer the hero brings you in and you get executed. Option two, if you didn't play nicely, which is where we are now, you put poor Spicer out of his misery and then put one last bullet into your own head. Just like you should have done a year ago."

"How did you know about that?" His voice was a whisper.

"Are you kidding? Man, it was all over the news for, like, *days*, you getting hurt. Who didn't know about–" He looked at him more closely. "Wait, did you–? You tried to kill yourself back then, didn't you?"

Noah couldn't answer. He closed his eyes and began to pray. *Please don't let it end this way, not for Spicer, at least. Please help me get him out of here alive, like I couldn't do for Donnie.*

"You did. What stopped you, huh? Couldn't follow through with it, or you just didn't do a good enough job of it?"

Shame and anger brought a flush to his face. "I don't know what stopped me. I guess God wasn't done with me yet." He didn't know where the words came from.

Ian scoffed. "You got religion, huh? Just in time to save your worthless life." He knelt in front of Noah, avoiding the puddles of sick on the floor. "You know what's so ironic about that? If you had gone through with it, Nigel Warner and Jennifer Sealey would still be alive, and you and your little pal wouldn't be sitting here with me.

How do you like that, huh? Is this what God wanted you to stick around for?"

He was right. What had been the point, if it all led here, to this moment? "Maybe it was so you would finally know the truth."

"Are you calling my sister a liar?"

"She was twelve, Ian, and in need of some serious psychiatric help. I don't have any idea what all she thought happened that day, but she couldn't have processed it the same way the rest of us did." He took another slow breath, feeling the itching pain deep in his lungs. "Just let Spicer go. He'll tell everyone I confessed to killing your brother. He'll corroborate your story. Better yet, he'll tell them I confessed to killing everybody."

He turned to Spicer. "I did it. I killed Nigel Warner and Jennifer Sealey. I killed Will Messer and Paula Stevenson eight years ago, too. I am the One O'clock Killer."

CHAPTER FORTY-TWO

They had just pulled away from Jerry's and Franks was putting an APB out on Ian Beaumont and the white 1998 Ford F150 registered to him, when Townsend's cell phone rang. "Townsend."

"Hey, it's Conrad. I got a hit on some prints from Nigel's wallet. They belong to a Peter Michael Lawrence. Did a stint for armed robbery back in oh-four. I emailed you his BMV photo."

"Thanks, Ward. We're on it."

A raindrop hit the windshield. Then a few more. Franks turned on the wipers as the sky opened up on them, sending torrents of rain down on the city.

"Yep. Hey, listen," Conrad said, "Neil's taking this pretty hard. Are we any closer to finding Noah, you think?"

Townsend sighed. "Tell him...that we won't rest until we've got him back."

Ward was quiet for a moment. "So that would be a no, then, huh?" He let out a slow, heavy breath. "I'll tell him you're doing everything you can."

"Yeah." Now was as good an opportunity as any. "Ward, what do you know about chloroform? Can it be made by someone if they have access to the right chemicals and equipment?"

"Uh, yeah, actually. It's not all that hard, really, but creating it from scratch by the average Joe is gonna get you a junky end-product. It would be harder to get dosages right without killing the victim and the side effects could be a lot more severe than the pure stuff." He fell silent as if realizing what he had said meant for Noah.

"What would he need?"

"A chem lab, basically. A fume hood and some other equipment and the right chemicals – bleach and acetone, chiefly – and a lot of time. It can take up to an hour or more for the right reaction to take place. Oh, and he'd need a gas mask when using it. It's not like in the movies, it's as dangerous to the attacker as the victim." Again, he went quiet a moment. "It's really nasty stuff."

"Okay, thanks. That's pretty much what we were thinking."

"Yep, you bet. See ya later."

"Yeah, see ya." He hung up and turned to look out the window, rolling this all around in his mind as he watched the warehouses and factories roll by, already drenched. Should he tell Franks that it was possible Harkham was already dead? Or that he soon would be from chloroform toxicity, no matter if Ian Beaumont decided by some miracle to let him go?

"What was that all about?" Franks asked.

"Ward got a hit off the prints on Nigel's wallet. Guy named Peter Lawrence." He pulled up the photo. Lawrence was a big block of a guy with a buzz cut.

"Let me see?" Townsend showed it to him. "That's gotta be the guy our High-flyer saw tossing the wallet. Anything tying him to Ian or Lynn?"

Townsend pulled up and scrolled through his record. "No, nothing in his record, but that doesn't mean he isn't. Or that he doesn't know anything that might help. He's probably the last person to see Nigel alive."

"Yeah, as he was mugging him less than an hour before Ian Beaumont killed him. That poor kid," Franks scoffed angrily. "Okay, so we have the uniforms pick him up. What did Conrad say about the chloroform?"

"I...just wanted to make sure we were right about him needing access to the University's chem lab." He looked out the window again. "We were, by the way. Ward said he'd need all kinds of equipment to do it."

"That's good to have confirmed, I guess. We can add theft and criminal trespass to his list of charges.'

Townsend sighed and turned back to his partner. "I'm sorry, that's not everything. I can't yell at you for withholding information and then turn around and do it to you myself. Pull over somewhere."

Franks threw a worried look over at him but slowed down and pulled over into the parking lot of the oyster canning factory. The rain pattered and plinked against the roof of the car, providing a percussive background. He gripped the steering wheel for a long moment once he'd parked, then turned to Townsend. "You're going to tell me he's dead, aren't you?"

Townsend's heart sank at the look on his partner's face. "I don't know that, and you don't either. Nobody does. But...but, yeah, Alan, it's possible."

He expected Franks to crumble, to break under the weight of the possibility. And maybe some part of him did, deep inside, but the rest of him steeled itself with determination. "Possible. But not certain. We could still find him in time."

"Dr. Lee, he said that chloroform was used to incapacitate Jennifer Sealey before Ian Beaumont beat her to death. But he said the dose she'd been given was high enough that she was probably near death before the first blow landed. I'm not saying that's what happened to Harkham – to Noah. But what we do have to prepare for is the medical attention he's going to need to survive the side effects."

Franks twisted his grip on the steering wheel. "Side effects?"

"I looked it up. Severe headache, nausea, vomiting, airway and skin irritation initially. Then liver damage or failure. Kidney failure. Pulmonary edema."

"Pulmonary...that's what?"

"Fluid in the lungs," he said as gently as he could.

"So, he'll drown, essentially."

"Yes. I'm sorry."

He closed his eyes. "How long?"

Townsend cleared his throat. "I mean, I don't really–"

"Twenty-four hours? Twelve? Two? Just a ballpark number, Casey. Just tell me if I should still be looking at this as a rescue or a – a recovery operation." His voice trembled.

"I think probably less than twelve, but a lot more than two is fairly accurate."

"And we've already lost," he glanced at his watch, "five hours." He hit the steering wheel with his palms three times, then leaned his forehead onto his left hand and his elbow against the car door, his fingers shoved into his hair. "And any more time we waste trying to find Ian and Lynn is only going to put him closer and closer to dying."

"But it also brings us closer to finding him."

"Marginally." He lifted his head, his eyes lighting up as a thought struck him. "Everything they've done so far has been a mix of smart caution and ignorant recklessness. They've been careful about fingerprints and DNA and trace, but Ian didn't seem to care that he'd be on tape going into Noah's office and apartment building. Guess he thought no one would be able to tell he wasn't just in there to clean. Lynn took advantage of the run-in with Noah and Jennifer Sealey to secure the bloody mug pieces to plant on Jennifer but didn't know her story about how that all happened would be blown out of the water by Walter's sneaky surveillance cameras. How much do you want to bet that they weren't smart enough to map out a route to wherever they took Noah that would avoid traffic cameras? Avoiding surveillance is their biggest, maybe their only weakness."

Townsend started dialing his cell phone. "I'll get Tyler on it."

Franks put the car into gear and pulled out of the parking lot. "I still have a feeling we're missing something to do with December of 2000."

"Maybe." Something tugged at his memory. Then it clicked. "No, definitely. Ah, why didn't I put it together already?" He hung up his cell phone and put a hand to his forehead.

"What?"

"You are absolutely right. Remember when I told you Harkham had killed someone in the line of duty?"

Franks nodded, looking at him with puzzled expectation. "Right, the bank robbery thing?"

"It happened on December fourth, 2000. He walked in on a bank robbery in progress. It escalated into a hostage situation. The guy got amped up and was about to shoot one of the hostages, so Harkham had to drop him before he could."

"Okay, but that was on the fourth, Neide said the girl at the bus station said the fifth."

"The suspect didn't die on scene. He died over eight hours later at the hospital – at twelve fifty-eight in the morning."

"Which is pretty much one o'clock."

"Exactly." He dialed the A/V lab again.

CHAPTER FORTY-THREE

Townsend was poring over the file from the bank robbery case while Franks was sitting on the A/V lab, going over the feeds from the handful of traffic cams across the city. The suspect Harkham had killed had been Donald Andrew Peters. But what really caught his eye this time was the fact that he hadn't been alone when he held up the bank. There was a note that his little sister, Raelynn Peters, had been with him.

The official statement that Harkham had made said that the girl showed signs of mental instability and that the suspect claimed he only needed the money to get her help. He had told the bank teller he only wanted thirty grand. Harkham argued this supported the idea that he was doing it out of desperation, not basic criminality.

He switched away from Harkham's account to the more complete report filed by the senior investigating officers and IAB. He flipped a couple of pages until he found the list of witnesses and hostages. Halfway down the list, he knew without a doubt that the cases from 2006 and now had their origins in that bank that evening in 2000.

Hostage name: William Messer, seventeen

And then, a few lines later:

Hostage Name: Stella Stevenson, sixteen

A cross-reference check confirmed that Stella and Paula Stevenson had been sisters. And, from the BMV photos he compared, they were nearly identical, even if Paula was two years older. It had just been mistaken identity. It also explained why a standard search wouldn't have revealed any connection between Will and Paula.

But maybe Meares did figure it out. The note Franks had been so sure was the key to all of this had said 'CMB, 2000 – connection?" CMB...City Mutual Bank. He just died before he had a chance to do what Townsend was doing right now. And Harkham never knew to look for a connection between the two cases.

But wouldn't Harkham have remembered Will's name? His face? Wouldn't the Stevenson name have struck a chord with him from that day? How could he have not connected the dots for himself?

And then he saw the bombshell:

Hostage name: Jennifer Sealey, twenty-three – bank teller

Had it been a coincidence that she ran into Harkham at the shop? He remembered seeing her talking on her cell phone just seconds before colliding with him. He pulled up the footage and watched the encounter again and again, paying close attention to each player in turn from start to finish.

What he had failed to notice the first time he watched it before showing it to Harkham was that Lynn didn't charge Jennifer for her food and drink. The money that Lynn handed to her wasn't change because Jennifer never gave Lynn any money in the first place. A payoff? To what? Set up the run-in between Harkham and Jennifer in front of witnesses so people would say he had a motive for killing her? As if such a small sleight would have triggered the man to commit murder.

Why hadn't Harkham recognized her? Hadn't she recognized him? If so, why would she go along with running into him? From the reports, Harkham had saved lives that day, including hers.

And who had she been talking to on the phone right before it happened? Lynn was with a customer, so it had to have been Ian. How on earth had he convinced Jennifer to stage the run-in – that it was just a harmless prank?

He shook his head. Too many questions and too few answers. This was all great for background and motive, except it didn't have anything to do with Lynn or Ian.

Or did it?

He flipped back through until he found the photo of Raelynn Peters. It had been taken at the hospital less than half an hour after her brother had been shot right in front of her. There was evidence that she had been crying at some point, but at the time of the photo, her expression was empty, devoid of emotion.

I've got all the time in the world, Detective. Not sure the same is true for your guy.

The look Lynn had given him was almost identical. He did the math. She was the right age. Raelynn Peters...Lynn Hopkins. They *had* to be the same person.

He delved into Raelynn Peters' history from that night on. She had been put into the foster system while the courts decided what to do with her. One side of the issue argued that she was an accessory to the crime and should be charged. The other side argued that she was just a child, and one with severe mental issues, so should be treated. She was bounced around between three different foster homes in as many weeks before a formal psychiatric evaluation was ordered.

The diagnosis was schizoaffective disorder. The District Attorney's office decided not to file charges against her, instead recommending she be committed to Twinwood Institute, a psych ward on the outskirts of town, until the age of eighteen. A chill washed over him when he saw who had signed off on the waiver of charges, even though it came as no surprise.

Gerald Warner's tight, slanted signature practically leapt off the page.

And with that one piece of information, everything began to make sense. Twinwood Psychiatric Hospital, as it was now called, had come under intense investigation a few years back after former inmates, as they were termed at the time, were able to bring to light the inhumane conditions and treatment they had experienced during their stay. If Raelynn Peters had gone to Twinwood at the age of twelve, she would have been a legal adult in 2006, and would have been released. What horrors she experienced while there, he had no idea, but he wasn't too surprised to see that she had been involuntarily recommitted to a different psychiatric care facility called the Fisher Institute in January of 2007, after being picked up for verbal and physical assault of a homeless man.

Reading further, he saw that she'd been released from that second facility eighteen months ago. He nearly spilled his coffee when he looked up the Fisher Institute's website and saw the care team photos. The third in the list, after Dr. Jeremiah Fisher and his co-founder and brother Dr. Martin Fisher, was Dr. Michael Coates.

He noticed the website hadn't been updated since 2012. Would Dr. Coates still work for them? He picked up his cell phone and dialed Neil's number. The criminalist picked up halfway through the first ring.

"Did you find him?"

"Ah, not yet, no. Sorry. I just need to ask you a question."

"Okay."

"Does your dad still work for the Fisher Institute?"

"Uh, no. It closed down toward the beginning of 2012. There was some sort of feud between the brothers who founded it and they dissolved their partnership. Dad went back to private practice exclusively after that. Why are you asking about this?"

"It came up in connection to some background info we found." Townsend did a map search for the address of the Institute and saw that the building was now being used as a drug rehab center. There was no way Harkham was there, then.

"For the guy who took Noah?"

"For someone who we think helped the guy who took Noah. We think they're working together."

"Okay, is it relevant enough to help you find him? I can give you dad's number."

Townsend smiled at the offer of help laced with the not-so-subtle recommendation that if this line of inquiry was even remotely a waste of time to move on to something else. "That would be great, actually."

Neil rattled off his father's number and signed off. Townsend then called Michael Coates.

"Hello?"

"Doctor Coates?"

"Yes. Who's this, please?"

"Detective Casey Townsend."

"Did you find Noah?" The question came fast, worry etched in the timbre of his voice.

"Ah, no, sir. Not yet. I–"

"Is Neil all right?"

"Yes, sir. He was the one who gave me your number. Listen, I'll cut to the chase: do you remember a patient named Raelynn Peters at the Fisher Institute?"

"Ah, Detective Townsend, I'm sure you'll appreciated that I can't divulge information about any of our patients."

So, he does remember her. "I do. But I have reason to believe she is directly involved in Noah Harkham's abduction."

"How? What on earth–?"

"I can't really explain it all now. As you can imagine, time is of the essence. All I need to know is if you can think of any place that has significance to her, any place they might have taken him?"

He sighed. "I wasn't her doctor. I was told there may be a conflict of interest with her case, so I kept my distance. I was just a consultant at the Institute, for the most part, because I specialize in mood disorders and the Institute was aimed more toward those with behavioral and social disorders. I didn't see her much."

"Did you know what the conflict was?"

"No. I asked not to. If I did have to interact with her at all, I didn't want to subconsciously treat her any differently than the other patients." He paused a moment. "How will any of this help with finding Noah?"

"Did you have photographs of Noah anywhere she may have seen them? Or did you ever talk about him? Was he ever there with you?"

"Did I–" He took an audible breath and let it out slowly. "I had a couple of photos of the whole family, Noah included, in my office, yes. And...let me see...I think he may have stopped by to meet me for lunch in the early days."

"Early days?"

"I started working there in 2007. I wanted to branch out from just private practice. My boys would sometimes meet me for lunch. But my schedule eventually got too erratic to make that feasible."

My boys. Noah was almost as much his son as Neil... "Thank you, Dr. Coates. That helps. Do you know who her doctor was? I don't need to know anything privileged, I just need to know where to start looking for Harkham. I know who has him, but that doesn't tell me where they've got him."

"It would have been one of the brothers. I'm sorry, I don't know which one. I only remember the girl at all because she's the only patient I've ever been told I might have a conflict of interest with."

"Well, sir, when this is all over, I promise to tell you why that was. Right now, though, I've got some calls to make."

"Of course. Uh, Detective Townsend?"

"Yes, sir?"

"Please let me know when you find him. I– I need to know when he's okay."

"Of course, sir. Thank you for your help." He hung up and ran a search for contact info for the two Doctors Fisher.

He found Martin Fisher's number first. But when he called it, it went straight to voicemail. He left a brief message asking for a call back, then went on to get Jeremiah's number. Before he could dial the other Dr. Fisher, a call from Franks came through. "Yeah, Townsend," he answered.

"I think I have something. Meet me in the precinct parking lot in ten?"

"All right. I have something, too. Turns out the guy Harkham killed in that bank robbery had his little sister there with him. Seems she had mental issues and he needed the money to get her help. She saw him get shot."

"She was there? Geesh. What happened to her afterwards?"

"Twinwood until 2006, then the Fisher Institute, where – get this – Michael Coates worked part-time. She was released eighteen months ago."

"So, she sees Noah or his picture, whatever, in Michael's office and decides to get revenge on him for her brother's death? How do the victims fit in?"

He filled Franks in on the connections between Will, Paula, Jennifer and the bank robbery, and Gerald Warner's part in all of it. He also shared his theory about Raelynn Peters and Lynn Hopkins being the same person.

"Well, we definitely have the motive figured out," Franks said. "But now the question is, how does Ian Beaumont figure into all this? And is Raelynn/Lynn the killer, or is Ian?"

"Or both?"

"Either way, I have it narrowed down to a two-mile area of town where they're holding Noah. Dockyard Row. I'm almost back to the precinct, I'll pick you up. Do either of them have ties to the docks?"

He opened a database and did a search for any property in their names besides their currently listed addresses. "Nothing that I'm seeing so far, but I'll keep looking."

"Great. See you in a few."

Once Franks hung up, Townsend put in the call to Jeremiah Fisher. After identifying himself to the doctor, he got straight to the point. "I know you can't divulge anything privileged about your patients, Dr. Fisher, but Raelynn Peters is involved in the abduction of one of our officers. I need to know if she has any ties to any place in the dockyards here in Riverdale where she and her partner may have taken him."

"Oh..." he took a moment that felt like a year as Townsend waited. "I think I can answer that."

"Really? Great," Townsend said, grabbing a pen and paper.

"Well, no, not great, because the answer is no. No, there is nothing significant about the dockyards to her, as far as I can recall."

"Oh. All right. Thank you for your time, Dr. Fisher."

"I'm sorry I couldn't be more help, Detective." He paused a moment. "Wait, you said she and her partner..."

"Yes. Does the name Ian Beaumont mean anything to you?"

"Ah, yes. Ian. He's sort of her stepbrother. Their parents were never married. She spoke of him often. He was a soldier, the Army or Marines or whichever branch. He was her hero."

Never married. That's why the connection didn't turn up. "Did she say anything about Ian and Dockyard Row? Or the port itself?"

"Uh... It seems like there was something, now that you mention it. Maybe his father worked in the area? Or he did? I'm not really a hundred percent sure. Sorry."

"That's okay. That might help. Thank you."

"You're welcome. Oh, and Detective?"

"Yes?"

"If you'd like, I would be more than willing to come speak with her when you bring her in. I may be able to get her to cooperate."

"We'll call you. Thank you."

They signed off and hung up as Townsend made his way down to the parking lot. Franks was just pulling up and within seconds they were on their way to the docks. Again. To think, they had been in that area earlier today without any idea Harkham was nearby...

Several patrol cars were also speeding off ahead of them. None had their lights or sirens on, though. "I thought we might need backup," Franks explained. "I've got six units meeting us there. Dark, so we don't spook them."

Townsend was accessing a property records database on his phone. Franks glanced over. "Got anything yet, or will we need to canvass the docks when we get there?"

"I'm looking into Beaumont's father's history. Raelynn's doctor says his dad may have worked somewhere in the area."

"Worth a shot," Franks said. "There are a lot of empty businesses in the area, though. It could be somewhere random."

He nodded but kept looking. At first nothing matched up, but when he went further back, he saw that Richard Beaumont – Ian's dad – had worked at a small factory in Dockyard Row for seventeen years. A simple Internet search showed that the company had shut down five years ago and was in limbo with a lawsuit tying up the company's assets.

"Got it. 3407 E Water Street. The old Reston chain factory."

Franks radioed the address to all responding units, reminding them to proceed without lights or sirens and to wait for them before entering the premises. Time seemed to crawl, or the city seemed to stretch out, because it took forever to get back to the area. Townsend eyed the clock: it was almost four p.m. Noah would most likely have already started suffering symptoms of pulmonary edema by now, if the chloroform had caused it. And if he was still alive. They would be cutting it extremely fine if he was, and even if they found him right away, there was no guarantee he would survive.

Their radios sputtered. "2262, 2914, be advised we are receiving incoming transmission from 3119's radio, on the distress channel. In your vicinity. Pinpointing location. Stand by."

"Copy, Dispatch. Please identify 3119?"

"Officer Andy Spicer, sir."

Franks looked at Townsend. "Spicer?"

CHAPTER FORTY-FOUR

———

<u>Monday, September 1, 2014 1:39 p.m.</u>

Ian's elation had shown itself as a terrible, burning glow of triumph in his eyes. But it was short-lived. Only moments later, he had grown sullen and had withdrawn to sit on the crate once more. Noah and Spicer exchanged a look.

"Did you hear what I said? I confessed. You've won."

"I know I've won. There was never any doubt that I would."

"Then—"

"You're done talking."

He was worried about Lynn, Noah realized. Or, the fact that she hadn't been there to witness their triumph had hit him and maybe now he was uncertain how to proceed without her. Noah worried that Ian would abandon all pretense of a plan and just shoot them both in the head and dump their bodies somewhere.

"Ian—"

"I said you're done talking. We're all done talking for now."

He had taken the gun and left the room, leaving Noah and Spicer to wonder what was going to happen to them now. He had stayed away long enough that Noah hoped he'd left the premises completely, but he soon discovered that wasn't the case. Ian had returned with a small cooler in one hand and an open soda can in his other.

Noah's eyes had zeroed in on that can. He was so thirsty. But Ian had just taken the cooler up onto the crate where he'd been perched before and brought out a sandwich wrapped in a plastic baggie and a cup of mixed fruit. He seemed to take enormous pleasure in eating and drinking in front of them. Noah had just hoped that he'd screw up and leave something behind that would have his DNA on it. But no, he'd very carefully eaten his meal and put all his trash back into the cooler.

"You know," he had said, "you could write up a handbook out of that notebook of yours and call it, 'How to get away with murder and frame other people.' Granted, it might only cater to a niche audience, but I'm sure you could make a lot of money off it. It certainly has been useful to us."

He'd refused to take the bait, refused to get riled. He was concentrating on not coughing. The itching pain in his lungs was slowly intensifying, feeling more and more like a band constricting around his chest. Maybe four hours or less to go. He wished he could write something, some sort of last will and testament or statement to tell his family and friends he loved them. He'd never been good about saying that to people and hoped they knew it anyway.

Almost an hour had now passed since his confession. What was Ian waiting for? He'd said he didn't need Lynn to finish this – so why wasn't he finishing it?

Ian's cell phone beeped. He dug it out of his pocket and read the message. A huge grin spread over his mousy features. "Looks like I won't have to see this through on my own after all. Raelynn will get to join us all very soon. Just like I expected."

So that was it. Ian had known somehow that Lynn would be released. Noah's heart sank; if Frankie and Townsend had had to let Lynn go, it meant they couldn't prove her connection to his abduction. If they couldn't prove her connection, they didn't know where he was.

And since they didn't know where he was...

I know this is a big ask, but I'm asking for a miracle here. At least let Spicer get out of this okay. Please. I don't expect you to bend over backwards for me after everything, but the kid had nothing to do with any of this. He deserves better.

Noah licked his dry, chapped lips. His head was still pounding, his nose and throat still burning. He was starting to feel ill again, too, which was probably as much from his kidneys and liver as from the chloroform. If it weren't for Spicer, he'd probably give up and provoke Ian into killing him now and getting it over with. As it was, he couldn't see any hope, even if they did get a miracle and he survived the day. What would happen after that? Days, maybe weeks in the hospital, for what? All so he could go back to the same pointless existence he'd been living.

Ian glanced up from the text he was composing. "I'm giving your good news to my sister now." He sent the text. "That's all I wanted, for you to take the blame. It was my idea to frame you, you know. Raelynn wanted you 'utterly destroyed,' her words. Took some convincing to get her to see it was the best option. Framing you would strip away everything you'd worked for, make you lose everyone you'd ever cared for, and in the end, you'd still die by lethal injection. She finally came around, but this has been eating at her, the waiting and planning. She wanted to find you the moment she got released and rip you apart with her bare hands." He chuckled. "She still might, when she sees you sitting there so helpless."

"Believe it or not, I understand that," Noah said. "If I had a chance to be in the same room with the man who killed my parents, I don't think I'd waste a single second."

"Ooh, so there is blood-lust in you, after all," he said with a grin. "And here I thought you the type who becomes a cop because you really want to help people. Turns out, you're a different kind of cliché. So, what would you do, if you had the chance?"

"I won't ever get the chance. He killed himself on scene just after killing my parents and the store clerk. He never even got to leave with the hundred and eighty-nine dollars from the register. The hundred and eighty-nine dollars he felt three innocent lives were worth."

"Wow, you're quite the tragic hero, aren't you? Does this poor, tragic orphan bit get you laid a lot? I bet it does. Chicks eat this sort of thing up." He grinned conspiratorially, like they were old buddies swapping conquest stories.

"I don't talk about my parents. With anyone."

"You're talking about them a lot with us."

"That's only because I wanted you to understand that what I did, I didn't do lightly. It was the hardest thing I'd ever had to do. If Donnie hadn't forced me, I never would have shot him. Especially not in front of Raelynn."

"You want me to feel sorry for you, is that it? For how my brother made you kill him? Oh, you poor thing." He cocked the gun and aimed it at Noah's leg. "Maybe young officer Spicer here gets one lucky shot off before bringing you in."

"Well, if he did, it would be with his gun, not that one, which I'm guessing is Donnie's that you somehow stole from the evidence room."

"Good eye, Detective. Oh, ha! Pun intended. But you're right, of course. That pretty little ballistics tech would see right through that. What's her name? Rachel? No, Robin. That's it. You know, I had considered snatching her up at some point and having some fun with her before putting her down. But as much as that would hurt your stoic little cousin, it wouldn't make much sense for you to do her like that."

He waved a dismissive hand as he got up and walked toward the door to the next room. "I mean, we could've made it work. Jealousy of their relationship, something along these lines. I mean, she is pretty hot for a science nerd."

Once he was out of sight, Noah turned to Spicer. "You hanging in there, Spicer?" The younger cop nodded, but his eyes were full of pain still. "I don't know how yet, but we're going to get you out of here. You heard him say maybe you get a lucky shot off before bringing me in – I think he's decided to go with option A again, now that he's gotten what he wants from me. Okay? So just hang with me a little longer, all right?" Spicer nodded again, closing his eyes to let a tear fall down his face.

Ian came back with Spicer's Beretta. "Now, should we have a little tit for tat, a little fun before the big hero moment?" He went to Spicer. "You a lefty or a righty?"

Spicer flicked a glance at Noah, then raised his right hand as much as his bonds would allow. Noah thought back to whenever Spicer raised his hand in class...and then grinned inwardly at what the cop was doing. Now, whatever happened to him and Noah, Spicer had just given the techs one more clue to put together the truth. He had paid some attention to his teaching, after all.

Ian placed the gun in Spicer's hand. The officer looked at Noah apologetically and mumbled something behind his gag.

"It's okay, Spicer. It's going to be okay." He braced himself for the impact and pain, but the sound of Ian's text alert made everyone freeze.

Ian made a frustrated sound and pulled the gun back out of Spicer's hand. He looked at the message on his phone and sighed. "Well, boys, looks like our little game will have to wait. Little sis is a bit upset that she's been left out of the festivities and wants us to wait 'til she gets here to have any more fun."

Noah let out a sigh of relief. Spicer looked like he could weep. Another new message alert chimed. Ian read this one as well, his expression becoming troubled. He wrote a quick reply and sent it.

"Something wrong, Ian?"

He looked up. "Nothing to worry about. Just a little delay, is all."

"Delay?"

"Just means we get to spend a little longer together than originally planned." He twirled the Berretta on his finger. "Too bad she doesn't want me putting any more holes in anyone in the meantime." He eyed Noah as if thinking of disregarding his instructions.

"What happens when Lynn gets here? I mean, you've got my confession, that means you're going to have Spicer bring me in, charge me, right?"

Ian grinned, a nasty, mean smirk. "You mean as opposed to the murder-suicide route? Relax. I'm pretty sure she'll want to stick with the original plan and send you to prison."

Thinking back on Raelynn's expression that day in the bank, he wasn't too sure about that. "I'll have to plead guilty, avoid a trial, you realize that, right?"

"What are you talking about? The trial is part of the plan. Your public disgrace and downfall and all that."

"But any decent lawyer will be able to get me acquitted. Hate to break it to you, but you shot yourselves in the foot by abducting me. There's no way anyone will believe I left of my own free will. If it goes to trial, you'll lose."

"You staged your abduction. You tried this whole time to make it look like you were being framed so no one would suspect you really were the killer. But you ran into Spicer somewhere along the way, and you were going to kill him, too, but you couldn't stand the guilt any more. So, you turned yourself in instead."

The prosecutor could make that play. Noah definitely had the knowledge and training to pull that off. Ian regarded him with a smug look as he thought it all through. "Okay," Noah said, "that could work."

"Oh, it'll work. And know this: if you're thinking that you can agree to confess now and recant later to save yourself from Death Row, you need to get that out of your head right now or there will be consequences."

"I won't, I swear."

"Good. Because if you ever try to go back on this, if you ever try to send the cops after us, I will track down everyone you've ever known, let alone cared about, and I will end them. And if that doesn't convince you to follow through, we'll start with random people you've never even met, until you finally learn to keep your promises."

Let's just work together and I promise to get you both out of here safe. Noah nodded. "I understand. I won't recant. I'll take the fall for all of it, just like you said. But *you* promised that if I did, Spicer will live. You have to keep that promise, too, or the deal's off."

"Deal?" He laughed. "This isn't a negotiation. There is no deal here, no agreement or transaction. His staying alive depends on you, just like it has from the beginning. You don't do what we say, he dies and so does everyone you love. That goes for the whole process, right up to the day they execute you."

A chill crept over him, but he could only nod his acceptance. Ian started to walk away but turned back. "Oh, and by the way, go ahead and settle in. You're getting about a two-hour reprieve. I suggest you start rehearsing the details of your confession. You'll want to make sure it's believable, or else–" he pointed the gun at Spicer and made a *grrrkk* sound as he drew one finger across his throat. Then he winked and walked away.

CHAPTER FORTY-FIVE

———

Two hours had come and gone, near as he could tell, and his body felt every minute of it. It had started to rain about fifteen or twenty minutes ago, the pattering staccato on the roof sounded almost peaceful. Ian hadn't left Noah and Spicer alone for a single moment, but was sitting on the crate against the wall, often catnapping. During those brief respites, Noah had tried to break the zip ties that held his wrists to the arms of the chair, but it was no use. Ian had used three for each arm and Noah didn't have enough energy or strength left to break them.

He next tried to slip his hand through the zip ties, since there was some slight give for when Ian wanted him to hold the gun. He got it part of the way, but his hand was too wide to go any further, no matter how he tried tucking in his thumb or maneuvering his fingers. He'd even tried forcing it, willing to sacrifice whatever skin he'd lose, but all he accomplished was making himself bleed. Spicer had tried the same, with similar results.

All the while, Noah's condition continued to deteriorate. The ache in his back was now constant and sharper, and his nausea and fatigue made him feel worse than that time he got food poisoning from bad clam chowder. Worst of all of this, however, was that the pain and heaviness in his chest was spreading. He was at the point where he could no longer breathe deeply and felt like he needed to cough when he tried. He kept his breathing as shallow as possible, so Ian wouldn't notice something was wrong. But breathing like this was starting to make him light-headed. Plus, there was a rattling deep inside with each breath, no matter how shallow. He tried to focus on freeing his hand and ignore the slow death building up inside him.

Eventually, Ian seemed to notice his attempts to break free. He hopped down off the crate and examined the restraints. "I suppose you had to try once," he said, tightening the remaining zip ties, "so I'll let it slide this time. But if you try to get free again, you and Officer Spicer will regret it."

Ian left him and began pacing in a slow circle, periodically checking his phone. Maybe something had happened, and Townsend was able to pick Lynn up again. Maybe Tyler was using her phone to track Ian's. Maybe–

The sound of a motion sensor alarm broke the long silence. Noah's heart attempted a leap. Frankie and Townsend had found them. They were going to be all right.

Ian took the gun and climbed a stack of crates against the far wall under the grimy window. He peeked out, gun ready. A moment later, he grinned and put the gun in his pocket. The sound of a motorized door opening somewhere, like a garage door, echoed through the building. Ian climbed down and went to open the door between this room and the next.

Lynn walked in. She looked just like she always had at the coffee shop, although this was the first time Noah had seen her in clothes other than her Jumping Beans uniform. She wore a thin, long-sleeved black shirt and dark maroon trousers. No one would notice right away if she had his or Spicer's blood on her.

She and Ian hugged once the door was shut behind her. "Do you have everything?"

She scoffed and patted the purse hanging from her shoulder. "Diego didn't have it ready when I got there, but after some persuading, he agreed to hurry things along."

"You didn't hurt him, did you?"

"Not for long," She shrugged, tossing the purse up onto the crate Ian had been perched on. "I put him out of his misery before I left."

Ian sighed. "What if we need him later? Dammit, Raelynn, you need to think these things through."

"Watch what you say to me, Ian," she snapped, her voice cold and dangerous. "Diegos are a dime a dozen anyway."

"Not of his caliber."

"I know what I'm doing." She turned away from him, and then froze when she saw Noah and Spicer.

Her expression hardened, and she pushed Ian out of her way and approached Noah. The look in her eyes made his sluggish heart race like he was a cornered rabbit and she was a fox about to devour him. "You," she said, not much more than a whisper, "broke your promise."

He could see it now: the little girl behind this woman's face. The same brokenness and cold, consuming hatred deadened her eyes now like it had when the cops carried her away from her brother's body that day.

"Raelynn, I—"

She sprang at him, knocking his chair backwards onto the hard, concrete floor. His head smacked the floor despite his efforts to tuck his chin in and he was dazed for a moment. Her fists buffeted his chest, and she snarled as she clawed at his face. There was nothing he could do; he couldn't fight her off with his hands bound, and a part of him didn't even want to. If she killed him now, it would all be over. No more pointless half-existence, no more watching from the sidelines as his dreams drifted further and further out of reach. Her face was inches from his, the hurt and fury in her eyes boring into him. She wrapped her fingers around his throat and smiled as she squeezed the breath from him.

Finally, Ian pulled her off and Noah was able to gulp in a breath. Ian had to keep his arms around her until she cooled off. "Enough! Didn't you get my message? He's going to confess. He's going to go to jail for everything, just like we wanted."

She was still throwing looks at Noah that rivaled those of any predator, but her body had gone slack. She brushed her sort of step-brother's arms away from her and turned to face him. "Like you wanted. I want to pull him apart with my bare hands."

"Raelynn, we agreed that if he died, it had to look like suicide to sell the story. But isn't this better? Didn't we agree this was the better option? He goes down for all four murders and they throw him in prison. Do you know what happens to cops in prison? And after all that, we get to see them stick the needle in his vein. All the misery and humiliation and ruin we could ever ask for and he still ends up dead. How is it not the best ending?"

She remained silent, staring at Noah lying helplessly on his back, gasping for breath. The fluid had moved around in his lungs with the sudden change in position and he couldn't hold back any longer. A coughing fit ripped through his body. Great, tearing coughs came one right after another for a full minute before he could regain some control.

Ian came over and righted the chair, which only made Noah sick again. He lurched forward as far as he could and heaved, but there was nothing left in his stomach but bile. He sat there, hunched forward and slack in his bonds, riding out the wave of misery, desperately trying to draw in air without coughing.

Lynn sneered. "Clean that up. Clean all of it up. This place reeks."

Ian's expression darkened, but he went through the door to the next room. He was gone several minutes, and Lynn spent the whole time pacing in front of Noah and Spicer like a caged beast. She suddenly stopped, her attention focused on Spicer. "Idiot," she said, shaking her head. "No one is going to believe you took him down with a bullet in your knee..." She knelt and checked his bandages, grumbling to herself. "I'll have to come up with something...as usual."

When she was done, she stood and faced Noah. "Why agree to confess? You'll only end up dead anyway, and your whole life, your name, everything you worked for will be ruined. Of course, that suits me just fine, but why would you agree to it?"

He had to take several slow breaths before he trusted his voice to answer. "What else could I do? If I don't, either Spicer and I or everyone I love dies. Besides," he said, panting, "you're right: this is all my fault. If I hadn't walked into that bank that day, I never would have had to kill your brother and you never would have had to fend for yourself in Twinwood. Alone...scared... You never would have killed Will Messer and Paula Stevenson, or Nigel Warner and Jennifer Sealey."

Her eyes narrowed as she considered his answer. Ian returned with a bucket of water and a mop. She stepped aside so he could clean the messes up. It didn't take him long to get it mostly washed away, but every moment felt like an eternity as Noah struggled to breathe without coughing up a lung.

"What's wrong with his face? It looks like he got burned."

Ian made a dismissive gesture. "It's from the chloroform. It does that sometimes."

She gave him a steely glare. "I *thought* we agreed you weren't going to use that on him after the screw up with the Sealey chick."

"Well, *you* got yourself picked up by the cops and I had to grab him alone. It was the only way I could do it."

"We can compare notes on who screwed up the most later. But for now," she said, turning to Noah, "sell it to me."

"What do you mean?" He was beginning to wheeze. Calm down...slow breaths...slowly...don't cough...not yet.

She wiggled her fingers in a 'come on' gesture. "We're that puppy dog of an ex-partner of yours and his creepy new partner. Tell us why you killed all those poor, innocent people." She pulled a pout.

Noah's mind felt mired in mud. It was hard to think through the pain and lightheadedness. "If...if Paula hadn't called you and your brother crazy, maybe I could have talked him into letting everyone go. And Will...if that little piece of shit hadn't tried to tackle him, I would never have had to shoot him."

He cleared his raw, scratchy throat. He was trying to recall confessions from past criminals he'd arrested, trying to find a motive that Townsend might buy. "Nigel was to hurt Gerald. He let the man who took my career, my *life* away from me get off with just a slap on the wrist. I lost *everything,* ending up half-blind, half-deaf and teaching a bunch of idiot cops who couldn't care less about what I've devoted my whole career to. And Jennifer...she just made the whole thing start going sideways by dropping the money, which wasn't even enough, and upsetting him – and then she had the audacity to call me a jerk when *she* ran into *me*? I saved her life – I saved everyone in that bank – by doing the most horrible thing I've ever had to do... a thing I was forced to do because of her and the others. It was their fault, their fault I had blood on my hands...and, since I was already tainted, what was a little more blood? Why not punish the ones who had caused me to murder a guy who was barely more than a kid right in front of his little sister, scarring her and me? I probably would have killed them all if Spicer hadn't stopped me."

Ian stopped mopping and stared at him. "My god, I believe him, and *we* did it." He chuckled giddily.

She gave Ian a small smile but turned her leaden glare back at Noah. "Almost. Almost, but not quite. You may have your own reasons to hurt Gerald Warner, but that doesn't fit with being the One O'clock Killer. No, you're going to say that you recognized me the first day you saw me working at Jumping Beans and it brought that whole ordeal back to you. You talked to me, apologized for ruining my life. I tried to forgive you but couldn't, and after I told you about the years of abuse – physical, emotional and sexual – that I endured at Twinwood, where the benevolent Gerald Warner saw fit to send me, you couldn't forgive yourself, either."

She began pacing again. "You have the part about getting your revenge on Will and Paula because you couldn't live with the guilt and anger of what you'd done right, and that you killed Nigel and Jennifer, would have killed the rest, to try to make it up to me because you were going crazy with guilt and needed my forgiveness."

She stopped pacing and leaned closer to him. "And when they ask you why you stopped with Will and Paula all those years ago, you are going to tell them it's because Rob Meares worked out that you were the one who killed them. And the guilt of being forced to kill your mentor, your partner, your *friend* was too much to live with. You retreated, mentally, and buried the memories so deep you actually convinced yourself that you didn't know who the One O'clock Killer was and let the case go cold."

Noah's throat constricted with emotions he didn't even know the name of. "But Rob– Rob died of heart failure." His voice was barely audible.

"You're the forensics expert, you know there are ways to mimic that."

Ian clapped his hands together and rubbed them vigorously. "Oh, this is *good*. This is *very* good, sis." He set aside the mop.

"I– I can't– not Rob, please. I'll say anything else you want, but please don't ask me to say I killed Rob." Tears pooled in his eyes.

She grabbed the revolver out of Ian's waistband in less time than it took Noah to blink. She pointed it at Spicer, who flinched and made muffled sounds of panic behind his gag. "I'm not asking," she said coldly. "I will kill him now unless you say it. Say, 'I killed Rob Meares because he figured out it was me. But then I couldn't live with myself, so I repressed the memories of being the One O'clock Killer.' Say it!"

He couldn't breathe, and not just from the fluid filling his lungs. "I– I killed Rob– Rob Meares because he figured out I was the One O'clock Killer. I couldn't– couldn't live with myself, though, so I repressed the memories of ever being the killer." He closed his eyes as the tears poured down his face.

She laughed, that bicycle horn laugh that made a river of ice slide down his spine. "Excellent," she said, gleefully. "Yes, now you are *exactly* where I want you to be." She stepped forward and straddled his lap, putting her arms around his neck and caressing his spine with the barrel of the gun. She put her mouth to his ear. "I bet you want me dead now, don't you, Noah?" She nipped his earlobe with her teeth.

He shivered. "No, not dead."

She sat back and looked at him, her brow drawn down over her dark blue eyes. "Really? I would've wanted me dead a long time ago, if I were you."

"You need help, Raelynn. Real help. You owe it to Donnie."

She hit him with the gun, in the same spot Ian had. "You don't get to say his name! Ever!" She screamed this just like she had screamed as a child inside the bank. "And what? You think I should go back to *Twinwood,* is that it? You think I deserve to be beaten and raped by the people who were supposed to keep me safe and get me sane?"

"No," he said, testing his jaw to make sure she hadn't broken anything else. "Nobody deserves what happened to you. I'm sorry you had to go through that." Shallow breaths...keep calm.

"You're sorry. Oh, well, that's okay, then. Let's just call this whole thing off and everybody gets to go home." She pressed the muzzle of the gun between his eyes. "You can shove your 'sorry,' Noah Harkham. I don't want to hear you say how sorry you are. I want to hear you being sentenced to death and then I want to hear your last breath as they put you down like a rabid dog."

He swallowed as well as his parched throat allowed, fighting the panic of another gun in his face. "I know you do," he said, panting. "And I get it. Believe me, I understand. But what then, Raelynn? Will my destruction, my death give you peace?"

"As long as you end up rotting in the ground like my brother, yeah. Yeah, I'm pretty sure it will."

"I hope that's true...for your sake." He felt that bottomless hopeless feeling again. "I know you don't believe me, but I am sorry for killing your brother...and I hope, someday, you will be able to forgive me... I want you to know, if I could go back, I would do everything I could to stop it."

"That's easy for you to say. But it doesn't change a thing. Donnie is still dead, and my life has been hell, all because of you."

There was a moment where time seemed suspended, during which he could see Raelynn consider pulling the trigger anyway. He looked her in the eyes and tried to brace himself for it. He was a dead man anyway, what difference would it make if it ended now or in a couple hours?

"Raelynn, please," Ian said, his voice quiet and careful, like Donnie's had been all those years ago. "It will ruin everything if you kill him like that now. Everything we've worked for, we have it – we just need to follow through with the plan. We're so close now, please."

She pushed Noah's head further back with the gun, but then lowered the weapon to point at the floor. "You get to live, for now. But I will *never* forgive you." With her face still close to his, she whispered, "And don't for a moment think all of this is because of my... illness. I keep my appointments and I take my meds, like a good girl. I know *exactly* what I'm doing. How else do you think we've managed to pull this all off?" She gave him a cold smile, then got off his lap and returned to Ian's side. "Let's get this show on the road."

Ian nodded. "I'll get Noah, you take Spicer, then."

Noah's pulse tried to quicken again. "Get? What do you mean? Where are we going?" There was no way he could hide his condition if he had to walk far. He was exhausted, and it took every ounce of willpower to keep from coughing. They would know immediately that something was wrong with him; it was happening too quickly to conceal much longer.

Ian came up to him with a pocket knife. "Don't worry about it. Now, hold still or she will kill Spicer if you try anything."

"I told you, Ian: you've won. I'm not going to fight this."

Ian paused and stared at him a long moment. Then he cut the zip ties holding Noah's hands and feet to the chair. The skin on his wrists was more sliced up that he realized, and his circulation, which had been constricted some before, resumed its arduous flow, making his fingertips tingle and blood ooze out of the cuts.

"Get up."

Noah stood slowly, using the chair to support his weight until he could trust his legs to hold. *Now would be a great time to throw us a rope,* he prayed. *I– I can't do this on my own. I need You. Please forgive me for all the years I hated You, blamed You... Please, don't let my arrogance and anger cost Spicer his life.*

Raelynn helped Spicer to his feet. He groaned, and his left leg buckled, but she caught him and supported his weight. As she forced him upright, Noah noticed Spicer still had his radio clipped onto his belt. The handset mic that was usually clipped on near his shoulder was missing, but the base unit itself was still there. The young cop gave him the barest hint of a wink. He'd done something with the radio while doubled over to get them help.

This kid is smarter than I ever gave him credit for.

"Come on," Raelynn ordered, pulling Spicer toward the door.

They didn't bother with securing their hands again; their conditions and the revolver in her hand and the Beretta in Ian's were enough to ensure their full cooperation. Ian force marched Noah to the door leading out into the other room and had him open it. Noah walked through and found himself in a garage-like area that served as a loading/receiving dock for whatever business this place had been. Inside was a white Ford truck, a beat up maroon Oldsmobile – and a patrol cruiser.

"All right, Spicer, in the front," Ian said, gesturing his gun between the cop and the cruiser.

"Relax, Ian, he can't do it on his own. Thanks to you," Raelynn mumbled. She brought the wounded officer to the driver's side of the patrol car and opened it. He looked at her uncertainly for a moment, but when it was clear she was helping him get into the car, he went along with it.

She took off his gag. "Can you drive with your leg like that?"

He ran a tongue across his lips. "I think so. But, where am I going? I don't even know where we are right now."

"You'll know when you get outside," she answered. "And you're driving back to the precinct."

"You're letting us go?"

She sighed. "Haven't you been paying any attention at all? You get to be the hero today, Spicer! You've caught the notorious One O'clock Killer, at tremendous personal peril, nonetheless. You'll get more medals than you'll know what to do with."

Ian shoved Noah to face the car's open back door. "Put your hands behind your back and hold still."

Noah did as he was told, and Ian put Spicer's cuffs on him. He felt it again, but worse than before. The urge to cough, his body's desperate attempt to purge itself of the fluid that was killing him, was overwhelming. He couldn't fight it any longer and gave in to a coughing fit that doubled him over. He had to brace himself with one shoulder against the cruiser to keep from falling. Hacking, wheezing coughs tore from him, leaving the taste of blood in his mouth.

Ian smacked the back of his head. "What's the matter with you? I said hold still."

Noah ignored him, immersed in his own world of agony. The more he coughed, the more it felt like he was drowning. He couldn't catch his breath and his brain kicked into panic mode. He tried to slow down and drag in a shallow, ragged breath, only to cough it back out – along with a large glob of bloody, thick fluid.

"What did you do to him?" Raelynn shouted.

He could hear Spicer calling out to him but couldn't respond. He couldn't do anything but cough up more bloody fluid and try to breathe. His eyes and nose were running, he was flushed and sweating. But he was cold and tired, too. He was incredibly tired.

"Nothing! I just handcuffed him and he started having a fit." Ian sounded panicked. He tried shoving Noah through the open car door, but he was too slumped and unresponsive for that to work. "Just get in there," Ian ordered.

Raelynn had already hit the button to open the overhead garage door and was coming around to see what was going on with him. She looked at the blood he was coughing up and grabbed him by the hair. "What's happening to you?"

Noah took a wheezing, shaky breath. "Do you want... to know why... they stopped... using chloroform?" He coughed again, feeling more blood burbled up into his mouth. "It has... a nasty habit... of killing the people... you use it on." He started to laugh, but only coughed up more bloody liquid and added it to what was already on the floor.

She growled out some vile sounding but mostly unintelligible profanity and released him. "This is your fault," she said to Ian. "If this goes south on us because of you, I swear you'll regret it."

She ignored Ian's sputtered protests and went around to the driver's side again. Grabbing Spicer by the arm, she hauled him out of the driver's seat and dragged him around to the rear passenger side. She pressed the revolver to Spicer's throat. "Get in the car or I kill him now."

Noah tried to stand up straight, but without the use of his hands, he had trouble balancing. "I'm getting in," he said, leaning heavily on the open door. "Please don't... hurt him."

More coughing doubled him over, choking up more of the fluid in his airway. He spat out another clotted glob and then panted for several seconds.

"Move it!"

"I... just... need a... minute." He fought to get air without triggering more coughing and took a few shallow breaths. But then the fit seemed to be over, leaving him exhausted and wheezing, his head swimming. "Okay... I'm okay..." He tried once more to get into the car, but only managed to go from leaning on the door to dropping to his knees.

"This isn't going to work," Raelynn said, practically snarling at Ian. "He'll die before he ever gets to confess. And even if he doesn't, there's no good way to explain his condition." She was quiet a moment. "We'll have to go with Plan C instead."

"Plan C? We don't have a Plan C," Ian said.

"You take Spicer and follow me."

She shoved the wounded cop at her almost step-brother, then grabbed Noah by the arm and dragged him toward the open overhead door. The rain pelted his body, soothing his sweat-drenched skin. She stopped in the middle of the empty gravel parking lot, with Ian and Spicer right behind.

"Uncuff him," she said.

Ian used the handcuff key to free Noah's hands, slipping the cuffs into his back pocket. "Now what?" he asked. "Besides us getting drenched."

"Cut off Spicer's bandages." She motioned the gun toward the cop, keeping a firm grip on Noah's arm

Ian did that, too, and then turned to her for further instructions. She grabbed Noah's hand and pried it open, slapping the revolver into it. "Now," she told Ian, "put that gun in Spicer's hand and shoot Noah."

"No!" Spicer tried to pull away from Ian, but he rammed his knee into the cop's wounded leg. Spicer cried out and stopped struggling.

Ian forced the gun into his right hand and pushed his arm upward. Spicer gritted his teeth and tried to resist, but Ian rammed his knee into the bullet wound again until he complied. Raelynn held Noah up, bringing the gun in his own hand up and aimed to a point just to

Spicer's left and above his shoulder. Noah was too exhausted to even try to fight her. *This is it, this is how it all ends.*

He wasn't sure if the thought terrified him, saddened him or was a relief.

An almost tangible calming presence surrounded him, and a scripture he didn't even remember reading came to mind: *Fear not, for I am with you; be not dismayed, for I am your God; I will strengthen you, I will help you, I will uphold you with my righteous right hand.*

Spicer was fighting tears. "Please don't make me do this."

Ian grinned. "Do what? Your job? Be a hero?"

"He didn't do anything! Don't make me kill him."

"It's okay, Spicer," Noah wheezed. "I'm dead either way... At least this way... will be quick." He attempted a smile.

"See? He doesn't mind, and you'll probably get all sorts of medals. Plus, Raelynn and I get to go live brand-new lives far away from here." Ian chuckled. "It's a win-win-win-win."

"If you don't shoot him now," Raelynn warned, "and keep to the story that he confessed to being the One O'clock Killer, I'll personally hunt down everyone you have ever known and loved and kill them. Same deal as we gave him, only for you now."

Vaguely, Noah became aware of movement out of the corner of his eye. Ian and Raelynn noticed it about the same time and turned toward the small factory building where he and Spicer had been held. Noah nearly wept when he saw Frankie and Townsend. Everyone started shouting, a confusion of chaos and orders to drop weapons swirled around him from both sides.

Raelynn grabbed Noah around the waist, holding him up in front of her and putting the revolver to his head. She inched them both closer to Ian. He was now only able to take the shallowest of breaths and was seeing stars in his dimming field of vision. If it weren't for Raelynn holding him up, he would have collapsed. Lynn shifted the aim of her gun toward Spicer instead of Noah suddenly.

"Raelynn, don't," Noah begged. "It doesn't have to end like this."

"Remember this, Noah," she whispered into his ear. "This is what happens when you break your promises."

He used the last bit of strength he didn't even know he had to break free of her and lunge sideways to knock Spicer to the ground.

Above them, shots rang out.

He heard a *whump* and saw Raelynn's body lying on the ground by his feet. "No," he moaned. *Not her, too.*

Ian was crying out her name. He was on his knees near Spicer, with Townsend cuffing his hands behind his back.

"Hark! Talk to me. Are you all right?"

It was Frankie. Frankie was really there. Noah tried to push himself up onto his hands and knees, but he was so weak and lightheaded from lack of oxygen. He tried to reach for Frankie's hand as he knelt next to him but collapsed onto his back instead.

He couldn't get a breath. He was going to drown.

So tired... he didn't want to fight anymore. He was dimly aware of Frankie trying to help him sit up, but all he wanted was to close his eyes and sleep. Finally sleep.

The last thing he was aware of was a sensation almost like free-falling, and someone saying his name.

Then–

Nothing.

CHAPTER FORTY-SIX

———

<u>Monday, September 1, 2014 4:02 p.m.</u>

Franks looked at him. "Spicer?"

Townsend shrugged, and the Dispatcher continued the transmission. "10-20 verified: 3407 East Water Street, same as target. Proceed with caution. Over."

"Copy, Dispatch. Out." Franks said his radio down and sped up, weaving through traffic. He had to flip on his siren for a moment a couple of times to clear a path, but as they approached the old factory, he and the other units all approached silently.

They got out and commanded the uniforms to spread out to check the windows and doors for any sign of Ian, Raelynn, Noah or Spicer. He and Franks took the front door, rain pelting them, and had the officer with them, Reynolds, use bold cutters on the chain securing it. The door itself was locked as well, so Franks used a lock pick to open it quietly.

He made sure Townsend and Reynolds were in position before opening the door. They walked into a small lobby with reception desk. Dust and dirt filled the air and covered every surface. There was no sign anyone had been in this room for a long time. They cleared the area and proceeded toward a set of double doors behind the reception desk.

Officer Adelmo spoke on the two-way, his voice coming in quietly through the radio's earpiece, affectionately termed an earwig. "Pole cam spotted movement in the rear of the building, southeast quadrant. Looks like a warehouse. Standby...target sighted. He's alive."

Townsend heard Franks let out a short sigh of relief. He stopped the others at the double doors. There was a panel of grimy glass in each door, and Franks checked the field of vision through each. "It's clear."

Adelmo continued his report. "I got eyes on four warm bodies total: target, two suspects and a second hostage. A uniformed officer, likely 3119. They're moving east out of the main warehouse toward another sector."

"Unit 6, fall back to our position," Franks ordered. "All other units, hold position on north and south walls. Stay out of sight. Units 1, 2 and 6 are going in behind suspects. Everyone, try to maintain the element of surprise to not jeopardize hostages."

A chorus of voices acknowledged the orders. The three of them waited a moment for Cox and Adelmo to catch up with them, then Townsend opened one of the two double doors. It slid open just as the rattling sound of an overhead door opening filled the air.

"They're leaving," Townsend said.

Franks pulled open the second door and they all rushed through into the abandoned factory's manufacturing floor. They ran through the plant, dodging derelict machines and equipment to a single door set into the east wall. There was no window inset to this door, so Townsend opened it cautiously.

It led to the warehouse. A stack of crates nearly blocked their entry and they had to squeeze past to go any further. He could hear voices and someone – Harkham – coughing somewhere ahead, and he and Franks halted the other officers. Townsend crept ahead, around another stack of crates and got a glimpse of the center of the room.

He clenched his teeth, not liking what he saw.

He gestured for Franks and the others and they all moved past the two metal chairs set facing each other. Then they passed the blood and partially mopped up vomit to another single door in the east wall. The sound of rain was louder now, and Townsend hoped it would mask their approach.

He couldn't hear Harkham coughing anymore.

That could either be a good thing, or a very bad thing.

They entered what appeared to be a receiving bay. Three vehicles were parked inside: Ian Beaumont's white F-150, a junked out maroon Olds, and what must be Spicer's cruiser. The cruiser's driver's side and rear right passenger doors stood open.

There was some sort of bloody fluid on the floor by the rear passenger door. They eased in further until he could see Ian Beaumont with a bleeding Officer Spicer, and Lynn Hopkins – Raelynn Peters, he corrected himself – with a very ill looking Noah Harkham standing out in the parking lot. The two pairs were facing each other, and Ian was forcing a gun into Spicer's hand and aiming it at Harkham.

But then Harkham noticed Townsend and the others. A beat later, the suspects spotted them as well.

"RPD! Drop your weapons," he ordered. The rest of the team issued orders for the suspects to stand down and drop their weapons as well.

"All units, close in," he heard Franks order. "Ian Beaumont, Raelynn Peters, drop your weapons and get on the ground. Do it now!"

Raelynn and Ian shouted their own orders back as the pair regrouped, using Harkham and Spicer as human shields. Once the other units formed up to flank them, Ian apparently decided the odds were stacked too high against him. He dropped his weapon and held up his hands.

Before Spicer could get clear, Raelynn turned her gun to his head, though she kept a firm grip of Harkham. Franks took a few steps forward and again shouted at her to drop her weapon. She said something in Noah's ear, then turned her head to solidify her aim at Spicer.

"No!" Townsend yelled.

"Don't do it!" Franks ordered.

They couldn't risk it, Harkham was in the line of fire. But he somehow broke free of her and lunged sideways, knocking Spicer out of harm's way.

Franks fired three shots. Raelynn squeezed off one round before dropping to the ground.

CHAPTER FORTY-SEVEN

———

Noah was running, the cold wind stinging his cheeks and pulling his breath to stream behind him like a dragon stoking up his fire. The tree loomed before him and, as he reached it, he threw his gloved hands up, grabbing hold and pulling himself into the notch between the main branches of the trunk. He kept climbing and soon found himself higher than the house he'd just escaped.

He'd never been up this high alone. It was scary up there, but his anger and hurt made him go even further up the slender branch. Besides, he was six now. He didn't need anyone's help. Especially not Daddy's.

Far below he could see Daddy chasing after him. "Noah, please stop running from me! Noah?" His father stopped and turned in a circle, not seeing him yet. He cupped his wind-chapped hands around his mouth and shouted. "Noah! Where are you?"

His grip slipped on the branch and his heart pounded with fear. He wanted to call out to his father to come get him down, but he was still too angry at him to ask for his help. But then his father looked up and saw him, his eyes going wide.

With a tremble in his voice, he said, "Noah, don't move! I'm going to come up and get you."

"NO!"

"Please don't move, Noah. Just stay still."

"Go away! You took her away! I hate you!" He shouted, while angry, shamed tears poured down his face. He'd never spoken to Daddy like that.

His father was at the base of the tree now. "Noah, please listen to me. I didn't take her away. Your grandmother, she– she had to go to Heaven, son. She's with God now."

He was sobbing now. "But why?"

His father was crying, too, he could see. The cold sunlight made the tears shine on his face. "Because– let me come get you down and I'll– I'll try to explain."

But Noah was already trying to climb down on his own, though he only got part way before his foot slipped. His hands were wrenched from the tree branch and he fell. Screaming, he saw the branch get further and further away as he rushed toward the ground. He squeezed his eyes shut. But, instead of hitting the frozen earth, he was suddenly in his father's arms.

"You caught me," he said, awed by the near superhero action.

His father hugged him close. "Oh, buddy, I would never let you fall." He lowered him down to stand on the ground and cupped Noah's face in his hands. "But please, don't ever run away from me again. I was so worried about you."

"I'm sorry, Daddy."

His father was surrounded by a bright, warm light, and the hands cupping Noah's face were strong and warm, no longer shaking and cold.

But then his father was no longer there. Instead, sixteen-year-old Noah knelt before two graves: his father's and his mother's. Unbearable grief weighed down on him, and the only way he knew to fight it was with bitter anger. Its heat spread through his body, burning his cheeks.

"Why?" he asked in a hateful whisper. "Why them?"

Behind him, a man stood silently with a hand on Noah's shoulder. There was a light that seemed to come from within and around the man that obscured his features. It gave the impression that the man was both more and less substantial than his surroundings.

Oblivious to this presence, Noah pounded his fists on the ground. "They were good people. They loved You – why did You do this to them? To me?"

The man moved closer, placing both hands on Noah's shoulders. "I know you are hurting, my son. But they are safe. They are with me."

"They loved you," Noah said again, through his tears.

"And they loved you. You can be together again."

"You took them from me," he sobbed, his forehead touching his hands clutching the loose dirt covering his parents. "I will never forgive you."

"Regardless, I will never leave you."

"I hate you," he whispered.

"I love you."

"I hate you!" Noah screamed into the air and pounded the ground with his fists again.

The man hugged him while he wept. "I love you my son. I will always love you."

Now the tears that spilled down Noah's face were for another fallen father figure, another lost family. The moment he had entered the hospital waiting room, he knew Rob was dead. Bonita Meares clung to him, sobbing. He held her, unable to find words to lessen the horrible pain losing Rob had caused them.

The man was there with them again. He wrapped his arms around them both and held them close. In his heart, Noah cursed coldly. *How could You? Haven't You taken enough?*

The man placed his hand on Noah's face. "I love you, my son. I will never leave and will comfort you, if you let me."

I will never forgive You.

"I will be here. I will wait for you. Always."

And now, now Noah was one of five officers surrounding Bobby Avalon. The drunk and high former boxer raised his gun, pointing it at Adelmo's chest. Noah was closest and shouted a warning as he tackled Avalon, knocking him to the ground. Again, the same man was there, and he place one hand on Noah's face and the other on Avalon's hand. When the gun went off, the bullet grazed the back of the man's hand instead of entering Noah's skull. It injured Noah instead of killing him.

And when Noah was lying on the grungy carpet in that rundown apartment, in the fiercest physical agony he'd ever known, the man knelt and placed his hands on either side of Noah's head, shushing him. "It will pass, my son. The pain will pass. I won't leave you. You will get through this."

He pressed his lips to Noah's forehead. Unconsciousness took him and temporarily released him from the agony.

———————

Then one night – that night when it had all become too much to bear – when death seemed preferable to the constant misery and the loss of everything that made him who he was, the man was there. He sat on the couch next to Noah, his arms around him, asking him to listen to Frankie, to give him the gun.

"I have wonderful things in store for you, my son. The way won't always be easy, but I will make you strong and I will hold you in my hands. My grace will sustain you. But you must choose to accept it. You must choose to come back to me. I will always be here. Please, stop running from me."

———————

Now Noah was back in the warehouse. He knew he was dying, could feel the slow drowning. He knew, too, that Spicer would die unless Noah gave Ian and Raelynn what they wanted, and, at that point, it was an easy bargain to strike. If he survived long enough to confess, he would die soon after, or he would be killed in prison, so it really didn't matter.

But when he could feel how fast his death was approaching, could no longer hide that he was dying, he feared Spicer would die then, too. *Now would be a great time to throw us a rope,* he prayed. *I– I can't do this on my own. I need You. Please forgive me for all the years I hated You, blamed You... Please, don't let my arrogance and anger cost Spicer his life.*

The man was there, too, just as he had been in all the other moments. He placed a hand on Noah's chest. "You *are* forgiven, my son. You will live; it is not yet your time. You still have a purpose to fulfill, though this part of it will be difficult for you. Know that I am here and will walk before you to guard your path."

―――――――

Noah found himself walking on a wide, rocky dirt track. His feet were bare and bleeding, his nostrils choked with dust. He was covered in the filth of the road and was weary beyond belief. He felt beaten, nearly to the point of death. Part of him wanted to take another step further down this road, but another part told him to turn around, he was going the wrong way.

Can I go back? Or am I too far gone down this road? But he thought back on what the memories – or whatever they were – had showed him, of the presence that had been with him through the worst moments of his life. He had begged Noah to stop running, to choose to come back.

Noah stopped.

He turned around.

The man appeared before him. He was as radiant as before, and the cleanness, the *pureness* of him made Noah feel ashamed of his unclean state. But the man threw his arms around him and rejoiced at their meeting.

"My son."

"Please, don't– I'm filthy. You'll get dirt all over you."

The man laughed, not in mockery or scorn, but in delight. "I have had the filth of the world placed upon me and have overcome it. Look, it is not I who am sullied, but you who are made clean."

And Noah looked and saw that what He had said was true. The dirt of his journey was washed from him and carried away on the wind; his broken and bloody body was restored to wholeness and the weariness and pain were lifted from him. And he was awed.

The man took his hand and walked with him, along another path, one that was green and beautiful, though narrow. It led them to a place that was familiar to Noah, one that filled him with sorrow and bitterness. It was the cemetery where his parents were buried, except now, Rob's grave lay next to theirs. There was a headstone for Noah as well.

Pointing to the graves, Noah turned to the man. "Why did You bring me here? Did You think I needed reminded of everything I've lost? Of everything you took from me?"

"Loss is inevitable; the flesh of this world is not meant to be permanent. But the perfected body of the world beyond, that is eternal. Your parents and your friend, their story here was done, but they are now with my Father. You can be reunited one day."

"But why, why take them from me? Why did I have to go through so much of my life alone?" Grief and bitterness poured out of him in a stream of tears.

"You were never alone. I have never left you. You have been surrounded by people who love you. They are all here now, pouring out their love for you. You will meet many more in the future who will love you, as well."

"You want me to go back, then, is that it? Back to a life that was meaningless and hollow?" Anger still seethed inside him. He'd lived with it so long, it was hard to let go.

"Noah, hear me: the meaning was there, but you chose not to see it. You are hollow because you tried to fill your soul with meaningless things. You tried to define yourself by the wrong things. You are not merely a cop or forensic scientist, and you are no less you if these are taken away. Nor any less when your sight and hearing were diminished. Your life had not ended, though you chose to see it that way." As He said this, the gravestone bearing Noah's name vanished. "You are my Father's creation. There is more to you, to your life. Let me fill the hollowness. Let me guide you and you will know life full and rich."

"But after everything that's happened... how can You... I hated You for so long. But in all those... memories, You were there the whole time. Why didn't I know it then? If I had..." he shook his head, shamed tears falling from his eyes. "And why would You want to help me, after everything?"

"You hardened your heart against me, so you could not feel my presence. But I never left you. Just as your father pursued you when you ran from him in anger, I have pursued you. Just as he caught you when you fell, I will always catch you. My son, you are everything to me. I will always want to help you."

He wrapped his arms around Noah, and he felt his anger melt away into shame. "My God, forgive me."

He laughed in delight. "Oh, my son, I already have."

Noah wept, but with joy now as the weight of bitter grief lifted from him. But there was something still troubling him. "I don't understand what's happening right now, though," he said, stepping back to look around. "These graves aren't even in the same state—where are we? Am I dead?"

"No, Noah, you are not dead. But neither are you fighting to live. I told you before that I have great things in store for you. It isn't your time yet. You need to wake up."

The darkness that had engulfed him these last few months was still there. "But I still feel the... *bleakness* waiting for me. I don't know what it is, but I don't want to face it again. *Please,* can't I just be done? I'm so tired and I miss them too much. Please, I can't do this anymore."

"That's because you've been trying to do it alone. But you don't have to. I will carry you. Let me guide you out of the darkness that ensnares you." He cupped His hands around Noah's face once more. "There is more for you. Be at peace, Noah. Let me lift your weariness away; let me be your strength."

Noah closed his eyes a moment. When he opened them, he said, "All right. I'm ready."

"Then breathe, Noah." He blew a pure, soothing stream of air that Noah inhaled deeply.

The breath entered his lungs, bringing new life to every part of his body. He fell to his knees and bowed his head to the ground. And there, in the dirt of his parents' graves, Noah Harkham relinquished his bitter anger and reclaimed his faith.

When Noah opened his eyes, He was gone, and Noah was no longer in the cemetery.

He was back, in a hospital. And more than that, he could see. With both eyes, he could see.

He should have been overjoyed by that fact and by the encounter he'd had, and a part of him was. But the darkness was still with him, just as he feared, making him feel guilty and ungrateful. These conflicting emotions roiled inside him and he put his hands to his face and wept.

CHAPTER FORTY-EIGHT

———

<u>Friday, September 5, 2014 2:33 p.m.</u>

"We're going to try removing the ventilator, now that his lungs are clear," the doctor told them. "We'll see how it goes, if he tries breathing on his own. The dialysis helped his kidneys and his liver function is improving, though I'm afraid there may be some permanent scarring. I'm hopeful that this will be minor, though."

"Can we see him?" Helen Coates, Noah's aunt, asked the question on everyone's mind.

"Let's see if his lungs will be able to do their job first. We may have to hook him back up again. I'll let you know when and if he's where he can he receive visitors."

"Thank you," Frankie told him.

Four and a half days had gone by since they'd found Noah at that factory. In that time, he'd only been allowed to see Noah briefly twice, and both times he'd been asleep. He hadn't regained consciousness at all yet. The doctors said he wasn't exactly in a coma, but he wouldn't wake up, either. *It's like he's just not fighting*, one doctor had said.

Given his mental state before his abduction, this news didn't come as complete a shock to him as it had to some of the others. Over the last couple of days, Frankie had discussed it with Noah's Uncle Michael, who indicated that he believed Noah was suffering from both PTSD and major depression. He'd said Noah had occasionally had bouts of depression ever since the day his parents were killed. He'd never been officially diagnosed, because he refused to see any of the psychiatrists Michael had suggested he see.

These bouts had always been short-lived and mild, so Noah had shrugged off any of Michael's offers to talk it through. He'd always been obstinate about not wanting anyone to analyze him, but he'd at least listen when Michael tried to help him. But once he'd lost his sight and hearing on the left side, Noah had shut down any and all attempts to get him to talk about how he was feeling.

All Frankie could do now was wait and hope his friend somehow found something to hold onto that would bring him back. He wasn't exactly a faithful Christian, but Frankie did believe in God. He'd been talking to Him a lot the last few days on his friend's behalf.

Frankie, Neil, Robin, Michael, and Helen all waited in the ICU's family waiting room for the next half an hour. Townsend had stopped by earlier to show his support and to update Frankie on the case against Ian Beaumont. Because he had shot and killed Raelynn Peters, Frankie had had to undergo an Internal Affairs review and hadn't been allowed to work the case until it concluded. He'd been cleared of any wrongdoing, and they even commended him for helping save the lives of Noah and Officer Spicer.

They told him he could go back to work once he'd seen the department shrink, which he had. But he still couldn't get the images out of his head; he'd put in for a leave of absence that was granted without question.

Once Ian had dropped his gun and surrendered, and Raelynn shifted her gun toward Spicer, Frankie knew she was going to pull the trigger. He couldn't risk a shot with Noah in the way, and helpless frustration raged through him. But, somehow, Noah had gotten free of her and pushed Spicer to safety in time for Frankie to take the shots that brought her down.

He replayed it in his mind over and over again. The look of fiery hatred on her face, then, as the bullets entered her body, how that fire snuffed out along with her life. There was a spray of blood that the rain caught and washed away. The sound of her body hitting the gravel would stay with him forever.

His hands began to shake now just thinking about her again. He balled them into fists and tucked them under his crossed arms. Just like in the aftermath of the Turner Heights fire bomb last year, where he'd gotten burn scars on his arms and chest, he knew it was going to take time and more sessions with Dr. Frazier before he'd be able to sleep at night. If Hark pulled through this, Frankie hoped he would finally talk to someone, too.

Robin saw the doctor approaching first and alerted the others. He came in and gave them a puzzled look. "He's breathing on his own. That's the good news. But he still hasn't woken up. That's what concerns me. I'm hoping that maybe if he hears your voices again, it will trigger something." He shook his head. "His brain activity is normal, very active, so we know something is going on in there. But... he just doesn't want to come back yet."

"But we can go in now, though, right?" Frankie asked.

"Yes, you can go in. No more than two at a time, and try to keep it brief. His body has gone through quite an ordeal and needs rest, but I would really feel better if he woke up first. I know that sounds paradoxical, but..." He shrugged.

"No, we get it," Neil assured him. He looked at Frankie. "I think you should go in first. He might respond better to you, after... everything that happened."

Frankie asked everyone if they minded, which they didn't, before following the doctor back to Noah's room. He'd have never asked himself but was glad to be the first one to see him today. If he did wake up, Noah might have questions the others wouldn't be able to answer. Besides, Frankie would need to call Townsend and have him come take Noah's statement.

Just like he had the last few days, Noah looked like he was sleeping. Frankie hoped that's all it was; from what he'd been saying, he'd barely slept at all the last few months. But if the doctors were worried, Frankie knew he had to try to wake Noah up.

He sat in the chair next to the bed, listening to the steady rhythm of the heart monitor. The EEG showed a bunch of wavy lines. He wasn't sure what that meant, but the doctor had said his brain was active. He figured that was a good sign. "Hey partner," he said. "What are you doing, huh? You've got everybody worried."

There was no response. He leaned forward and grasped Noah's arm. "Listen, Hark, you're safe now. Okay? Spicer's safe, too. You saved his life. So, you really need to wake up now."

He waited, but nothing changed. "Please, Hark. Don't just... give up like this, okay? Don't make what I–" His voice choked up. "Don't make what I did be for nothing." He sniffed. "I know it's completely selfish to say that, but I don't care. If you die, you'll have made me kill a girl for nothing and I won't let you do that."

There was a soft knock on the door. Frankie sniffed and looked up to see Joyce Collins peeking in through the doorway. "I hope you don't mind," she said, coming in a shutting the door behind her. "They told me there could be two of us in here at a time. I can't stay long, so they said to come on back."

"Of course," Frankie said, getting up to give her a hug.

She held a small bunch of sunflowers in a vase, which she placed on the window sill. "For when he wakes up," she said, taking Noah's hand in hers. "He told me once his great grandfather had grown up on a sunflower farm. He said they were one of his favorites." She smiled up at Frankie. "How's he doing, honey?"

"They can't figure out why he won't wake up."

She rubbed Noah's hand between both of hers. "He will. When he's done."

"Done?"

She nodded. "He's been wrestling with a lot of anger, a lot of guilt, and a whole lot of doubt. It takes time to wrestle with God, but when he's through, he'll come back to us." She smiled. "Just wait and see."

"What if he...doesn't?"

"Oh, I wouldn't worry about that, baby. I've known Noah Harkham a very long time and I know that in his heart, he loves God and has a lot to live for. He just has to be willing to let go of some things before he can move forward with his life. It was the same with my Danny, you see. They're an awful lot alike in some ways."

"Did he ever let go of it? Your husband."

"Yes, but only toward the end. But," she smiled again, "he did find peace." She held out one hand to him and he took it in his own. "And Jesus said to them, 'Why are you afraid, O you of little faith?' Then he rose and rebuked the winds and the sea, and there was a great calm."

She leaned down and kissed Noah's forehead. "I'm praying for you, baby. For Him to calm that storm in you." She then stood and squeezed Frankie's hand. "And how are you faring, honey?"

He managed a smile. "I'll get there."

"Yes, you will. I'm praying for you along the way, too."

"Thank you. That... that actually means a lot right now."

She squeezed his hand one more time and, with a glance at the clock, said, "I'll leave you with him now. I just wanted to check on my boys."

Frankie walked her to the door and hugged her again. "Thanks for coming by. If he can hear us, I think he'll be glad to have heard your voice."

She kissed his cheek. "Take care, Alan."

"You, too, Joyce."

When she was gone, he turned back to Noah's still form. He had hoped to see some change, but there was nothing yet. "I have to go now, Hark. Your family wants to see you, too. But please, please try, okay?"

He turned and, just as he got to the door, he heard a slight increase in Noah's heart rate. He looked back to see Noah turn his head toward the window.

"Hark?"

Noah mumbled something but went quiet again. Frankie watched for another minute and was just about to leave when Noah took a deep breath. He shifted his position and brought his hands up to cover his eyes. He lay like that for a moment, and Frankie realized he was crying.

"Noah?" Frankie called out quietly.

Noah sniffed and turned to him. "Frankie?"

He grinned broadly. "Yeah, buddy, it's me." And then, without really knowing why, he asked, "Where have you been?"

Noah looked at him with a strange expression. "I don't think you'd believe me if I told you."

Remembering Joyce's words, Frankie went back to sit in the chair. "Try me."

CHAPTER FORTY-NINE

———

<u>Tuesday, September 9, 2014 9:20 a.m.</u>

Noah was sitting in a chair putting on his shoes when Neil arrived, tapping his knuckles on the door as he entered the hospital room. "Hey," he said, "glad to see you out of bed again."

Noah smiled. "Yeah, good to be out of it." He tied off his shoelaces. "You know, it's ironic. Before all of this happened, I couldn't sleep more than a couple hours a night and would've given anything to be knocked out. Now, I feel like I've slept my life away."

Neil reached out a hand and helped him to his feet. "You haven't missed much. The trial won't start for another month or so and there hasn't been much else going on. No major crimes, anyway."

"But I missed Nigel's funeral." Noah let Neil help keep him steady as he made his way out the door. He was still a little shaky and tired quickly, but the doctor told him he should make a full recovery, other than some minor scarring on his liver that would need monitored.

"The Warners understood." They made their way down the long corridor. "Gerald said to tell you he hopes you make a quick recovery. They wanted to come see you here, but the press has been swarming this place. And their house."

"The press? What do they want here?"

"Are you kidding? Everyone wants to interview you and Spicer. What happened in that warehouse is national news."

354

Noah frowned. "How is Spicer? I tried to see him a couple times, but he was always in PT."

"He'll be fine. Thanks to you, he says."

"He's the one who got the distress call out," he said as they got to the nurses' station, where he signed his discharge papers.

The nurse insisted he be escorted out of the hospital in a wheelchair, despite his protests. "Protocol is protocol," she told him, so he relented.

She wheeled him to a side entrance by radiology, rather than the main exit. Once outside, Neil helped him to his SUV, which he'd parked out of sight of the main parking lot. Noah got in, and once they'd circled through the lot, he could see Neil hadn't been exaggerating. The place was crawling with reporters and news vans, waiting for him to exit the building.

He frowned again. He wasn't sure how to feel about their interest in his case. He certainly didn't feel like a hero of any kind, nor did he feel like he was a victim whose story of survival could help anyone else. He just felt blessed to be alive and wanted to put the whole thing behind him.

He also felt guilty and confused. Even though his encounter while he was unconscious had given him hope of getting better in the future, he still felt the oppressive black cloud hanging over him. He was still irritable and emotional but felt less and less like he was going to fall apart. *Yeah, definitely not hero material.*

"Hey, do you mind if we make a stop on the way?"

Neil glanced over at him. "No. Where?"

"The cemetery? There are a few people I need to pay my respects to."

He nodded. "Of course. But..."

"But?"

"I'm not supposed to tell you this, but there are some people at your place to welcome you home. Family, friends, people from work."

Noah sighed. "Seriously?"

"Yeah, man. It's a big deal, you surviving. People are glad you're okay and they wanted to let you know that."

"And I appreciate that. It's just...I'm not good with parties. Especially not for me. You know that."

"I know," he said, turning onto the road heading toward the cemetery. "But this one time, you're gonna just have to get over it. We're happy you're alive, Noah. Let us be."

Noah went quiet a moment, his throat tightening up. Eventually, he said, "Thank you. And thank you for telling me and not letting it be a surprise. I'm not sure anyone would have liked the reaction I'd have had if I'd been taken off guard, after everything..."

"That's one reason I told you." They were stopped at a red light. Neil gave Noah a sympathetic frown. "You've been through a lot the past few years. I don't know how you've kept it together as long as you have."

Noah shifted in his seat. "I still don't have it together, Neil. I'm not sure I ever did."

The light changed and half a block later, Neil pulled onto Cemetery Drive. He parked his SUV by the main entrance, where there was a directory of grave site locations. Noah went into the little shelter that housed the directory and flipped through the laminated pages inside the large red binder. There were scraps of paper in a little wooden holder; a pen was chained to the holder.

Noah looked up the sector, row and plot numbers of four names. The location of the fifth grave he planned to visit was already known to him, though he'd never been able to get himself to visit it more than once before. They walked slowly; Noah needed the exercise after so long on bed rest, but his muscles weren't quite up to normal speed yet.

On the way to the first grave, Noah remembered something. "Frankie said that Paula Stevenson wasn't even the one who was in the bank that day. It was her sister, Stella." They approached her headstone. It was rather plain, he thought, which made him feel a little sadder for her.

"Ziehring wasn't able to keep a lid on the whole backstory," Neil said. "The papers have let it out that you and the others were targeted because of Donnie's death... Stella Stevenson will have seen the story by now, I'm sure." He looked away. "I can imagine how she must be feeling," he said, his voice somber.

Noah studied his cousin from the corner of his eye. "I've been meaning to tell you," he said, still facing the grave. "Well, trying to figure out how to tell you, more like..." He sighed and started over. "Something happened to me while I was, I guess comatose or whatever you want to call it. It made me realize that I've been holding onto a lot of things I should have let go of a long time ago."

He paused. "It wasn't your fault, Neil. I should never have let you think that or treat you like it was. I'm sor–"

"Don't," Neil interrupted in a raw voice, not looking at him. He took a deep breath in through his nose, the muscle of his jaw twitching. "It *was* my fault. If I hadn't been crying so much–"

"You were a kid, Neil. And a man was pointing a gun at you." He blew out a breath and rubbed a hand across the back of his neck. "Man, I should never have let you carry this so long. I am so sorry."

Noah could see a tear slip free to slide down Neil's cheek. "I'm sorry, too," he whispered. "I'm sorry it happened. And I'm sorry it ruined us both for so long." He still didn't look at Noah as he said this, keeping his gaze fixed on the ground in front of them. But when he was finished speaking, he threw a guarded glance at his cousin, his eyes red-rimmed.

Noah pulled Neil into a hug. "It's okay, man. We're okay." He released him after a moment and gave him a small smile. Then he knelt before the headstone to touch his fingertips to Paula's name etched into it.

They moved on to Will Messer's grave. Then Jennifer Sealey's and Nigel Warner's, both of which were still mounded over with fresh dirt with only a place marker where their headstones would eventually go. By the time Noah got to Rob Meares' grave, he was exhausted and out of breath, but he forced himself to face his mentor and friend one last time.

Neil gave him some space for this one, seeming to understand how much more personal and important this visit was than the others. Noah knelt and brushed away some stray grass that had clung to the rugged black stone from the last time the lawn was mowed. "It's over now, Rob," he whispered. "The One O'clock Killer case, it's solved. Finally. Thanks to you, actually. You put it together for me, but I never saw it. I'm sorry it took so long to get it right...and at such a high cost."

He sighed. "I wish you were still here, partner. But I've got good people looking out for me now. One of them's a lot like you, too.

I wish you could've met Frankie, you'd have liked him." He had to pause and clear his throat before he could continue. "Anyway, I just thought you should know it's done. It's over."

Noah touched his fingertips to Rob's name, as he had with each of the others. But he lingered a little longer here before getting up and joining Neil on the walk back to the SUV.

CHAPTER FIFTY

They rode back to Noah's apartment in comfortable silence. As he slid the key into the lock, he made a mental note to get the apartment manager to change the lock the next day. He took a breath, let it out, then turned the key to enter the apartment, ready to feign surprise. But there was only Robin and Frankie, seated at his dining table with a cake between them.

"Hey, Thunder Cloud," Robin said with a warm smile, getting up to give him a hug. "Good to see you."

"Good to see you, too," he replied.

When she released him, Frankie gave him a quick hug and a thump on the back. "Welcome home, Hark."

"Thanks, Frankie." He couldn't help but look around.

Robin giggled, and Frankie went over to the kitchen doorway and rapped his knuckles on the door frame. Noah's aunt and uncle, Joyce Collins, Simon Lewis and Jake Saddler, Conrad Ward, Bonita Meares, John Reynolds, Officers Adelmo and Byers, Drs. Barnes and Weymouth, and Gerald and Miriam Warner all filed out into the living room. They each shook his hand or patted him on the back, offering greetings and best wishes.

"Surprise," Robin said.

The only thing Noah could think of to say was, "How did you all fit in there?"

Everyone laughed, and Neil ushered him over to the cake, whose candles Frankie was now lighting. "Glad you're not dead," Noah said, reading the sentiment written in yellow icing.

Frankie grinned. "We thought it was the most fitting thing to say."

"We thought about just 'Congratulations,' but since it was such a pyrrhic victory," Robin said with a glance at Gerald and Miriam, "we went with this instead."

Conrad threw an arm around his neck and gestured to the cake. "You gotta blow out the candles, man."

"Oh, is that how this works?" Noah asked dryly. He took a deep breath – reveling in the fact that he could again – and blew out the candles. "Hope I wasn't supposed to make a wish," he muttered as the others clapped.

Conrad thumped both hands on Noah's shoulders. "All right, let's divvy up this thing. Guest of honor first, of course," he added with a wink at Robin.

Robin began cutting pieces and putting them on plates, handing the first one to Noah. He thanked her and grabbed a second plate, taking them both to give to Gerald and Miriam instead. He turned back to everyone else and held up a hand to get their attention.

After they all fell silent, he said, "I want to thank all of you for being here. But Robin and Frankie are right: this isn't exactly a victory celebration. I don't know how much of the story you all already know, but I want to take a minute to tell you from the beginning."

He took a steeling breath before continuing. "In December of 2000, I walked in on a bank robbery in progress. I was just a rookie, fresh out of the academy, and I was in way over my head. I tried to talk

Donnie Peters, the guy holding up the place, into letting everyone go and surrendering. I, uh, I promised him and his little sister, Raelynn Peters – he had her there with him. Why? I'll never know. But I promised them everything would be okay, that I'd get them both out of that mess safely."

He watched the cops in the room react to this. "Yeah, I see you guys grimacing. Never promise anything you cannot guarantee, right? Right. And this is exactly why. Predictably, it all went south, and I had to neutralize– no, I *shot and killed* Donnie right in front of his little sister. This already troubled child's world was shattered and she, uh, she grew up abused and traumatized by the people who were supposed to help her. She grew up wanting revenge."

He stopped to swallow. He hadn't spoken this much in the days since it all happened, and his voice was getting tired. "It was a simple domino effect. But, you see, I set it all in motion. Donnie and I did that. It is because of that day, because I failed to resolve the situation peacefully, that Gerald and Miriam lost their son. Doesn't matter if anyone thinks it was my fault or not, that is still true. And I can never– I can never take that back." He had to stop to regain control of his emotions. "And I can never make up for that."

Gerald touched his arm and Miriam took his hand in hers. The three of them were now crying. "I may have survived," Noah said, sniffing, "and Spicer, but four other people did not. I would like us all to take a moment of silence to honor the victims."

Everyone bowed their heads and he could hear sniffling all around the room. He prayed for those lost. He prayed for guidance to live the rest of his life in a way that would make good on the second chance he'd been given.

After several seconds, Gerald cleared his throat. "Thank you, everyone. We appreciate this very much." He turned to Noah and regarded him a moment, tears still trailing down his face. "But the fact is, Noah, it is a miracle you survived, and this tragic case was solved. And that should be celebrated. So, please, everyone, enjoy the party." He shook Noah's hand and Miriam hugged him tearfully. But all he could do was nod, his throat felt too constricted by emotion to speak.

After a while, it did begin to feel like a party. People were talking, there was cake and soft drinks, and somebody put on some music. Since it was Noah's New Wave playlist, he figured it was Neil. Eventually, though, the noise and the crowd got to him and he snuck off to his bedroom. He shut the door and opened the window, breathing in the fresh, but warm, air. He took several slow breaths, savoring the feeling of air filling his lungs – a feeling he hoped to never take for granted again. A few moments later, he heard a soft knock on his door.

"You okay, baby?" Joyce Collins asked, opening the door just a crack.

He smiled and opened it the rest of the way. "Yeah, I'm okay. It just got a little much there for a second."

"I understand," she said, her hand on the doorknob. "Would you like this shut or left open?"

He gestured for her to come in. "Actually, could I ask you something?"

She stepped into the room. "Of course. Anything; you know that."

He chafed his knuckles on his thigh. "I did some research, while I was still in the hospital. I was wondering, was it...depression that your husband suffered from?"

She nodded. "Yes. Depression and PTSD."

He nodded, looking at the floor. "I think... I think that's what is happening to me." He looked up at her. "Why I've been acting the way I have, feeling the way I've been feeling. Does that sound right?"

"Could be. What will you do now?"

"I don't know just yet," he said, shaking his head. "I feel like it makes me ungrateful or wrong somehow to still have this hanging over me when I was just saved from dying quite literally by God's mercy and grace."

"I'm no expert on the mind or soul," she said, placing her hands on his arms, "but seems to me the mind is a strange and complex thing. I am elated to see you've let God back into your heart, Noah. I can see His light all over you. But healing your mind will take time and patience and a whole lot of faith. But God is faithful, He'll see you through this." She rubbed his arms, smiling warmly.

He smiled at her. "Thank you, Joyce. You always say exactly what's needed."

"I'm just a messenger, honey." She touched his face and gave him a mock stern look. "Now, the guest of honor can't keep hiding out at his own party." She tilted her head toward the door. "Come on back, now."

"Yes, ma'am." He smiled and followed her to the living room.

There was a knock on the apartment door, but Neil answered it before he could. It was Townsend. Noah got to them just as Neil was shutting the door. "Townsend, hey," Noah said.

He handed Noah a 2-liter of ginger ale. "Franks said this was your favorite?"

"It is, thank you. Come on in and get some cake."

"I can't really stay, sorry. And sorry I was late. Uniforms picked up the guy who mugged Nigel before he was killed."

"Did he say anything? Did he witness it?"

"Ah, no, but he did confirm seeing Raelynn hanging around the area. Looks like it's as we thought: she killed Nigel, Paula and Will, and Ian killed Jennifer Sealey and," he made a vague gesture toward Noah.

"Abducted me and Spicer, yeah. Do you know how Ian got in here so easily?"

Townsend shifted his weight from one foot to the other and furrowed his brow. "Um, yes, actually. He said you left your keys on your desk during a class one day a few weeks ago. He swiped them to make copies and then put them back on your desk where you left them before the end of the day."

A chill stroked his spine. "I made it all pretty easy for him, didn't I?"

Townsend's expression was grim. "He would have found a way, regardless. He was very determined to help his little sister get vengeance. He's been calling it a war and, apparently, it's one he felt obligated to help her fight."

Noah nodded. "That's what he called it in the warehouse, too. I guess he felt like he owed her for being gone while she was being victimized at Twinwood."

Frankie caught up with them, with Dr. Barnes in tow. "Casey, hey," he said in greeting. "Get you some cake?"

"No, thank you. I need to be going. I just wanted to stop by."

Noah shook his hand. "I don't think I've officially said this yet, but thank you, you and Frankie. If you two hadn't found us when you did, I wouldn't be here."

Townsend smiled. "Glad we got there in time. Take care." He gave the doorknob a pointed look. "And you should probably change your locks."

"I definitely am."

After Townsend left, Noah turned his attention to Frankie and Dr. Barnes. The ophthalmologist gave him a lopsided grin. "Have you told everyone the good news yet?"

"Some," he replied, noticing Frankie's own big grin. "I think I'll let it circulate on its own from there." He was glad to have his eyesight back to normal. But that was it: he was only glad. Not elated, thrilled or ecstatic and overawed by the miraculous recovery a full week ahead of expectations.

"Oh, yes," Barnes said as he reached into his pocket of his shirt and withdrew a pair of glasses whose frames were thin and dark grey. "These came in today. Since I knew I would be coming here, I volunteered to deliver them."

Noah eyed the glasses a second before taking them. His left eye was ever so slightly weaker than his right eye now, and Barnes told him he would require reading glasses for close work like reading or using his computer or phone. At least for the time being. "You didn't have to do that. I could have picked them up."

Barnes shrugged. "Ah, saved you the trip."

"Thank you."

"Let's see them, then," Barnes said.

"Now?" Several of the others had gathered around and were watching. He conceded and slipped the glasses on. After a few moments of checking the fit, Barnes stepped back.

"How are they?"

"They suit you, Noah," his aunt said, and Bonita agreed.

"Yeah, they make you look like you're actually smart," Neil added.

"Oh, ha ha."

Robin leaned toward him. "Just an FYI: the hot nerd look is really attractive to a lot of women. Just saying."

"Uh, thanks, I guess." The right lens was clear glass, no prescription, but there was a slight prescription in the left lens that made a distorted effect on everything he looked at far away. He got out his phone and brought up his text inbox. He didn't need to squint, like he had while in the hospital; the words were sharp and clear. "They work," he told Barnes with a smile.

"Fantastic, fantastic," Barnes said, clapping his hands together. "Now, maybe things will start to feel a little more normal for you."

He wanted to say, *Normal? Nothing is ever going to be normal again, not after the warehouse.* He'd had nightmares the first few days after coming out of his semi-coma. If it hadn't been for the sedatives they finally started giving him, he would have gone mad. Or *madder.*

"Maybe, Doc. Maybe."

12:17 p.m.

The party went on for another half hour or so before it seemed like there had been some unspoken signal for everyone to clear out. Neil, Robin and Frankie were the last to leave, after insisting on cleaning up the place for him. Once he was alone again, he called the building manager, Jim, to request his locks changed. Jim said he'd heard about what had happened and was already planning to get them changed just as soon as Noah was out of the hospital. He said he'd take care of it before five o'clock that day.

Noah thanked him and tried to settle back into his home, but the fact that his family had tidied up for him while he was gone made him feel almost out of place. He went around and moved a few things that were in the wrong spot. When he tried going into the bathroom, he felt like he was being watched. Twice he thought he saw Ian or Lynn reflected in the medicine cabinet mirror, and his heart jackhammered in his chest until he left the room.

He deliberated only a moment before grabbing his keys and phone and exiting the apartment. He double-checked that the door was locked behind him and then took the stairs down. The elevator was apparently fixed again now, but he had no desire to get in it again so soon. He didn't remember any of the trip from the apartment to the warehouse, because of the chloroform, but Frankie and Neil had filled him in.

His intention was to catch the bus, but once he got outside and started walking, he didn't want to stop, no matter how tired he got. Forty minutes later, he stood in front of a wooden door with a frosted glass window inset. He paused, his hand halfway to the handle, and took a deep breath. He let out a slow exhale, studying the gold words painted on the glass.

DR. MARIA FRAZIER, MD Ph.D.

PSYCHIATRY, TRAUMA COUNSELING

When the last of the exhale left his lungs, he turned the handle and walked through the door.

AUTHOR'S NOTE

I want to thank you. If you are reading this, it probably means you've read this book all the way to the end, and for that, I am glad and grateful. I hope you enjoyed it, and, if so, I hope you will let me know. If not, please let me know that, as well. Readers make authors as much as authors make readers.

I've been accused of enjoying making my characters suffer. I've been accused of taking delight in maiming, torturing, scarring and/or disabling them. To an extent, okay, that's a little true – but only because I believe that it is through their struggles that we get to know and come to care about them.

I love my characters. I hate it when they're hurting, or scared, or lonely or confused. I hate when they feel vulnerable and helpless. But it is during these time that they've shown me who they really are. It is during these times that I feel closest to them, and love them more, for all their human frailties and surprising dignity and strength.

I hope you feel the same way.

I also hope that, if you found you can identify with some of the struggles Noah has been going through (or the Barlowes, Frankie, Townsend, the Warners, or Ian and Lynn), you will reach out and ask for help to get through. There is no shame in needing someone to give you a hand, to give you hope and to guide you back to life the way God meant for it to be: Full, rich and meaningful.

That is my hope whether you believe in God or not. I want you to be well and safe. I want you to know that you don't have to be perfect, you just have to be you. And know, again, whether or not you believe in Him, God loves you.

You're probably thinking that's just a load of greeting card sap. And, it does sound like that, granted; but that's because humans can't express the Divine well with our mundane words. But please know that it is true, nonetheless.

Please know that you are not alone in what you are feeling. You are not alone in your fear, desperation, hopelessness or pain. There are others like you, going through what you are going through. Feeling what you are feeling. Contemplating what you are contemplating.

Reach out. It's okay to need help, to need people – it's how we were created. Calling one of the numbers below could be the one thing that changes everything for you. I pray you'll make that call.

Samaritans Completely Confidential Hotline

When you need someone to talk to 24/7

(212) 673-3000

U.S. National Suicide Prevention Lifeline

1-800-273-TALK (8255)

Veteran Crisis Line

1-800-273-TALK (8255) – Veterans Press 1

Kristin Brooks Hope Center Hopeline

1-800-784-2433

Crisis Text Line

Text DBSA to 741-741

National Veterans Foundation Hotline

1-888-777-4443

Rape, Abuse, and Incest National Network (RAINN) (24 Hours)

1-800-656-4673

National Domestic Violence Hotline

1-800-799-7233

National Council on Alcoholism and Drug Dependence Hope Line

1-800-622-2255

Gulf War Veteran's Hotline

1-800-796-9699

COPLINE

800-267-5463

Cop-2-Cop

1-866-Cop-2Cop

Don't miss out!

Visit the website below and you can sign up to receive emails whenever J.I. O'Neal publishes a new book. There's no charge and no obligation.

https://books2read.com/r/B-A-MNEF-VOEQ

BOOKS 2 READ

Connecting independent readers to independent writers.

Did you love *Time of Death*? Then you should read *Impact: A Riverdale PD Series Prequel*[1] by J.I. O'Neal!

[2]

Noah gazed at the still, small form and sighed. Franks was right: it was always bad when it was a kid... Long glossy black curls obscured her face. One hand lay on the asphalt, pale as milk. She looked so still and perfect.

It is spring, 2006. Three months after Detective Sgt. Noah Harkham lost his partner - and mentor - Detective Sgt. Rob Meares to a sudden death he gets the news he's been dreading: he's been assigned a new partner, Detective Alan Franks.

On their first day, the pair get put on a hit-and-run that left one young girl dead and two families forever altered. When a witness leads them to a member of one of the city's most powerful families,

---

1. https://books2read.com/u/me2GaE

2. https://books2read.com/u/me2GaE

the two must put aside their differences to close the case- and keep their star witness alive.

"Impact is a hard hitting 'who done it' that makes you want to buckle up and ride right along with Detective Sergeant Noah Harkham."

-Katelyn Hensel for Readers' Favorite

Also by J.I. O'Neal

Riverdale PD Series
Impact: A Riverdale PD Series Prequel
Indiscriminate: 5th Anniversary Revised Edition
Time of Death

Stell-Ore War
The Crew of Cartage 15
Stell-Ore Justice